Ex
Libris

LIZ HYDER

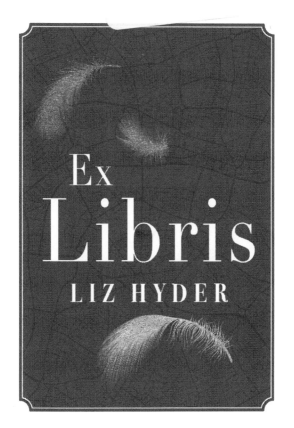

The
Gifts

ABOUT THE AUTHOR

Liz Hyder has been making up stories ever since she can remember. Originally from London, she now lives in South Shropshire. She has a BA in drama from the University of Bristol, and, in early 2018, she won the Bridge Award/ Moniack Mhor Emerging Writer Award. *Bearmouth*, her debut young adult novel, won a Waterstones Children's Book Prize, the Branford Boase Award and was chosen as the Children's Book of the Year in *The Times*. *The Gifts* is her debut adult novel.

www.lizhyder.co.uk

 @LondonBessie

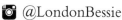 @LondonBessie

The Gifts

LIZ HYDER

MANILLA PRESS

First published in the UK in 2022
This edition was published in 2022 by
MANILLA PRESS
An imprint of Bonnier Books UK
4th Floor, Victoria House, Bloomsbury Square,
London, England, WC1B 4DA
Owned by Bonnier Books
Sveavägen 56, Stockholm, Sweden

This is a work of fiction. Names, places, events and
incidents are either the products of the author's
imagination or used fictitiously. Any resemblance to
actual persons, living or dead, or actual
events is purely coincidental.

A CIP catalogue record for this book is
available from the British Library.

ISBN: 978–1–78658–075–7

Also available as an ebook and an audiobook

1 3 5 7 9 10 8 6 4 2

Typeset by Palimpsest Book Production Ltd, Falkirk, Stirlingshire
Printed and bound in Great Britain by Clays Ltd, Elcograf S.p.A.

Manilla Press is an imprint of Bonnier Books UK
www.bonnierbooks.co.uk

What a piece of work is a man! How noble in reason, how infinite in faculty, in form and moving how express and admirable, in action how like an angel, in apprehension how like a god!

—*Hamlet*, Act 2, Scene 2, William Shakespeare

Pinion

noun

The outer part of a bird's wing including the flight feathers.

verb

1 *Restrain or immobilise (someone) by tying up or holding their arms or legs.*
2 *Cut off the pinion (of a wing or bird) to prevent flight.*

origin

Late Middle English: from Old French pignon, *based on Latin* pinna, penna *'feather'.*

October, 1840
Shropshire

The bark is rough under her hands, scratching at her palms and fingers as she stumbles between the trees. She retches violently, her body jerking and shaking as the convulsions push her forward, deep into the clutches of the forest.

Copper and bronze leaves dance around as the wind shoves at her, roars like a rushing river. She is aware of everything. Breath and heartbeat. Colour and sound. The smell of the dank autumnal air. All of it heightened somehow. More vivid, more *real*.

She coughs, chokes in agony, tears streaming down her face as she gasps for breath. Make it stop, she begs, silently. Whatever hell this is, *make it stop*!

She had left the cottage mere hours ago. A bright autumn day, a long walk in the low golden sun. She had desperately needed to clear her mind. Scout was gone, her beloved companion buried just this morning. She had seen to it herself. Sobbing tears of anger as well as sorrow into the thick clay soil as she had dug his grave. His faithfulness for so many years cut short by some poisoned meat from who knows where. Her pleas to Walter to help her find the dog's murderer had fallen on deaf ears. Her half-brother disliked the black-and-white pointer only marginally more than he disliked her. 'My father's exotic bastard,' she had once heard him call her as she left the drawing room. The words had cut into her, carving at her heart, as his friends had laughed, the sound of them echoing down the long hallway as she had fled.

And now she was fleeing again. Distraught at having buried her most loyal, most faithful of friends and reeling from her loss, she had done what she always did when she was unsure of herself – she walked. Walked until her feet were sore and the fog in her head began to slowly lift.

She had gone beyond the field edges of Juniper Hill, heading round and up towards the peak of High Vinnalls when she'd seen it. Out of the corner of her eye, something in the ditch by the side of the narrow path. She had thought it was a branch at first until her eyes adjusted to the muddy fur. A badger, long dead now. She turned it over, gingerly, with the scuffed toe of her boot. One of the paws had rotted clean away, leaving just the white coral bones. A hand reaching out. Fingers not unlike her own. She held her palms in front of her, turned them over and examined them. Flesh over bare bone, knuckle and sinew. A flash of understanding. A moment of wonder deep in her heart and brain alike. Was this what Scout's soft, leathery paw had been hiding too? A hand more like hers than she could have imagined? And what of his heart, his brain . . . ? Her mind had whirled, spun on its heel and fizzed off in a million and more different directions. Had that not been less than an hour since?

She gags again, a dry empty bark like a wounded fox. Harder this time, more painful. The next retch throws her to her knees at the edge of a small clearing, palms damp on the forest floor. The sun disappears behind the clouds for a moment, throwing her into the forest's grey shadows. She cries out, roars, as a searing pain cracks across her back, twists her agonisingly over herself once, twice, and then a third and final time.

The wind drops and the world stops.

All becomes silent – not even a solitary bird sings.

A weight of *something* sits behind her, a shadow of a presence. The pain has gone, burst right out of her, drained all her energy too, but *something else* sits on her shoulders now. Scarlet blood drips down from them onto the back of her hands. She has survived – for now at least – when she feared she might not. Breathless and shivering, she sits slowly back on her haunches, not daring to look behind. The skirt of her dress is sodden with damp autumn leaves. Birch and beech. Oak and larch.

Come, Etta, she says to herself. Come. *Open your eyes.* Whatever it is, the worst must surely be over. Wrung out and exhausted, she edges slowly to her feet, wobbles as she comes to stand. But she has no need to turn her head. The sun emerges from the clouds above, stretching Etta's shadow far in front, taking her breath away with it.

It is impossible.

It cannot be.

But there before her stands a winged silhouette. The shadow lifts its arm to its face and she sees herself, *feels herself*, as her hand softly touches her own tear-stained cheek and the birds resume their orchestra.

She turns her head, half dazed as if in a dream. And yet

there they are. Russet wings, larger than an eagle's, fanning slowly out from her shoulders. Part of her. She lets out a short laugh, a yelp of disbelief, as thoughts tumble through her head, a discordant jumble of noise.

A branch snaps, crackles through the air. Etta glances up to see a youth at the opposite edge of the clearing, eyes wide, confused and scared. A poacher, looking for something for the pot. Tensed and primed, ready to spring, his crossbow is already raised towards her, hands trembling.

'No,' she says, holding her hand up as if to ward him off. '*No!*'

But the word has barely left her mouth before the bolt flies towards her, slicing through the air. Her feet no longer touch the dank leaves of the forest, but instead hover an inch or so above it. She has no time to consider this, this sense of being both herself and *something more*, before the bolt thuds home, knocking her backwards and forcing her to the ground. Her breath rasps, bubbles up inside, thick with crimson blood. The boy's boots thud towards her, his face swimming into view but she can no longer find any words within.

She gasps for air. Newly formed impossible wings dig hard into her back as she looks up at the canopy of trees. Papery leaves whirl down towards her in a cascade of colour. Remnants of the summer past. It reminds her of something and she grasps for the memory, deep in the labyrinth of her mind: the tiny motes of dust trapped in the sunbeams of her father's library when she was a child. Patterns in the air. Angel dust, he used to call it. Angel dust.

Etta smiles as her eyes close, the darkness already settling in.

Eight days earlier
LONDON

The pocket watches are already being pulled out by the time Samuel Covell cries, 'Time me, gentleman, please!' to the baying crowd of spectators crammed tightly within the small operating theatre at St Peter's Hospital.

Edward Meake, his best friend and dearest rival, watches from the side, a faint amused smile on his lips as Samuel flamboyantly wields a long sharp knife in one hand and a bone saw in the other, both of which he will shortly use to amputate the patient's leg. Edward's elder by a handful of months, Samuel and he had first bonded when they both studied medicine some many moons ago. They had dissected, dissolved, sliced and preserved in the name of science and got royally drunk numerous times in the name of friendship. Samuel was Edward's closest friend and he loved him almost as much as he envied him.

Samuel, basking in the glory of all eyes being upon him, hands the saw to the dresser who assists him. He holds his preferred knife aloft one more time to the packed auditorium, standing room only in all four tiers, a final charming smile, and then, 'Gentlemen! Let us commence!'

No matter how many times Edward has borne witness

to or taken part in an amputation, they still thrill him to the very marrow. The tick of the watches, the thrum of the saw, the glorious risk of it all! The knowledge that you could save a man's life or destroy it in an instant, all with but a single slip of a knife.

Samuel inhales deeply as the eager audience jostle for the best view before he deftly inserts his knife into the patient's thigh, slicing swiftly through the flesh around the lower part of the femur. The man screams once, loudly, through the stick clamped tightly between his jaws before promptly passing out. Better for him that he does so, thinks Edward. Samuel has been known to take the top off a man's testes on more than one occasion in his quest to be the fastest in London.

As the dresser bends in to tie off the man's arteries, Samuel reaches for the saw. Tourniquet tightened, the bone now exposed higher up the thigh, Samuel leans over and begins, pinning the now limp patient down with some not inconsiderable strength. Edward counts just eight long strokes before the stump is set free. With a flourish, Samuel stands back up, bows to the crowd and drops the severed limb with a dull thud into a waiting box of sawdust.

'Forty-two seconds!' cries a member of the audience, to groans of assent.

'Ah,' Samuel tuts, shakes his head. 'A tad slower than usual, but one would be hard pushed to witness a finer demonstration in our beloved capital. Is that not so?' Ever the showman, he bows again to a round of applause, before returning his attention to the unconscious patient. Working swiftly and closely with the dresser, Samuel ties off the smaller blood vessels, thread in mouth, before leaving his assistant to stitch the flap of loose skin back over the stump.

Satisfied with his work, Samuel steps back from the operating table, a fever of elation across his face. He catches Edward's eye and Edward cannot help but return the grin, even as Samuel goes to clap him on the shoulder and Edward ducks swiftly away from his friend's hands, red with blood.

'Was that not well done, my friend? *Truly well done?*' Samuel's eyes are bright and wild, cheeks flushed with both his achievement and the heat of the crammed room. He wipes his hands on his already stained coat.

'I believe there is nothing I cannot do if I put my mind to it!' Samuel exclaims, high on euphoria. 'The age of science is upon us and we are at the vanguard.' He leans forward, whispers in Edward's ear, '*And yet, are we not in our own way gods you and I, eh?*'

It is a phrase that will play upon Edward's mind in the days to come, words that will rack him to his core, keep him awake in the small hours until he is half-driven mad with it. For now, though, he simply shakes his head, a wry grin writ large upon his face.

'Come, Meake, I need a drink!' says Samuel. 'For what is man if he cannot imbibe the finest of liquor after saving another's life? *Let us liquor up!*' He laughs to himself as he struts out, still in his blood-encrusted frock coat, footsteps muffled by the sawdust scattered thickly on the floor. He leaves the hubbub of the crowd behind, knowing full well that they know to find him at the Blood Bay.

Edward follows close behind, glancing back at the patient lying prone on the bloodied table. A more careful man,

Edward would have gone for accuracy over speed, for success over showmanship. He would still be finishing up on the operating table even as Samuel delights in his first taste of beer in the tavern around the corner.

'To friendship!' Edward says as he raises his tankard to Samuel and towards the smoke-stained ceiling of the Blood Bay.

'To *success*, Meake!' says Samuel, as his ever-growing fan club of young medical men gather around him. 'For any fool can have friends, but only the gifted obtain success!' And with that, he downs his beer in one, slamming the empty tankard down on the curved wooden counter, calling noisily for more.

Edward watches Samuel in the small beerhouse, watches the clamour of others around him, bees to a honeypot, even as he is himself edged to the sidelines. A twinge of envy rattles through him as he leans against the brown matchboard walls in the corner of the room. He knows that he is not as charismatic as Samuel, not as natural a performer nor as tall or broad. Yet he comforts himself for a moment as he allows his thumb to feel the smooth, cold metal of the wedding band that his wife insists he wear. For Edward has something Samuel does not. Samuel may be the better known, the fastest, most flamboyant surgeon in all of England but when Samuel returns home, staggering drunk, to the cold sheets of an empty bed, Edward will return instead to the warmth of his own home and the arms of his dear wife, Annie.

She remains the only prize Edward has yet beaten Samuel to, but for now, at least, it is enough.

Mary takes the creaky wooden stairs quickly. She is small and light of foot, but the harsh croak of Mrs Barrett's reprimand follows her up to the first floor and beyond. She is regularly told off by her landlady for being noisy despite the fact that, as Mary would one day love to point out, Mrs Barrett hasn't seen fit to put even threadbare carpet on the stairs beyond the first landing.

The two paper-wrapped pies that Mary carries are hot in her hands and she is both hungry and eager to share her spoils. By the time she reaches the third and final floor, she is breathless and full of laughter but, after a brief struggle to open the door with her hands full, her smile turns to dismay. Her beloved, kind-hearted Uncle Jos is once again knocked-out drunk.

Uncle Jos, red of face and portly of stomach, is slumped over the worn wooden table that doubles as a writing desk and a dining table, although, truth be told, it is used for far more than that implies. It has been a ship on the high seas, a cave full of dragons, a tent in the wilderness and many more play scenarios from Mary's somewhat unconventional childhood. These days, it is more often than not covered in articles and notes from Jos's work or pieces of material for dresses, waistcoats and the like, for Mary is a dab hand at sewing and often helps with costumes for the penny gaff. But for now it is simply a plain table, an arm and headrest for a drunk man and a lost soul.

An empty bottle is clutched tightly in Uncle Jos's right hand and Mary gently prises it from his fingers, sniffing it with distaste before putting it to one side. Sheets of paper are scattered in front of him, most blank and just one half-filled with writing. In the midst lies his precious notepad, full of scribbled hieroglyphs decipherable only to a handful of others. Mary glances over it, huffing to herself. Another unwritten piece, no doubt with a looming deadline.

The fire is low and the evening is getting chill. She prods at the embers with the poker, taking out her bad mood with angry jabs until the flames yawn themselves back into life, brightening the corner of the cramped little room. It is still too dark to work, though, and so she must light a candle too. She brings it close, throwing a circle of light onto Uncle Jos's small notepad. Slowly, thoughtfully, she reads the half-written piece before scanning his notes, flicking through the pages to unravel the article he should have finished hours ago.

Uncle Jos snorts and mutters to himself in his drunken haze as Mary makes a start on finishing his piece for him, the words scratching themselves onto the page in front of her. He has taught her well without even knowing it. She has read so many of his articles over the years that mimicking his turn of phrase comes naturally to her.

Mary is a fast and economical writer and there is still

some semblance of warmth in the pies when, with great satisfaction, she places the final full stop on the page. She is halfway through a sigh of relief when there is a knock at the door. It is not too late for visitors – after all, she is used to Uncle Jos's tipsters calling with a snippet of news in exchange for a coin – but no one is expected tonight.

Mary straightens both her dress and posture, takes a moment to check herself in the faded mirror on the bare plaster wall. She pinches her cheeks to put a little colour in them, but there is nothing to be done with her uncle. She will have to send away whoever is calling for no one else must see Jos like this.

She opens the door a crack, but both her mouth and the door fall open at the same time and somehow he is already within before she can think to make an excuse.

He is even taller than she remembers, his hair as wild and curly as ever. It's as if his hat is sprung off his head simply from the power of his compressed curls. He is all limbs and angles and energy, an eager young colt made human.

'Hmm,' he says, as he carefully places his hat on the table and nods towards Uncle Jos. 'How long has he been like this?'

They are too familiar in many ways to need the usual civilities of introduction, but she is irked that he has not at least attempted it. He is part family, part friend, part something she is not yet sure of. This is Richard Gibbs, journalist, wit and consumer of coffee in large quantities. He is as fiercely intelligent as his sparkling eyes suggest, but also profoundly shy behind his recently discovered cloak of confidence and they both know it.

Richard had been a big part of their lives since Uncle Jos trained him up as a young court reporter some six years ago, but, just as swiftly as he'd been incorporated into their little circle, he had departed from it. An unexpected offer of a senior job in Edinburgh eighteen months ago had been irresistible. No one could blame Richard for taking up the opportunity, but Jos had felt abandoned. He had not been easy with his forgiveness, and yet, at George's funeral, he had fallen upon Richard almost as a long-lost son. In the two months since, Richard's letters had become considerably more frequent. Mary too had been sorry to see Richard leave; he was glorious company and had always treated her as his intellectual equal. And now, here he was again. More outwardly assured now that he'd reached the grand old age of twenty-three but, underneath it all, still the same old Richard.

'How long?' he asks again. 'Please, Mary.'

She looks at him for a moment, head to one side.

'Well, good evening to you too, Mr Gibbs,' she says, with a faint air of sarcasm. 'What a pleasant and unexpected surprise. We had not been expecting company. I trust you have been faring well since we last met?'

'Miss Ward.' Richard bows, ashamed for a moment. 'Mary. Forgive me. I had not meant to offend. Only that . . .'

'I am quite well, thank you,' she says, archly. 'I trust you are too. And how was your journey from Edinburgh, Mr Gibbs?'

Richard isn't sure what to make of this unexpected sharpness. The black mourning dress becomes her, although he's surprised to find her still wearing it. She catches his puzzlement, reads him like a book.

'Uncle George was as a father to me,' she says, and Richard nods. Of course. Two months for an aunt or uncle, a year of mourning for a parent. His gaze wanders to Jos again and Mary softens.

'He has been like this since George died, but it has become worse of late.'

Richard glances at the finished article on the table, having already noted the ink stains on the fingers of Mary's right hand.

'I see that, despite his obvious inebriation, he is still managing to write,' Richard says, the corner of his mouth twitching. Mary starts towards him but he has already snatched up the piece and is reading it. She watches him in silent apprehension as the fire spits in the grate.

He inhales deeply when he is done. 'Ha! Very good,' he says. 'Oh, well done, Mary. Bravo! You've captured his voice exactly. Good Lord, were it not for the change in hand, I would not even be able to see the join!' He smiles at her, a warm grin that lights up his entire face, and she cannot help but smile back.

'Your secret scrivening is safe with me,' Richard says, putting a hand to his heart as he takes a seat. 'We shall talk about Jos and what is to be done, but first a more pressing question.' He leans forward. 'Are you going to eat *both* of those pies or can you at least donate one to a poor, starving reporter?'

Mary rolls her eyes and pushes a pie over to him before pulling out one of the wonky wooden chairs for herself, catching it against the scrap of tatty carpet underneath which she pokes back with the toe of her boot.

'Since when have you been a reporter again?' she asks. 'The last I heard from one of your most *irregular* missives, you were happily ensconced in an editorial role. Is that not so, Mr Gibbs?'

The formality of her calling him Mr Gibbs annoys him and it delights her to see it. She has missed him. Richard's mouth, however, is already full of pie. He has never been, nor will he ever be, an elegant eater.

'Mmm, delicious,' he mumbles as he chews. 'Saved from starvation at last!'

Mary snorts with laughter. She is sure that some would be scandalised at this spirited young man being alone in her company with Uncle Jos fast asleep beside them but she cares not a jot. He is one of my oldest friends, she thinks, warmly.

Richard, meanwhile, is still adjusting to this new Mary, the young woman sitting opposite him with a smile playing across her lips. Before he left for Scotland, she was but a girl. Yet when he saw her at George's funeral, he was startled at how grown-up she had become. He had felt the shock almost as much as he had George's swift demise. And now here he is again, with this sharp-witted young woman with eyes as black as coal.

'Well?' she says, trying to hide her smile, as she neatly prepares to bite into her pie. 'I have never known you to be *quite* so hungry that your food takes precedence over one of your interminable yarns, Mr Gibbs.'

'Why, thank you.' He nods, taking her dig exactly as

they both knew he would. 'In short,' he says, 'I am returned! The non-prodigal son! Well no, not actually a son—'

'Returned to London?' she says, interrupting him. 'For good? Really, Richard?'

He grins, gratified by her reaction as he takes another large and messy bite of pie.

'Don't tell me,' she says, trying to hide her pleasure and failing miserably.

'Therein lies a tale!' they both say together, as they have done many times before, him with his mouth full.

'Therein lies a tale indeed . . .' Richard says, wiping his mouth with his sleeve as he smiles. And he does not, cannot in fact, take his eyes off her for even a moment.

It is the colour that strikes her first. The sun glinting off the emerald glow, a pebble of reflection hidden amongst the stony shingle beach where Natalya sits, mending a fishing net. It is beautiful. A rounded piece of green glass, sanded smooth by the rough seas. It is worthless. It is irresistible. It feels solid in her hand, weighty, as if it holds a thousand stories within it.

She takes a moment to stretch her back, stiff from sitting, breathes in the scent of sea-salt mud flats. The landscape around Mersea fascinates her. Estuary life so similar yet so different to the sea-faring islands from which she has travelled so very far.

Natalya wonders what London might smell like, what fragrances and stenches might linger in its streets and rivers. Not long now, she thinks to herself. In exchange for food and board, she has been retying and fixing the nets of a few of the local fishermen. They knew a good deal when they saw one and so too did Natalya. She had turned up in the eye of a storm, exhausted and wet through, dripping torrents of rain from her worn woollen clothes. She was taken in by one of the local families, fed soup and hearty meals, given a bed and a warm welcome worth more than its weight in gold. One more day, she estimates, looking at the net, and she will be done. One more day and London beckons.

The trade card her cousin sent some years back has long since disintegrated on her journey south but she can still see it in her mind's eye. An illustration of a compass and, above it, in various typography – BM Calder. Mathematical Instrument Maker. 428 The Strand, LONDON. Benjamin – the black sheep of the family. Like myself, she thinks. If you could have predicted her life for her, read the runes at her birth, Natalya should be married by now, bairns in arm, settled peacefully on a smallholding on one of the scattered northern isles. And yet, here she is. Disowned. Shamed into leaving. The wind catches one of her boot-laces, loosening it so it flaps against her boot for a moment before being retied.

A young baby cries, its yowl carried on the breeze, and Natalya feels the sound pierce her heart like a flint dagger. It is time for her to go. One more day to finish the work, to make good her promise, and then she must move on, blown on the wind like one of the gulls . . . She runs her finger back over the smooth green glass. A story is coming to her, one that she will save for her last night. Natalya has become fond of the three young children in the small house she has been staying in. For the past few weeks, as she worked on the nets, recovering her strength, she has told the children strange tales as they were put to bed. Tales of mermaids and shipwrecks, lost islands and angry giants, fairy folk and talking birds and of grand palaces drowned in thick snow.

Natalya places the glass nugget by her side, one small pebble amongst a million. She wonders what manner of bottle it might have come from, what jar or glass, what forgotten life it once lived. The last story before I vanish, she thinks to herself, and she smiles out at the wide-open skies.

The groom has fallen over. Annie noticed it earlier but there were people coming and going – visitors, tradesmen, patients, the hubbub of the day – and no opportunity to fix it until Edward had left for the hospital and all became calm. The couple stand under a glass dome, groom at a peculiar angle, matching smiles fixed in clay, surrounded by handmade artificial flowers. A wedding present from Annie's since departed mother, they guard the short but imposing entrance hall from their viewpoint on the large oak sideboard.

Annie gingerly lifts the fragile dome, noting with irritation the traces of dust on her finger – Sarah has not been thorough with her work again. The groom topples over into her hand. A little clay Edward looks up at her with green eyes and she smiles back at him before turning him over, noting a hairline fracture running up along his back. She traces a finger over it, tenderly, before placing the figure back in the correct position and picking up her own clay self, dark blonde hair, rose-plaster lips. She remembers her mother painting it, laughing as she did so. 'If you cannot be happy on your wedding day, Annie, when can you?' *Oh*, thinks Annie and, for one terrible moment, she feels the loss of her mother anew.

She sighs as she gently replaces the bubble of glass, sealing the clay couple back into their own little world. Edward is late again, out drinking with Samuel, no doubt. Sometimes, she wishes they were still back in their old home. There seemed to be so many more hours in the day then, time enough for them to linger in bed, warm limbs entangled as the sunbeams broke through the gaps in the curtains.

Annie is tired of this new house not feeling like their own. Edward's reputation grows with the small but increasing stream of patients and their purse swells accordingly, but she knows all this, the luxurious carpets, the new-fangled gas lighting that Edward had insisted upon, the extravagant wallpaper, it all *costs*. She notes the daily newspaper placed so that patients may pick it up throughout the day. Anyone who can afford 5d for a mere four pages of news (three if the advertisements are discounted) is surely someone with influence. It is ridiculous, thinks Annie. This façade, this show of having money in order to persuade others that you too have worth.

The door to Edward's consulting room is ajar and Annie goes to pull it shut, but cannot resist a quick peek inside. Neat and orderly – shelves of books along one wall, a vast cabinet full of bottles and concoctions along another – it is even more meticulously organised than when she last looked. The furniture in here is new too, she notes, with a frown. It is not her place to question her husband's spending but she cannot help but feel he has been profligate, pushing their means to breaking point. *Patience, Annie!* She reprimands herself. It is an investment for the future. When Edward is more established, there will be time enough for lazy days and indulgence.

Later, as Annie readies herself for bed, she studies her reflection in the dressing-table mirror. Over her shoulder, the brass four-poster with its heavy blue drapes and crisp white bedspread reflects itself back at her. It is a bed to linger in, a bed as much for comfort and caresses as sweet dreams, the same bed in which they spent their wedding night. *Three years married*, thinks Annie, *and still no child*. This house should be *filled*, not just with friends and art and light, but with children too. She feels their absence almost as a presence, ghosts in the hallway, a faded dream of those who have not yet come to pass. She runs her hand gently over her abdomen, hopes that perhaps *this* will be the month in which her luck will turn, for surely a baby would bring her and Edward closer than ever?

'There is always hope,' Annie murmurs softly to herself as she climbs into bed, for there is one other amongst their acquaintance whose advice has not yet been sought: the best man at their wedding and Edward's longest-standing friend. It will be hard for Annie to talk openly with Samuel Covell about such a private matter but it is clear that, despite finding nothing wrong, previous physicians believe the fault must lie with her and so, she reasons, it must surely be her that now finds the cure. Edward had always been against the idea of consulting Samuel but, Annie thinks, having exhausted other possibilities, it must be worth a try now. For all his faults, Samuel has an excellent reputation for achieving the impossible. As for Annie, she will make herself brave – for what greater proof of her devotion could there be than in providing her husband with the much longed for babe in arms?

Etta has still not decided what to name this rickety structure that she sits in. It is something more than a cabin and yet, in many ways, much less. Built from scrips and scraps of wood, it is more like a beached ship than a proper outbuilding and yet it is, she thinks with satisfaction, the one place that is entirely her own. The cracked pane through which she peers, looks out onto the darkening south Shropshire hills, bracken, gorse and broom jostling for position amongst the trees. She is high up here and, on a clear day, can see some considerable distance. In front of her, a series of small plants crowd the shallow, painted windowsill. They are to overwinter here as best they can – *Kniphofia uvaria*, *Verbena bonariensis*, *Macleaya cordata* cuttings and a handful of small *Lunaria albiflora* plants, a favourite of hers that she forgot to sow earlier in the year. Their tiny leaves reach towards the light as she brushes them with her fingertips, feeling the fragile strength of each plant in turn. Scout lays his head on her knee and she pats his black-and-white velvet head, tickles his soft ears.

Behind where Etta sits, the wooden walls of the cabin are covered with sketches, notes and uneven shelves crammed precariously to breaking point with finds from her meanderings: birds' eggs and tiny fossils; unusual pebbles of all colours and patterns; dried flowers and leaves pressed flat into heavy books waiting to be added to her herbarium; and a whole raft of books, periodicals and other publications she has devoured over the years. There are small paper packets of seeds saved from past experiments or collected from the wild (and occasionally, illicitly gathered from over the wall of someone else's garden). Fennel sits next to forget-me-not and foxglove, lupin next to lunaria, each twist of paper, each packet neatly inked and labelled in Etta's clear and precise handwriting, filed according to her own, rather irregular, system – her whimsical and deeply personal preference for the musicality of the name in Latin or English. She knows neither her father nor her old friend Matthew Lawley would have approved of such a scheme, but it works perfectly well for her – and besides, they are both no longer here to reprimand her.

Today has been a most excellent day, for Etta has recorded a sighting of *Pinguicula vulgaris*, known more commonly as butterwort, at the head of the beautiful and often muddy Mary Knoll valley. It is something else with which to arm herself against Reverend Grant, botanist, snob and general irritant. He dismisses all of Etta's finds, despite her dogged persistence in trying to convert him into seeing her as an asset rather than a rival. I shall write to him tomorrow, Etta thinks, taking out her notebook and looking at the rough but competent drawing she made of the delicate, pale purple flower earlier. Bringing the lamp nearer to her, she carefully copies the sketch, improving it as she does so, for this is the version that will be sent in the morning to Henry Underwood. Dear Henry. He is compiling a list of county flora for Shropshire and Herefordshire and she is sure he will be interested in her latest discovery.

'And here,' Henry had said to her, throwing open the side gate to his family's garden with a flourish all those years ago, 'is the *theatre*!' The auriculas, of all colours – purple and white, blue and lilac, scarlet and cream, burnt orange and lemon – sat in neat pots arranged on wooden tiers nearly five feet high and she had clapped her hands with glee to see them all.

'Ricklers, painted ladies, bear's ears,' he had said. 'Most excellent names of course, but I do rather like the word auricula itself. And of course there's so much you can do with them, so many different types – doubles, stripes, alpines, borders – one can create one's very own unique version with only a little effort.'

Henry had fuelled Etta's existing passion for the natural world, shared books and knowledge with her, encouraged her inquisitive nature. Once, some years back, Etta had high hopes of being more than mere friends with this polite and enthusiastic man who had shown genuine interest in her for who she was. Alas, fate had decided otherwise when Henry had met the pretty, vacuous and extraordinarily wealthy Miss Emily Swinnerton at a dance.

'As if he would have been interested in you!' Walter had scoffed as Etta's heart had cracked. 'You would be nothing more than a curio to a man like him. As if he would marry *you* of all women when he has the freedom to choose.' *Freedom to choose*. His words had stung deeply.

Etta is happy for Henry, though, she has remained fond of him and they have continued to correspond long after his marriage. Emily is kind and sweet although Etta knows she does not challenge or stretch him. Perhaps that's what he wanted, she thinks as she prepares her writing materials on the scratched old desk in front of her. Someone pliant, a wife who will endorse and support, not a 'difficult woman' as her half-brother often calls her. 'Knowledge is a dangerous thing for a woman to have!' Walter had barked at her on more than one occasion when he'd found her reading in their father's library.

Never mind, Etta thinks. I am perfectly happy on my own anyway. Scout yawns and stretches himself out behind her, claws scratching the floor as her pen scratches the paper, reminding her that she is never really alone. Her canine shadow, he brings her endless joy.

'Dear Mr Underwood,' she begins, remembering that one of Henry's numerous offspring has a birthday coming up and she must not forget to send her best wishes to little Emilia. She sits and writes as the sky turns jet black outside, stars stretching themselves out like flickering candles across the night sky.

ST PETER'S HOSPITAL.- The autumn course of lectures at this prestigious London institution commenced yesterday in the theatre of the hospital. An introductory address was delivered by the renowned surgeon Mr Samuel Covell in the presence of a large number of students shortly before he commenced one of his famously swift amputations. He began by stating that the institution had been founded by Dr Nicolas Bowley for the reception of the sick poor, who stood so much in need of proper medical treatment. Since that period (1831), a school had been established, in connection with the hospital, for the instruction of students in medical and surgical practice. Mr Covell's own lecture series will consist of an exposition of the principles of medicine and the application of these principles in the management and cure of diseases. Ample illustration is to be afforded by drawings, preparations, and *postmortem* inspections. It is almost unnecessary to describe the advantages to be derived by current students from the connection between the school and the respected hospital and Mr Covell recommended that students attend to their duty with cheerfulness and alacrity.

In proof of the estimation of the renowned surgeon's own labours, we may add no less than 100 students attended the lecture to receive its benefit.

Edward is fury itself. He throws the newspaper down, making the breakfast things rattle as it hits the table. It is rare for him to lose his temper and Annie waits patiently for him to speak. She knows exactly what the article says as Edward has now read it out twice in its entirety before huffing over extracted highlights.

'It's the cheek, the *damned cheek* of it. My oldest friend and—' Edward runs his hands through his hair, rage silencing him for a moment.

'He did not mention it last night then?' Annie ventures, looking into the depths of her tea.

'Would I be so angry if I had known about it earlier? He knows *full well* that the entire series of lectures were developed between the *two* of us – "Mr Covell's lectures"! – he's taken all the damn credit! Not even a single mention of me, St Luke's or the endless work I've put into the venture!'

'Perhaps the journalist—'

'Perhaps *nothing*, Annie. Samuel knows precisely what he is doing. You have no need to defend the rogue. The only fool here is me for trusting my oldest friend not to stab me in the back. I will not *stand* for it!' He stamps his foot like a stubborn toddler, making Annie jump.

'Edward! Please!' Annie reaches out a conciliatory hand, but this new dining table is too big and he is too far away. She is about to appeal for calm but he is in no mood to listen to anyone's thoughts or opinions apart from his own.

'I cannot bear to look at it a moment longer,' he says. 'Forgive me, Annie dear, forgive me.' He storms out leaving Annie on edge and Sarah, the maid, with eyes rounded in delight, storing up all the details to be repeated at length to Mrs McGilliveray in the kitchen later.

Betrayal. That is what Edward feels as he heads up the newly carpeted stairs to the first floor. Anger and betrayal. Samuel always has it so easy, as if his life was greased ahead of him before he was even out of the womb. His family connections eased his way into St Peter's whilst Edward trails behind at the less prestigious St Luke's, fighting tooth and nail for every tiny foothold. Yet this was supposed to be a joint initiative, showing the two hospitals working together, hand in hand, for the greater good. If only Edward had arrived at St Peter's earlier, he would have caught the end of the lecture, would have seen what Samuel was doing. He curses, though he knows the fault does not lie with him.

Later, on his rounds at St Luke's, Edward sees the eager faces of his young students hanging on to his every word. He is respected and liked by them – but it is not enough. He needs more students to pay for his lectures, more patrons for his private practice and, most importantly, a senior and *salaried* role at one of the more prestigious hospitals. He has been spending beyond his means for some time, investing in his future, in *their* future together, his and Annie's. Their union came, he believes, with the promise of his ascension in the medical world and he cannot bear to disappoint her.

The operating theatre in his own hospital is empty as Edward pushes the heavy door open and steps inside. The newspaper stated that over a hundred attended Samuel's lecture – Edward is lucky to have seven on his rounds with him. And yet, deep down, he knows he is as talented as Samuel – if anything, more accomplished. He breathes deeply, lets the fire of his ambitions restore him before noting the inscription high up on the wall. *Miseratione non mercede.* For compassion not for gain. He must have seen it a hundred times or more, but today he feels reprimanded by it and bows his head to pray. He has found that he has taken to praying more regularly of late. He is a good man, is he not? Perhaps then the Almighty will hear his prayers, reward him accordingly. Edward's lips move silently as he prays for the helping hand of God, prays for his wife to be blessed with a child.

The sounds of the city outside, thinly muffled by the brick walls of the hospital and the chatter of sparrows on the glass roof, accompany Edward's pleas until a thud interrupts his thoughts. He looks up to see a large, grey-headed bird, russet and white-barred chest, yellow unblinking eyes, pinning down a cock sparrow with razor-sharp talons. Edward is not squeamish, he could hardly have become a surgeon if he were, but he has no stomach to watch the raptor pluck and devour its meal and so, after a last look around the empty operating theatre, he returns to the wards.

By the time the inevitable note arrives from Samuel – grovelling excuses scratched in haste, blaming the journalist for a loose-tongued conversation oiled by afternoon drinks – Edward's anger has cooled. He knows that any of the lectures Samuel holds will, in content at least, be no better than his own. Granted, it is too late for this season, but perhaps spring could mark the commencement of the joint venture they had planned. A new year, a new start. Yes, Edward thinks, and perhaps this time I shall pre-empt the announcement myself, give Samuel a taste of his own medicine. He smiles at the thought before scribbling a short note in return, forgiving his friend but not troubling to disguise his disappointment in him too.

After dinner, Edward takes one of the black and tan mongrels he has been keeping in the basement for a short walk before killing it. The dog eagerly follows him back to the inky depths of the underground rooms, hoping for a titbit of some kind but instead finds itself lifted up onto Edward's stained but clean dissection table. The dog's tail wags, thinking it is a jolly jape of some kind until Edward ties its mouth closed. Whimpering, it tries to wriggle away, paws skittering against the table, panic in its eyes as Edward restrains it, tightly buckling up the leather straps until the dog lies pinioned. Edward pats its velvety side one last time, feeling its heart flutter under his palm.

'Good dog,' he says, before holding its head still and inserting a long needle directly into the dog's eye. He ignores the whimpering as the dog spasms, jerks and shakes out its final death throes as the needle pierces its brain. He waits, quietly counting to himself, until the dog is still.

It is as clean a way as any to kill an animal and one he has done many times previously. Whistling to himself, he opens up the still warm corpse. The superficial femoral artery that he deliberately tied off has rerouted itself, shifting and pushing into smaller, narrower blood vessels like a tributary rerouting its way to the sea. He already knows that it works, for this is not the first time he has attempted such a thing, but he wished very much to see it again. For, if it is possible to do such a thing with a dog, might it not also be possible to save a man's limb using a similar technique?

Later, when Edward lies in bed, he hears the echoes of the dog's faint whimpers in his mind. It is in the name of progress, he says to himself, shaking the memory from his ears. All in the name of progress.

He rolls over, reaches out to Annie who murmurs in her sleep. He runs his hands over her, warming himself on her back, her shoulder. He feels the warm softness of her breast in his palm, heartbeat and muscles below, the pleasure of her nipple hardening underneath her nightdress as he gently rubs at it. She drowsily turns towards him, arms reaching out, pulling him to her. It has been a while, he thinks. There has been so much to do of late – unpacking and setting up his consulting room, study, and dissecting room as well as his existing hospital duties – that Edward has increasingly come to bed exhausted and long past midnight.

He kisses her, slowly at first, then harder, more urgently, hand sliding up underneath her nightdress, bare limbs, warm skin, before she lifts it up herself, wriggling out of it and throwing it to the floor. He throws his own night-shirt off and rolls on top of her, the weight of him pinning her down as he pushes her thighs apart. Annie giggles for a moment, gasps as he sinks inside her with a groan, pressing against her. Passionate and gentle but briefer than he would like, when he is done, he rolls off, one arm around his wife even as he falls asleep, gently snoring himself towards daybreak.

Annie lies awake in the dark, her husband's arm a dead weight upon her. His disagreement with Samuel sits uncom-fortably with her and she has a pang of regret at having approached Mr Covell for advice. It is too late now, she thinks. An appointment has already been made and she must surely stick to it.

'It is a very large house for just the two of us, is it not?' she had said when Edward had first taken her to see the house where they now lived.

'Not at all, my dear!' he had replied. 'There's a whole room that is to be your studio, the basement rooms will be perfect for my research and the back room, well . . . ' He had looked at her meaningfully, squeezed her arm and smiled. 'It would make a fine nursery, would it not? God willing.'

Annie shifts, edges herself away from the uncomfortable damp patch left in the middle of the bed. Why do women not talk more openly of these things? she wonders. Of marriage and babies, of lovemaking and damp sheets, of hopes and dreams. She wishes she could paint it somehow, capture this wave of emotions with her brushes and oils. She thinks of Edward earlier, at the breakfast table. She would like to have sketched him like that – green eyes ablaze in his handsome face, black hair fierce and untameable.

Edward murmurs, turning over and away from her in his sleep. Gently, so as not to wake him, she runs a finger down his naked back, feeling the bones of his spine like marble beneath his warm skin. She thinks of the crack in the plaster figure in the hallway downstairs and smiles to herself.

'I love you,' she whispers in the darkness. 'I've missed you.'

The beer boy from the brewery is most put out when Mary instructs him not to call around anymore. 'But it ain't my fault if people do indulge themselves too much is it, miss? You can't blame the supplier for over-consumption, can you?'

It is only very reluctantly, and after the offer of a small bribe, that he finally agrees to her request. 'Cheeky beggar,' she murmurs, as she heads westwards, away from her poky lodgings on Folgate Street and along Primrose Street towards Moorgate. Uncle Jos is still abed, laid low with a frightful headache, but Richard has at least delivered his piece, or rather *her* piece, to the publisher. He is back! she thinks to herself. Richard said he'd become tired of Edinburgh, missed the wonders of London, but she knows there must be more to it. Both jobs he has taken, part-time reporter for the *Morning Express* and assistant editor at the *New Weekly*, could be seen as a step down from his more senior role in Edinburgh. Perhaps Richard feels he owes Uncle Jos a favour in return for his kindness towards him? And Richard was very fond of Uncle George. *He is fond of me too*, she thinks, suddenly unsure of the warmth that tickles beneath her skin.

The pie seller shouts out a greeting from the other side of the street where he's setting up for the lunchtime crowds and she waves back with a grin before wrapping her shawl tight to ward off the cool October air.

By the time she has negotiated the City's busy throng and arrived at Mr Gidley's Button Emporium on Cheapside, her good mood is tempered a little for Gustavus Gidley, known more widely as Mr Buttons, is a demanding employer with an exacting eye. She waits for him to approve of her work – sets of buttons tacked neatly onto stiff blue card, ready for sale – whilst she glances around the shop, an endlessly fascinating place packed with tiny wooden drawers crammed full of buttons and fasteners for every occasion.

Mary had been scraping a living from helping Jos with his research – note-taking, bookkeeping and the like – and from additional snippets for Cousin Lou and the penny gaff, a low-rent local theatre. It wasn't much but it was enough – until George died. Now Mary's piecemeal work is nowhere near enough to keep both of them afloat – and Jos's writing has become increasingly erratic, his reliability affected by the alcohol he seeks solace in. With both George and his income gone, Mary and Jos had already been forced to downsize to a cheaper part of town, their roomy lodgings in Holborn but a distant memory.

'Good,' says Mr Gidley, primly. 'Satisfactory.' He reaches behind him and counts out new buttons to be prepared for sale. 'Here,' he says, sliding them over the counter along with the coins he owes her. It's not much but it's work she can do from home, work that can be fitted in around her medley of other everyday tasks. Although neither Mary nor Jos would admit as much, Mary is the only maid they have since they moved to Folgate Street – up early to clean and blacken the hearth, empty the chamber pots, clean and sweep to stave off the scourge of black beetles. She feels the weight of responsibility – rent, food, even the cleanliness of their rooms – lies heavy upon her shoulders.

'Make 'em neat girl!' instructs Mr Gidley as Mary goes to leave, his attention already elsewhere in the shop.

'Yes, sir,' Mary says, trying very hard not to poke her tongue out at him as he looks the other way. The coins rattle in her hand as she leaves the shop, the bell ringing loudly before the door slams shut behind her.

Natalya shifts on the edge of the narrow bed as the three children bunch together under the worn old blankets, eyes wide, feet fidgeting, impatient for tonight's story. It will be a special one too for they know it is their last – tomorrow, their storyteller departs for the bright lights of the capital.

'Are you sitting comfortably?' Natalya asks softly and three little faces nod eagerly back at her. The chair in the corner scrapes and she looks up to see the children's mother join them.

'Then I shall begin,' says Natalya. 'Once upon a time, in a land not so very far away, there lived, by the edge of the big blue sea, an old farmer with his three daughters, No One, Nothing and Nobody.' She counts them on her fingers one by one and the children do the same.

'No One, the oldest, was tall, dark and as strong as an ox, Nothing was small, fair and as fleet of foot as a fox, and Nobody, the youngest, well she was somewhere in-between. They toiled every day, from dawn 'til dusk, farming a narrow strip full of hard stones and stubborn pebbles between the deep woods and the big blue sea. But their lives had not always been like this. The farmer had once been a king, ruling wisely and kindly with his beloved wife until, alas, a fever struck her down and she died. Weighed down by sorrow, weeks passed before the king realised his wife's lucky gold ring, set with the Emerald of Wisdom, had also been lost. Without both his wife and the precious stone, the king's power floundered like a fish out of water. Ousted by a distant cousin, he fled to a far corner of the land, renaming his daughters so none would know their true identity.

'"If only I had not lost your mother! If only I had not lost her ring!" he had said to his daughters a thousand times or more as they sat by the small hearth of an evening, warming their weary limbs on the flickering glow of the fire.

'Time passed and the three daughters blossomed and bloomed like spring flowers. One year, autumn shivered her bones and gave way to a cold, hard winter. Their last surviving cow withered, breathed her last, and the sisters knew they could not continue. As they dug a grave, a man on an elegant white horse came riding past. It was clear from his beautiful clothes and his thoroughbred steed that he was a man of wealth. He looked over the three young women and his eye settled on No One.

'"You cannot marry a stranger!" Nothing and Nobody told their sister. But the wealthy man promised them money in exchange for her hand, money that would pay for a new cow, new tools and a better strip of land. No One, determined to save her sisters, settled the matter herself and the next day she was gone, swallowed up into the deep woods. She travelled for days through ice and snow before arriving at a huge stone palace where she was to live. Weeks passed until, one day, No One's husband told her he must go away. He handed her the keys to the entire palace. Dozens of keys for dozens of doors. Bedrooms and store cupboards, kitchens and cellars. But there was one key, a small golden one, he told her she must not use.

'"You can do anything you wish," he said. "You can go anywhere you like but there is one thing you must never do and that is to enter my private room. None must cross its threshold bar me and me alone."

'And so No One explored the whole palace whilst her husband was away. Every door locked and unlocked a dozen times or more. Every corner of every room explored, every shelf examined. All except one. Her husband's private chamber. She put her eye to the keyhole, looked through into the darkness. Put her ear to the keyhole, heard only silence. And so it was that curiosity got the better of her.'

'She opened the door!' cries one of the children.

'She did,' Natalya says, with a smile. 'But can you guess what lay inside?' Three little heads shake at her and the youngest starts anxiously sucking her thumb.

'When No One unlocked the door, she found rows of shelves, empty save for two large glass bottles, and a huge barrel filled with black tar. She looked into the barrel and saw, floating on the top, a golden ring with a familiar green stone.'

'The Emerald!' cries the oldest child and Natalya nods.

'"My mother's ring!" cried No One. She reached in but the tar was burning hot and scalded her fingers, staining her hands no matter how hard she scrubbed. When her husband returned, he saw the marks on her fingers and was furious. "You have tricked me!" he yelled. "You have betrayed my trust!" He picked her up, carrying her into his secret room and throwing her into the barrel of tar.

'Six months passed and summer came, the forest shimmering with heat, as the sisters' father became increasingly frail. One day, the man on the white horse returned. "Your sister ran off with another and so I must choose myself a new bride," he said, and this time his eye fell on Nothing, the middle daughter. Again, there was an offer of money, again her younger sister and their father refused but Nothing could see that life was still hard, her father sickening more each day. And so it was that Nothing headed off with her newly betrothed, disappearing into the deep dark forest on his white horse and onwards to the huge stone palace. Weeks passed until, one day, her husband told her he would have to go away. "You can do anything you wish,"' he said.'

'You can go anywhere you like!' interrupts the oldest child.

'But there is one thing you must never do,' says Natalya. 'And that is—'

'To enter my private room?' a little voice suggests.

'Quite right,' Natalya says, with a smile, before continuing. 'It was as before. Again, the keys were handed over and just like her inquisitive older sister, Nothing opened every door a dozen times or more, explored every corner of every room. *All except one.* The small golden key felt as if it burned through her hand. And so it was that Nothing opened the door to the secret chamber. So it was that she too saw the golden ring with the emerald in it, singed her fingers on the tar and met the same fate as her older sister, drowned in the huge barrel.

'Months passed and the man on the white horse returned to the farm one final time. "I will go willingly," Nobody said to her father. "For it is the only way I will find out what happened to my sisters." And so Nobody accompanied the stranger on his white horse into the deep woods and to the huge stone palace where she was to live. Until, one day, her husband said he would have to go away . . . '

Natalya smiles at the children and they take their cue, chanting along. 'You can do anything you wish. You can go anywhere you like but there is one thing you must never do and that is to enter my private room. None must cross its threshold bar me and me alone.'

'*Ah,* thought Nobody. *A secret chamber.* As soon as Nobody's husband was over the horizon on his white horse, the first door she opened was the one with the small golden key. She entered the forbidden room and looked around, suspecting trickery of some kind. She examined the shelves, looked carefully at the two large glass bottles – one labelled The Water of Life, the other, The Water of Death. She peered into the barrel of tar and saw the emerald ring but she looked beyond it too, only to see her sisters' faces staring up at her from the oily depths. Nobody reached for The Water of Life and poured it into the barrel. Only when she had shaken out the very last drop were her sisters returned to her, rubbing their eyes as if they had been fast asleep. She told them all that had happened before pouring The Water of Death into the now empty bottle labelled The Water of Life.

'When the man returned, the trio of sisters were waiting for him. They threw him off his horse and fled, taking their mother's ring and all the man's other treasure with them. The man, injured and furious, stumbled down to his private chamber where he took up the bottle labelled The Water of Life. He drank swiftly and deeply and, within moments, he was dead. The three sisters returned home, joyful to be reunited, joyful too to have reclaimed their mother's precious emerald ring. Their father soon recovered his health and, shortly afterwards, word reached them that his distant cousin had died. The throne the farmer had once ruled from was left empty but there was one, they all agreed, who had earned the right to take it. And so it was that Nobody, the youngest of the sisters, became queen of all the lands, ruling wisely, kindly and *always* wearing the Emerald of Wisdom.'

Natalya pauses for a moment, reaches into her pocket to pull out the sea-smooth round pebble of green glass she had found on the beach the previous day. 'But look,' she whispers to the three attentive faces. 'Before I leave, I must entrust you with something very special. You must promise to take great care of it.'

'The Emerald of Wisdom!' cries the youngest child and three pairs of hands reach out to take it.

'Careful, careful!' says Natalya. 'You must share it between you fairly! Now, sleep awhile and see what stories your dreams will bring.'

Natalya kisses their foreheads in turn, saying goodnight to each of them, before turning in for the night. As she wraps herself in a blanket before the fading kitchen fire, she fizzes with a mix of fear and excitement about what the morrow will bring. Her cousin Benjamin, the talented young apprentice, the scandalous upstart found in bed with his master's wife in Kirkwall – Natalya has not seen him for years, wonders if he might even recognise her. 'Mathematical instrument maker' the card had said. Compasses, telescopes, navigational devices. He must surely help her to gain a foothold in the city, to start afresh. Her family had disowned him as they had her. If anyone will understand, it must surely be him. It was by chance she had seen his trade card before it was thrown out. Chance that she had tucked it away and kept it safe. It is engraved in her memories, etched in her dreams – 438 The Strand. And tomorrow, she thinks, hugging herself, she will finally be there.

She hopes the letter she sent her cousin some months back, forewarning him of her arrival, reached him safely. Her journey south has been difficult, challenging her far beyond anything she could have imagined. It has been irregular too, full of unexpected stops and starts, weeks shifting to months and passing seasons, impossible for any reply to reach her. Besides, she thinks, with not a little pride, Benjamin must be so busy with his business right in the heart of the capital.

One of the children cries out in their sleep and Natalya feels her heart tug. This could have been her life. Children and bedtimes and stories. Washing and cooking and mending. A young family to feed and love and cherish. This *should* have been her life. She shakes the thought away.

Tomorrow is a new start.

Tomorrow is a new story.

Elton, Shropshire

7th October 1840

Dear Sir,

My dear Reverend Grant, I am afraid your letter has only this moment reached me. I was out on my observations yesterday and my maid only saw fit to pass me your missive this morning.

Thank you for your considered and most detailed response to my recent finds although, in all honesty, I feel your advice that I should simply draw and paint the plants I note is perhaps a little misplaced. I am, as you know, a tolerable rather than gifted artist. I do, however, believe that my observations as a botanist may be more valuable than my sketches. Henry Underwood certainly agrees and, as I mentioned previously, is incorporating some of my recent discoveries in his countywide study of both Shropshire and Herefordshire.

I am sure you will be most interested to know that I recently sighted *Pinguicula vulgaris* at the neck of Mary Knoll valley, not far from Ludlow, one of only several recent discoveries I have recorded in the local area. I have taken the liberty of correcting your own list for Shropshire in which, as you will see, I have found a handful of omissions, no doubt the result of an errant printer's lack of attention.

I enclose the annotated list within.
With high respect, I am . . .

Etta pauses, her anger barely contained under the societal game of politeness. Reading his letter again, she feels irritated anew, the heat of her annoyance spreading over her like a rash. How dare he, a man of the cloth, dismiss *her* as a hobbyist when she has devoted many years of her life to the study and understanding of plants? Is it not true that *he* is in fact the hobbyist?

She simmers as she looks over her old writing desk, out of her small bedroom window to the clouds skimming across the sky. Her reflection reminds her of the panes in her father's hothouse, the moss garden next to it that she created with him. All gone now. The hothouse converted from a place of experimentation to an extension of the kitchen garden, filled only with fruits destined for the table. The moss garden planted over by Walter himself, turned into a formal flowerbed containing the most mundane of varieties. Her father's herbarium sent away to a distant relative in Cornwall, far from Etta's reach.

Etta sighs, leans forward to unlatch the window, allowing her anger to subside with the cooler air. The more one sees, the more one learns, the more one realises how little one actually *knows*. Light, cold, rain and heat – each of these things affect every plant. As seasons shift and stretch across the year, so too do all living things. Even *ourselves*, she thinks ruefully. The Reverend Grant looks but he does not *see*. Perhaps she ought to give up with him. She recalls reading something about James Easthope, the orchid expert, establishing a garden in Kent. Perhaps he might be interested in her findings? She thinks of the burnt-tip orchid she came across near Downton and resolves to write to him.

Scout nudges her hand and gives a short impatient bark of instruction.

'Yes, yes. Nearly time for our walk, my friend,' she murmurs as he reaches up and licks her ear, making her laugh as she pushes his velvety head gently away.

With high respect, I am most eager to hear your response.

She signs her name with a flourish. *That will irk the old goat*, she thinks with satisfaction.

'Come on then,' she says, as she stands, stretching out her stiffness as far as she dare without tearing the tightly fitted sleeves of her dress. 'Come on.'

Scout yelps, dancing in circles of happy anticipation, before Etta opens the bedroom door, freeing him to pelt noisily downstairs. She follows, smiling to herself, as she puts on her bonnet and coat before venturing outdoors to brave the chill autumn air.

All are still abed when Natalya creeps out of the Harrisons' little weatherboarded cottage, softly pulling the heavy wooden door closed behind her. The morn is yet to fully arrive and the stars still twinkle in the darkness. The sunrise lingers beyond the horizon, a faint glimmering of light tentatively reaching up.

Natalya loves this time of day, a time for fishermen and farmers. The dawn chorus is already in action as the birds puff up their feathers and sing off the night. Gulls circle above as she pads down to the small harbour where the boat awaits high tide. She has slept badly but a mix of adrenaline and excitement courses through her veins, lighting her eyes and making her fingers tingle.

As the captain readies the boat, the early glow of the day slowly spreads itself along the horizon, peeping up above low clouds. Grimmelings, Natalya thinks, the first gleams of daylight.

She has heard so much about the capital on her journey south, good and bad: the greatest city on earth, where opportunities are plentiful, where anyone can start afresh; the dirtiest, noisiest, most unruly place where chaos reigns and the streets are packed with robbers. She imagines the truth must surely lie somewhere in-between.

'First time to London?' asks the captain and Natalya nods.

'My cousin lives there.' She smiles. 'It will be the first time I've seen him in years. He's an instrument maker, mathematical, not musical. He's exceptionally clever.'

'Expect he is, miss. Well, best o' luck. Boat at Maldon'll take you on up the Thames. The Harrisons'll be sorry to see you go.'

'And I them,' she says. 'They have been very kind to me.'

Natalya clears a small space to sit in the stern as the captain hoists the sail. She pats the pocket of coins she'd managed to save tied tightly under her dress, feels the faint musical sound of them as if they were wishing her luck. As the boat sets off out of the harbour, she daydreams, imagining all the ways in which she could be reunited with her cousin, imagining his premises, the busy streets, the crowds, the noise. All the months of travel, of turning her hand to any work that needed doing, of sleeping in barns and borrowed beds, all the miles she has travelled. All the heartbreak and loss – it has all been leading to this.

I am ready for you, London, she says to herself as her heart flutters. City of dreams, wonders and rewards, I am ready for you . . .

When Annie enters Samuel's consulting room, she finds him reclining leisurely in a grand armchair the other side of an imposing walnut desk. It is the first time she has sought medical advice without her husband being present and she looks around a little nervously, taking in the lavish furnishings as she does so.

'Mrs Meake, please . . .' Samuel says, motioning for her to sit. 'Is Edward *very* cross with me? He's always finding fault with me for something or other. I could have done better with the mix-up over the lectures, but . . . Well, what's done is done.'

'I am not here to reprimand you, Mr Covell,' Annie says, smoothing her dress down as she adjusts her position. 'Certainly not on Edward's behalf; he's more than capable of doing that himself.'

Samuel looks at her, intrigued. 'So, what does bring you here without him then?'

'Please, Samuel. You must not rush me. It is . . .' Annie looks at the floor, her face reddening. 'A most *delicate* matter and I had thought to seek your professional advice. It has been three years . . .' she says, tactfully.

'He has been at St Luke's longer than that, surely?'

'Since the *wedding* Samuel . . . It has been *three years*.'

'Oh,' says Samuel, understanding dawning upon him. 'I am no expert in such matters but, please, permit me to recommend some of those who—'.

'Samuel! I have already seen *everyone* in London – Edward has made sure of that. The one person we have not yet consulted is *you*. Surely you can at least hear my plea? Surely, as his best friend, you owe him that? *Please*.'

'Does he know you are here?'

Annie shakes her head. 'No. I wanted it to be—'

Samuel interrupts. 'I must say you've put me in a most uncomfortable position.'

'Well,' she says, 'treat me as you would any new client.'

He frowns for a moment. 'In that case, *Mrs Meake*, I assume you have already tried a change in diet, a little more exercise? Loosening your corset?'

She nods in reply.

'And your menses, they are regular?'

'I believe so, yes.'

'And, forgive me for asking, but it is a necessary question. You are *intimate* regularly. You and your husband.'

'Of course,' says Annie boldly, looking him directly in the eye. He is enjoying this a little too much, she thinks.

'Well, I hope you've not been reading too much – there is a school of thought that believes the blood may be drained away from the uterus and sent to the brain. I find that extremely unlikely but it is perhaps worth trying all things. Sea salt and mushrooms should be added to your diet in greater quantities, and an increase in the amount of oysters you eat might aid and abet. I assume you can talk to your cook about more specific inclusions in your meals?'

He runs through a great long list of other theories and remedies, taking the chance to show off his knowledge, making Annie's heart sink as she hears the same familiar advice and unpleasant cure-alls she has been offered a dozen times or more. An underdeveloped cervix as the result of an indolent city lifestyle, injections of weak silver nitrate, acetate of lead or carbonate of potash within the uterus – and the reliable cure-all of an application of leeches to the affected area. He has, she ruminates sadly, nothing new or revelatory to add to the information she has already acquired.

'And I believe that is the last of the options presently available to you, although, as I say, it is not *really* my area of expertise,' Samuel says, having concluded with the notion that she lie prone on a couch for at least two hours a day, something Annie feels would be a considerable waste of time.

'Thank you for your advice, Mr Covell,' she says, a little sharply. 'I had hoped you might be able to shine a new light on the situation but it seems I must leave disappointed.' She feels ashamed as she stands, although she is at least grateful there has been no physical examination. Almost all of her appointments had been such as this, a conversation with no need to remove even a single item of clothing. But there had been one, a surgeon who thought she might have a uterine tumour, who probed her most intimate parts with a long, thin metal instrument whilst she lay on her side, skirts drawn up, knees to her chest, silent tears falling. She feels the same shame now as she had then, a flush of heat and humiliation.

'You will, of course, not breathe a word of this to Edward,' she says, a command rather than a question.

'Of course.' Samuel bows his head as he refuses her offer of payment. 'A patient's confidentiality is always kept by any reputable medical man.

'Just one thing more, Mrs Meake,' he says as Annie goes to open the door. 'Have you considered, that in fact, the problem may not lie with you?'

'What exactly are you inferring?'

'I am *inferring*, dear Annie, that perhaps the fault lies, well, *with your husband* . . . It is at least a possibility, is it not?' He smiles at her sympathetically but the slight is clear. It had been years ago now, but she knew he had once felt sore at her favouring Edward over him. Surely he couldn't *still* feel any resentment? He is supposed to be Edward's friend, his *best* friend!

'For goodness' sake, Samuel!' she snaps, angry tears welling.

'Do not be cross with me, Annie! I have to ask these things,' he says, with a faint smile. 'As a medical man.'

'In that case I believe our appointment is thoroughly at an end. Good day to you, Mr Covell,' she says, fuming, trying to hide the tremor in her voice as she slams the door. She holds onto her tears until she is safely home where, humiliated and offended, she washes herself thoroughly, as if to erase the memory of the meeting from her skin. Always willing to believe the best in anyone, she had believed, or perhaps wanted to, that Samuel's treatment of Edward and the ruin of their joint lectures was a genuine error, a clumsy oversight, but now she is not quite so sure.

It is not the usual sort that Peter King drags from the murky Thames with his hook. She is older, for a start. Silver hair and pale white skin. She looks in good nick, he thinks to himself, as if she had but fallen asleep underneath the waves. Can't have been in long else the fishes would have nibbled. The woman carries no coin, for her clothes are missing and she wears just the sodden dark cloak. Good quality, though, and worth a bit, he thinks.

He notes with interest – and more than a little surprise – a glimpse under the cloak of long and detailed tattoos on each arm, curling up from the elbow towards the shoulder. Faded now, as if they were done some years back, a vine, still green-leafed, winds itself up and around her left arm. On her right, a snake with a large flat head, forked tongue out as if tasting the air. Both are inked with skill and artistry, not the blunt jabs and blurrings from a prison cell. It is most unusual for any woman to wear ink on her skin, let alone something as large and intricate as these.

The wet woollen cloak makes the body heavy, but Peter has spent a lifetime hauling dead weights. He hoicks her out and into his boat as the rain starts to tap down. By the time he returns to shore, fighting against the tide to row his precious cargo safely back, the rain has become first sleet and then tiny hailstones, little grey pellets that bounce off his raggedy hat.

It is only as he drags her out of the boat and onto the dilapidated wooden pier that he sees what else she carries, what emerges from her shoulders. Stumbling backwards, he drops her on the ground, cursing to himself.

As the hailstones clatter down on him, he sits, dazed for a moment, before a grin near splits his face in two. He looks around to check that there are no other witnesses before scrambling to his feet and wrapping the cloak tightly back around the body. He throws her over his shoulders and, gripping her close, takes her back to his lodgings as fast as he can.

As the boat makes its way steadily up the Thames, welcomed first by a smattering of fog then heavy rain that shifts to hailstones, nothing could have prepared Natalya for the capital proper – the biggest city in the world. The sea gradually narrows to a wide river as they sail up it, passing boats of all shapes and kinds and sizes. Ships ancient and creaking, long cargo ships, steamboats puff-puffing away, and a most peculiar ship with strange, angular sails of which she has never before seen the like. 'A junk,' she is told. 'All the way from the East.'

The smell is as overpowering as the noise: fish and sewage, smoke and steam, ammonia and industry all combine into something peculiar, unfamiliar and noxious. Her eyes don't know what to look at next, the multitude of crafts jostling for position on the water, the sheer unpredictable chaos of so many people milling around. There are the buildings too, so many of them, stretching off as far as the eye can see. And all around *so much noise* that her ears are as overcome as the rest of her.

A man with a red hat catches her eye as he heads in the opposite direction, past her and back out to sea on the largest vessel she's yet seen. On her right, a small, vulnerable boat with a man fishing something out of the river . . . a body, she realises with a shudder. To her left, some other new building is being constructed and, just along from it, a boat is upended like a great snail's shell, men running over it like ants to repair the hull. It is all so much to take in. With a sense of panic, she wonders if she is ready for this, if she could *ever* be ready but it is too late now, for the boat is turning in, heading towards the river's edge and the quay it will shortly dock at.

The crew busy themselves, all hands on deck, and Natalya is glad she took the opportunity earlier of asking for, and memorising, directions to the Strand. She has no map, no guide and no friendly face, only her wits and an old, faded address lodged in her memory. The weather clears just as Natalya's boat creaks to a halt and she disembarks into the chaos of the waiting crowd. In the blink of an eye, she is swallowed up in her entirety, disappearing from sight as if she had never really been there at all.

Today is the day in which Edward's life changes. He does not know this yet, he is mainly consumed with irritation at Miss Frankie Webster – not, of course, her real name – a 'tart' with whom Samuel (and quite possibly half of London) had been familiar with some years back. He is surprised at just how far she has fallen in the years since he last saw her, long before his and Annie's paths collided. The area around George Row, better known as Jacob's Island, is a most insalubrious part of Bermondsey and he would like to depart from it as soon as possible. It is only the distinctive name of one of his aristocratic patrons calling in a favour that could possibly have brought him here. The stench of poverty and desperation mingles with that of the Thames – rotting weeds, animal carcasses and dead fish – making his nose wrinkle and his heart sink.

Frankie has aged a decade or more and her gums are turning black. A few teeth are missing and he wonders who on earth would pay for her services now. He presumes that the Right Honourable Member of Parliament for Bedfordshire must either have some long-standing affection for her or that something akin to blackmail is in the offing.

'Ain't easy this life, my love,' she'd said as he examined her. The sores were not painful, she confirmed as he looked at her groin, an area that had once held such extreme fascination to so many men. She would not be able to afford the mercury pills, but Edward gave them to her anyway. He suspected they were doing her more harm than good, but what else could he offer, bar a few spare coins?

As he washes his hands in the cracked bowl in the corner of the threadbare room, there is a knock at the door. Frankie pulls down her skirts as she yells for whoever it is to bloody well enter and a boy bursts in, a scrappy wisp of a thing with a forgettable face.

'Someone said there was a surgeon here,' says the boy, staring at Edward as Frankie, with a toothless grin, jerks her head towards him. And so it is that Edward finds himself following the boy to the riverbank just a handful of minutes away from Frankie's unsavoury chamber. A maze of wooden boards leads down to the water's edge where a handful of boats bob up against each other. Dozens of flimsy wooden shacks perch above at the lip, tiny rooms half-propped up by decaying poles set deep in the dirty river mud – a tower of playing cards, threatening to topple in, to be carried away by the tide at any given moment. Edward can hear babies screaming, raised voices shouting. People live here, he thinks, torn between shock and disgust. People actually *live* here.

The door is low as Edward enters the patched-up hovel, straight into a tiny room with cracked windows. A body is already laid out on a small wooden table, covered over with the cleanest thing in the room, a grey cloth which, Edward knows instinctively, must once have been white.

'I see I am come too late,' says Edward. Having just removed his hat, he immediately goes to put it back on, noting only that the man has, for some reason best known to himself, placed the body face down.

Peter King fixes him with a glare. The boy watches from the doorway until Peter throws him a coin, which he catches with glee before running off.

'Less haste, sir. Tarry just a moment,' Peter says. 'Ain't it true you're a surgeon?'

Edward nods.

'And you do sometimes take a body for, y'know . . .' He motions slicing through the air with his hands.

'I am afraid I do not dissect my fellow humans,' says Edward with a note of pride, although what he actually means is that he *no longer* dissects humans. He has sliced and diced many a person in the past, women, men and children ('smalls' they are called, their tiny bodies paid for by the inch).

'Might you be interested in a curio, sir? A body with some distortion to it perhaps?' Peter offers.

Edward frowns at him. 'What manner of curio?' he asks.

'Ah well, see, sir,' says Peter with glee, 'something most unusual. Something I ain't ever seen the likes of afore and I warrant you ain't neither.'

Edward raises an eyebrow at him.

'I think you'll find it ain't *quite* human,' Peter says and, with a flourish, throws the sheet off the body.

Edward cannot breathe. His chest aches hard as if someone has punched him.

It is impossible.

But there it is.

A naked woman with two small wings growing out of her shoulders, like a baby bird fallen too soon from the nest. Her arms are tattooed, ink twisting and winding around the upper part of each but Edward is interested only in the impossible. When he eventually brings himself to speak, it comes out in a croak.

'If it is a fake, it is an excellent one,' he stutters, heart hammering as he steps forward.

The woman faces away from him, silver hair to the nape of her neck, pale flesh rising from shoulder bones into small, feathered wings. Edward has been offered many a bogus body over the years, mermaids, mermen and the like. This is no fake though, the moment he saw it – *her* – he knew. This, he thinks, is something else. Something new. Something *miraculous.*

Edward lightly traces his fingers over the still damp feathers, examines the woman's shoulders.

'She is as real as you or I,' Peter says as he fancies that a sale will be both shortly forthcoming and most advantageous.

As Edward slips into professional mode, his faculties are restored. 'How much?' he asks, still not taking his eyes away from the creature.

Peter names a price three times what he thinks he might get. He is thirsty and desires, no, *needs* a drink sooner rather than later.

Edward merely nods and they shake hands.

''Tis a most unusual specimen, ain't it?' says Peter. 'I

coulda charged you four times that for it,' he adds wistfully, wishing already that he had done so.

'It is well done,' says Edward, heart thumping in his chest. 'Most well done. I wonder how they were stitched on?'

It is only later when Peter is once again rolling drunk that he regrets having sold his angel so cheaply. If only he could remember the name of that surgeon . . . He wishes, not for the first time, that he could write, wishes too that he had made a note of some kind. He angrily turns his room upside down in hope of finding a clue, something that could be used to squeeze more money out of the fellow who bought the winged woman. Alas, he cannot find evidence for any of it. No proof at all of the strange wonder he pulled from the river, save for more coins hidden under his bed and some vivid and most unsettling dreams.

Mary and Uncle Jos stand, with Richard, by Uncle George's gravestone outside St John's, their old church in Holborn. It is a sorry sight, the small stone already gently leaning to one side as the ground sinks beneath it, bells ringing dolefully from the church tower above.

'Come,' says Richard, taking Jos by the arm who, at this stage, is already wiping his tears away. 'George would not have wanted us to be unhappy, is that not so?'

Jos is resistant to being dragged away though, sorrowfully turning his hat round and round in his hands. 'What ever will I do?' he cries. His voice is raw and distraught and it breaks both Mary and Richard's hearts to hear it.

'I think a warm pot of tea and a bun will restore us no end. Come,' says Richard, firmer this time, but poor Jos is so distressed by it all that, the moment they return to Spitalfields, he insists on going straight to bed.

'I thought it would be a good idea,' whispers Mary, aware of how thin the walls are, as she lights the fire for some much-needed warmth.

'The graveyards are fit to burst all over London,' Richard shakes his head. 'If I'd realised earlier, I would—' He silences himself, seeing how much he has hurt her, thinks of the stories he has heard – bodies rising to the surface, shallow graves and bodysnatchers, corpses broken up and dismembered to fit into ever-smaller holes. As increasing numbers of people cram into the city, so too rises the number of dead that must, likewise, be accommodated.

Richard sees Mary on the verge of tears and sighs. 'Oh Mary,' he says softly. 'It was done with good intention, that's all any of us can do, is it not?' He goes to take her hand, but she flinches away.

'All I've done is make him more miserable than before,' she says, sadly. 'I thought – oh, I don't know what I thought, Richard. Perhaps that it might help him to say goodbye again, to think more of the living than the dead. I only want Jos to return to us, to want to *live* again.'

This time, she lets Richard gently take her hands. It has been some time since he has done so; last time, he thinks, it may have been helping her cross the road some two years back but now, *now* it feels very different indeed. He feels the soft warmth of her skin as a rush of heat that travels straight to his heart.

'Let us talk to him,' he says. 'Perhaps he's feeling a little brighter now he is home.'

'It might be better if *you* talk to him. Nothing I say has made any difference, but maybe you might. After all, he loves you almost as a son.'

'And I repaid his kindness by abandoning him,' says Richard, thoughtfully.

'No,' Mary says firmly. 'You cannot always stay by his side and he's long forgiven you despite the fact you did no wrong. You're not an apprentice for life, Richard.' She takes her hands away and goes into her small bedroom, leaving the door open behind her. Richard waits a moment before following her to the doorway. He has not seen her room before and is startled by how tiny and bare it is.

'But where on earth are all your books?' he asks, puzzled, realisation slowly dawning on him of the wider consequences of George's demise.

Mary cannot bring herself to answer straightaway. Oh, how she misses her old, commodious bedroom with its high ceiling and large bookcase. Now she has but a windowsill, which is too precariously thin to balance anything of significance on, and a small ledge above the fireplace. Most of her books had to be sold before they moved and she misses them deeply.

'They've gone away – on exciting new adventures with other readers,' Mary replies, trying to be cheerful as Richard notices the pile of buttons on her bed, the squares of stiff card they are to be sewn onto. She hastily covers them before picking up a blanket. 'You can take this into him. Besides,' she says, boldly, 'a lady's boudoir is not for the likes of your eyes, Mr Gibbs.'

'I'll talk to him,' Richard says as Mary walks out past him and he follows her. 'I'll do whatever I can to help you both. I promise you.'

'Thank you,' Mary says. 'And, Richard . . . Please don't mention the buttons to him. I need to make ends meet somehow and I can't take better-paid work in a factory or shop, not if it means being somewhere else all day. I can't do that and look after him and, well, everything else.'

'Could you not, perhaps, write more pieces for him?'

Mary snorts at the suggestion. 'I would happily do so but I don't think Uncle Jos would be too keen on me taking over his work on a regular basis – do you? Besides, there's no such thing as a female journalist.'

'Not yet,' Richard says. 'But there are women writing essays, stories, novels. Someone of your talents should not be doing menial work. It's not fair.'

'No, well,' says Mary, 'it may not be fair, but what else am I to do? I'm being as resourceful as I can. We are surviving – that's the main thing.'

He looks at her for a moment before heading into Jos's room, softly pulling the door shut as Mary puts the kettle on above the small fire in the grate. She feels ashamed that he's seen what she must do for her extra pennies. Still, Mary thinks, at least buttons are clean, not like the phosphorus from match-making that nibbles away at your jaw.

She looks over at Uncle George's empty armchair and wishes with all her heart that he were sitting in it, looking back at her with his twinkly-eyed air of mischief. It had not, in any sense, been a conventional family set-up, but it was the only one Mary could now recall. Jos and George had been the best of friends, bachelors together, after becoming pals in one of the city's many gentlemen's clubs. A clerk and a journalist, they bonded over their love of pen and ink, the satisfaction of getting things just so and a shared passion for both the printed word and each other. Mary could not, in truth, remember a time without them. She knew the story, of course. Her own parents killed in a shipping accident when she was not yet four, she had been thrown upon the mercy of Jos, her mother's last surviving brother. The bachelors had, between them, agreed to take on the unexpected role of surrogate fathers to the tiny dark-eyed girl. It had not occurred to the outside world that the two men loved each other as much as they loved her. It was unspoken, a love that hid in hallways and private rooms, a love that dared not show its face in public.

Jos and George had been Mary's fathers and more, saving her from the workhouse, encouraging and nurturing her. They had even once, to their collective amusement, engaged a governess for her. One of George's fleeting acquaintances, Miss Wiltshire had lasted but a few months before resigning, saying that she believed Mary was more than capable of educating herself through her own reading and wit.

The kettle starts to whistle and Mary sighs as she pokes the fire beneath it. She remembers Miss Wiltshire's parting words to her, words she has gone over many a time in her head since. 'Don't forget – "Ignorance is the curse of God, Knowledge the wing wherewith we fly to heaven." Keep reading, Mary, keep devouring all those books you love so much.'

That's all very well, Mary thinks, but all of my books are gone.

'Oh, thank goodness you're here!' cries Ellie, blonde curls bobbing, as Annie is shown into the chaos of her best friend's bedroom, clothes of all kinds strewn over the bed.

'Devon is calling!' Ellie says, waving a letter at her, and Annie takes it, reading the first few lines to discover that Ellie's sister Lizzie has given birth to her much-anticipated firstborn. Other women seem to find it so easy, Annie thinks, a twinge of envy rippling through her.

'Nearly a month early!' Ellie continues. 'There's nothing for it but to go down and help and I had *so much* to do here! Come, let us have tea! Now, what was it you wanted to talk to me about?'

Annie inhales. She can hardly bring herself to tell Ellie why she is really there. Bruised from her earlier consultation with Samuel, she had meant to confide all in her best friend, seek her advice, be soothed with sympathy, but she has no wish to talk of her own desire for a baby, not when the conversation revolves around the arrival of another's.

'No matter,' she says, forcing a smile. 'It's a breath of fresh air to see you, that's all.'

'Oh, it was so much nicer when you were nearby! How is the studio coming along? And you look thinner, are you eating properly?'

Annie lets her friend's words wash over her as she is led through to the quiet coolness of the morning room at the back of the house. Ellie is always like this when she is excited, thinks Annie, fondly. A torrent of thoughts and whimsies. Since Annie's mother died, joining her father and sisters in the little cemetery in Playden, Ellie had become Annie's only family. She had always felt more like a sister than a friend and Annie had become increasingly grateful to her for her friendship and ever-jovial company. Yet both of them had been so busy of late that they had barely seen each other. Annie sighs, goes over her meeting with Samuel again in her mind, as if she could rewrite what happened more to her satisfaction.

Ellie's voice calling her name jolts her back to the present. 'Annie, dear! You haven't touched your tea. You are not poorly are you?'

'No. No, in fact, there's nothing that can be found wrong with me in any way,' she replies, her voice tinged with a sadness which Ellie is too preoccupied to hear.

'Well, that is excellent. In which case, you can help me finish the last of my packing. There are some books I wanted to lend you too. Oh, I *shall* miss you! It feels like an age since we saw each other and now I am to be snatched away from you again!'

'And I shall miss you. Very much so,' says Annie, feelingly

– her only confidant taken away from her. 'But you will be back soon enough and I must not be selfish. Lizzie needs you more than I do.'

Ellie leans forward and squeezes her arm. 'Oh, Annie, what on earth would I do without you? You are a veritable angel!'

Natalya is confused. She is standing outside 428 The Strand but it appears to be the wrong address for it is not Benjamin Calder's establishment but a Jeremiah Heath, Globe and Map-maker. 'I don't understand,' she murmurs as cabs and carts rattle along the busy street behind her. 'This can't be right.'

The bell rings above the door as she enters into a light-filled wood-panelled room, packed with globes of all sizes, beautiful, tactile objects that Natalya instinctively goes to touch. As her fingers draw near one, there is a loud cough.

'Can I help you, madam?' says a tall thin gentleman with tufts of white hair spouting from the sides of his head and a bald patch on top. He wears small glasses and a frown.

'Oh, I beg your pardon,' Natalya says. 'I-I'm, well, I'm looking for Mr Calder, Mr Benjamin Calder.'

The man looks at her blankly.

'Benjamin Calder, the mathematical instrument maker? I was led to believe . . .'

'There is no one of that name working here, madam,' the man says, coolly.

'Well, perhaps his establishment has moved?'

'We have been here for nearly three years now, madam. I am afraid I cannot possibly say who was or wasn't at this address before then.'

'*Three years?* But I have come . . . I have come so far!'

Natalya feels as if all the breath has been squeezed out of her. Of all the scenarios she had imagined, she had never considered that Benjamin would not be here. That she would have come all this way, fighting her way southward, earning her passage in a piecemeal fashion for months on end, *for nothing*. She thinks for a moment: his trade card, it had been in her possession for some time after her aunt had gone to throw it out. Can it really have been three years ago?

'Does madam need a seat?' says Mr Heath, quickly fetching a narrow wooden chair into which she sinks, heart tumbling in her chest.

'Peggy!' he cries. 'Come here, please.' There is a sound of footsteps running on stairs before a small maid appears, bobbing a curtsey and staring at Natalya.

'This woman is looking for a Mr Calder. Do you recall anyone of that name?'

Peggy screws up her face in concentration. 'Mr Calder . . . ?' she mutters.

'Benjamin Calder,' says Natalya. 'A maker of mathematical instruments. Compasses and—'

'Oh, the Compass Man! Ben the Compass Man? From the far north? Blond wiry hair and a liking for the ladies?'

Mr Heath coughs politely at his maid's indiscretion.

'I'm afraid that does sound rather like him,' says Natalya. 'I'm his cousin.'

'Oh, miss, I'm sorry then, miss.'

'Sorry?' says Natalya. 'What for?'

''Cause he ain't here anymore, miss. Not for years now. Went bankrupt. Ended up in the workhouse. Don't think he lasted there even a year. Sorry, miss.'

'So where might I find him now then?'

Peggy glances at Mr Heath before looking back at Natalya.

'He ain't anywhere you'll find him, miss. He's . . . well, I'm sorry to have to spell it out for you, but he's *dead*.'

The shock hits Natalya like a punch in the stomach. A pauper's grave for her cousin. This world is full of injustice, she thinks, bitterly. She recalls the letter she sent to him, ink like liquid hope as she had scribbled her best wishes to her cousin, let it fly south as if bound on wings. Her words, her hopes, evaporated now, her letter to a dead man incinerated in the kitchen hearth long ago.

Before Natalya is sent on her way, Peggy sits her downstairs, gives her a hot cup of tea and tells her as much as she remembers, about Ben the Compass Man and about the notorious Camberwell workhouse that devours the lost, desperate and desolate like a hungry furnace.

'You must think I am very green,' Natalya says, sadly. 'To have come all this way, to have chased a dream so far.'

'Not really, miss,' Peggy replies. 'Wish I'd never heard of the workhouses neither. In some ways, I think you're brave.'

'Or foolhardy.' Natalya grimaces. 'And now I am to be punished for it. All alone in a strange city and not even a bed to sleep in.'

'Plenty worse than you in this city though, miss. And there are places with beds all around. But you get what you pay for.' Peggy picks up the empty teacup. 'If you don't mind me saying, I'd say go home, miss. I'm not sure London is a place for the likes of you.'

Natalya thinks for a moment. Is this it then? Time for her to pivot on her heels, make her long way back to the family who disowned her? *They will never accept me.*

'You said you thought I was brave,' Natalya says, as she goes to stand. 'Well, a brave person doesn't run away. Besides, isn't this the greatest city on earth? So let me see what opportunities it can offer up.' She nods to Peggy. 'Thank you for the tea,' she says. 'I'll show myself out.'

She rises up from the basement steps to a side passage leading back out to the Strand. At the far end of the passage, she can see the chaos of the capital, framed, as if a living portrait, by the narrow brick walls either side of her. Hooves and wheels, noise and people, an endless labyrinth of buildings and streets.

'Come on then, London,' Natalya whispers to herself, determination rising. 'Let me see what manner of place you really are.' And she steps out of the frame and into the maelstrom.

She lies on her back on Edward's dissection table, thin and angular, still slightly damp from the river. The wings have nearly dried already; creamy white in colour, they are large for a bird, perhaps just over a foot in length. On a human, they look strangely small, not large enough to be of use and yet . . .

Edward stands in the corner; he cannot do anything but look, eyes staring greedily at his prize. The wings are flesh and bone and feather, attached to her as firmly as his own arm is attached to his shoulder. How and why it is so, he does not know. It should not be possible and yet here it is.

He steps forward, looks closely into his angel's face – her unseeing eyes, blue-grey lips – before gently lifting her. He takes her left wing in his hand and opens it out, lingering on the feathers, parting them with his fingers, feeling the soft barbs and hooks.

This is God's will, Edward thinks to himself as the feathers tickle his palm. An answer to his prayers. This wonder that the Almighty has laid at his feet, this gift from heaven, it will enable his own ascension in the world. His route into the Royal Society, the Society for the Promotion and

Advancement of Knowledge, this will be the making of him. Recognition. Success. *Fortune*. All by the grace of God.

Footsteps tentatively echo down the basement corridor and Edward hastily folds the wing back, covering the body with a cloth. No one is allowed in this part of the depths bar his own self. There is a bell to be rung on the console table in the hallway if he is to be disturbed and, much to his annoyance, he hears it ring out.

Lord Douglas waits upstairs in Edward's consulting room, fingers tapping impatiently. Edward has visited him previously at his grand mansion as befits his status but on this occasion Lord Douglas was 'passing by' and thought to ascertain the opinion of his admirably discreet surgeon on a most personal matter. Samuel had initially been Douglas's first choice as consultant but he had soon decided that Edward's calm and thoughtful nature made him a better pick. Douglas, although married with a variety of offspring – some, indeed, actually with his own wife – also has a liking for rough, paid encounters with both the fairer and less fair sex. Alas, this has taken an inevitable toll on his health.

Edward neither knows nor cares for Lord Douglas's predilections, his sole focus is to keep this wealthy ally on side both for his reputation and his purse. Douglas has had a chancre on his penis before and a bubo in the groin. The symptoms had abated for a while, but are now returning and he is most desperate to stop the itching in his trousers. More hydriodate of potash, Edward thinks.

'Ah, Lord Douglas, what an unexpected pleasure,' says Edward, all charm as he shuts the door to his consulting room behind him, noting with dissatisfaction that Douglas has placed his ample being on Edward's own favoured armchair. He has no need to ask his patient the reason for his visit as he rubs and scratches at himself like a dog with a flea.

'Damned nuisance,' mutters the aristocrat, hands down the front of his trousers. 'Damned nuisance, Meake!'

Annie, watching from the stairs, sneaks down to the basement as soon as Edward shuts the door on his consultation with Lord Douglas. She knows that he had returned from whatever client he'd seen in plenty of time for lunch, for Sarah had told her so, but he had remained mysteriously absent from the dining table. She had sat, instead, on her own, appetite waning as she thought of her husband's late nights working away downstairs. Curiosity about what could possibly still be keeping him from her has finally won over and she heads, determinedly, down to the maze of dinginess below. She weaves past the small servants' hall as the open-flame gas lamps flicker and hiss, turning right to pass the kitchen and diminutive but well-stocked wine cellar before a final left by the tiny blue-wash laundry room and along the hallway, clad recently with wood below the dado rail to hide the rising damp underneath. She moves swiftly past the narrow console table with the bell sitting on it, past Edward's small study on the right and straight to his dissecting room at the far end.

She stops. Inhales. There is a corpse in front of her.

Covered by a sheet, it is still a body, a shell of a person. Someone who once lived and breathed. Someone who laughed and dreamt and loved. Annie is well used to death – many have been lost in her lifetime and more, she knows, will come – yet it still unnerves her, making her pause in the doorway, hand grasping the surround to steady herself. It takes a moment for her to recover her senses.

There is a smell of death in here too, mingled with chemicals and sadness. Bottles of pickled and preserved organs and creatures sit looking down at her from the shelves. Disembodied eyes staring back at her from jars, thin winding strips of what look like sausages curled tightly up. Lizards, mice, moles and rats floating in small vessels filled with semi-clear liquid. Bones and skulls, empty-eyed, gaze blankly down at her. Her husband's dissecting room is part museum, part morgue and as mesmerising as it is repellent.

Annie looks down into a vat positioned near the doorway and sees the head of a dog just below the surface of the liquid. She recognises him as the same one that Edward took for a walk only the other day.

'Oh,' she says, sadly. She had been rather fond of that dog, played with it on more than one occasion. And now it was to be another specimen, flesh and fat melted away, reduced down to bones and labels. She has been down here before, once or twice, when they first moved in. It is not as if she was ignorant of what medical men must do in order to progress their understanding, but still . . . The acrid smell of chemicals, the knowledge that the friendly dog with its wagging tail and gentle licks is no more, it pains her.

Perhaps Edward is trying to create immortality in his own way, Annie thinks. Like the pictures she draws, the paintings she makes. A landscape, a person, an animal, she replicates them on paper and canvas, a moment in time captured, preserved. Perhaps he too is doing the same with these bones, giving them a new life. But she cannot shake away the thought that it is wrong somehow.

She takes a deep breath before stepping inside. In their early-wedded days, back in the old house, Annie would help her husband by sketching the strange and beautiful creatures that ended up on his dissecting table. An unusual giant fish from Billingsgate clad in all the colours of the rainbow, a sad tiger cub from the zoo, killed by its own mother. She no longer has the stomach for it.

She slowly approaches the body. Edward had promised her, before they were married, that he would no longer open up a person unless, and this was to be the only exception, it were one of his former patients. He had persuaded a handful of them – those with the most interesting cases – to sign a document granting him permission to hold an autopsy on their body after death.

This must be one of them then, thinks Annie, as her fingers close around the corner of the cloth and she starts to lift it. But she has been down here longer than she realises and the consultation is finished, Lord Douglas sent away with a cream and some pills.

'Annie! What are you doing?' Edward is in the doorway and Annie drops the cloth immediately, like a naughty child caught in an act of mischief.

'Nothing! I simply wanted to . . .'

'Wanted to . . . *what* exactly?' Edward's voice is calm and quiet, but his eyes tell a different story. It is worse, Annie thinks guiltily, than if his voice were raised.

'*Lift it then,*' he says, a challenge in his voice. 'Go on.'

Annie looks at the shape underneath the cloth and has no desire to really see what manner of person lies underneath. She shakes her head.

'Do you not trust me?' Edward says as he steps towards her, holding out his hands. A moment passes before Annie realises that he is expecting her to step forward too. 'Do you not trust your own husband, Annie?'

'Of course,' she says, taking his hands in hers. 'Of course I do, Edward.'

'Then all is well,' he says, smiling at her. 'Trust is all that I ask.' He kisses her on the cheek before motioning towards the door. 'Now, I must get on.'

'Of course. Yes. It's only . . . Will I see you at dinner tonight?'

'I hope so,' he says, with a quick smile before turning away from her and beginning to busy himself with his instruments. 'I hope so, dear.'

Annie trembles as she leaves the room, her own footsteps pattering back at her from the flagstones as she walks hastily away and straight up the two flights of stairs to her bedroom where she locks the door behind her. Whenever Edward worked at home, he would always make the time to sit and share meals with her. There had only ever been a handful of exceptions, when Edward had been called away to embark on an urgent operation. Yet today, it is clear that there had been no such emergency. It is rare for them to have a cross word or be cold towards each other but for him to be keeping such things from her – *a body in the basement*. And yet, is she not keeping secrets from him as well? Her consultation with Samuel . . . Oh, if only Ellie had not been called away!

Edward, meanwhile, is barely thinking of his wife at all. In the basement, gingerly, carefully, as if not quite believing his own luck, he lifts the cloth, revealing the impossible winged woman underneath. He is not prepared to share his secret with anyone yet. It was God's will, Edward thinks, *a sign* that Annie did not lift the cloth. The Almighty has entrusted me, Edward Algernon Meake, with an angel and I must tell *no one* else of it. God has chosen me for this, *me alone*.

Many years ago, Edward had disobeyed his reverend father's wishes for him to follow in his own footsteps. There had been arguments, unpleasantness, but Edward had known, been absolutely certain, that medicine was the right path. *Look*, he thinks, look at what it has given me, Father. Here is the higher calling you wished for.

Edward resumes his watch on the impossible body, thoughts falling from his mind like rain until they start, slowly, to settle like snowflakes into a semblance of a plan.

Scout is busy at work, noisily demolishing a heavy stick Etta found for him some days ago and which, to his great delight, he rediscovered under a hedgerow this morning. The wet chomping of his jaws is revolting and yet strangely comforting, Etta thinks, with a smile, as he runs ahead of her as they head towards Elton Hall.

It is a large and impressive building from both front and back. Three elegant and imposing storeys of red brick, a cluster of thin chimneys stretching up towards the sky. It is the home in which Etta spent her formative years and which was taken from her, after Papa died, by the resentful Walter. The old gatekeeper's cottage she has found herself relegated to – out of sight, out of mind – suits her modest tastes but, even with the additional shelves in her cabin, she only has a little space for books and is forced to sneak in the back door to raid the remnants of her father's old library and to return previously borrowed tomes.

There is bustle around the Hall as always: comings and goings of suppliers, servants and horses. Many of them know Etta by sight and acknowledge her presence with a nod but she is distant from them, both one foot above and one below, straddling the social strata. They know her late mother had been a freed slave, her father the master of Elton, but with the master buried and long gone and Walter's lineage secure with his three motley sons, no one need longer pretend that Etta might inherit anything more than her little cottage and small stipend and so she is treated accordingly, a novel eccentric who wanders the hills, preferring her own company to that of others.

Scout whines as Etta leaves him by the back door. He had been banned from the house ever since he had given Walter Junior a nip when the boy roughly pulled his tail. No blood had been drawn and Etta had passionately defended him, but Walter Senior had been insistent and so the ban remained in place.

The Hall is a grand place, built for comfort and show, and yet it had been Etta's home for so long, the place where she grew up, learnt to dance and play piano, the place where she started her first collection of birds' eggs and ferns, where she first fell through pages of books into whole other worlds. The place where Henry Underwood came into her life. The wide wooden staircase curving up, the high ceilings, ornate plaster and large windows – it is a house of light and learning and, once upon a time, Etta's laughter too.

Bertie, the youngest of her nephews, stands and watches her with his thumb in his mouth, a habit he has not yet grown out of. He will run off and tell his father that Etta is in the house and Walter will find her, as he always does, in the library. It is there that their ongoing differences mutate into something sharper and nastier.

'You cannot always use the coach when you require it,' her half-brother snaps, following her polite request. Etta's lips are pursed but she says nothing in return.

'You assume—' Walter continues but she cuts him off, a hand up to silence him.

'A "no" is sufficient answer in itself, Walter. If it is inconvenient, I do not need to – nor indeed *wish* – to hear the reason why.'

He is startled at her answering him back.

'I suppose it is for another of your self-indulgent trips to see old—'

'It is no matter what the request was for, dear brother, the fact remains that it's clearly not convenient and we shall say no more upon the matter.' She goes to leave, but Walter will be damned if he'll let her have the final word.

'In future, when you wish to visit the library, Etta, you will let me know in writing in advance. We have some important visitors over the coming weeks and I do not wish to—'

'You do not wish to be associated with your "exotic" sibling?' she says, sharply.

'How *dare* you?' he growls. 'How dare you speak to me like that in my own house?'

'How dare *you* throw me out of my own house when you know perfectly well Papa left it as much to me as he did to you?' She speaks calmly but her words are full of fire. There. It is out at last.

He boils with fury, a laugh of outrage.

'That will I assume you are referring to went missing and was never found – as you well know. The estate could only be divided up according to his last dated will.'

The will you drew up and had him sign on his deathbed when the opium had numbed both his strength and sense, she thinks angrily.

'He was my father and *this was my home*,' she says, now on the verge of tears.

'No, Etta,' he says firmly. 'No. This was never truly your home and it never will be. You do not belong here – you never have.'

She takes the book she was looking for as hot tears spill down her face. It is the most she has spoken to Walter for some time. The worst thing, she thinks, as Scout bounces along the path ahead of her, is that perhaps he is right.

Despite being the city to end all cities, London's rumour mill is both as efficient and inaccurate as that of any small rural town. When someone with an ear for a story over-hears Peter King's drunken, meandering tale of a woman with wings plucked from the river, it spreads, slowly at first like spilled ink on a page. In a handful of days, it will have picked up enough speed to make its way from the riverbanks and docks, along ragged streets and tumbledown slums, past grand houses and noisy markets, dodging and weaving around carriages, carts and omnibuses, lingering at numerous other taverns on the way before finally making its way up three flights of stairs to the top of the irregularly shaped house that is home to Jos and Mary Ward. But all that is yet to come – for now, it is simply one of many overheard conversations in the Blue Boar this night. There is always bragging to be witnessed in this place, strange tales of impossible things, but Peter's is strangest of all. Propped up against the uneven walls of the tavern, his inebriated ravings are caught by more than one set of ears – and so it is that the embers of the old tale of the Angel of the Thames are once again set aflame.

Natalya's first night in the capital is not at all what she had expected. Far from enjoying the warm hospitality of her cousin, she is instead squashed up in a bed with two other women in a cramped, overpriced room that smells of boiled cabbage and onions. It was not the first guest house she tried, but it was the first affordable one with any semblance of cleanliness. She is already planning ahead, working out how much she needs to live on, how many days she can get by, counting her coins secretly in the guest house privy, as though they might duplicate themselves by the act of her doing so.

The city is so alive, much more than she could have imagined, a creature that never sleeps, streets throbbing like blood in its veins. Giant windows in tall buildings stare down like watchful eyes, a dragon perhaps, roaring with the sound of industry and wheels, of hooves and feet.

Natalya mourned as she walked the streets looking for both work and a bed for the night. Benjamin is gone and with him her dreams of a new life too. She rebuked herself. How could she have been so foolish as to not consider that misfortune may have plagued him as it has her?

'Sorry, miss,' she has heard a dozen times or more. 'Nothing going.' She has been asked for references she does not have, notes of recommendation she cannot magic from thin air. There is piecemeal work, small, badly paid jobs to be done at home but she has no home in which to do them and no means of getting one.

'I can turn my hand to anything, I am a good worker, hard-working and strong,' she has said to anyone who might listen. But her voice is soft and it is a strain to make herself heard above the noise of the streets. The capital seems to be for those who shout the loudest, draw most attention to themselves, she thinks.

As darkness descended, the streetlights blazed like constellations, erasing the real stars above. It made her feel as if she had come adrift. She hadn't realised how much she needed those bright pinpricks to navigate herself, to anchor her to the solidity of life. Instead, she feels as if she is floating in some in-between place, some in-between state.

She sleeps badly. The two other women with whom she shares the bed fidget and kick in their sleep. Snatches of vivid and strange dreams call to her of the wild seas of home, of low, inquisitive clouds, and the thick, cold mist that descends upon the isles like a wolf pack.

Natalya stretches herself awake, prepares for her first full day in this strange, bewildering place until she realises, with a jolt, that the pocket under her dress is no longer there. Despite feeling as if she has not slept for more than a few minutes, she has been robbed during the night by fingers more nimble than she could have imagined. Panicking, she checks her clothes, hoping beyond hope that the pocket has simply slipped down, but it has vanished into thin air and she is left only with a few spare coins hidden in her boots. Her companions for the night are long gone, names and destinations unknown. In a city of nearly two million people, there is no hope of finding either them or her money.

Natalya pours cold water from the jug on the washstand into the bowl, splashes it over her face, washes her hands. She dare not undress. There are no locks on the doors and her trust in people has disappeared along with her money. I have survived worse than this, she thinks. And so, I must survive this too. She shakes her hands dry, touches the space where her beloved grandmother's ring used to sit until she pawned it on her journey south. The mirror on the washstand is cracked and a jagged version of her face stares back, startled and bad-tempered.

'I can turn my hand to anything, I am a good worker, hard-working and strong,' Natalya whispers, setting her jaw. Today is the day I will find work. Today, is the day in which my luck will change.

Annie has been so busy of late that she has neglected both her art and the setting up of her studio. This new house is so much bigger than the old one and, with only two current members of staff, there is much to organise and supervise. Hearths to be cleaned and blackened, rugs to be beaten and swept, food to be bought and prepared, suppliers to be approved of. There is a seemingly endless stream of things she must herself be consulted on, everything from menus and suppliers to laundry and cleaning and, on top of it all, so much dust and dirt. At least when they lived in Bloomsbury, the large green square opposite had been a much-needed refuge but here, in the City, they have no outdoor space bar the back yard with the privy and that is hardly a place one wishes to linger in.

Come, Annie, she says to herself. Focus. For at long last, after nearly three months, she has finally carved out a little time for herself and she plans to use it to its full advantage. She talks to her materials as she unpacks, laying them out for the first time since they moved here. This little room is all hers. It is not yet arranged exactly as she would like, but that will come in time as she becomes more familiar with how and where the light falls during the day. She smiles to herself as she lays out her old sketchpads, brimming with moments and memories, her old canvases of forgotten days, yet to be mounted and framed. Today is a day for restoring order to chaos – sketchpads on shelves, canvases stacked against the wall and, when all have found new homes, she looks over her old materials: papers, brushes, inks, charcoals, watercolours and oils. There is such delight contained in the sheer range of coloured paints, names so pleasurable to say out loud. Annie relishes the sound of them, feeling as if she tastes the very essence of the colour as she does so.

'Chinese White and Cobalt Blue. Indian Yellow and Rose Madder. Viridian and Cobalt Violet. Cerulean Blue and Green Oxide. Vermilion and Carmine.'

Annie has a few brand-new glass syringes from Winsor and Newton that she is extremely proud of, but most of her oils are in sealed bladders which she must pierce with a tack, working as swiftly as possible before the liquid inside dries into an unusable solid. None will be opened today, though, for she dare not waste a drop of her precious paints until she knows the final shape of her painting.

She runs her fingers over the tightly woven threads of her canvases, the tactile nature of them pleasing her immensely. Canvas and oils, paper and watercolours. It is like alchemy, this ability to transfer an image of life itself from the brush of imagination onto a blank canvas, a white sheet of fresh, empty paper.

Edward is preoccupied, that is all, thinks Annie, reassuring herself as she readies a preparatory sketch. Of course she had been disturbed to find the body in the basement, to see the corpse of the dog too, but whatever Edward is now working on is not for her eyes. It's only that he had *promised* her he was done with cutting up cadavers. The look in his eyes when he found her in his dissecting room contained a strange glint she had never seen before. She wonders if she might be able to capture it on paper . . . Today, she will try, half-hoping that if she sketches it well enough, she will somehow draw it out of him — that the natural balance of things will be restored and he will once again resume his practice of coming to bed at the same time as her. For, as she is only too well aware, without regular intimacy, there cannot be any fresh hope of a baby.

'Oh, now that is odd!' says Annie out loud. She does not quite have the quantity of paper and ink she had remembered. No matter, she thinks, after a brief but thorough search. I have enough for now. She starts to sketch Edward's fierce green eyes and soon she is lost deep in concentration.

Friday 9th October, 1840

Specimen – female. Age – early 50s? Height – 5 foot 5 inches. Two large tattoos on upper arms. Left arm, some kind of vine. On the right, a snake, a cobra of some kind. Both faded, indicating age. One single mole approximately a quarter inch in diameter on the underside of the left foot in the arch. A single irregular mark around the upper right thigh – likely from boat hook, approximately six inches by two. No other identifying features.

Wings emerge as extension of lower scapulae. On external examination only, they appear to be linked to trapezius and, suspect, rhomboideus major and minor.

Wings are lightweight, movable and easily manipulated. Similar structure to those of a large bird of prey, a buzzard or kite. Wing bones appear to be hollow.

Humerus, radius, and ulna appear well developed and strong. Wing length from shoulder to tip, a little over 17 inches when fully extended.

Edward has already begun. The weather is cool but the body will not be preserved indefinitely and he must get to work. He sketches alongside his notes as he works, using the ink and paper borrowed from Annie's study, remembering all that she – a considerably better artist than he – has taught him and wishing, for a moment, she were there beside him. *No*, says a voice in his head. Tell anyone else and your secret is lost forever. *You* are the one who has been chosen. Not Annie, not Samuel, *you* and you alone.

'I, Edward Meake, am the man who discovered an angel,' he says to himself. 'I will preserve her skeleton for all eternity.' He hums to himself as he works, composing paeans to the Almighty as he does so.

The tattoos had unsettled Edward at first – a snake and a vine. Was this a message of some kind? A message of the Garden of Eden, of the first betrayal? His thoughts wound around him like thread on a spool until, gradually, he became less focused on the content of the tattoos and more on their being a means of identification. Yet, he reassured himself, what woman of repute would possibly allow herself to be scarred in such a way? It is a conundrum but one that fades as he concentrates his mind on the dissection. For, as God has surely foreseen, the woman's tattoos will soon be rendered into nothingness during Edward's process to preserve her skeleton and he takes comfort in the thought.

What will an angel be like on the inside? he ponders. Do they look as we do? Torn between science, wonder and belief, Edward takes a deep breath as he makes his first incision.

The wind is fierce up on the banks of the steep and uneven hill known as Brown Clee. It blows all the thoughts around Etta's head as she stops for a moment near the old earthworks at Nordy Bank to catch her breath on the ascent. She closes her eyes for a moment, feels the wind rushing around her, roaring in her ears. She thinks of all the other people in past times who have trodden this same route, this same path, smelt the same damp earth of autumn and felt the wind scouring their faces. She thinks of those who once lived within the banks of the hill fort, imagines them turning, looking back towards the distant hills, the same view she now looks at herself. Etta smiles. This is her world – these paths and lanes, holloways and tracks. She can trace them in her mind's eye, feet retreading the same footprints, month after month, year after year, engraving herself into the ground. She knows these hills as well as she knows herself, years of familiarity allowing her to see the finer details that few others would observe. From lichen to ladybird, from a hare's form to the scrape of a lapwing's nest, she feels the seasons unroll around her.

I am the breath in the soaring wind, the heartbeat in the

thunder. I am the hills and the holloways, the meres and the mosses, the fields and the ferns. She remembers Walter's words from the other day and grimaces. *No*, she thinks. It is not *I* that do not belong here, Walter, it is *you*.

Etta laughs as the wind suddenly does its best to dislodge her bonnet and she grabs at it, holding it tight onto her head. Scout races ahead through the tall bracken, his black-and-white head bouncing up for a quick check of his position before disappearing again below the curling brown ferns. She calls him back, mindful that he doesn't go too far towards the quarry at Abdon Burf.

She has not visited Woodbank for some time, situated as it is, nearly five hours on foot from Elton. Since Walter had slowly withdrawn access to the carriage, Etta's visits to Dorothy, her elderly nursemaid, have become increasingly infrequent. When Etta was brought to Elton Hall after her mother died, Dorothy had become almost a second mother to the young toddler. The wiper of snotty noses, provider of comforting hugs, the person who tipped her out of bed in the morning and tucked her safely back up at night. It had been Dorothy who had once, after Etta scratched her arm when playing in the woods, bound up the wound with spiders' webs to close the skin. It had been Dorothy who pointed out old country remedies that lay hidden in plain sight amongst the forests and hedgerows. And it had also been Dorothy who had found Etta hiding in the wood store, aged six, face stained with tears, dress still wet after Walter, then an uptight, envious little boy of eleven, had pushed her into the lake.

As she had grown up, Etta had remained fond of Dorothy

– although unable to see her in person as often as she would like, she still sent notes and seeds to her and would, on occasion, receive the same in reply. When Etta looked towards the double peak of Brown Clee on the eastern horizon, she would often think of Dorothy, finding comfort in the knowledge that her old nursemaid was still happily, albeit slowly, pottering away somewhere near the top.

Over the years, Etta had asked for and received advice about a number of things from Dorothy. She will surely know how Etta should best handle the situation with Walter – as the person who has known them both the longest, she is well placed to advise on how best to ease the growing tension between them.

Etta has imagined their conversation the whole way here, but, alas, she is to be disappointed. The first sign that something is wrong comes long before Etta steps foot in the house. Dorothy's garden, her pride and joy in which she battles the elements year-round to create an idyllic space filled with flowers, fruit and more, is curling at the edges, brown and decaying, old beanpoles with yellowed pods flapping in the wind like tiny rotting flags, flowers decomposing to mush, mouldy apples and leaves scattered amongst the overgrown paths. Etta had expected to find Dorothy out here, bent double with age and squinting in the daylight, putting the garden to bed for the winter; she would never normally leave her garden in such a state.

It has been six weeks or more since Etta's last visit and she is dismayed by what she finds. True, her nursemaid had become increasingly hard of hearing, her eyesight worse in low light, but she had not expected matters to deteriorate quite so quickly. Etta steps into the small parlour, her heart cracking as Dorothy's eyes, glazing over like frosted glass and no longer their old lively self, turn towards her in the doorway.

'You always were my favourite,' Dorothy whispers loudly as Etta seats herself in the chair next to her and they sit together in silent companionship for a while, looking out of the window towards the shifting clouds stretching themselves over the hills. Dorothy does not seem in pain, there is that at least, thinks Etta sadly, noting that her old nursemaid is already dozing off. But one of her oldest friends is being erased in front of her and soon, she thinks, it will just be her and Scout.

Dorothy has long since fallen asleep, knitted shawl tucked over her knees, when Etta rises to her feet, but the movement wakes the older woman, and a look of startled fear comes over her.

'Who let you in?' Dorothy cries as she peers at Etta, confused and scared. 'Who the devil are you?'

Etta tries to comfort her until Mariah, Dorothy's younger sister, dashes in having heard the commotion from upstairs where she'd been changing the bed linen. 'Oh goodness! It's only Miss Lockhart, Dorothy! It's just Etta! Have you been having one of your dreams again?' Nothing she says seems to soothe her sister and Etta is ushered out of the room, bewildered and hurt.

'Don't take it to heart, please, Miss Lockhart,' says Mariah, joining her by the front door. 'Yesterday, she didn't even recognise me when I tried to get her out of bed, but an hour later, she was right as rain. It might be best if you went now, though. I'm so sorry you had to see her like this. She's not good with visitors at the moment. Perhaps you could let me know in advance next time, if you might be planning to visit? I can at least try and prepare her a bit.'

'Yes, of course.' Etta swallows, doing her best to hold her emotions in check. She knows that Mariah is only doing her best to care for her sibling, but the words still sting regardless. 'I understand.'

'Thank you for coming all this way,' Mariah says, embracing her tightly for a moment before handing Etta her bonnet. 'She was always awful fond of you, you know. She always said you had some kind of spark in you.'

Etta only just manages to make it out of the house before the tears come, the fierce wind drying them on her face as they fall. It will be the last time she ever sees her old friend.

Mary is jostled and shoved in the midst of the crowd as she struggles to push her way to the edge, her bonnet askew. She has lost Uncle Jos at the harvest fair in Greenwich Park and wishes for nothing else but to find him and return home.

The chaos is deafening, stalls selling all manner of things from gingerbread and oranges to penny toys. There are coconut shys and fortune tellers, wandering musicians, whole throngs of men and women shouting, singing, drinking and eating. There are giants and giantesses and a theatre troupe – for some reason known only to them – dressed as Romans. Spiced nuts, pickled salmon, alcohol and cigars mingle in Mary's nostrils, making her cough.

Jos had solemnly promised her that sobriety was within his grasp and she had thought a cheap day out at the fair might help cheer him, distract him from the drink. Alas, no sooner had they got their bearings than a throng of rowdy young men had separated them.

Mary finally squeezes her way out of the crowd, only to stumble over a muddy guy rope and into the doorway of a tent where a fortune teller sits.

'Oh, dear me, poppet!' the woman says, looking up from her crystal ball and adjusting her turban. 'You look in a state and no mistake.'

'I'm afraid I've lost my uncle,' says Mary, as she catches her breath.

'Sit down, my love, I'll read your fortune,' the woman says, smiling.

'Thank you,' says Mary, 'but the most pressing thing is that I find my uncle. If your fortune-telling can do but that, I'd be more than grateful.'

The woman eyes Mary up, decides she won't get a fare from this one, and gives her a wink. 'He'll be in the tavern, dear, they always are.'

'Ah, but he no longer drinks!'

'Ah, well,' says the woman, 'I fear he'll still be in the Rose and Crown whether you like it or not. Let's hope not too much the worse for wear, eh? Sure you won't have your fortune told? I could tell of the sorrow within you; I could tell of a handsome young man who's got his eye on you! Ah, I see *that* rings a bell!'

'I must be going. Really. I'm sorry to have disturbed you.' Mary steps outside, heat rising to her cheeks, as she hears the words of the fortune teller behind her.

'Ah, I don't need to read your fortune, lovely, you will make it yourself, eh?'

Later, after Mary has spent the little money she was hoping to spend at the fair on a cab home instead and Uncle Jos is drunkenly put to bed, she allows the tears to come. The shame of knowing they would not be able to get the train back to London Bridge as her uncle was so inebriated; the way the cab driver looked her up and down before charging her what she knew was above the odds for the five miles home. How will I make my own fortune? *How?* Mary thinks, cheeks damp upon her pillow. I cannot abandon Uncle Jos; both he and George looked after me for years, it is surely only right that I do the same in return.

She wishes Richard had been there to help and blushes in the darkness. The handsome young man was but a guess from the fortune teller; the mourning dress she wears for George, it was easy enough to assume sorrow. Mary is eighteen now; it is not much of a leap to assume she may have interest from a young man somewhere. But *Richard* – Mr Gibbs. He is a *friend*, an old family friend, she tells herself firmly. Besides, she thinks wistfully as she stares at the cracks in the ceiling, he likely still sees me as a younger sister. And she does not dare allow herself to think, to hope, otherwise.

Samuel is talking, words pouring out of his mouth like beer from the tapped barrels at the Cheshire Cheese on Fleet Street where they sit, but Edward is barely listening. He thinks only of the winged creature in his basement, the secret of her existence growing within him.

'Tricky fellows, journalists – you know how they are, charming the words out of your head before you've even thought them through yourself.' Samuel takes another swig of his port wine, careful to mind his new blue brocade waistcoat and yellow necktie, both of which he is extremely proud of.

'It was never my intention to announce the lectures on Tuesday, Meake,' he says, apologetically. 'I truly believed the first of the autumn season began *next week* as you know – but I found myself in a pickle from the board and rather had to run along with things. I clean forgot that damn journalist was loitering. I should, of course, have mentioned it to you but I'm afraid with the exhilaration of the theatre and'– he holds up his glass – 'the devil drink in me, I clean forgot.'

'And how fares the amputee?' Edward asks, wrangling his thoughts back to the present.

'Ah, alas he expired yesterday. A great shame as he'd looked to be recovering rather well. There was an excellent amount of pus on the stump, most laudable but, unfortunately, it was not to be.'

Samuel eyes Edward for a moment. 'Do forgive me, Meake, you are my oldest, dearest friend and I would be most mortified to have given you offence when none was intended.' He waits for an answer, but Edward has disappeared back into his own head and Samuel mistakes the silence for something else.

'Dammit, man, say *something*, for goodness' sake. I cannot bear your long silences! Well, look, if you will not forgive me so easily, perhaps this news will raise some cheer.' Samuel clears his throat, dramatically. 'I have put you forward with the highest of recommendations for membership of the Society for the Promotion and Advancement of Knowledge. They are due to convene shortly and will consider it at the very next meeting. Is that not capital, my dear friend?'

Edward smiles. It seems his next move has already been played for him. Membership of that prestigious society would give him an extra air of authority – a philosopher of science as well as a practitioner, a true thinker.

Samuel sees the smile and allows himself a sigh of relief. He had not meant to upset Edward, only that he does have a tendency to get carried away in the heat of the moment. But no harm done, he has got away with it, as he knew he would.

'You say nothing, Meake, but I see from your expression that it pleases you! I cannot guarantee they will accept you, of course, but despite my own very recent membership, I am not without influence. I will do my damnedest to get you in.' Samuel slaps Edward on the shoulder. 'Another drink?' he asks.

Edward nods. 'Why not?' He does, after all, feel like celebrating.

'I've been meaning to ask,' says Samuel. 'Not just after the delightful Annie of course but your father too. How is the aged Meake?'

Edward shakes his head as a pang of guilt stabs at him. 'Alas, with setting up the new house and extending the practice, there has been much to do.'

'You should go and see him again, tell him of your news. It might do him good, perhaps you too.'

Edward nods. He knows this is true but he cannot bear to see the man whom he thought of as indestructible, a great bear of a figure, reduced to a jellyish quiver, unable to argue with and disapprove of him. It frightens Edward, reminds him of his own mortality – yet he knows at some point he must return to the family home, perform his duty as the last surviving son.

As Samuel waves the head waiter over for pudding – today's is lark, kidney and steak – and more port wine, Edward allows his eyes to close, relishing the thought of the secret in his basement. He has already put a plan in motion to protect his discovery – a wrought-iron gate across the entrance to his part of the basement, a single key to be held only by him, just like his private door to the yard that he had created – a necessity in order to keep any unsavoury deliveries from the neighbours' prying eyes. Discovering Annie so close to his prized angel had unnerved him. If his gift from God is to truly remain a secret, he must keep it secure under lock and key until such time as he is ready to reveal it. All else is well. God will guide him in all things.

'Here, Meake, let me charge your glass, let us drink a toast to happy times ahead.'

'To happy times ahead,' says Edward, raising his glass. 'To happy times indeed.'

Natalya is hungry. She had grown used to eating as and when the opportunity arose, knowing her next meal might be some while away, but three weeks of good, regular food are easy to become accustomed to. Her few coins are being saved for a bed for the night and the pit in her stomach grows harder and emptier with every hour. She has nothing of any decent value left to pawn and is puzzled at how hard it is to gain a foothold here. Perhaps Peggy the maid was right. *This city is not for the likes of you.* There is always the option of a boat back to Mersea, back to the Harrisons' little cottage – providing she can raise the funds – but Natalya dismisses it out of hand. She'd already mended all their nets and what other work would there be? There must be no going back. Only forward. And yet the divides between those with and without in the capital are more like a chasm than anywhere else she has been. Rich and poor jostling for space, brushed nap of top hats that cost more than rent for others, extravagant dinners at restaurants beyond the reach of those who walk past, glancing in at the golden glow of money and privilege. Huge houses, modern and old, in the same street, some crammed with dozens of people, others populated more by servants than the affluent families who rent them.

She summons up the last remnants of pluck to tell stories in the new, cheaper, guest house she finds, hoping for a coin or two in return. The eager faces cram in around her, clinging onto her every word. She tells two long stories and is begged for another, only giving in after much pestering.

'Then I shall begin,' she says. 'Once upon a time, in a land not so very far away, there was a young girl with eyes the colour of the sea and waves in her hair. She lived upon an island, small enough to walk the coastline in a single day yet large enough to be lost on. The girl spent her days in a cove filled with small shells, all the colours of the rainbow and, every day, she would look out at the sea. In winter it would be fierce, all bluster, wind and rage. In summer it would be calm and silver, smooth as a mirror looking back at her.

'The girl had heard tale of the Mother of the Sea, as had all those who lived upon the isle. The spirit of the waves themselves, ebbing and flowing with every moon that passed, the Mother of the Sea was the deity to whom one would ask for safe passage from storms.

'The girl was seen as simple by many on the island, losing herself in daydreams as she played on the shore, so much so that any work she was given was soon forgot – cows unmilked, a plot of land undug, chickens unfed. And so the girl was left by herself, to wander in her world of dreams. If only they had looked more closely, paid more attention, they too would have noticed that the girl's own moods came and went with the seasons, shifting and stretching with every pass of the moon.

'One year, when autumn was coming and the plants yawned themselves back to sleep, the weather changed. The horizon darkened as if angry with the world. The clouds grew black with rage and the waves reached up to the sky, white-flecked with furious foam, spitting and hissing as they raced for the island.

'The boats were already out, the menfolk at sea, their vessels thrown about like corks, pitching and turning helplessly in the boiling waves. Panic spread around the island like a fever as women and children raced to the harbour, anxious to see their brothers and fathers, husbands and sons, their friends and family return safely.

'But the girl was not with them. The girl was on the hill above, watching the angry waves gleefully toy with the tiny boats at their mercy. She felt the rage in her own self too, at the boy who threw a stone at her earlier. The boy who was on his way to his first full outing as a fisherman. His stone had grazed her forehead, glancing off it, a red smear on her fingers when she touched her head, a sore bruise welling up beneath.

'She thought of him out there, crying for his mother, wanting to come home, and for a moment she felt glad. Until she remembered the others – her uncle, her cousins, her distant relatives. They might have abandoned her, but she would not, in turn, abandon them. She knew what she must do, had always known somehow.

'She calmed herself, slowed her breathing, thought of the golden sun of spring warming the earth. She walked down the hill towards the sea, not to the harbour but to the cove nearby, *her* cove, in which the small shells were all the colours of the rainbow. She walked, determined, head held high, arms outstretched, feet tickled by the long sandy grasses of the machair until she reached the shoreline, and still she walked, the tiny shells crunching under her feet. One of the women at the harbour spotted her, cried out, as the other faces turned to look. And still the girl walked. For she had understood what she was, *who* she was, with the sea in her eyes and the waves in her hair.

'They cried to her, the women and children, called to her to stop, but their voices were like so many gulls in the sky and still she walked, walked until her feet felt the first white waves frothing around her ankles, walked until she was waist-high in the raging sea, hands held out in supplication as the water tried to push her back, all the time the full realisation of who and what she was dawning upon her. She walked until her head was all that was visible above the rolling waves, walked until she had gone from this land and into another life. And as she disappeared, swallowed up by the sea, the rage too went from the world. Dark clouds melted to fluffy white and the boiling sea calmed itself, sighed, settled back to quiet. And the boats, with their menfolk, swearing, praying, weeping, begging for home, the boats were softly, gently nudged back towards the harbour, bringing with them nets brimful with armies of silver fish.

'And so it is, that one night, every autumn, all the islanders gather by the harbour to sing songs around a fire in memory of that day, when a girl with eyes the colour of the sea and waves in her hair, stepped into the wild and angry ocean to save them. And every autumn, now, there is a man, once a boy, who remembers a stone he threw, who remembers the rage in her eyes as it hit home – and every year, his is the loudest voice singing in praise of the Mother of the Sea.'

The room bursts into applause when Natalya has finished but, alas, there is not even a single coin for, like her, everyone else in the guest house lives a hand-to-mouth existence too.

London is baffling to Natalya; she cannot see the night skies, hear the same wild birds she is so used to. The city is unreadable – *not a dragon after all*, she thinks, *but a chimera*, a mish-mash of creatures all mixter-maxter, ready to bite the unfortunate, the poor and the unlucky.

She longs to see the horizon again, to see and smell the sea stretching off into the far distance, that beautiful, endless water that leads to everywhere – that flows out of the Highland rivers, from the wilds of the Norwegian fjords, from the Thames in London, all of it mixing together, connecting everything, just like the great white river of the Milky Way up in the night sky.

All those stars, all those cities, all those people, she thinks as she drifts off to sleep, connecting them all in her mind's eye, the patterns she sees around her echoed in the constellations of her dreams.

Edward is late again. He missed supper and Annie was forced to eat alone in the large, empty dining room with Sarah's baleful eyes upon her, every mouthful watched, everything she did monitored to be reported back to Mrs McGilliveray.

Annie's hairbrush is filthy as she brushes out the day's dirt. An earlier venture to Winsor and Newton in Rathbone Place to replenish her supplies meant she had been outside for longer than intended. The dust and smuts here take some getting used to, but perhaps one day, with Edward's growing reputation, they might be able to afford to move further out, beyond the edge of London where there are still green fields and space to breathe. Camden, Chalk Farm, perhaps even Walthamstow if it were not too far from Edward's place of work.

As Annie plaits her hair for bed, she recalls the first time she laid eyes on Edward, the picnic at the top of the hill in Greenwich, the cold mirror of the Thames snaking away through the heart of the city. He had startled her with his beauty, with his sharp cheekbones, wide smile, untameable dark hair and those green eyes like a mossy pond. He looked more like a poet than a man of medicine. And there was Samuel too, taller, broader, more confident in his charm than the elegant Edward, but it was not he who captured the young Miss Harding's heart.

Edward had seemed fascinated when Annie took out her watercolours to capture the view, had asked questions about her preferred suppliers, the artists she admired most. He had watched her working, paid attention to every brushstroke, and admired her ability to capture the cloudy sky on the dappled paper. He had extolled the virtues of painting before confessing, shyly, that he had never once been to even a single exhibition. She had laughed, catching his eye, and he had smiled back, a smile brimming over with promise.

'Enough of art, Miss Harding, come, let us move to literature,' he had said, resuming his place on the picnic rug and idly chewing on a long strand of summer-dry grass. 'After all, we have covered medicine and art and we have discussed the weather at great length as is the English tradition. And so, my next question – who is your favourite poet?'

'I had not realised medical men were so interested in art and literature,' she said, archly.

'We medical men are interested in all things! For is not the ability to save a man's life a form of poetry in itself? So, come, your preferred poet, Miss Harding!'

'I am not sure, in all honesty, I have such a thing, Mr Meake.'

'Ah, not a lover of poetry then . . . alas, alack!' He

pretended to be wounded in his heart, rolling onto his back and chuckling.

She had laughed merrily. 'It's more that I tell stories in pictures rather than words. That's all.'

'Come, Miss Harding, then what of music?' he had asked and she had suddenly found herself blushing. 'Surely you must dance?'

All else in the park suddenly seemed far less interesting than this elegant man with his intense looks and easy company. All else faded into the background. The others a little way off under the dappled light of the chestnut trees. Samuel deep in conversation with Lizzie, Ellie eating strawberries somewhat suggestively in front of Mr Bigsby, the man she was later to marry, and the others, friends of Lizzie's, distracted by chatting, eating and laughing. And there *he* was, in front of her, Edward Meake, with his green eyes and inviting smile.

'Let me tell you of a song, Miss Harding,' Edward had said earnestly, leaning towards her. 'It is the title of one of my favourite poems. Not mine, of course – my talent doesn't lie in being a wordsmith – it comes from the pen of a William Davenant and they are far prettier words than I could ever muster.' He had sat up, fixed her with a piercing gaze and did not look away once, did not blink, as he recited it. He had repeated it to her when he proposed and again on their wedding night as he had removed her clothing, exploring her for the first time.

It came as little surprise that he liked the operating theatre so much, Annie thought. There was an actor eager for an audience somewhere deep within him. Her lips move slightly as she recounts the poem to her reflection in the mirror, plaiting the last of her tresses, half-lost in the memory.

> 'The lark now leaves his watery nest,
>   And climbing shakes his dewy wings,
> He takes your window for the east,
>   And to implore your light he sings;
> Awake, awake, the moon will never rise,
> Till she can dress her beauty at your eyes.
>
> The merchant bows unto the seaman's star,
>   The ploughman from the sun his season takes;
> But still the lover wonders what they are,
>   Who look for day before his mistress wakes:
> Awake, awake, break through your veils of lawn!
> Then draw your curtains and begin the dawn.'

Annie had known then, as the skylarks rose behind him in the park with exquisite timing, as her heart quickened and her breath lay suspended between them, she had known then that this was the man she would marry.

She climbs now into the empty bed, knowing that Edward will once again be distracted by his work well into the small hours. His fascination with work feels different now, sharper somehow, *as if he is infatuated*. A flicker of envy rises and she dismisses it. We are still settling in, she reassures herself. I must be patient. Edward's obsession with his work, this too will pass. All will be well again. All will be well.

The small roast joint makes the entire room smell more delicious than Mary can almost bear. After Sunday service at Christ Church, they returned to Folgate Street to find Richard waiting for them with a roast dinner – a small joint of mutton, potatoes and more, roasted in one of the nearby baker's ovens. Mary is so overwhelmed by this act of kindness that she feels close to tears but, instead, recalls the fortune teller's words at exactly the wrong moment, blushing a deep shade of crimson which she disguises, not entirely satisfactorily, in a bout of pretend coughing.

'Ah, Richard! You needn't have gone to all this trouble,' beams Jos. 'But as you have, it would be a shame for it to go to waste! Shall you carve or shall I?'

'I'm happy to do the honours if it suits?' says Richard. 'And I've also brought a small present for you,' he adds, looking at Mary.

'A present?' she asks, puzzled. 'But this is present enough, surely?'

'Ah, now, well . . . I do actually want something in return.'

'Aha,' says Mary, recovering her wits. 'So it is an *exchange* rather than a present.'

Richard holds out his hand to reveal a small book, which he gives to her.

'A novel!' Mary says gleefully. '*Catharine* by Madeleine Martin. But what could you possibly want in exchange for this?'

'Well . . . I, er, I wish you to write a review of it,' Richard says as Mary's surprise silences her for a moment. She looks to Uncle Jos first who smiles and shrugs.

'Richard, I—'

'No, Mary, you are more than capable and it can be published under a pseudonym if you like, but there it is. I've already spoken to Mr Ashman, the editor of the *New Weekly*. He read the piece you finished the other day for Jos and was most impressed. This isn't a commission from me, but from him. A *paid* commission.'

Mary doesn't quite know what to say. It is a kindness but it also marks something else, a shift to a new phase in her life. A tantalising new world opens up to her.

'It's not improper, is it, Uncle Jos?' she asks.

'Mary,' says Richard, interrupting. 'You have a gift with words and it would be a great shame – nay, I believe a *crime*, if you were not allowed to use it. Tell me I'm wrong, Jos, I dare you.'

Jos shrugs. 'It is entirely your choice, Mary,' he says, though all three of them know that the money is not just useful but essential.

'See it as a trial,' Richard says. 'There are so many new pamphlets and books being published, the whole of the magazine industry is in need of new blood. There's no reason why you should not be amongst them, is there?'

'In that case, I accept both your gift and your request, Mr Gibbs – and I thank you,' says Mary, failing to hide the delight in her voice.

'One more thing,' says Richard as he goes to slice the joint. 'You must do it in your own voice, not mimicking that of Jos.'

'But I don't know what it's like to write as myself!' she protests.

'Then it's about time you found out,' Richard says. 'Now, pass me a plate before this drips all over your table.'

'I propose a toast,' says Jos. 'With tea, if you like, in this new age of temperance I'm embarking on – and which I am most determined to adhere to after a few recent, shall we say, slips, for which I apologise profusely. A toast! A toast to my little Mary who has grown up into a most remarkable young woman.'

Mary glances at Richard, catching his eye, and this time, it is his turn to blush.

'I really do think we might try to find a church closer to home,' mutters Annie as the cab lurches them forwards on the journey to Bloomsbury. It is not only the expense she objects to but the distance too, eating into their precious time together on a Sunday – the one day of the week when she has any chance of having her husband to herself.

Edward smiles, pats her hand. 'But this is *our* church, Annie dear, this is the best place we can attend in all of London. Besides, the possibilities held within the walls of St George's are worth much more than a return cab fare.'

Annie smiles wryly. She knows full well that what her husband *really* means is that it is most advantageous for them to continue to attend St George's despite it being nearly two and a half miles away from their new home. There are dukes in attendance, Lord Douglas and his wife, and a dozen others from the landed gentry, House of Lords and more. It is a church to be seen in, a church that connects the highest echelons of society with the rising stars of the future.

Edward helps her out of the carriage, smiling at her as she steps down. He seems more like himself today, Annie thinks, feeling relieved as she clasps his hand tightly – perhaps his work in the basement has come to an end?

The church is already filling up by the time the Meakes enter, up the wide stone steps and past the heavy, metal-studded doors. No matter how many times Annie comes here, somehow the space always feels new. Perhaps it is the high windows letting in so much light, the ceiling stretching up towards the sky; or perhaps it is simply the luxury of having her beloved husband by her side that makes Annie feel blessed as she takes her place next to Edward. All is well, she thinks as the sun streams down upon the balcony on which they sit, along from Lord Douglas, overlooking the less well-do-to congregation below. Until, that is, the Reverend Pennyworth begins to speak in his usual soporific tone.

'God sits upon the throne of His eternity,' he drones, 'inaccessible to change, unapproached of death, the same yesterday, today and forever. Amen.'

His flat tones echo around the church, reverberating off the stone pillars, and Annie is grateful both to the architect of St George's and to God Himself that she cannot quite make out all the words. The acoustics are worse from the balconies but at least it means Annie can tune out of the sermon and in to her own imagination instead. She sketches the congregation in her mind, a woman with an unusual bonnet, the hunched man with a worn-out military jacket, Lord and Lady Douglas dressed in their finery with their bored offspring who, like Annie, are trying to stifle their yawns.

Edward, meanwhile, is casting his eye over the church-goers below. He spies Miss Bewdley near the front, an anxious older woman who has worried herself thin and who he finds strangely irritating, before focusing his mind back onto his prayers. He thanks God for his devoted wife, for his livelihood; above all he thanks God most profoundly for bestowing the extraordinary gift of the angel upon him. Edward finally finished his dissection in the early hours of this morning, confident that God would not object to him doing such a thing on a Sunday for, after all, it was the Almighty's work that he was doing. He has confirmed that, bar her glorious wings, the angel is anatomically identical to a regular female – and yet she is *so much more* than a mere daughter of Eve.

Edward puts his hands together for a moment and prays for one more thing – for what harm can it do? – and so he asks, again, for a child to be given to them. A baby, fresh with all the joy of a new life. A gurgling baby boy whose laughter would echo around the room that is to be the nursery. Edward would dress him in miniature versions of his own attire, play with him in the evenings after work, hear him learn to speak, see him take his first, halting steps. We would be a *family*, he thinks to himself. Complete. It is what society expects of them too; for what is marriage for, if not for children? He looks at Annie beside him, reaches for her hand, and she smiles warmly back at him.

At the end of the sermon, Reverend Pennyworth announces with a great show of woe that his mother is very ill, meaning he must go to the Highlands to see her. There is an audible ripple of approval – and relief – throughout the congregation as they learn they are to be left in the capable hands of Reverend Rogers.

'Did you know they are taking the unicorns down?' asks Annie on the way home as the cab lurches them eastwards.

'What unicorns?' laughs Edward.

'On the church tower, the unicorns and the lions there; they are taking them down. Miss Bewdley told me on the way out whilst you were conversing with Lord Douglas. I think it's a great shame. I rather liked knowing they were there.'

Unicorns eh? thinks Edward. Unicorns atop a church tower. Well, well. Almost as strange as an angel in one's basement. If only, he thinks, with a twinge of regret, he was able to share the joke with his wife.

Etta is a heathen. Ah no, that is not quite the case, but she certainly no longer attends church. She had argued with Papa over it and they had reached an agreement by which she agreed to attend only if she didn't have to truly listen. It was a strange compromise but it had worked perfectly well until her father's death when she felt that she had kept her part of the agreement but that he, alas, had ducked out of his. It was not that Etta did not believe in the higher power of God per se, only that she believed He lived in one's own heart, inside one's soul, not within the four walls of a building.

Increasingly, though, she wonders if God has a most peculiar, nay, even cynical sense of humour. There are the strange things she has witnessed that do not fit into the neat category of God's plan – the lamb born with two heads, destined to end up as a taxidermied curiosity in a sideshow; the triple-flowered aquilegia with unusual colours, an unexpected spring visitor to her small garden; the albino red kite she saw flying over Stokesay Castle. And there were more, many more. Deformities, peculiarities, even the evaporation of the memories of Dorothy, a devout churchgoer – were these really all experiments from a higher being, part of His grand plan? And what of the fossilised shells that lay within so many rocks scattered across the land? The idea that the world was fixed, unchanging – if this were so, then how came creatures from the sea to be atop the highest hills in the county?

The letter, a reply from James Easthope, had been mistakenly sent to the Hall instead of Etta's cottage and it is only on Sunday that Betsy, still dressed in her clothes for church, delivers it to Etta directly and she eagerly tears it open.

I am afraid I am extremely busy with my own garden project at the moment but I thank you for your interest. I believe female hobbyists have much to offer the world of botany and wish you luck with your own endeavours.

Etta rips it up in frustration, throwing the remnants onto the fire. There is still no reply from Henry Underwood. She pulls on her boots, tying them with a double knot, before throwing on her thick overcoat to march her annoyance out in the rolling hills, Scout ever-present by her heels.

Miss Bewdley wrings her hands at the shabby figure standing below her, halfway up the steps to St George's. 'Please, won't you come in?' she offers.

Natalya hesitates. She had bared her soul with her stories, exposed her heart last night and been left with nothing in return. There was one woman who had shaken her hand, thanked her most profusely for her tales but, when Natalya awoke with the sunrise, that very same woman was quietly unlacing her boots in order to steal them. Despite her drowsiness, Natalya managed to kick the would-be thief hard in the face, prompting her to hastily run away.

There are now no more coins after Natalya spent her few remaining ones on a penny loaf and last night's bed, and the nights are drawing in. Winter is coming and Natalya can feel in her bones that it will be a cold one. It is chilly already, even by October standards. At least she has her boots – despite the thief's best efforts – and the clothes she stands up in. They are not as clean or presentable as they once were, darned and patched so often that the original garments may well have been lost to posterity, but they are, at least, warm.

She had paced her way through the capital, wandered past grand architecture and tumbledown slums, walked through Leicester Square and past a large, cleared area that is soon to become Trafalgar Square. And now she is lost in the labyrinth with no thread to find her way out.

'No. No, thank you,' Natalya mutters, shaking her head. She had not realised her feet had taken her towards a place of worship. She refuses to step inside one ever again. Not after what happened. She has no need for redemption, for has she not been punished enough? Punished by her family. Punished for love. Punished so many times, losing first her lover, then . . . no, she will not allow the memories back in.

Natalya turns from the church, steps away and spots, for the first time, the huge stone unicorn tied tightly onto a large wooden pallet at the bottom of the tower. It is rendered beautifully, a wild animal with nostrils flaring and a long thin horn stretching skywards. It seems as ridiculous to Natalya that people believe in gods as unicorns. For are they not, in the end, all simply stories?

It is only as Natalya dozes off to sleep in a cold stone doorway that reeks of dog and cat and vermin, that she realises her head is, perhaps for the first time, empty of her own tales. And, what is somehow worse, is that even if it were not, there is now no one for her to tell them to.

Uncle Jos is shivering and tucked up in blankets by the fireside as the dawn breaks and the sparrows outside chatter from the rooftops. Mary knows enough of such things to realise that it is the continued withdrawal from drink making him unwell, but she cannot help but feel excited too. A story reached their ears last night, after Richard's surprise meal, when one of Jos's tipsters had turned up with the tall tale of an angel dragged from the Thames.

'Oh, but that's nothing new!' Jos had said. 'The Angel of the Thames is as old as the hills – first sighted back in the days of the Great Fire of London and appearing at perilous times in the capital's history. It's simply a myth that surfaces from time to time, bobbing up as a nonsensical tale every few decades or so.'

'Hmm,' Richard had murmured thoughtfully. 'But surely it's different *this* time?'

'Yes!' Mary had said. 'If there's an actual body, it would be proof that angels exist! It must be worth looking into – if only to be dismissed as nonsense.'

It had been agreed that Jos and Richard would set out to examine the story further, sharing the results between

Richard's two papers as well as the various publications that Jos supplies, from the *Public Ledger* to the satirical *Odd Fellow*. But it's clear now that Jos is not well enough and so Mary will accompany Richard instead, reporting back all that she finds in order for Jos to write it up. It doesn't occur to Jos that it might be inappropriate, for Richard is simply a close family friend, an honorary older brother to his niece. Jos has thus far remained blissfully ignorant of any signs otherwise, not noticed the warmth with which Richard looks at Mary, the spark in his eyes when he does so. And so it is that Mary finds herself alone with Richard in one of the many less respectable parts of Bermondsey, the air thick with the pungent smell of the tanneries and nearby knackers' yards.

'This whole yarn reminds me of the ghost of Whitechapel,' Richard says as they approach the thin crowd that is starting to gather by the edge of the Thames. The first coffee stall has already set up to take advantage of the expected numbers and a strange atmosphere is brewing.

'It was one evening, not long before All Hallows, that a rumour started to spread. A ghost had been seen at Whitechapel Church,' Richard whispers in Mary's ear, bending down to do so. 'Two young boys had first spotted it.'

'Always a sure sign of a prank,' says Mary.

'Well, quite. And then, of course the numbers that had seen it, or claimed to have seen it, started to swell. Soon there were whole crowds waiting to see the spectre. Coffee stalls, hot pies, roast chestnuts – free theatre for all of East London. Until that is, the ghost was caught . . .'

Mary laughs. 'Let me guess – a man in a bed sheet?'

'Worse, it was the curate!' says Richard, as Mary descends into helpless giggles. 'He pleaded temporary insanity and was back at work within two months after a small but significant fine,' he adds, with a grin.

'And his congregation?' asks Mary.

'The largest it had ever been, at least until the novelty wore off.'

A roar emerges from the thin crowd and they see a young man flying a small white kite. There is laughter and a faint air of hysteria.

'The angel! 'Tis here! And looks mighty like a kite made from a nightdress!' shouts one wag.

'I fear we won't find out much from this rowdy lot,' mutters Richard but he is soon proved wrong. Despite the noise from the steamboats, boatyards and the usual rattling of the nearby roads, Mary manages to extract a great deal of information from the handful of mildly inebriated old sops that loiter near the water's edge. In fact, much to Richard's undeniable respect, she does a considerably more efficient job of finding the next clue than he does. It is not long before the two of them are heading back upriver towards Southwark Bridge, in search of the ramshackle walls of the Blue Boar and a boatman with a yarn.

Much to her disappointment, for it would not be seemly for her to venture within the tavern, Mary is deposited at a haberdashery around the corner where she whiles away the time pretending to eye up ribbons for a new bonnet. Sometimes, Mary thinks to herself with an audible tut that makes the shopkeeper look up with a frown, it is most frustrating to be a woman.

The boatman is not hard to find, propped up on one elbow at the bar and surrounded by an eager crowd who interject, laugh, and yet hang onto his every word. But Peter King – for of course it is he – is drunk again and his story shifts and ebbs like the tide, every time he repeats it. The angel was alive when he found her, the wings were this big – no, *this* big – growing in size exponentially like a fisherman's tall tale.

Richard is, unfortunately, recognised by one of the other men in the Blue Boar who, seeing the potential for a coin, explains that Mr King is not in fact the man who found the body of an angel, it was him, John Floyd. And that of course opens the floodgates to all the other men. Richard is soon forced to flee the scene, squeezing himself through the rowdy crowd and back onto the street. The only fact he has managed to ascertain is that the body of the supposed angel, if indeed there ever was such a thing, was purchased by a surgeon. Richard knows full well that he will not be the only one who has gleaned that information and it's of little use anyway. It's clear there will be no sense from the drunken Mr King for some time – if at all – and there are almost as many surgeons in the capital as there are journalists. This isn't quite true, of course, but with so many new hospitals opening or expanding and ever-rising numbers of medical students swarming to the capital like ants to a picnic, it does sometimes feel that way. What little Richard has learnt is not enough to write up into anything of substance, the crowds not sufficiently impressive yet, but it will make tomorrow's paper as a passing mention. Richard knows that by reporting the story it will only add fuel to rumour, but he will keep an eye on it in case it develops into something more.

Mary is most animated as they walk upriver and discuss their findings, heading over London Bridge and back towards the City. 'We *must* find that surgeon – what if the body of an angel truly had been found? What a story that would be!' she says, eyes bright with excitement.

'Alas, I fear there is no surgeon to find,' replies Richard. 'It's most likely a rumour started simply to create a few coins for men struggling at their livelihoods. It's a ruse and no more. Like the ghost of Whitechapel.'

Mary looks at him. 'Or perhaps it *is* something? Something wondrous . . . *What if?*'

'If I'd followed up all the "what ifs" I had encountered in my years of journalism, Miss Ward, I fear I would no longer be in the job. After a while, one does develop a feel for things, a sense of whether a story has legs or not. And I am afraid I don't feel that churn of excitement in my stomach for this particular tale.'

'Hmm,' says Mary. 'It's such a shame I could not come with you, I am certain I could have found out more.'

'I'm afraid the Blue Boar is no place for a young lady.'

'And instead I had to entertain myself with the tedium of ribbons and bonnets.'

'I don't make the rules, Mary,' says Richard. 'I wish I did.'

'No,' says Mary thoughtfully, 'I wish *I* did.'

'Well, that would be quite something I'm sure!' Richard chuckles. 'Ah, before I forget,' he says, speaking more loudly as a phalanx of cabs clatters past, 'how are you getting on with that book?'

'Thank you for that kindness,' she says. 'I've already started it and am much enjoying it.'

'It is not a *kindness,* Mary,' says Richard, earnestly. 'It is simply that your talent for words should not be wasted.'

'Well, it's certainly more fun to be paid to read and write than to sew buttons onto card. I hadn't realised being on the trail of a story was so much fun.'

Richard frowns. 'It's not always fun, Miss Ward, and I would hate for you to be given the impression that it is. There are serious matters to be reported upon – crimes and punishments – as well as the silly and trivial.'

Mary shakes her head. 'If there's even a grain of truth in this story, then it may not be as silly and trivial as you seem to think, Richard. But either way,' she says with a grin, 'I rather think I should like to do more of it.'

Edward re-examines each and every one of his angel's organs as he methodically places them into individual jars. He must preserve and label everything, meticulously record every detail. He must see to it all himself – from dissecting and note-taking to mounting the finished skeleton. His new iron gate in place, Edward feels considerably more secure going about his work in the basement – even if his wife was clearly unhappy about its installation.

'It's like my private door to the yard, simply a mechanism to keep the servants' and neighbours' eyes from my work,' Edward had said with a smile, although both he and Annie knew full well that it was also to keep her out. It is inconvenient that he cannot yet tell her all, but, Edward reasons, she will be more than grateful, more than understanding, in due course.

A wave of tiredness comes over him, the consequence of too many nights with not enough sleep, as he seals up the last of the preserving jars. He sits for a moment, exhausted, head in his hands, and a memory of a dream from last night comes back to him like a wisp of smoke. He cannot recall the details, only a feeling of humiliation, a sense that people were laughing at him. A flicker of fear rises, for the possibility of being seen as a laughing stock fills Edward with dread. He knows miracles can be faked. The travelling fairs, the circuses of freaks, all those fakeries he has seen that can and should be palmed off as bogus. His exquisite angel does not belong with them, but in the realm of wonder, in a museum or a church, a cathedral – why, even in St Paul's itself!

The enormity of his task suddenly overwhelms him. He looks again at his angel, flesh and skin already being rendered down to bone. He is immune to the smell of such things, has been for many years now. From maggots and beetles to quicklime, he has tried numerous different methods but, in recent years, had settled for his own recipe, a secret mix of caustic materials that would strip the flesh in under a week but leave the bones intact, ready to be further cleaned before assembly and display. The chemicals prickle at his nostrils. Have I done the right thing? he asks himself as he scratches at his sideburns. Should I have shared this, should I *now* share this with Samuel, with Annie?

Guiltily, he recalls Samuel's words from the other night. 'Are we not gods, you and I?' No! *We* are not gods, he thinks, flushing with shame, we are merely tools in the hands of the Almighty. He will do with us whatsoever He wishes. He will guide us, guide *me*, as He sees fit. Edward falls forward, onto his knees, prays to clear his exhausted mind. He prays to banish doubts and guilt, he prays for further guidance, and he also prays for forgiveness.

He neglects, this time though, to pray for a baby.

It is a most excellent find, thinks Etta. A tiny, detailed fossil of a fern, unfurled for a summer long ago. Small and neat, it would easily fit into a child's palm after having flaked off from the side of the holloway. Above it, stands a similar-looking fern, a clump of *Dryopteris filix-mas*, turning copper at the edges as autumn beds in.

Etta examines the fossil, turning it over in her hand. She prises up a lump of clay from the rutted path and pushes it gently into the indentations, leaving it for a moment before peeling it away to reveal the fern itself, raised up into proud form, breathed back into existence. She taps the fossil, thoughtfully, with a muddy fingernail. Can it really be that the world was created in such a short space of time?

Later, when Etta has reached the summit of High Vinnalls, she pauses, sits on a low rock with some difficulty – clothed as she is in bulky skirts to ward off the autumn chill – and takes in the glorious view over Mortimer Forest towards Ludlow, Titterstone Clee's pointed summit framing the horizon. She lets her mind meander for a while, ponders the names of ferns and their origins. She thinks of horsetails, clubmosses, and quillworts, of spores and fronds and of rare ferns like the prized *Vandenboschia speciosa* and *Osmunda regalis*. She closes her eyes for a moment, thinks of whinchats and wheatears, of hoverflies and moths, of miniature landscapes amongst the mosses, whole other tiny worlds that offer endless new discoveries. She loses herself in her thoughts before her mind wanders back, returning to join her where she sits, sketching both the fern she plucked from the side of the path and its fossilised sister too.

Etta sketches intermittently, thoughts punctuated by the need to just sit and observe, to *see*. To watch the clouds wend their merry way across the sky, to hear the distinctive sound of a pigeon's wings slice through the air, feel the grasses and trees sigh as they sway in the breeze. To feel the world around her soak into her bones.

When the last stroke of her sketch is done, Etta muses on how fortunate she is to have a small stipend, enough to allow her the luxury to wander, to think, aside from the day's necessary routines and demands. If only everyone could have this, she thinks. If only all could be granted the freedom to imagine, to learn, to expand their minds. She is grateful to have been born into wealth but she knows too that the money came from the sugar trade, a plantation in the West Indies sold long ago when she was far too young to remember. She had wrestled with her thoughts and feelings for some long time before slowly making her peace with it as much as she ever would. Or so she had thought until her father died. So many questions she wished she had now asked, so many gaps in her knowledge never to be filled, for the dead can no longer be interrogated – their secrets buried alongside them in their caskets, for better or for worse.

A male stonechat calls to her from the top of a nearby hawthorn, interrupting her thoughts, and she smiles to herself as she turns the page of her notebook, sketching his outline as he flicks his wings. The day shifts around her, sun slowly arching across the sky. Morning stretches to afternoon and onwards to dusk as Etta sits and watches, thinks and works in the low, golden October light. Her mind dances with the birds in the bright blue sky, swooping down through copper-edged trees and out to grasslands and pastures, flitting between branches and hedgerows. It is only when the robin starts a tuneful melody to ward off the gloaming that Etta realises it is getting late and she must hurry home before the curtain of darkness falls. But the day has not been wasted. All of this – the fossil, the ferns, the patterns she sees, the absorption in the world around her – all of this has helped set Etta on a path that there can be no turning back from.

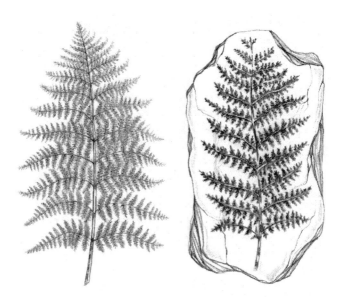

The Rookery is the worst of places. It is mere spitting distance from the glory of the towering pillars of St George's, Bloomsbury and yet it is hell itself. It is the worst of slums, piss and excrement mingling with despair and starvation. Ragged children with pinched cheeks run barefoot past overflowing privies and crammed buildings that creak at the seams, filled with bedbugs hidden in the walls that, like so many tiny vampires, come out nightly to feast on their victims. There is drunkenness and drugs, all manner of things in which to dull the ongoing pain of hunger and hopelessness.

Natalya is tired and broken by the time she emerges. Her wanderings have taken her right through the Rookery and she surfaces now with dull eyes that cannot unsee the suffering she has witnessed. Humans living in worse conditions than livestock, in crowded, stinking colonies, not able to see the horizon for buildings stacked on top of each other, not able to breathe clean air into their lungs.

What little money she had is gone and she finds her accent is mistaken for somewhere else. Doors shut in her face, opportunities that dry up as she approaches.

Her options are fast running out. Natalya knows she could sell herself for a handful of coins but the streets are already crowded with other women forced to do so and her body remains precious to her, to be shared only with the one she loves. It is the sole thing she possesses apart from her clothes, and it is likely just a matter of time before she is forced to sell the best of them. She has seen men and women padded up with old newspapers under their too-small coats and winter is not even here yet. She refuses to enter a workhouse, not after all that Peggy had told her, where desperate workers were forced to do hard and even dangerous work in exchange for meagre portions and an uncomfortable bed. She will not allow herself to go down that route, *she will not.*

She returns, feeling lost, to the steps of St George's but it is late now and the kind old woman she met previously is no longer here. Unbeknownst to Natalya, Miss Bewdley is abed only some small distance away in the part of Bloomsbury that is for the well-to-do. Slums just hundreds of yards from the wealthy.

Natalya huddles up behind one of St George's stone pillars as a cold wind tickles and wraps around her, blowing dust and fragments of rubbish into tiny whirlwind clouds before disappearing. She shivers. It's cold and she's too aware of the risk of being robbed to allow herself to doze.

Instead, she spends the night in a state that is neither awake nor asleep. Some might call what she sees visions, others the result of an exhausted mind that cannot afford to drop its guard. The clock strikes midnight and the one remaining unicorn and lion at the top of the church tower remain impassive as Natalya sees the world unwind around her as vividly as she sees her own hands, feels her own heart beating within.

She sees the clock on the tower turn back in time, at first minute by minute and then faster, faster, hour by hour, from sunset back to the brightness of noon, to the dark of the night sky before. People rush past backwards in a blur of activity, the aisles in the church behind her fill and empty, fill and empty and then – ah – the tower of the church is removed, taken down brick by brick by the very same hands who built it, the whole building dismantled along with the others around it as the world spins backwards.

She sees time shift to the distant past, sees bodies in the graveyard rise again, flesh puffing out their hollow cheeks until they become as rosy as in life. Their hair regrowing into thick tresses from translucent white to the prime of youth, they grow younger still, to children playing in the street until all the graveyards are emptied, until the buildings shift, mutate into older structures, brick to timber, stone to wood, roads to tracks, lanes to paths, parks to forest, railings to grass.

Natalya has no sense of her place in this. She is simply a witness, watching the world turn back in time, so many lifetimes for humanity and but a blink in the eye of the stars above as they spin, rotate, dance on their axis and bow for applause.

She stands, eyes open, dazed, hands out as if appealing for something or someone. She is not sure if she is awake, if she has been granted access, borne witness, to something extraordinary or if this vivid vision has but sprung from her own imagination. Has she dreamt all this, the world turning in the wrong direction? And if she could have gone further back, beyond the dance of the stars – what then? What other strange wonders might she have seen?

It is early morning and a boy tugs at her hand. It is Charlie Meckin, one of the street urchins who linger around this patch hoping for a bit of work.

'You all right, miss?' Charlie asks. 'You all right?' But there is no reaction.

One of the other boys stands there, mocking her strange position as if she were a statue, and Charlie shoves him away.

'Leave off,' he says. 'Leave her alone.'

And so they do. And Natalya, palms out, stands in silence, dazed and immovable, as London begins a new day.

THE MORNING EXPRESS, Tuesday 13 October 1840

SOUTHWARK.- Last evening a numerous public meeting took place at the Three Tuns, Southwark, to discuss recent alleged sightings of a phenomenon known as the 'Angel of the Thames'. The story dates back to the Fire of London when a vision of a winged creature was seen hovering above London's great river as a portent of troubles to come. Rumours of a winged figure have been circulating for some days, started, it is believed, by a boatman who is said to have pulled from the river a woman's body with unusual features. The result has been a small but growing crowd gathering in and around the jetties of the local area. Mr Martin Woodman, recently elected Alderman, stated that the crowd should be cleared in order that the boatmen and others may go about their business in the usual fashion without hindrance. The resolution was seconded and unanimously carried, after which the meeting separated.

There is a small cluster of white feathers on Etta's pillow-case in the morning, in her hair too. They must have worked their way out of the pillow overnight and she collects them, one by one, into a tiny handful, before opening her bedroom window and releasing them, watching them drift down into the garden below.

Scout is behaving strangely today. She soothes him, strokes his soft black velvet ears and he returns to his usual self as they walk together in the autumn mud over the remnants of the ancient fort at Bury Ditches. There was enough space for him to sit with her in the mail coach from Ludlow to Bishops Castle but instead she made him run alongside. It is the first time since he was a boisterous pup that she has been a little unsure of him.

The efforts of their expedition are at last rewarded by the sighting of both a male and female hen harrier, the auburn female full of subtlety, the silver-white male like a statue breathed into life. There's another treat too, a flock of redwing that she watches feasting on berries in the hedgerows. She smiles, their pretty red flanks reminding her of the red-backed shrike she once saw, years ago now, when she was walking here with Henry Underwood.

'My goodness!' Etta had said as she spotted it perched atop a gorse bush, the male's distinctive reddish wings, dove-grey head with a handsome black mask across its eyes. 'The butcher bird! Can it really be?'

Henry's eyes had gone straight to it. 'Dammit, Miss Lockhart, you're right! I've never seen them this far inland, only on the Welsh coast.'

'I wonder where its gruesome larder is? All those poor insects impaled on thorns . . . I should very much like to see it! I do so hope it stays, such a charismatic little bird,' she said as it suddenly turned away to scan the landscape, dark red back glistening in the May sunshine.

'Oh, how beautiful!' Etta had breathed. '*Beautiful!*'

'Yes,' Henry had said. 'Beautiful.' But when Etta turned to look, Henry was already watching her, his eyes agleam. He had, she realised, been looking at *her* when he had spoken. Heat rushed to her cheeks and she had returned her glance to the small bird, overwhelmed by both shyness and rising hope. She had felt as if she were dancing on air; that look in Henry's eyes, she had felt it deep in her heart, known it for what it was. But two days later Henry had met Miss Swinnerton and Etta's hopes had crumbled into dust.

As she walks back home, Etta feels suddenly worn out. Saddened by her old nursemaid's decline and by Walter's continuing antagonism towards her, tired of being made to feel as if she is a nuisance in some way, of constantly being dismissed as a mere hobbyist. The exhausting, never-ending struggle to be recognised for her own self, acknowledged for her achievements. She knows that she cannot possibly be alone, there must be others out there who are equally frustrated – their minds and findings rejected purely because of their sex. If only, she thinks, we could find each other, be seen for ourselves without having to fight for it, if only we could have the same encouragement and societies as men do, rise up as equals!

Scout yelps beside her and she smiles. It is hard to be self-pitying for long when there is a joyful companion, brimful of enthusiasm, by one's side, she thinks as he bounces up on his hind legs, tail wagging eagerly.

'Of course you could come too,' Etta whispers to him. 'Beloved pets would have a *very* important role to play in my vision of arcadia.'

Scout barks an acknowledgement before charging off along the lane, daring her to follow him, and Etta laughs, lifting her skirts with a grin, and running headlong after him.

Natalya is sitting on a pew inside St George's as Miss Bewdley brings her a cup of weak tea, boots tapping on the floor as she approaches. Natalya cannot recall entering and yet here she is. *Inside a church.* That sacred space she had promised never to return to, for God abandoned her and so she, in turn, abandoned him. She feels hot all of a sudden, heat welling up in her head, and she undoes her bonnet, letting it fall to the ground.

She cannot muster any words, her mind still entirely consumed with all that she saw – or dreamt – last night. She sees now that everything is interconnected, everything. The motes of dust that fall down from the windows in the church, the people milling around on the hectic streets outside like busy ants. It all seems so simple. She looks into the cup, the liquid whirling in circles as it does between the skerries back home when the tide pulls out and the low-lying islets emerge.

The sun shines in and Natalya looks up at the ceiling, at the streams of dust that dance and bathe in the low golden glow, so much like the hazy band of star-filled light reaching across the night sky. She sees now that these connections, these patterns all around, the rivers and tides, the great clouds of dust and light in the Milky Way, they are not to her mind the work of a higher being – it is simply a matter of *seeing*, a leap of the imagination to join them all.

Open your eyes.

She stands abruptly, cup falling to the ground, smashing into a thousand porcelain splinters. She retches, her body jerking and spasming uncontrollably, as Miss Bewdley rushes to comfort her.

Whatever is happening to this young woman is far beyond Miss Bewdley's abilities and she thanks God that she knows exactly who to call for. That taciturn surgeon who comes every Sunday with his much friendlier wife. She scribbles a note and gives it to the first boy she finds outside with an eye for a job.

Young Charlie Meckin, for it is he who takes the note, runs east towards the Meakes' home as Natalya lies fitting on the floor of the church. Miss Bewdley tries to reassure her, hoping this seizure will soon abate and that the surgeon will swiftly arrive. She is so busy fussing around that she clean forgets to pray, to ask God to soothe the young woman's pain.

Cousin Lou – no one dare call her Louisa – isn't really Mary's cousin in much the same way Uncle George wasn't her real uncle. A friend of the family who was closer to George than Jos, inevitably Mary has seen less of her since his death. Small and pretty with a neat figure, she's a regular performer at The Curtain, one of London's most popular penny gaffs, but when Mary turns up to the cluttered storage space that doubles as the dressing room, she's surprised to find that her cousin isn't there. Instead, there's a small young man with a naughty look, a terrible moustache and his trousers down by his ankles.

'Goodness!' says Mary, averting her eyes. 'I am so sorry, I had—'

But the peals of laughter that emerge from the young man's mouth are not those of a man but the distinctive gravelly laugh of her beloved Lou.

'I couldn't have planned that finer myself!' Lou says, helpless with giggles. It is not often that Mary is rendered speechless, but as she takes in Lou's disguise of false side-burns, moustache and trousers, she really is lost for words.

'It's good, ain't it? It's for a new act, and judging by your reaction, I think it'll work marvellously!'

Mary puts down the garments she's made in the only space available – atop a large birdcage containing a scruffy-looking parrot that pecks at its own wings.

'Ah, ta,' says Lou. 'Here, let me pay you for that,' but Mary shakes her head.

'It might need altering now that you appear to have lost your ample bosom.'

'Cheek!' mutters Lou. 'Look, it's just bound around with cloth. It's uncomfortable but you get used to it after a bit. How's Jos? Still drinking?'

'Well, he promised both me *and* Mr Gibbs that he would stop and—'

'Ah yes, I'd forgot the giraffe was returned. And how is Richard of Gibbs?'

'Same as ever.' Mary tries not to blush as she retrieves the dress she has made and shakes it out, indicating for Lou to step into the opening at the back.

Lou's eyes sparkle with mischief. 'Mary . . . ?'

'Richard has been very kind,' says Mary firmly as she lifts up the dress, pulling it together tightly.

'All right!' complains Lou. 'I'm only teasing. No need to squeeze a body's lifeblood out! Now, come on, tell me how Jos really is and how *you* are too. Will you watch the show after? It's a treat to have you here.'

And so Mary tells Lou about Jos, about her button work but nothing more about Richard – the book review he's requested, the Bermondsey outing, the flutter of excitement she feels when she sees him. It is her guilty secret and hers alone.

Later, as Mary watches the show from the wings at the side of the stage, she lets her mind wander over the rabble of dirty boys in the pit, the mothers with babies screaming over the action, the crammed balcony where the audience have paid an extra penny for a better seat. As Lou bounces out onto stage, Mary idly thinks how much she would like to run her fingers through Richard's unruly hair if only he were there beside her. Startled, she stops herself, for no good can possibly come of thinking such a thing.

The audience roars and Mary is brought back to earth by the sight of Lou provocatively flashing her ankles under her petticoats. Mary smiles too, for her cousin had earlier asked her to make a new outfit – to be produced as fast as possible and for which she would pay handsomely.

'Why, it's the talk of the town!' Lou's reflection had said, winking back at Mary from the dirty mirror in the dressing room. 'Make us some angel wings, pet!'

Edward objects most strongly to being called away from his work but the scruffy urchin standing in front of him is most insistent. There is such a commotion in the hallway that Annie cannot help but hear and she interrupts her meeting with Mrs McGilliveray in order to intervene.

'Why, if Miss Bewdley is calling you, then you must surely go!' she says to Edward.

'Please, sir, she was most insistent,' says the boy, fidgeting where he stands.

'I will accompany you if need be,' says Annie. 'But whatever the matter is, Edward, I don't believe Miss Bewdley would call on you for anything other than an emergency.'

And so Edward finds himself dashing across town in a cab, thoughts tumbling over themselves as the vehicle bounces over the uneven road surfaces. This is an inconvenience, Edward thinks, feeling put out. By the time he arrives, his mood has worsened and the sight of Miss Bewdley waiting for him all of aquiver does not alleviate matters. The sun has gone in, taking refuge behind the clouds and St George's feels darker inside than usual.

'Well, Miss Bewdley?' he says, abruptly, looking around the empty church.

'She was here a moment ago, Mr Meake, I—'

There's a sound in the far corner, underneath the carved wooden stairs that lead to the upper balcony in which Edward and Annie sit every Sunday. It is the sound of a creature in desperate pain.

'Hallo?' says Edward, interest now piqued, as he steps forward. 'Please, I have come to help. I am a surgeon, a medical man, one of the best in London.'

A figure is crouched under the stairs, wrapped in a blanket and shivering. She retches and shudders, clearly in pain, as Edward moves closer to her, reaches out a hand.

'Do not touch me!' she says fiercely, in an accent from far away, and Edward stops, surprised.

'Please,' he says after a moment, his voice echoing around the empty church as he places his medicine bag on the floor, lifting his hands up as if in surrender. 'Let me help.'

The figure underneath the balcony slowly moves to stand, still jerking unevenly. Both Miss Bewdley and Edward instinctively step back as she emerges from the darkness, strangely beautiful, brimming with power. Natalya's eyes are wild, a whole other universe contained within. She is possessed, thinks Edward. She is possessed and here in the house of Our Lord.

But Edward is wrong – she is not possessed. She is *changing*.

She roars at him, this creature that is both woman and something else. It is a sound of fury, of pent-up anger, of pain and deepest sorrow. It is a sound to break hearts as it bounces around the white walls and lodges in Edward's soul.

He steps towards her but she backs away, moving around the corner of the heavy wooden pews until she faces him, in front of the altar, shivering and shimmering with sweat. She howls in unbearable pain as she fights whatever is happening to her. Tears stream down her face, splashing onto the cold stone floor of the aisle.

Natalya falls to her knees, blanket slipping from her shoulders. There is an almighty crack as if the beams supporting the roof of the church have split asunder, yet the sound does not come from above but from deep inside Natalya herself as she kneels, her back to the altar. Edward and Miss Bewdley watch, transfixed, as another crack twists the woman's spine into an impossible curve, the noise reverberating hard around them in their ears and chests. Then a third, final twist when the frightful snap is accompanied by a scream so loud and long that Edward fears the woman must surely die.

But she is not dead.

She is not dead at all.

Edward cannot speak. Cannot move. Cannot breathe. All he can do is stare in wonderment.

The woman crouched in front of him, from her back, there emerges – but no, it is impossible.

And yet there they are. Huge, soft white wings, splattered with scarlet blood. They rise from her back, newly formed. He saw them, *witnessed* them burst forth from her shoulders in the exact same place as his angel from the river. This is not a death but a birth, a *transformation*.

Miss Bewdley collapses to her knees and prays, but Edward remains standing. He thinks of the angel skeleton in his basement. He had not dared ask for a live specimen and yet God has granted him this! A breathing, *living* angel with wings as large as she would need – his mouth falls open as he thinks of it – *to fly.*

Edward swallows, regains control of his limbs for a moment to walk slowly towards her, but he can only manage a handful of steps before his legs give way to the enormity of what he has beheld and he too falls to his knees.

'Dear God,' he murmurs, unable to take his eyes off this new prize in front of him.

Natalya looks at him, exhausted and scared, brimming with rage and tears.

Edward stares at her. He thinks fast, adrenaline surging. He must take this precious new creature to his home as a matter of urgency, take her to his basement until he can work out his next move. One of his holding rooms is empty since he dissected the dog. As for Miss Bewdley, she is the only other witness . . .

'It is a miracle!' whispers Miss Bewdley, interrupting his thoughts, wonder woven through her voice. 'It is a miracle! *From God Himself.*'

Natalya struggles to her feet, still fighting this extraordinary change that has swept over her, but she is unbalanced by her wings, by the new weight upon her shoulders. She mutters something but Edward cannot make it out. She tries again, her voice growing louder each time until the words cannot be misunderstood, cannot be unheard.

'A miracle from God?' she says, as she stands above Edward, still on his knees, looking up at her. Her wings unfurl, fanning out in front of him. 'But there is no God!' she says, spitting out the words with a fury.

'*There is no God!*' she screams, and it echoes around the whole of St George's.

It is the last thing Natalya says before she falls in a dead faint.

The dark wooden box is tucked away neatly under the bed where it has lived since the move. Annie pulls it out, gently blows the dust of the city off and traces the initials of her maiden name inlaid in brass on the lid. ACH. Annabel Charlotte Harding. She opens the lid to explore the treasure within. Mementos of the past – pressed flowers from picnics long gone, coloured pebbles combed from childhood daytrips to Dungeness, a smattering of beads from her mother's favourite necklace that snapped all those years ago, scattering the beads across the dunes at Camber Sands until they were giddy with laughter as they looked for them. There is more too – precious notes brimming with passion that Edward sent her when they were courting. But none of these are what she is after.

She rifles through until she finds what she was looking for. Feathers. Of all different sizes and colours. The iridescent blue of a jay's wing, the distinctive speckles of a guinea hen, little linnet feathers – oh, how she misses the linnets from the Kent fields with their melodious song! The only time she comes across them now is in a cage, ready for sale, destined to be hung up in the gloom of the indoors.

Ah, now this is what she wanted! Silky white feathers from a swan, collected from the Serpentine in Hyde Park.

She takes one out and holds it to the light, brushing her finger against the creamy barbs. The Angel of the Thames. *Such a beautiful idea*, she had thought when she read about the story in the newspaper. The guardian of a city, coming to warn of danger. That spark she saw in Edward's eye, she believes she is drawing it out of him through her sketches, but the results have pleased her so much that she has decided to paint him next, capturing his beauty, but this time transposing it onto the divine – like the Angel Gabriel himself or even the mythical Angel of the Thames. The idea excites her terribly, quickening her heart as she works. She will make him *spectacular*.

Annie is in a good mood too for she has had word that Ellie is newly returned from the country after her trip was cut short. After the entire extended family descended upon poor Lizzie, Ellie felt she could better support her sister by handing over money for hired help and vacating the premises. Annie is longing to see her dear friend, to share her idea for her new painting. She won't tell Edward of Ellie's return though – he can be somewhat disparaging towards Annie's painterly friends, seeing them as irreligious, unmotivated and too liberal for their own good. He had not been sad when Marcus, Annie's beloved painting tutor, left for the continent and his tolerance for Ellie, in particular, has waned in the years since he and Annie were wed.

A knock at the door interrupts her, Sarah's muffled voice from the other side. 'Sorry to disturb you, ma'am, but Mrs McGilliveray says she must consult with you upon the butcher's bill. Will you be available to discuss it at some point today?'

'Yes, Sarah, thank you. Please let her know I shall be down shortly,' Annie says with a sigh. Her new creation must wait a little longer, for now at least.

Thanks to Edward's extremely generous dose of laudanum in her cup of tea, by the time he leaves St George's, Miss Bewdley is lost in a deep slumber. He is hoping she will remember nothing of the events they have witnessed, for there will be no evidence when she comes to, bar a single missing blanket and the remnants of a broken teacup. As she slept, propped up in the corner of a pew, Edward took the opportunity to cover his newly fledged and now unconscious angel. He gently folded her wings, wrapping her tightly in the blanket that had fallen from her shoulders before stepping outside to hail a cab.

Heart thumping, Edward bundled his semi-prostrate angel, bonnet loosely tied back on, out of the church and straight into the carriage. One of the many ragged urchins that hung around the area like flies had hovered hopefully, offering to help but, when the boy got too close for comfort, Edward batted him away. He wanted no further witnesses to this creature whom he had claimed, nay been given by God Himself. The boy had fallen backwards into the street as the cab lurched off but it was of no matter. Edward needed to get his angel back to his basement, to study her, to understand her. He had been chosen and everything that stood in his way must be swept aside.

She half-wakes in the cab, pushing away the bottle of laudanum he puts to her lips to calm her, but Edward is strong and she is weakened by her transformation; he manages to get a fair amount into her mouth. She is a beautiful creature, he notes, not in the first flush of youth but younger than his wife. He wonders what lies underneath the patched clothes she wears. Is she too like his Angel of the Thames? A woman in all ways, bar those miraculous wings?

She sleeps now as the cab rattles them eastwards, along Theobalds Road and Clerkenwell to avoid the notorious Holborn traffic, down Goswell Road before a sharp turn towards Bishopsgate that almost knocks them both off the seat. As he steadies himself, Edward notices a handful of feathers poking up out of her blanket and he carefully covers them. He feels torn between excitement and confusion. Think, Meake, *think*! He must sneak her into the house without any witnesses. He praises the Almighty for giving him the foresight to create the private back door to his basement workspace. Fumbling in his waistcoat pocket, he holds the key tight in his hand, cold metal pressing hard into the hot flesh of his palm as he tries to focus his thoughts. Will she need food, this angel? Water? What do these creatures eat and drink?

He cannot ask questions of her yet and he is a little grateful, in truth, of that being the case. She said such *terrible words*, the words of a heathen, within the walls of the church. A jolt strikes him as he studies her face, the bow of her lips, pale cheeks, dark blue eyes, half-closed and unseeing. This stunning creature, this angelic form, could she be something other than what he hopes? Could she be, he thinks to himself, heart plummeting, a *fallen* angel?

The cab stops around the corner from Edward's home, at the end of the dark passageway leading to the back yards of the houses in the short street known as St Mary Axe. Before Edward steps out, he wraps the blanket tightly around his sleeping angel once more, checking her wings are fully concealed before pulling her out and carrying her over his shoulder. The cabbie looks the other way, minds his own business – the passenger had said he was a surgeon, true enough, but truth be told he was far more interested in the proffered tip than why a gentleman of such apparently high standing should be taking a semi-conscious lady to a back alley off Leadenhall.

Edward manages to smuggle his prized possession into the basement without anyone from the house seeing. Or so he thinks, but Sarah is watching from the small laundry room window where she has briefly hidden herself for a moment's respite. She sees him carry something into the basement that she will recount later that evening to Mrs McGilliveray 'looked awful like a body'. They will both shudder as she says it, despite sitting close to the fire.

The newly installed wrought-iron gate that demarks Edward's part of the basement from the servants' area is not now enough, he realises, with a twitch of irritation, for prying eyes can see right through it. After he has gently laid his drugged angel down on his dissecting table, he takes an old oilcloth from the empty holding room to cover the gate. Using short pieces of wire, he fixes the tough cloth on securely, piercing the ends through and twisting them together before cutting a small hole by the keyhole so he can access it from both sides. Now, not only can no one else access his working area, none can see into it either.

Heart racing with both relief and the weight of responsibility, Edward returns to his angel. She lies where he placed her, face upwards, creamy white wings overlapping the table on both sides. He leans towards her gently rising and falling chest, hears her breath, listens to her murmurings and feels a frisson of excitement. God alone has entrusted this miracle to him.

Edward puts his hand on her forehead and she feels warm to the touch. He removes her bonnet, sees her brown hair stiffened with dirt. He wants to undress her, examine her, this exquisite being that now lies before him in his care.

His holding rooms still have old straw mattresses in them from when Edward and Annie first moved in, something for the dogs to sleep on. Edward held a greater number of animals then, all of whom – bar the last mongrel – have subsequently departed from this life in one or other of Edward's many experiments. It will be easy enough for him to steal a clean sheet from upstairs, a few more blankets too. Yes, he thinks, musing to himself, I will put her in the empty cell at the far end of the basement; she will be unable to be heard in there given how thick the door is and, even if she tries to make a noise, the one remaining dog, prone to howling at the best of times, will soon drown her out.

A plan forming in his head, at least for the next few days, he allows himself to relax a little, his angel now safely ensconced in a controlled area that only he has access too. She is *all his*, a live specimen that none can doubt. He gently turns her over onto her front, laps up the sight of her wings – oh so much grander, so much more spectacular than those of his river angel!

There is much to do, Edward thinks. He must mount his river skeleton as soon as the bones are stripped of flesh, rebuild her in wires and metal, reattach her wings so she stands as upright as in life but *this*, oh this warm *alive* being in front of him, with her soft breath and smooth cheeks, this new angel takes precedence over *everything*.

Edward's thoughts whirlpool as he runs his fingers through her feathers, soft and incredible, yet as real as the City outside. A wave of happiness rolls over him as he strokes the curved back of her neck, gently touches the bloodied rips in her clothing where the wings burst through. He is so absorbed by his thoughts that he nearly forgets to dismiss the handful of other patients waiting for him upstairs. None of them are important, not any more. There is only his angel now and all that she will bring him.

She is his most magnificent gift. He smiles to himself, holds his hands together and prays, thanking the Almighty for this incredible, this miraculous and most timely present that has been bestowed upon him – Edward Algernon Meake.

Mary works through the night on Cousin Lou's costume, making a narrow gauze harness to slip over Lou's arms and sit behind her shoulders. In the early hours of the morning, she sends a lad from the street off to Leadenhall Market as soon as it opens.

'They 'ent the best ones they had, but they was the best for the money, miss,' says the boy, out of breath as he hands over the white goose wings.

'Plenty good enough for the stage,' says Mary, holding them up before handing him a coin in exchange.

Dashing back to her room, she finishes the costume as quickly as she can. It wasn't the neatest job but Lou had wanted them as soon as possible and Mary needed the money. When all is done, she wraps the wings in paper and string and heads to the penny gaff, treating herself on the way to an early breakfast of piping hot coffee and 'two thins', slender slices of bread and butter, from Mr Pippin's booth near the Hen and Chickens. It's cheaper and more convenient than attempting to make anything at home given that they have no kitchen; besides, she likes the snug little booth – Mr Pippin is always polite and cheerful, his crockery clean and relatively uncracked.

Mary hums to herself as she moves onward towards Greville Street, holding her package tightly as she goes. The usual ragtag rabble of scruffs lingers outside the shabby theatre but there's one in particular that catches Mary's eye. A blond boy with round blue eyes and a distinctive cut, fresh and red-raw, down his face. He looks away, ashamed, and Mary feels guilty for having stared.

'Oh my! You've done a marvellous job!' Lou slips the wings on and dances delightedly around the small dressing room. 'Strong enough to last a good few weeks afore everyone's tired of the Angel of the Thames – they're perfect!' She kisses Mary on the cheek and Mary laughs, pushing her away.

There's a rap at the door and the boy with the cut on his cheek comes in with a note. He avoids eye contact but seems captivated by Lou's wings – thin fingers reaching out to touch them until Lou slaps his hand.

'No, Charlie! Only I'm allowed to play with these. No grubby little hands, please.'

Charlie looks ashamed and dashes out, slamming the door behind him.

'Ah, I've upset him now. Poor lad,' says Lou. 'Such a pretty face ruined. He'll find it harder to get bits of work lookin' like that.'

Mary looks at her, curious. 'Why? What happened?'

'Charlie? Oh, he does the odd job for us, keen as mustard and handy when a key's been lost – he's got a knack for pickin' – but he's not skilled enough to help with much else. So, he hangs around further in, Bloomsbury mostly. Yesterday, there's a woman taken sick inside one of the churches, I forget which, so Charlie is sent off to fetch some medical gent. He comes back in the cab with him, waits outside 'case anything else needs doing, and eventually the gent comes back out with this woman wrapped up like it's the dead of winter. Charlie goes to see if they need help, carrying the fella's bag or something, and the man whacks him round the face with it! Well, the metal in those big clasps cuts him right down the cheek. Cab whirls off, hooves missing him by inches, leavin' him knocked down in the road. He was lucky to get up 'fore somethin' else ran him over.'

'Good Lord!' says Mary, shocked.

'I know! Man of medicine and all, you'd have thought he'd mop up injuries that he caused himself. Anyway, funny thing is, Charlie swears there was something peculiar about the woman.'

'Peculiar?'

'Mmm,' says Lou as she looks at her wings in the mirror, trying to decide her best angle, 'somethin' about her shoulders, like she was a hunchback or suchlike. And he said there was somethin' odd pokin' up out the blanket she was wrapped in.'

'Odd how?' asks Mary.

'Feathers,' says Lou. 'Just like these, I suppose,' and she idly strokes her wings in the reflection.

But Mary has already left, running out of the room as fast as she can in search of young Charlie. That little spark of excitement that Richard talked about, knowing when there is truth in a story, it is balled up inside of her, quickening within. She knows it is impossible, that there is likely a perfectly simple explanation, but she cannot stop her impulse, cannot stem her curiosity without finding out more.

As she bursts out of the theatre, she catches Charlie's eye but a look of fright comes over him and he runs. And even though Mary knows it's not a genteel thing for a young lady to do, she lifts her skirts high and pelts straight after him.

Annie is in high spirits over breakfast for her husband is returned to her. In the small hours of last night, Edward had tiptoed in, gently waking her with soft kisses. He had desired her as breathlessly and urgently as she had him, burning for each other like fire as they had when they were first married, and Annie knows full well that happy children are made from happy couplings. She smiles at him over her teacup, her handsome husband fizzing with energy. All is well with the world, she thinks, the body in the basement long put out of her mind.

'It is the most wondrous thing, Annie dear,' he says to her as they prepare to part at the base of the stairs, Edward to head down to the basement and Annie to go upstairs to change before a visit to Ellie. 'A gift. A miraculous discovery. More than I could ever have dreamt of. For both of us.' He kisses her on the cheek before descending the stairs, humming cheerfully to himself.

Annie changes swiftly, a lightness in her heart that grows until she is brimming over with happiness by the time she arrives at the Bigsbys' house on Sandland Street. But Ellie has a most delicious and unexpected surprise in store, for it is not just her dear friend that awaits.

'I am afraid I have been rather mischievous,' says Ellie, a gleam in her eye. 'For I am not the only one newly returned from afar. Come,' she says, squeezing Annie's hand and taking her into the drawing room.

The tall figure by the window turns around and it is all Annie can do not to burst into tears.

'*Marcus!*' she cries, running to him, hands out to greet him, for it is her beloved drawing master. In the four years since she last saw him, he has become a little more grey around the temples, the lines upon his forehead more deeply scored, but he is still as delightful as ever.

'My dearest Annie,' he says, tears in his eyes and with an unfashionable glow of hot summer days from his time on the continent. 'My dearest Annie.'

It is not until late afternoon that the effects of both the laudanum and the exhaustion of her transformation begin to wear off and Natalya slowly surfaces from her strange and frightening dreams into a nightmare more terrifying than any she could have imagined. Her eyes open slowly only to find herself still in darkness. She feels groggy, heavy-headed as if she has awoken from a bewitchment in one of her own tales. A jolt of reality hits her as she lifts herself up onto her elbow, senses the lumps on her back. She turns her head, feels the strange weight of the wings sitting behind her.

Not a dream after all.

It is impossible that they should be there and yet there they are.

A thin line of light shines in from around the bottom edge of the door. It is not much to see by but she tries to stand, feels dizzy and, thinking better of it, crawls on her knees over the rough flagstone floor towards the faint glimmer. Clambering up, she realises with a rising sense of fear that not only is the door locked, but there is also no handle. She rattles at the door, thumps at it with what little strength she has left until a dog howls close by. Startled by the sound, Natalya feels the damp brick walls with her hands, rough under her palms, a tickle of air coming from above. She reaches upward to feel the holes of a grate against her fingers. Another cell, next to hers.

'Hullo?' she whispers. 'Hullo?' but it is only the dog that answers, whining in reply through the grate.

Where am I? Natalya wonders. There's an air of cool dampness, scratchy salt crystals forming on the surface of the bricks. The unfamiliar weight of her wings unbalances her for a moment and she stumbles, blunting her knee on a low table. She yelps with pain, starting the dog off yowling all over again. Natalya reaches out, feels with her hands, slowly reads the story of the room she is trapped in. The small table has a thickset candle that went out some time ago, the wick cold to the touch. There's a jug and bowl of water in which to wash, a tankard of weak beer and some bread and cheese, which she eagerly gulps down, eating so fast that her stomach cramps swiftly in response. She swigs the beer too, only regretting it afterwards. The man in the church, he was a surgeon, she remembers, and all have heard tales of how they practise their craft. Yet he must surely want me alive, she thinks, else he would have done away with me already.

Her wings stretch themselves behind her, fanning themselves out as far as they can in the small room. They feel so odd and yet, somehow, as if they have always been there. She turns, feels the flicker in the air as the wings, *her* wings, move behind her. She reaches out, strokes an impossible feather before frightening herself. *What have I become?* she thinks, fearful, as her wings furl back up and she collapses back onto the uneven mattress.

Why has this happened? Natalya wonders. *Why me?*

She is a sinner.

A heathen.

She has brought shame upon others through her sins. Upon her family. She hugs her knees tight to herself. Feels them warm against her belly, against the absence of the bump that once sat there.

She is a sinner for she gave in to love, to lust. A mother outside of wedlock. And a heathen too, for how could any mother believe in a God so cruel as to steal her child away?

Her heart falls, crashes down to inky black depths of despair.

It is her first day with wings. It is also her first day as a prisoner.

Etta calls for Scout but he does not come. She had let him out first thing in the morning as she always did for his early wander around the garden before waiting for her to join him after her own ablutions are complete. But today he is not there, not in the garden at all, not by her rickety cabin hidden in the undergrowth at the far end, not in the cool shade of her small fernery in which he sometimes likes to sleep on a hot day.

She calls his name again, for the twentieth time or more. This is most unlike him, she thinks, puzzled. 'Scout? *Scout!*'

But there is no answer, none at all.

'Miss Lockhart, Miss Lockhart!' Betsy stands in the back door, red-faced, breathless from running. 'It's the dog, miss!' Betsy gasps back her tears. 'It's Scout.'

He is collapsed, a black-and-white heap, halfway down the path to the main gates at Elton. Etta runs to him as fast as she can, holding up her skirts, not caring that she is bonnetless or without her coat. Betsy runs after her, trying her best to keep up.

Scout lies on his side, wheezing, short breaths coming irregularly. His eyes are glazed and his heart is slow. He has been sick and there is blood in it. His brown eyes roll to Etta's face and he tries to lick her hand but his mouth is dry. He whimpers, struggles to breathe – he seems so very, very tired.

His chest rises and falls, rises and then falls one last time. One more small, gasping breath and he is gone. Eyes staring into nothing, the moisture slowly drying on them as she watches.

'No,' says Etta, disbelieving. 'Scout!' She strokes his soft velvet ears, runs her hand over the smooth furrows of his ribcage, willing it to rise again. 'Scout . . . come on, boy, come on.'

But his ears no longer hear his mistress's voice. She lays her head on him, cheek to his still warm chest, waiting to hear the thud of his heart, of his tail, but all is still, all is silent.

Betsy's tears run quietly down her cheeks. Her mistress is most peculiar but she is fond of her in her own way. Betsy has never known anyone love an animal like her mistress loves this dog and it breaks her heart to see Etta's distress.

Etta cannot move, cannot stand, cannot contemplate life without her beloved companion. He is her *everything*. She had known that he would leave her one day, some distant day, but not yet, *not yet* – she is not ready for it. She feels herself unravelling. When the sobs come they are hot and angry, breathless and raw. Her whole body heaves uncontrollably, chest so tight she can barely breathe.

When Etta spots the chunks of meat that Scout had vomited up, flecked with blood, she sees the telltale signs of poisoning. A burning rage rises in her, the likes of which she has never felt before. It is a power too. She feels on the verge of something, an understanding, and yet all seems so cracked, so disparate.

She will bury him by the side of her cabin, she owes him that much at least. When she finally manages to stand, sobs abating, she looks down at the still body of her dearest friend and her mind feels strangely clear – fresh like the air after a thunderstorm.

Today is the day that Etta changes.

Charlie Meckin will not be talking for some time, thinks Mary wryly as the boy stuffs himself with buns, cramming them into his mouth as if he has not eaten for days. She had managed to follow him through the maze of streets towards Holborn, briefly losing him until he stepped out from an alley in front of her.

'What d'ya want?' he'd said, half-scared, half-bravado. 'Why you following me?'

An offer of a coin and some buns was enough to gain his trust and now Mary and Charlie sit on a bench in a leafy square underneath a sycamore tree that, with every small gust of wind, sends down a shower of winged seeds.

''S'like when I caught a jackdaw last year down Coptic Street,' Charlie says. 'It had a broken wing so I tucked it up in my jacket to take home. That's what she reminded me of, the lady in the cab.' And with that, he stuffs most of the last bun into his mouth.

Mary thinks for a moment before telling the boy all that she knows, everything about the Angel of the Thames story, and Charlie nods as he chews.

'It can't be true though, can it?' asks Charlie, crumbs trickling from his mouth. 'I mean, an angel, miss. An *actual* angel! And here in London!'

'It sounds impossible,' Mary says, eyes glittering. 'And I'm sure it is. But, wouldn't it be fun to find out? Just to make sure.'

'But how?' asks Charlie as he finishes the bun. 'You're just a girl. No offence.'

Mary grins. 'None taken. D'you think you could tell me where the surgeon lives? The one who took the woman away, who hit you with his bag?'

Charlie nods. 'Yes, miss, just off Leadenhall. I went inside and everything.' He sticks his dirty finger in his mouth and pokes it around his teeth to mop up any last remnants of currant and baked goods.

'That is a filthy habit,' says Mary, pulling a face at him. He pulls one back and she laughs before a movement catches her eye – a policeman, approaching from the corner of the square.

'Ecilop,' she whispers to Charlie and he sits up, startled. He had no idea this young woman knew any Cockney back slang. It's the language of the streets and yet she seemed so proper . . .

Mary stands, holds out her hand to Charlie. '*Take it*,' she insists and he does so.

'Good morning, officer,' Mary says sweetly, in the most refined voice she can muster. 'My young charge and I were enjoying the last of the autumn sunshine. What a glorious day.'

'So it is. Good morning to you too, miss,' he replies as

they walk past him, giving a nod to Charlie as if he vaguely recognises him.

It's only after they have left the square and are back on the busy streets, leaving the policeman far behind, that Mary realises Charlie is still clutching her hand.

It is Wednesday and Edward is once again walking the wards of St Luke's with his students. He has been doing this for long enough now that he works automatically, charming his patients with a smile, commanding his pupils' attention and respect. He plans to keep to as much of his routine as he can in order to avoid suspicion, paranoia softly rising within him. To keep his angel from the servants' ears and eyes, he laced her beer with just enough laudanum to keep her quiet. She'll need feeding when he returns but then so will the dog and that will give him excuse enough to take food from the kitchen again.

There is an inner confidence that has been growing in Edward since he acquired the body of the river angel, but now, with a living specimen in his possession, it has become something else. Others might call it arrogance but to Edward it is simply an acceptance of God having chosen him above all others. This is his due, he believes, and he has worked hard for it, prayed more than any other man – so much so that he has garnered the attention of the Almighty Himself.

When Edward returns home, heading in the back entrance and straight to his basement, he unlocks the door to the small room, his heart thudding as he looks in at his prize. Her candle has long gone out and she lies asleep on the mattress, lips parted, hair ruffled. He relights the candle, leaving a few spare matches beside it, and she wakes, groggily pushing herself up on her elbow and glaring at him.

'You are awake then,' he says.

'What right have you to keep me here?' Natalya demands.

'Every right,' Edward replies, captivated by the vision in front of him, her beautiful wings framing her lovely face. 'I am a man of science and I wish to study you.'

She says nothing, only stares at him silently.

'Where are you from?' he asks, waiting for a response that does not come. 'You will not say where you have come from then?'

Her lips remain still, but her eyes pierce him. They are a rare dark blue, intense like the sea before a storm.

'Perhaps at least you can tell me your name?'

A faint smile plays across her lips for a moment before disappearing.

'Nobody,' she whispers.

'Nobody.' Edward sighs. 'Well, judging by your clothing, that much is true. Well, Nobody,' he says. 'I wish to examine you.'

She glares at him, before slowly shaking her head.

'I will do it with or without your permission,' Edward says, calmly. 'It is God's will. That is why you are here. That is why you have the gift of the wings.'

Natalya narrows her eyes, but she is too tired to argue. She sinks back onto the grubby mattress, scowling at her gaoler.

Edward is irritated by her silence and they stare at each other again until he blinks first.

'God granted you those wings and He has given you to me. I will do unto you whatsoever He guides me to.' He leaves, slamming the door to behind him, before returning after a short while with more opium-laced beer, knowing her thirst will eventually get the better of her.

After his own supper, at which – to Annie's dismay – he fidgets and is most ill-tempered, Edward returns to the basement, collects his fallen angel, drugged and dozy, and carries her to his dissecting room. He removes each and every one of her items of clothing calmly and methodically, examining how the wings ripped and pushed through corset, chemise, dress and coat. He labels, catalogues and boxes everything, layer by layer, until his angel lies naked on his dissection table.

Edward runs his fingers over her bare breasts, probes her ears, eyes and nostrils, listens to her heart, feels the undulating bumps of her ribs before turning her onto her front. He examines with cold-hearted concentration her beautiful white wings, measuring and studying them, before turning her back over. He hesitates for a moment, and then dares to push apart her thighs and examine her internally too. To his astonishment and repulsion, he discovers his angel is not only no longer a virgin but has, at some point, given birth.

He does not understand. There was no child with her, no ring on her finger. A fallen angel, then. Or is she simply – as she said – a nobody, a freak of nature who God, for reasons known only unto Him, has blessed? Edward is bewildered. He prays for guidance, prays for something, anything to soothe his confusion. He sits, staring at his naked angel, watching her breathe, chest gently rising and falling as the light from his gas lamps flickers around the room.

This is a test. A puzzle to solve. God is testing him, asking him questions, but he does not know the answers. He has no idea what to do next.

Annie lies in the dark, thinking over her day as she waits for her husband to come to bed. It was such a joy to see Marcus again. She had felt so happy when she came home, her beloved Marcus returned, cheerfulness restored. And then supper came and Edward was bad-tempered and secretive once again. Annie had mentioned, in passing, to Ellie and Marcus that Edward had been a little erratic in his behaviour of late, but she dared not say more for fear of being disloyal. She would have been more frank if it had just been her and Ellie but she had not wanted to reveal more in front of Marcus, for he had never taken to Edward.

Marcus had helped Annie so much, lifted her talent from that of accomplishment to real skill. It had been how she had first met Ellie too — through Marcus's drawing school for young ladies. Ellie had not been without proficiency but they had all known it was Annie who had the innate gift. Annie and Ellie had taken extra classes, offered gratis, for Marcus swiftly became fond of the company of these two, very different young women. They had spent many happy hours wandering the Kent coastline, venturing inland for gentle hills and low valleys, all the while sketching, talking and laughing. The trio had remained the best of friends until Marcus had gone overseas, less than eight months after Annie turned down his proposal and shortly after she had accepted Edward's. She had not seen him since.

He was too old for me anyway, thinks Annie ruefully, although she knows he had loved her dearly, perhaps still held some strong affection for her. And perhaps fourteen years was not so very much of a difference in age. Yet it might, in some ways, have been a marriage of convenience too for she knew – though would never say it out loud – that Marcus had almost as much of a soft spot for handsome young men as pretty young women. But his affection for her had been sincere and he was a man of integrity – he would surely have been loyal as a husband, she thinks.

In the early hours, when Annie wakes, the bed remains empty beside her. 'He will be a good match for you,' Annie's mother had said all those years ago, having been impressed both by Edward's future prospects as a surgeon and his clear affection for her one surviving daughter. Annie had been so happy at the thought of it all, a husband who cherished and respected her, their own house in London where all things seemed possible – exhibitions and galleries, parks and picnics. The first year or so had been so much fun, full of dinner parties and dances, but as Edward's ambition slowly grew, the number of engagements diminished in turn as his work took precedence.

Last year, her mother's health had started to decline, at first slowly and then, in late winter, with sudden speed. Annie had been forced to move back to her old family home in Rye to help look after her and Ellie had become even more of a support. Letters bouncing between the two, Ellie had visited Annie in Rye more often than Edward had, something Ellie still brought up every now and then as an example of what she considered to be Edward's dereliction of duty. And then, on a bright spring day in March, her mother had died. Annie had been by her side, witnessed her last gasps for breath, heard the death rattle in her throat, felt the warmth slide out of her mother, disappearing into the ether. It had not been a smooth or kind death and she feels distressed each time she recalls it.

The family house, *her home*, had been sold but it had fallen into disrepair and did not fetch as much as it might once have done. The money had taken a while to come through and, when it eventually did, prompted their move from Bloomsbury to this spacious new house with its large basement and impressive rooms. It worries her to think of it now. So much money spent – on the rent, on alterations, on furniture and furnishings, on Edward's equipment for his work.

'You worry too much,' Edward had said to her with a smile when she tried to raise it with him before they signed the lease. He had been stern with her the second time, after they had moved in, then finally short with her when she had attempted to discuss it a few weeks ago. All she owned, all she had ever owned, belonged to Edward now. She doesn't feel she can bring the subject up again; besides, does she not trust her husband? To love and cherish him – that is what she vowed in the eyes of God on her wedding day – and, she thinks guiltily, to obey. She must be a dutiful wife, support and encourage him. That is her role is it not, the angel of the house?

Annie washes her face, dresses herself to the sound of the sparrows chittering outside. Sometimes, she thinks, it is as if her husband is developing two different personalities, each on the face of a coin that is tossed at random. She wonders on which side the coin will land today.

FOR ONE WEEK ONLY
THE CURTAIN THEATRE

THE ANGEL OF THE THAMES

THE MYSTERIOUS LADY!
SOIRÉES FANTASTIQUE

Astounding Wonders – Inconceivable Transformations –
Startling Illusions – A Temple of Enchantment

ROBERT THE SORCERER! ! !

THE MAGIC KALEIDOSCOPE – THE SEAT OF TIME

A PLEASING AND VARIED FEATURE IN THE ENTERTAINMENT IS THE PERFORMANCE OF THE

GOBLIN SPRIGHTLY

WITH VOCAL AND INSTRUMENTAL MUSIC

Miss L. Scott will preside at the Piano-Forte

Doors open at Half-Past Seven; The Angel appears at Eight; Children under 13 Years of Age,
Half-price in the First and Second-Class booths only Tickets (and for Reserved Seats Numbered)
may be had of the Printer

Printed by D. Fulton, Oxford Yard, Brompton Lane, London

Etta's hands are tied. She wakes with a jolt and a sharp pain down one side. For a moment she cannot recall anything, her mind a puzzled blank, until flashes of the day before flicker through her mind. The strange sickness in the woods, a boy and a crossbow. *Scout.* She feels the loss anew, a rush of grief fresh in every vein.

She feels hot, sweat trickling down her forehead. An old blanket covers her and she rouses herself, tries to kick it off, before realising, with fear, that there is something across her mouth, a cloth that tastes faintly of salt and stale milk. Rough straw prickles beneath her as her eyes focus and she finds herself in a rickety old barn, light shining in through gaps in the timber, bales of hay stacked up in irregular towers.

Etta's shoulders feel stiff, as if something lies upon her. Ah, her breath is sucked out. *The wings.* They feel as strange as if she had sprouted another limb and yet, in many ways, that is precisely what they are – two newly grown limbs, joined in but a moment by bone and sinew, muscle and blood.

It was not a dream after all. She is confused and groggy,

but she knows something impossible has come to pass – her doubts about the church have been growing week on week and yet this has happened to her of all people. She must examine herself, understand what has happened as much as the why. But where might she be now? This is not her home, this is nowhere she knows. She has never seen this barn before. And there is no Scout to defend her. *Scout.* She is alone, helpless and, it seems, hopeless too.

A movement in the far corner of the barn catches her eye. The boy with the crossbow sits in the shadows, watching. She tries to communicate that she is no threat but the gag over her mouth is bound too tightly for her to do so and she is soon forced to relinquish her efforts.

The boy, Thomas Marshall, sits and watches her, confused and wary. He has seen her before, this noble-looking woman with brown skin and dark, tightly curled hair. He had seen her many times with her big black-and-white dog, watched them from afar as they wandered through the woods – and now that self-same woman has grown wings, turned into an angel. He saw her, as his hand slipped and the bolt flew from him, he saw her *hover above the ground*. He has not told *them* of that though. He wishes he had never said anything, wishes he had left her there to die. But it is too late for regrets now. He shivers as he looks at her. *What is she?* He watches her close her eyes, trying to take in all that has happened, knowing that she too will be wondering what will become of her. But that, he knows full well, is no longer in either of their hands.

Edward is not expecting Miss Bewdley at all, let alone for her to call this early in the morning. He bustles her into his consulting room, shutting the door firmly behind her.

'That young woman in the church . . . it is just . . . oh, Mr Meake, I was so dreadfully concerned. I did not dream it, did I?' Miss Bewdley wrings her hands as she speaks making Edward's skin crawl with irritation.

'She was most unwell I'm afraid, Miss Bewdley, yes.'

'But the wings! She had—'

'*Wings?*' says Edward, a faint smile rising. 'Sorry, Miss Bewdley, *wings* . . . ?'

Miss Bewdley looks at him, deep into his eyes. 'I thought – I could have sworn Mr Meake, truly. You say, hand on heart there were no . . . '

'Wings, Miss Bewdley? The young woman at St George's was taken most badly with some sort of fitting sickness and I had to remove her as speedily as I could. Miss Bewdley, do you *really* not remember?'

'Oh, Mr Meake! Are you sure? It's just, I had the most peculiar dream . . . that she grew wings, actual wings, in the church itself.'

'There were no wings, Miss Bewdley,' Edward says with a show of great solemnity. 'You seemed most distressed by her sickness and I'm afraid you fainted. I would, of course, have stayed with you but I needed to seek further medical attention – to no avail, though, for I'm afraid the young woman sadly passed away in a fit.' He had not thought to lie but it comes so naturally, funnelled from somewhere deep inside, that Edward feels strangely calm as he speaks. This is God's will, he thinks.

'Forgive me for neglecting to check on you since,' he continues. 'I have been busy with my other patients but I can at least offer you something for your nerves, Miss Bewdley, if you will permit me? I am sorry, though, that you have come all this way only for me to be unable to share good tidings with you.'

Miss Bewdley is confused, he can see it upon her face. 'Could I perhaps have a little word with your dear wife?' she ventures.

'No, I would rather you didn't,' he says firmly. 'She has been unwell herself of late.' He leans in, lowers his voice. 'You know, Miss Bewdley, we have been over three years married and we are still not blessed with a child.'

'Oh, I am most saddened to hear that, Mr Meake.'

'Thank you. It troubles my wife a great deal at times.' He nods at her before turning to his large cabinet on the far wall, opening it to pull out several small bottles which he mixes into a single empty one, sealing it with a stopper. He carefully wipes the bottle with a small cloth before handing it to her.

'Tincture of opium, Miss Bewdley, it will help with your

nerves. It is oft used for bronchial problems but I have found it to be soothing for a range of concerns. I could not help but notice you wring your hands rather a lot and, as a medical man, I know that repetitive movement is often caused by the nervous system.' He shakes his head as she goes to make some motion of paying him.

'No, no, Miss Bewdley, you have always been very kind to us. I am most grateful to you for bringing the distress of that poor young woman to my notice. Please, no, there is no payment due, it is the least I can do.'

Edward dismisses her, seeing her to the front door himself with a sigh of relief before returning to his consulting room. He locks the door behind him, falls to his knees and prays.

Natalya wakes up screaming but there is no one to hear – bar the dog in the next room who howls back at her. She sits up, catching her breath as whatever nightmares were plaguing her slip from her sleepy grasp.

I am not wearing my own clothes, she realises with a jolt. This rough nightdress, this old coat, they are not mine. She is no longer wearing a corset or even a chemise. *He has undressed me*, she thinks, shocked and angry as she runs her hands over herself, a twinge of soreness below. *What else has he done?* She feels violated, knowing her captor has undressed her, *examined* her. Anger and resentment rise in her. *How dare he?*

She straightens her thoughts. The drink her captor has left her must surely be laced with something. Natalya is familiar with the numbing effects of laudanum, had taken it many times before realising it did little to comfort her. She had come to realise that pain, her own deep grief, could in fact be harnessed, transformed into power. A ball of anger, growing hard like a knot of scar tissue, giving her strength. This surgeon, this man, knows *nothing* of this, she thinks. Who is he, this *monster* that believes the heavens have ordained him?

She stretches, feels her wings fan out through the holes he has cut in the nightdress. Why her? Were the wings somehow connected to the vision she had? Were they connected to the patterns that she now sees everywhere? Patterns big and small. Her fingers graze the rough brick wall. What then if all of life is like this? Made from building blocks too small to see, smaller than grains of sand. What if *everything* is like this? From the stars in the sky to the pebbles on a beach. What if *we* are made from such things too? Creatures of dust and wonder . . .

A flash of memory washes over her. Of love and safety. Of desire and passion. Of the way she felt ablaze when she looked at the new farmhand, an all-consuming burning that took over her mind, her body, her entire soul. How she could think of nothing else but when she would see him again, of how much she wanted to touch him, *all of him*. How she could see, reflected in his eyes, those same flames smouldering for her. His warm hands in the dairy, his slow unlacing of her that first time. Of his lips on hers, hands and limbs entwining, of bare skin, pleasure and pain and teeth-clashing urgency. Endless nights and days of snatched moments, forbidden love. She cannot bring herself to say his name for it hurts too much. *The reason why she left.* She had risked all only to be banished, left with a swelling belly, a vanished lover and, worst of all, a lost child too.

No, Natalya thinks as she strikes a match to light the candle stub, illuminating the small cell. It is no good dwelling on the past. She had stepped out of the role her family had carved for her, trodden a fresh path. She must think about the now. She has blasphemed, sinned, lost her faith, and now she has become impossible. A cruel joke from God, punishment for her faithlessness – or is it, as her captor seems to think, a gift? Whatever the cause, she thinks, I must get out of here, away from this dank basement, this terrible city, this *man*.

She doesn't touch the beer. She knows she will need a clear head to come up with a plan and food is harder to lace than drink. She stuffs the half-loaf into her mouth, ripping off chunks and gobbling it down. She must stoke the fire in her belly. She has seen animals cornered before, both on the farm and in the wild. The aggressive bull, the cow that will not be parted from its calf. She thinks of them, channels their wildness, as she looks at the porcelain jug, the washing bowl.

If I am to be treated like a cornered animal, then I shall behave like one.

A plan starts to form and, by the time she has eaten the bread, she is ready. She takes the jug, empties the water into the bowl and holds it up high above her head before dashing it to the floor.

The shards are plentiful. She carefully sifts through them to find the biggest, the sharpest one.

And then she waits.

'Big, ain't it?' says Charlie as he and Mary stand, looking up at Edward and Annie's house from the opposite side of the street. Mary nods, taking it all in. Three storeys including the basement, it is much wider than the houses around it and considerably larger than Mary would have thought even a relatively affluent surgeon could afford in this part of town. She wishes she could unlatch the front wall, peel it back as if it were a doll's house, to see what really lies within.

The row is terraced, other buildings joined onto both sides of the Meakes' residence, a higgledy mishmash of architecture spanning some two hundred years or more. A handful of steps to the left lead up to the front door, a gate in the railings to the far right leads downstairs to a small paved area and straight into the servants' hall in the basement for deliveries and trade.

A figure appears at one of the windows and Mary's eyes are drawn towards it. A woman with dark blonde hair stands, looking back at her, wearing a green dress the colour of grass and a puzzled expression on her face.

'Come,' says Mary, taking Charlie by the shoulders and

guiding him away. 'Let's see if there's a way in round the back.'

Annie watches them from the window, the young woman dressed in black and the small boy, sees her take his hand and lead him away. She feels unsettled by them, by *her* in particular, the way she looked up at her. St Mary Axe is not usually a street that strangers linger in.

When Annie returns to her study, she lays out her collection of feathers, one by one, by size and colour, by beauty, finding solace in the ritual of repetition until she is lost in her thoughts. She looks at the canvas she is to paint her angelic Edward on, examines it for imperfections and, when satisfied, scans through her preparatory sketches, marking up her favourites to refer back to.

Later, she idly sketches Marcus as he was when they first met. Elegant in both his dress and manner, he had moved like a dancer. He had a sharp mind, and occasionally a sharp tongue, but he was always excellent company and frequently generous and kind. Dear Marcus, she thinks to herself, his greying hair suits him, makes him look most distinguished. She smiles to herself before a flutter of guilt spreads within as if, simply by thinking such a thing, she were being disloyal to her husband.

Miss Bewdley is not expecting visitors and does not recognise either the eager young woman or the blond boy with the red mark down his face.

'I was given your address by someone at St George's,' says Mary as she hovers in the half-opened doorway. 'Please, may we come in? We shan't take up much of your time. My name is Mary Ward and this is Charlie Meckin. We are looking into a series of strange events and I believe you might be able to help us.'

'Goodness!' says Miss Bewdley. 'I'm not at all certain that I can, but I will do my best.' She opens the door wide and Mary and Charlie enter her rooms, as small, sparse and neatly ordered as the woman herself.

'It concerns something that happened earlier this week,' says Mary carefully. 'A woman taken ill, within the walls of St George's.'

'Oh, gracious me. Please, I do not wish to talk of such things,' Miss Bewdley says, wringing her hands as if she is washing them. 'I'm afraid the young woman you speak of has since passed away and I have nothing further to add. Please, I would rather you left.'

Mary notes the medicine bottle near the window before she continues. 'The name of the surgeon who attended the woman. It is a Mr Meake, is it not? Of St Luke's Hospital?' Mary looks Miss Bewdley in the eye, although she already knows the answer having earlier ascertained it from the hard-pressed maid whitening the steps at Edward's house.

'Please,' says Miss Bewdley, opening the door for them to leave. She does not know these people, does not know what to say or how to possibly explain to them what she believes she saw.

'I do not wish to pry and I certainly wish no one any harm, Miss Bewdley, but I think you should know' – Mary leans in and speaks quietly – 'Mr Meake is responsible for the injury to Charlie's face.'

A flicker of emotion runs across Miss Bewdley's face as she looks at the deep cut, still red-raw, on the young boy's cheek.

'Miss Bewdley, please. We only wish to know the truth! What was wrong with the woman?' Mary begs. 'What happened inside St George's?'

Miss Bewdley ushers them out, the young woman first and then the boy. Charlie stops in the doorway, putting his foot against the door as she goes to close it.

'I saw the feathers, miss,' he says, holding her glance for a moment before taking his foot away.

Miss Bewdley slams the door shut, gasping for breath. Is this a trick? Did Mr Meake put them up to this? Oh, how she wishes the Reverend Pennyforth were here, the voice of reason! She holds her shaking hands out in front of her. If the boy had seen feathers too – but no. The Meakes are an honourable family. Mr Meake and his wife, they are loyal to the church. It was simply a dream, as Mr Meake had said, a trick of the senses. And yet, she thinks, when she mentioned wings to Mr Meake, there came into his eyes a glimmer of recognition . . .

It is only later, after Miss Bewdley has taken a few soothing drops from Edward's bottle, that she decides she should, *must* in fact, confide these peculiar events in someone. She scribbles her letter to the Reverend Pennyforth as fast as she can – a peaceful sleepiness already beginning to come as the drug-filled tincture begins to sink in. When she is done, she asks her neighbour to send it for her and only then does she finally allow her weariness to overcome her.

When Edward unlocks the door, his angel is ready for him, lunging at him with the shard from the broken jug. He is caught off guard, the plate of food he carries knocked to the floor as she jabs at him. The dog goes berserk in the next room, howling and throwing itself against the door as Edward and Natalya tussle. He grabs her wrist before she can reach as far as his neck but her anger gives her strength and she slices at him. He hits her fist hard on the brick wall until she is forced to drop the shard but his left arm is torn and bleeding badly.

He smacks her around the face, knocking her to the ground. 'You are mad,' he gasps, clutching at his wounded arm. 'You are *mad*!'

She glares at him as she pulls herself back up to her feet, her attempt to escape foiled – for now at least. She sees the wound she has caused and is glad of it. Perhaps he too can suffer some of the pain that she has been forced to.

Edward is truly shaken. He feels his pulse under his hand, the blood pumping out of him. He leans in the doorway, catching his breath.

'Once upon a time, there was a man,' Natalya says, not

taking her eyes from him. 'A surgeon, who thought he was his own God. He thought he could do unto all the world's creatures whatsoever he wished. He coveted them, sliced them up—'

He steps towards her and slaps her hard on her cheek.

'I do not know what you are,' he growls, 'but I will *not* have you behave like this.'

This creature, this is no *angel*, this is no woman, this *thing* in his basement, it is nothing but an *animal*! Raging, he slams the door, locking her in. He must attend to his arm as a matter of urgency. He stumbles to his dissecting room, removes his waistcoat, peels his bloodied shirt from himself until he stands there, pale and topless, heart racing, shivering from both the cold and the shock.

He will replace porcelain with pewter. She cannot hurt anyone with that, he thinks, trying to calm himself. He wipes the blood from his arm so he can see the damage more clearly and is relieved to discover it is at least not an artery that has been lacerated.

Edward is used to sewing one-handed as he works, holding down a patient and stitching with his right hand but this is the first time he has had to do it upon himself. The wound is not as deep as he first thought but it is rough and jagged. He flexes his fingers to check for nerve damage and is satisfied. Wincing as he does so, he washes the wound before stitching it closed, tying it tightly off and biting the suture with his teeth. He reaches for a bandage, unrolling it, before wrapping it firmly around the whole of his forearm, tying it over his palm and around his thumb.

When he is done, he slumps down into the solitary chair in his room, breathless and exhausted, arm numb and sore. She is a wild creature, *wild*, he thinks. Those words she had used too. 'A surgeon who thought he was his own God.' They remind him of what Samuel had said – *are we not in our own way gods?* – yet how could she have known of that? *How could she possibly have known about that?*

He trembles, prays a moment for guidance and then, for the first time in a long while, he buries his head in his hands and lets himself weep.

Peter King's shack by the edge of the river is not hard to find. It is also not somewhere Mary ever wants to revisit, even in the bright hours of daylight. She wishes Richard could have accompanied her but today is deadline day for the *New Weekly* and she is thankful that Charlie is at least with her – he may be just a boy but he is resourceful and good company. Mary hasn't told Uncle Jos yet, but Charlie stayed in their lodgings last night. She smuggled him into her room after Jos had gone to bed and they slept top to toe like she used to with Lou when they were little. He had helped with her button work too, sorting the mixed pile into matching sets on her bed, cutting the card into neat squares and even depositing them at Mr Gidley's for her when she was done.

King is not in his hovel but is instead down by the river, working on his shabby boat, upturned like the shell of a tortoise, on the end of the rickety wooden pier. It is here Mary eventually tracks him down only to find him in a mournful mood, hungover and maudlin.

'Everyone's saying now it's *their* Angel, that they dragged this or that outta the river or they seen it flyin' round and it's all mischief it is. Mischief to discredit an honest fella. As long as the likes o' me and Him' – he motions to the sky – 'know what happened, that's all that matters, eh?'

'And so what *did* happen, Mr King?' asks Mary. 'If you don't mind me asking.'

Peter King narrows his eyes at her, suspiciously. 'Said it oft enough, ain't I? And if it bears repeating then I'm afraid a payment should be forthcoming.'

'I'm afraid I carry no coins with me today,' says Mary, innocently, although this is not quite true. 'I simply want the answer to one question.'

He nods and she continues. 'You sold the body you pulled out of the Thames to a surgeon, that's correct, isn't it? Can I ask you his name?'

Peter scrunches his face up with concentration before shaking his head. 'I've tried and tried but it ain't stuck.'

'Was it' – she hesitates for a moment, knowing full well that by even suggesting it, he might agree just to get rid of her – 'a Mr Meake?'

His face lights up. 'Leek, that's it! Leek.' Charlie and Mary exchange a glance and Peter clocks it. 'It were Leek, like the vegetable.'

'And did you make a note of it somewhere?' Mary asks.

He glances at her askew and she remembers, with a blush, that it's unlikely he is able to read and write.

'I made an adequate note up 'ere,' he says, tapping his head.

'Could you describe him to me?'

'Tallish, dark hair, pale.' He shrugs, describing both Edward and what could be nigh on half of London's population.

'Anything else?' she probes.

'He'd been to see one of the tarts round the corner, what for I don't rightly know. I asked her what he was after and she clamped up.'

'Pray, could you tell me her name? Perhaps we could try asking her?'

'Frankie. Frankie Webster, but you won't get nothin' outta her. She got taken off to the workhouse and none o' us knows which.'

Mary tries one final time. 'And there's nothing else you can tell us about him?'

'He looked like those sort o' men always do,' says Peter, returning his attention to a particularly tricky-looking hairline crack on the bottom of his boat. 'Hungry look in his eyes. And I tell you summat for nothin' too. I wish I'd never sold that body, wish I'd never found it neither. It's bought me nothin' 'cept trouble. Cursed, I think it is, *cursed*. And I hope it's cursed him who bought it too.'

'Do not fuss, Annie! It is simply a dog bite, nothing more.'

Edward's words come to her again as Annie watches him sleep in the soft light of daybreak. His arm is bandaged almost from the elbow to the hand, a large wound simply for a dog bite. He had not come to bed until the early hours. She had felt the warmth of him slip under the covers beside her, reached out to touch him, but instead her hand glanced upon his left arm and he cried out in pain. *He is not well*, she thinks as she looks at his exhausted face, red eyes telling of tears she knows must have fallen earlier.

Annie has only ever seen him cry once before, at the crimson lumps that slipped out of her in the bathtub in the early days of her only pregnancy. She was not yet three months gone. The small tin bath had turned into a torrent of scarlet and they had held each other tightly, weeping into each other's arms the whole night. It must be over two years ago now, she thinks ruefully.

This house was supposed to be a new start, the place where they grew their family, a house full of children and life. Instead it seemed to Annie to be increasingly full of secrets. She reaches out to stroke Edward's face but her movement wakes him and he grabs her arm tightly, roaring at her.

'Get away! Get away from me!' A moment passes before he recognises where he is, sleep falling away from him as realisation dawns that he had very nearly hit his own wife.

'Annie!' he says, as she peels herself away from him, breathlessly. 'Annie, my love, I am sorry . . . please, forgive me.'

But she is already halfway out of the room, an imprint of his nails, red-raw crescent moons, dug deep into her arm.

Natalya broods in the dark cell, her few matches long since used up. Her captor has abandoned her without further drink or food since she attacked him. Was that yesterday or only hours ago? Time is lost down here in the gloom when all she can do is sleep or think.

She has shouted and screamed, bashed the door with her fists, kicked it with her worn old boots, but all that happens is the poor mongrel yowls next door. He is clever, she thinks, putting a dog in there, masking any sounds she makes. If only there was a window she could break. If only there was something, *anything* she could do . . . I must outwit him, she thinks, running through scenarios in her head. What does he want me for? What is his ultimate will?

Then a new idea emerges. Unsure of whether or not she has the courage to go through with it, she sits, arms curled around herself. She closes her eyes, remembers herself as a girl on the long beach at the Bay of Stove, feels the soft crunch of the tiny, brilliantly coloured shells under her feet, sees the long sands stretching so far away, as if she could walk straight out onto one of the other islands to another world, another life, selkies mournfully calling to each other in the distance, bonxies scouring the skies like pirates, the lazy waves rolling in and out like sighs. She remembers the smell of salt sea air, terns ducking and weaving over her head, fragile as paper, the cry of the kittiwakes, gannets plummeting like falling stars down into the sea. Their island names – pickieterno, kittiwaako, solan goose – roll off her tongue into her memories. She cannot go back to the remnants of her family and nor would she now wish to. But the wild runs through her veins, the freckles on her arms forming tight constellations like the sky above, the sea reflected in her dark blue eyes as she reopens them, staring into the darkness.

I have nothing to lose, she thinks. This world has taken everything from me. All I have are my wits and my body. I did not ask for these wings, for any of this. It is he who started this war with me and if I am to see the sky again, if I am to walk out of here, then I must fight him in return.

She sets her jaw, determinedly.

Etta opens her eyes and she is a young girl again, back at Elton Hall and Papa is newly returned. 'Papa!' she cries, running barefoot over the grass towards him.

'Etta! Come back here this instant!' cries Dorothy, but Etta's small feet bounce off the grass, tickling the soles of her feet, as she pelts towards her father, delighted to see him, slowing only when she sees that Walter – as immaculate in his clothing as Etta is dishevelled – is already waiting by the carriage. Walter, prim and proper, glares at her as the door opens and their father steps out, but her beloved Papa does not see her. She calls to him but he looks straight through her, as if she were invisible. She calls again, shouts until her mouth is dry, a sense of hopelessness dawning, panic beating hard in her heart.

She wakes with a jolt. She is still in the barn and it was but a dream. Memories and imaginings jumbled together like a badly ravelled ball of wool. It is dark again outside and she wonders how much time has passed. Her side hurts from the crossbow wound, a dull ache that pains her every movement, and she feels feverish and strange, the wings on her back digging into her.

The boy approaches and Etta backs away, frightened, until she realises he is simply bringing her water. He pulls her gag down, holds the flask to her dry lips and she drinks deeply, greedily. When she is done, she turns her head away.

'Where am I?' she croaks and the boy's eyes widen with fright. He shakes his head and goes to pull up her gag but she jerks her head away. 'Am I still in Salop?' Etta asks and he nods. 'What is to become of me?'

He shakes his head. 'No more questions. Sorry, miss.' He sees the tear roll down her cheek as he pulls the gag up over her mouth before returning to the corner of the barn. His back towards her, for he cannot bear to see the sadness in her eyes, he contents himself with whittling the end of a stick into the shape of a bird's head.

Edward is furious, hands trembling with anger as he reaches for his instruments. His fallen angel lies unconscious, face down on the table. Her wings hang limply from her shoulders, both at a strange angle. The humerus on each is broken, splintered at the very top where the wings join her shoulders, yet the rest of the wing, from the ulna down to the furthest, longest feather at the very tip remains remarkably intact. The damage, though, is done. His angel is broken. Broken in a fit of uncontrollable rage.

He holds out his sweating hands, watches their shaking as he prays.

The Lord giveth and the Lord taketh away.

Steady my hands, O Lord, so that I may now do what must needs be done.

Let me finish this.

Lord, hear my prayer.

He is as ready as he will ever be. A deep breath as he holds out her left wing, uses his bone saw to begin removing it. She is not conscious but still, he hopes, cruelly, that she can feel the pain as he removes the wing. It takes him less than an hour to remove both wings, carefully severing them as close to her shoulders as he dares, feeling her warm body beneath his hands. He mops the wounds clean before bandaging the two short stumps tightly, lifting her up to wind the bandages over her shoulders and around her chest.

She is still alive.

When he has completed his work, he looks at her prone body with venom. He roars out loud, a wail of despair and rage. Her separated wings, those beautiful, miraculous wonders, lie underneath the table to one side, their stumps bloodied. When some semblance of calm has returned to him later, he will clean them, remove the broken feathers, restore them to at least a little of their past glory, but they are already much diminished by having been removed from their true owner.

He breathes deeply, tries to calm himself. His feet unsteady, he topples backwards until he stands by the doorway, grabbing at the post to keep upright as he gazes at the scene before him.

It is as if it has all been completed in some sort of feverish daze, a nightmare of rage and fury, a nightmare that ended only in tragedy.

'What have I done?' he wails softly to himself, breathless with horror as he slides down the doorway, looking upon his newly wingless angel as he crumples to the floor.

'What have I done?'

When Uncle Jos returns home, Mary and an unfamiliar young boy with a distinctive cut across his face are waiting for him at the table. Mary looks furtive somehow, a disobedient child about to confess a misdemeanour.

'Dearest Uncle,' she says, as she takes his hands. 'This is my new friend, Charlie Meckin, and we have been following a story.'

'Hmm,' Jos mutters. 'Have you indeed? Well, I think you had better tell me the full tale but I'm afraid your audience will not just be myself but Richard too. He is following behind with strict instructions to bring baked potatoes, though I was not aware we had *another mouth* to feed,' he says, pointedly, as he eyes Charlie.

'Please, sir, I don't eat much anyway,' says Charlie, eyes full of fear.

'I will share with him,' says Mary, heart gladdening at the thought of seeing Richard just as the tall young man himself strides through the door, bending down to avoid hitting his head on the door frame. He juggles three hot potatoes wrapped in paper from hand to hand to avoid burning himself.

'Ah, Mary.' He nods with a grin. 'Good evening – oh,

and to the young fella too. Good evening, sir. Good job I bought the very largest potatoes; there should be enough for all of us providing the young gentleman is staying to sup?'

'Mary and the young lad have been on the trail of a story,' says Uncle Jos and Richard smiles, as he tumbles the potatoes onto the wooden table.

'Have they now?' he says, intrigued, taking off his hat and pulling out the last of the chairs. 'And I bet I can guess which story too – am I right, Miss Ward?'

'It is a most peculiar tale, Mr Gibbs,' Mary says as she holds his gaze for a moment before leaning forward eagerly. 'Full of strange wonders. And it's time we shared with you all that we have found.'

'Ah,' Jos holds up a hand, 'forgive me, Mary, but I am somewhat ravenous and I feel we must eat first and then you can tell us all.'

It is late by the time Richard finally leaves Folgate Street. As he walks back out into the streets, still full of life even at this late hour, his thoughts are divided between the thrill of an impossible-sounding story and his regard for Mary. She has become, he thinks, with affection, a most remarkable young lady.

Poor Richard is so distracted that he's not looking properly as he crosses the road and a cab nearly runs him over, the driver yelling blue murder at him. Richard waves an apologetic hand as the cab rattles around the corner and he rebukes himself. The near miss reminds him of a terrible accident he witnessed once, as a cub reporter, long before he left London. A line of schoolchildren was walking along

Gray's Inn Road as a dray was being emptied of its barrels of beer, an everyday occurrence that happened numerous times around the capital, but on this occasion something made one of the horses panic. The horse had reared, the mare alongside it panicking too and they bolted forward together, heading straight for the children. It happened so fast that Richard froze for a moment just as a short, stocky man ran towards the horses, grabbing at their reins to stop them. In the blink of an eye he was pulled underneath their hooves. The horses slowed, came to a halt as the brewers' men ran in panic towards their steeds. The children screamed as Richard rushed to the man trapped underneath the unmoving wheels. One eye shut, face covered in blood, he was already dead. Yet, in one impulsive moment, he had saved all those children.

Henry Weston, that was his name. He had been awarded a medal for his bravery but that, as Richard thought ruefully at the time, would not have been much comfort to his widow and children. That day, Richard made a vow to never pause if he were ever to find himself in a similar situation again. But today, he thinks, it's simply a timely reminder that he should be more mindful when crossing the roads.

He watches his step all the way back home to his own modest quarters on Fetter Lane, distracts himself with thinking of Mary and Charlie's tall tale. It is an extraordinary story, he thinks, utterly fantastical and yet . . . could it really be that there *is* something to it?

It is only when he lights a candle in the hallway of his own lodgings that his smile disappears – for there is a letter waiting for him, sent all the way from Edinburgh, and written in a familiar hand.

The wings are gone.

Natalya wakes in the dark, lying on her front, her shoulders bandaged so tightly that she struggles to lift her arms, feeling only soreness and a stabbing pain as she pushes herself up.

At first, she feels relief. She is glad they are gone. *Glad*. She no longer cares what caused them to grow, why they sprang from her shoulders. They were not wanted, not desired by anyone other than *him*, her captor. And now they are no longer here. She wonders what he has done with them. Her back aches, a dull pain that sharpens as she shifts.

And then, seemingly from nowhere, a sob comes from deep inside. A single, solitary sob. *My wings. They had been so beautiful.* She hardens herself. Tries not to remember the strange sensation of being able to move them, fan them out without seeming to move her shoulders at all. The sense is so strong that, for a moment, she feels as if they are still there. She inhales deeply through her nose, refuses to cry. She will not let him have any further power over her.

She reaches forward, feels around with her hands only to discover that there is no food in her cell. Only a pewter jug with watery beer. This is her punishment then, she thinks. But he wanted her for her wings; without them, what prize can she possibly still be? Worry rises within like a drop of ink in water, clouding everything.

What does he want with me now? Why does he still keep me here?

She closes her eyes, tries to absorb the darkness around her, channel it into a story, just as her grandmother taught her to as a child. But she finds little comfort in it for she has come to realise that the monsters in life are not the same as those in tales – they are far more dangerous.

Edward sits with his father, takes his gnarled hand, arthritis twisting the knuckles like the branches of an old oak tree, holds it tight as he sits on the edge of the bed. His father's piercing eyes look up at him from a face that, Edward thinks, now resembles a half-melted candle more than the man who raised him. A cruel fate, Edward muses – for he believes his father's mind is working away as well as it did before the stroke robbed him of speech – for one so fiercely intelligent to be trapped in a body that no longer obeys one's will.

A carriage rattles by outside and Edward is reminded of his own childish glee in the coach and horses that used to take them to St Laurence's every Sunday when he was a boy, his father the very model of a reverend, well loved and kind to the villagers, but stern and taciturn with Edward, the less favoured son. All hail Jacob, the golden boy with a golden future, destined to follow in his father's footsteps until an outbreak of scarlet fever left only Edward and his pious sister Harriet. Puzzled by his older brother's death, Edward had been set on the path of medicine ever since, disappointing his father by turning his back on the clergy, dismaying him further by his marriage to Annie.

'You are marrying *beneath* you,' his father had barked, storming out of the parlour after Edward's declaration and heading straight to St Laurence's to pray for his son to make a better choice. It is where we engaged in our first serious row, thinks Edward guiltily, in the house of the Lord Himself.

Edward leans in, puts his mouth close to his father's ear. He has been longing to share with someone else the news of his gifts – the excitement and fear, the turmoil in his head. Whilst Annie sits downstairs in the parlour with his mother and sister, Edward makes his confession.

'I have seen an angel,' he whispers, softly. 'I know you were disappointed in me, Father, but I never abandoned God and now He repays me accordingly. *Angels*, Father. *I have seen angels.*'

He sees the trouble in his father's eyes, his own eager face reflected in the old man's pupils. 'I said I would make you proud one day, Father, and so I shall. God willing, that day is dawning soon, I *promise* you.'

His father's mouth opens and closes emptily, a murmur of some forgotten word rumbling around his tongue before being swallowed back down.

'I saw her wings grow from her own back myself,' Edward says, smiling with wonder. It is the first time he has spoken about what happened in St George's. But then, as he recalls last night, his smile fades, falls from his face like rain. The removal of the wings. His prized specimen no longer complete. *The Lord both giveth and taketh away*. He inhales – he only did what he was compelled to do . . .

★

In the carriage on the way home, Edward reads through the newspaper he brought with him only to find out that the Douglases are to host a masquerade ball to which, he deduces, he has not been invited. Perhaps Lord Douglas is ashamed of his surgeon? These upper echelons of society, they are so hard to infiltrate. If only he had more money to buy his way in! His inheritance, if only he could have accessed it, would have solved their financial problems for a considerable while, tiding them over until such time as Edward was ready to reveal his gifts. Instead, he has been speculating, seriously overspending with both the house and its contents long before his angels arrived.

He glances at Annie, sitting beside him. He has not dared tell her, but he's already sold some of the jewellery she doesn't often wear. She hasn't even noticed, he thinks, as she gazes out of the coach window. I will buy her a *thousand* times more jewellery one day, when all can be made public. He knows, though, that matters have become more complicated with his living specimen now without her wings.

He tries to distract himself, imagines the Douglases' ball, sees himself entering their grand mansion dressed in all his finery, pictures the Douglases welcoming him in as an equal, not as a subservient. Ah, he thinks, a germ of an idea spreading. *The ball.* Lady Douglas will want a spectacular outfit, will want to be the talk of the town, reported in all of London's many newspapers. She will want something *unique*, something to garner the attention of the press . . . and if the wings could earn him favour with the Douglases and a little money, well, it would be worth it in more ways than one. A short-term loan, he thinks; as a loan rather than a gift, he would be assured of the wings being returned. He will see the Douglases on the morrow at St George's and can suggest it to them then. His head whirls. So much to think about! He sighs, closes both the paper and his eyes. *God guide me in this, God guide me always.*

Annie, meanwhile, cannot wait to be home. She finds Edward's mother and sister tedious and trying. She had known full well that the family had been against Edward marrying her. People, she had thought more than once, with ideas above their station. They were, after all, not the family of an archbishop but merely of a reverend to an Essex parish. She had sat with the two women all afternoon whilst Edward was upstairs, listening to the tick of their intrusive grandfather clock and trying to think of a neutral subject to discuss. It has given her a headache and she wishes nothing more but to return home as swiftly as possible.

Annie turns her head to look at Edward and cannot decide if he is asleep or simply avoiding conversation. She studies him, wishing he would talk to her, tell her what's really on his mind. She feels the tender bruise on her arm from where he grabbed her in bed. He had later apologised profusely to her, held her tightly, willed her to forgive him. *He is a gentle man*, she tells herself, for he has never before shown any malice towards her – or indeed anyone else.

'Edward,' she whispers quietly, as the carriage rattles them home. 'Edward . . .' But he either doesn't hear or pretends not to.

The movement of the cart jerks Etta awake and she finds herself lying under a heavy oilcloth of some sort, hands and feet still tied, wings tightly wrapped up behind her. *Wings*, she thinks with a wave of horror, *my wings*. She has passed the last few days in a feverish state and yet the impossible is still real.

She tries to gather her thoughts into some semblance of order. Was it grief that caused the wings to grow, anger from losing Scout? Her delving into the natural world? *What, then?* She cannot fathom it, cannot make sense of it. Why would a divine power choose her above all others when her faith was beginning to shift and ebb like the moon's waning? Etta's fevered brain tires with questions as the wound in her side throbs painfully.

She is in a cart, that much is certain. As it bumps and lurches over the uneven track, aggravating the ache in her side, she hears the sounds of an October day, buzzards kewing, cattle lowing, a soft breeze in the trees. There is a noticeable chill in the air, the oncoming harbinger of winter, and she is suddenly glad of the weight and warmth of the oilcloth.

She is on the move, then, on her way to somewhere else. She tries to shift under the sheeting, roll it off just to glimpse the sky, to feel on her face the rain she hears beginning to patter down. But the oilcloth is heavy, tied down securely onto the cart and she cannot summon any strength to push it off.

In the barn, the boy had confirmed they were still in her home county, but she is unsure of how much time has elapsed since then. Worst of all, Etta muses, she has no idea of where she is now being taken.

Shortly after the Meakes' return home, there is a new patient to see Edward, a small, lively young woman with dark eyes and hair, dressed neatly, if a little shabbily, and accompanied by her husband, a tall young man with a mop of unruly hair.

'It is about my uncle, sir, rather than my own health,' the young woman – a Mrs Biggs – says once they are settled in Edward's consulting room. She has an intelligent look and speaks confidently, yet he finds her strangely hard to place.

'He has been most poorly of late,' Mr Biggs interjects. 'He has, I regret to say, taken to the bottle rather heavily and we wished to secure the advice of a medical man.'

'But I am a surgeon,' says Edward. 'Although I have some knowledge about such things, I feel a physician proper might better suit your requirements.'

Mary fingers her fake wedding ring; it is a little too tight and annoying her. 'But, sir, you have come recommended from so many people, we thought you might be able to help, given that it is somewhat of a delicate matter.'

'What is the cause of his fondness for the bottle? It is the root of the problem that must surely be tackled first.'

'His dearest friend died a little while ago,' says Richard, with a glance at Mary. 'I'm afraid it hit him rather hard.'

'And you have discussed this with him already, I presume?' Edward asks Richard.

'We have *both* done so, sir,' says Mary, a note of irritation in her voice at being ignored. 'But, alas, talking does not seem to get us very far.'

They discuss Jos for a little while longer until Edward's patience begins to thin and he fobs them off with a bottle of laudanum to cure Jos's nerves.

'I heartily recommend, however, that you take your uncle to see a proper physician,' says Edward with a smile, impatient to get rid of them as he goes to open the door back to the hallway.

'Thank you, Mr Meake,' Richard says. 'And I must say too, it's *fascinating* to see a surgeon's consulting room like this. So many books! So much knowledge! I wonder though, forgive me for being inquisitive, but do you still dissect bodies?'

Edward eyes him coolly before shaking his head. 'Only those old patients of mine who have given prior consent to do so in their wills. It is but a handful of people.'

'But if a curio came along, would it not be tempting? Something *unusual* in some shape or form?' asks Richard. 'Something that fell into your hands, say, or was fished out of the river – something offered for purchase?'

Edward frowns. 'It would, of course, depend on the circumstances,' he says calmly. 'But I would certainly not hesitate to report someone snatching bodies for that purpose for, as I'm sure you know, Mr Biggs, it is *illegal* these days. Now, I am sorry to rush you, but I have much other work to be getting on with.'

'Just one last thing, sir,' Mary says. 'Forgive me, for it is an odd question, I grant you. But, do you believe in angels?'

Ah, he was not expecting *that*, she thinks with satisfaction, as a flush of fear and surprise ripples across his face.

'I am not in the least sure what you mean, Mrs Biggs,' he says, his mouth suddenly dry. 'Good day to you both.'

As Edward ushers Mary and Richard out of the house, Mary takes a fleeting look behind her. The woman she saw the other day up in the first floor window is now standing at the far end of the hallway clad in a deep blue dress, watching Mary in return.

'Who was that, Edward?' asks Annie as he slams the front door shut with a bang.

'No one of importance,' Edward replies and disappears back into his consulting room, shutting the door behind him.

Annie stands in the hallway looking at the closed door. It is odd, she thinks to herself, but she is sure, *certain* in fact, that it was the very same woman who had been watching the house the other day.

'Mr Biggs!' Mary catches her breath as she and Richard pause in the relative quiet of an alleyway off Leadenhall. 'Why not use your real name?'

'Oh Lord! I panicked,' says Richard, embarrassed. 'Suddenly wondered if he might have heard of me and before I could rein my own arrogance back in — of course he wouldn't — it was too late.'

'Did you see his face when I mentioned angels?'

Richard nods, serious for a moment. 'It does feel that there *is* something odd going on, something unsavoury perhaps. Although I do think it will turn out to be rather more earthly than miraculous.'

'It unsettles me too,' she says. 'But surely that is why we must find out the truth? I couldn't live another day if I didn't at least try.'

'No,' says Richard with a note of admiration. 'I believe you could not. It took courage to go in there and to question Mr Meake. I don't think many women would have had the pluck to do what you just did.'

'Well, I don't think many men would either,' she retorts.

'Oh, Miss Ward,' he says. 'There's very little that gets past you, that at least I am sure we can both agree on. Unfortunately, though, we do not have much more to go on with Meake. He admitted he would take a curiosity, but he also said he'd report it to the correct authorities and, having already checked this morning, I know no such curio has been registered. And a suspicious look is merely that, no more, no less. It is intriguing, admittedly, but hardly any form of proof.'

He checks his pocket watch. 'Now, come, I have a meeting at the offices of the *New Weekly* within the hour and you, Miss Ward, must make haste with that review of yours.' He offers her his arm and they walk together back into the maze of the city.

It is merciful, thinks Edward, that membership of the Society for the Promotion and Advancement of Knowledge is so restricted given how small the meeting room is on the second floor of the tavern. It is not the Society's usual meeting space, as he well knows, but the club they usually convene in is being refurbished; besides, as Samuel had said earlier to him, the Blood Bay offers most excellent repast and ale and pie is always conducive to convivial conversation.

Edward recognises some of the twelve men already seated. Samuel, of course, then there is the engineer, Simon Thomas, the writer Jonathan Davidson, the philosopher Christopher Snow and the publisher James Hedges. The rest he knows only by repute. As Samuel introduces him, Edward looks around at the faces of these important men, their eyes on him for the first time. *Oh, you will remember me!* he thinks to himself, confidence rising. You will remember this day for many years to come!

Edward takes to his feet, presents a short lecture about himself and his work as he had been forewarned that he must. He talks about his brother Jacob's death and how, by studying medicine, he believed he could help human-kind. He touches on his experiments on animals, bangs his fist on the table with enthusiasm when he talks about his passion for surgery. Samuel nods encouragement at him throughout and, too soon, Edward thinks, he must end his address.

'But, gentlemen, let us be guided by reason, by experimentation, by science – but above all by God! He has given us brains in order that we examine and explore, in order that we improve the world around us. He gave us this world, all of His creatures, and we must always – in our work and lives – be guided by Him.'

There is applause when he is finished and he bows before sitting back down.

'Thank you, Mr Meake, for your most edifying lecture,' says Davidson. 'I am intrigued to know where you see your work taking you next. Is it in the realm of experimental surgery like Mr Covell here?'

'No, not quite,' Edward replies, smiling at the sea of faces, enjoying the sensation of a captive audience. 'It's something I am not yet at liberty to discuss but I can assure you that it is something *utterly extraordinary*. Something that, and I say this most sincerely, gentlemen, will shake the very foundations of our science and philosophy.'

'So much so he's not even whispered a word of it to me!' laughs Samuel, a glimmer of envy in his eyes.

Edward dare not say more, *not yet*. It is so tempting to tell them, this panel of distinguished men whose favour he craves, but he restrains himself. The young woman from earlier in the day flickers into his mind, the one who asked about angels, and a shiver passes through him. No, no, it was a coincidence, he thinks, simply an inquisitive young couple discussing a story that had all of the capital talking. He absentmindedly scratches his injured arm before stopping himself. He'd examined it earlier and found pus crackling on the skin into yellow crystals. It seemed to be healing well, he had thought, before re-bandaging it with a clean dressing.

The Society vote 9–3 in favour of Edward's membership and he and Samuel relocate downstairs to celebrate after the others have left.

'Congratulations!' says Samuel as he drains his glass. 'You are now a fully-fledged member of one of the greatest intellectual clubs in the whole of England. Now, in return, *you* must tell me what on earth you are working on that has got you so excited and secretive! The last time I saw you anywhere near this animated was over your infernal modern lighting which I still maintain you paid over the odds for. So come, what is the cause of this new excitement?'

Edward smiles at him. 'It would hardly be a secret if I told you!'

'Are you still put out about those lectures? It was an honest mistake, Meake. Come, what is this intriguing thing you are working on? Surely you can tell me?'

Edward shakes his head. 'You may cajole and nag me all you wish, Sam, but I shall remain tight-lipped.'

Samuel laughs and refills their glasses. 'Well, I shall pressure you no further but let me instead tell you of something that amused me greatly. I had a most peculiar and entertaining letter. This will make you laugh, I'm sure. Lord, people will make up anything for the chance of a coin.'

He rummages in his coat, pulling out a letter. 'Aha! Here! Now, do you recall that nonsense about the Angel of the Thames?'

'A load of gibberish made up by some boatman, wasn't it?' Edward replies, picking up his glass and hoping Samuel will not notice his trembling hand.

'Exactly so! Unfortunately, the papers added fuel to the fire by endlessly covering it and so the timewasters that are inevitably attracted to such nonsense build on it by targeting the gullible and the stupid.'

'So, what exactly is in this letter of yours?'

'Well,' says Samuel, glancing down at it. 'According to one Mr George Marshall, he is in possession of an angel and he wonders, Meake, if I might like to purchase it.'

Edward swallows. 'A pretty concoction of fakery and illusion. Dead presumably?' he says, his heart thumping so loudly he feels as if all in the tavern can hear it.

'But no, my dear Meake! No! An *alive* specimen and in the Midlands of all places! Good Lord, as if God does not have enough work to do without sending a messenger to those godforsaken wastelands. Here.' He hands the letter to Edward. 'Read it for yourself, I think you will find it most amusing. I almost admire the fellow's cheek for having the audacity not merely to come up with such a crazed plan but to follow through with it too.'

C/o The Unicorn Inn,
Ludlow, Salop

Dear Mister Samuel Covell,

It has been brought to my attenshun by means of the news-papers that you are one of London's most highly respeckted surgeons. It is most fortuitous that I came across your name for I have something I believe will be of much interest to you.

Tis an angel, sir, much like the storys from the great capital about the angel of the Thames. Well, sir, we have our very own angel up here in Salop. My own flesh and blood, my own son, did with his own eyes see the angel fall from heaven itself, see the wings sprout from her very back.

She was I am sad to say, injured during her capture. She is still alive for now – but I daresay could easily not be if you would prefer such a thing.

I am prepared to sell the angel to you, sir on receipt of one hundred pounds. Tis a large price I know but tis what she is worth.

Please keep this in confidence, sir and if you do not wish to purchase such a unique creature, I would like to know at your earliest convenience so I might offer her to other interested parties.

Yours in sincerity,
George Marshall

'One hundred pounds, Meake! One hundred pounds!' exclaims Samuel. 'Have you ever heard such damned cheek?' He snatches the letter back from Edward, rips it up and throws it into the nearby hearth where they sit.

'I shall obviously ignore the rogue, but it has, at least, afforded me some amusement. Meake? You look thoughtful.'

'I'm sorry,' says Edward, trying to remain calm as his heart continues to pound, 'I was thinking of my wife, is all,' he lies, glad that he managed to memorise both the name of the letter-writer and the address from which it was sent before it was incinerated.

'Ah! Dearest Annie, is she quite well?' Samuel asks, concern in his eyes.

And Edward, so overwhelmed, so absorbed with the possibility of a third angel – a veritable holy trinity of gifts – realises with a jolt that he does not, hand on heart, truly know the answer to Samuel's question.

In the darkness of her cell, Natalya has disappeared into her head, the power of her imagination sculpting pictures and stories to sustain her. If she focuses all her energies, she can be back at a moment in time, back on her beloved islands. She can blow the clouds clean away, feel the ice-cold foam of the shallow waves tickling her bare toes. She lets her imagination wander as she walks the beaches of her mind, conjuring up tales of sea serpents and dragons, of wandering minstrels plucking notes of sorrow and laughter from their lutes as they travel the land. She weaves yarns of thorn-filled forests, snowy mountains and life-giving springs, of great battles on plains that stretch as far as the eye can see. She spins stories of love and kindness, of bitterness and revenge, of peasants and royalty, of magic and myth. It is the only way she has to pass the time down here, her defence against going mad.

The dog is distressed. She hears it howling and hums to herself to drown it out, to loosen the knot of anxiety sitting hard within. She hasn't touched the bread her captor left. She will starve herself, wish her own body and soul out of existence. She will resist him at every turn, fight him with every part of her being.

The door is unlocked and Edward enters with a newly filled tankard of watery beer, a thick candle and a few matches. He puts them down, sees that she hasn't touched the bread and grabs her face tightly with one hand, turning her towards him and forcing her to look into his blazing eyes.

'Starve if you wish, Little Miss Nobody,' he says with a sneer. 'What, pray, do you think will be achieved by it? It's of no matter to me if you starve yourself. There's another of you out there and I have sent for her. Do you understand? *Another one.*'

He leans in, his face just inches away from her. 'And yet,' he says thoughtfully, quietly as if talking to himself, 'for all your faults I would still rather have you alive. I had believed you to be something exquisite, something wondrous, but I see now that you are all wickedness. Perhaps you are proof of the very Devil himself?'

He eyes her for a while before letting her go, slamming the door and locking it behind him. Natalya hears him rummaging in the cell beside hers, the dog's fearful whimpers echoing through the walls.

Another with wings, she thinks. *Then I am not alone after all.* Perhaps this other person will be an ally. A glimmer of hope sparks within her. She waits a while until the noise stops and her captor's footsteps fade before falling upon the bread, stuffing it in to her face in greedy mouthfuls. I will need my strength now, she thinks. *Another one like me.*

'Miss Bewdley is unwell,' says Annie, as she takes her seat next to Edward on the balcony at St George's. 'Perhaps we should call on her?'

'No, no,' her husband replies, as she takes his hand. She feels the bandage looped around his palm from the dog bite, rough against her own skin. 'I will do so alone. For however kind and compassionate you are, Annie dear, you are not a nurse. Besides, rest and recuperation is what Miss Bewdley needs most. I would say more but I cannot break a patient's confidentiality.'

He is behaving strangely again today, Annie thinks, all fidgety and secretive. She had tried to speak to him last night, before he left the house. 'Edward. *Please* talk to me, tell me what ails you, husband dear. Perhaps I can help resolve whatever is occupying your mind so much?'

'All in good time, Annie,' he had said, patting her arm. 'All in good time.' She'd watched him hail a cab in the rain, disappear inside on his journey to this Society he was so fixated on joining. She had wanted to call him back, plead with him, but instead she had simply watched as the cab rattled off down the street. *He didn't even kiss me goodbye*, she'd realised as he disappeared from view.

After the service, Annie waits for her husband outside, watches him talk to Lord Douglas on the steps of the church, shaking hands as if sealing an agreement. He laughs freely as the low October sunlight catches his handsome face and it reminds her suddenly of Green Park, the first time she and Edward attended an exhibition together, a hot stuffy afternoon in late summer . . .

The gallery at the Royal Academy had been packed full of people, a whirlwind of colour and scents, opinions and noise. Marcus had invited Edward in an attempt to get to know him better, to include him in their circle of friends. Annie had spied Edward the moment he arrived, her heart warming as he scanned the room, his obvious look of relief as he spotted her in return.

'Miss Harding!' he'd said when he finally reached her. 'I had thought a packed operating theatre was a maelstrom of chaos but it has nothing on this. I cannot even make out a single picture! Which somewhat undermines the point of the event, does it not?'

Marcus had waved them over, shaken Edward's hand with vigour. It was too noisy for Annie to hear their conversation but when Edward turned back to her, his face was flushed.

'Come,' he had said, leaning towards her, warm breath tickling her ear. 'It is so very crowded in here, Miss Harding. Would it not be pleasanter to stroll through Green Park in the fresh air? Perhaps we could return a little later when it is cooler and less congested?' He'd smiled, held out his hand, and she was unable to resist. They made their way through the crowd, dashing across the road in front of an omnibus and taking haven in the park's green swathes.

'You don't care that much for art then, Mr Meake,' Annie had said with a smile as they slowly walked together along the neatly ordered paths.

'Ah! That is not a fair accusation, Miss Harding. It is perhaps true that I do not care for art as much as an artist like yourself may do, but I am very interested in all things – as any man of our age must be.'

They had walked a few more yards before he stopped and turned to her, the sunlight glowing behind him like a halo around his head.

'And, as you know from Greenwich, Miss Harding, I do very much appreciate a good picnic,' he had added. 'Perhaps we could return here, to the park, at a later date and you can educate my woeful medical brain on the wonders of art – in exchange for some delicious delicacies spread out on a picnic blanket? Come, what say you, Miss Harding? Might you indulge me, I beg of you?'

Oh, the picnics! Annie smiles, remembering them with delight. So many glorious picnics as summer turned to autumn and love turned to a proposal. A ring in the palm of his hand, his fingers tracing her lips so very gently before he had kissed her for the first time, the way he'd looked at her with those green eyes shining, the way he held her hand so tightly as if she were the most precious of jewels.

The touch of Edward's hand jolts her back to the present as he hails a cab to take them around the corner to Queen Square. She watches him disappear into Miss Bewdley's building, bottle of tincture in hand, and cannot, for the life of her, remember the last time Edward took her on a picnic, perhaps May of this year? Months ago, certainly not since they moved to St Mary Axe where there had been no dinners out and but a handful of social engagements. Work had taken precedence over everything. It's as if he's always trying to *prove* something, Annie thinks – but to whom? *To whom?*

She recalls Marcus's words to her after that same exhibition. 'Tread carefully, Annie. He's a man who doesn't like to admit the boundaries of his own knowledge and I am always wary of such men.' She had dismissed it at the time, put it down to Marcus's own fondness for her, but his words surface now like bubbles in a pond. When Edward returns to the cab, there is a frenetic look in his eyes and it troubles her, like a buried insect tickling from deep within.

When Etta wakes next, she is lying atop a freshly made bed, cold and shivering. She is in a small bedroom, sparsely furnished, with old curtains that are pulled closed. A fire is dying in the narrow grate and the youth who shot her is asleep in an armchair beside it.

Etta goes to move but her hands are still tied together, her ankles too. A gag remains over her mouth and she focuses all her energies on pushing it off. Using her tongue as a tool, she concentrates on pushing the gag down and away from her mouth until, after what feels like an age, it finally slips off. She takes a single deep breath before screaming as loudly as she can. The boy wakes, runs over and throws himself upon her, holding his hand over her mouth, a petrified look in his eyes. In desperation, she tries to bite him but he pins her down.

'You won't be here for long,' he hisses. 'You'll be on the move soon enough.'

'Please! My brother, my friends, they will be looking for me.' She struggles to speak as he presses his hand down.

'No,' he says, easing the pressure a little, 'Ma says everyone'd be ashamed of you. She says you're Satan in disguise, that an angel can't look like you.'

'And what do you say?' she says, quietly.

He sits back on his haunches and looks deep into her eyes.

'Don't matter what I say,' he says, pulling the gag back up. 'Never does.' He lifts up her head and reties it twice as hard so it digs into the corners of her mouth.

Etta watches him as he returns to his chair by the fire. He won't even look at her. 'Please,' she tries to say. 'Please.' But the gag is too tight. She saw it in his eyes though, a flicker of compassion. But she fears it will not be enough to save her.

Uncle Jos is out on one of his night-time walks, the first since his renewed resolution of sobriety. 'I must test myself alone, my dear,' he had said to Mary as he went to leave. 'I cannot always have a chaperone to ensure I stick to the right path. Seeing the dregs at closing time will, I hope, remind me why I must never venture down that route again.'

Mary had nodded and taken his hands. 'I loved Uncle George too,' she said. 'With all my heart. And I love *you*, very much indeed.'

'I know. I know, dearest Mary. But it will only be when you are older that you will understand – when your own heart has been taken and, God forbid, you feel the loss of it. Only then will you truly understand what this is like.'

The fire is already low when there's a rap at the door and Lou lets herself in.

'Any chance of a cocoa?' she asks, looking around. 'Well, this ain't a patch on the old place, but still, it's decent enough even if it is a little hard to find at night. Oh, I'm glad you kept that at least.'

They both look at George's old empty armchair for a

moment in silent remembrance before Mary breaks the quiet.

'I forgot you were coming,' says Mary, prodding the fire back to life before noticing that Lou's placed a package on the table. 'What's that you've got there?'

'Turns out the angel has become such a success that this ain't needed for the moment.' Lou grins, mischievously. 'Besides, I thought you could do with a bit of fun.'

Mary picks at the corner of the package. 'May I . . . ?' she asks, puzzled, and Lou nods. Mary carefully unwraps it, keeping both string and paper to be reused for some other purpose, before bemusedly holding the garments up in front of her.

'But what on earth do you expect me to do with *these*?' she asks, confused.

'Well, there are a few holes that need fixing but, I dunno, Mary, love, I had thought you might consider *wearing* them!' Lou laughs wickedly. 'Y'know, you might find it rather thrilling!'

'Sarah, what exactly is this please?'

Annie is confused. There is a huge parcel on the kitchen table, over four feet long, wrapped in layers of paper and addressed to Lord Douglas.

'Don't rightly know, ma'am. Sorry, ma'am,' replies Sarah. 'Mr Meake asked for it to be sent. Said it was delicate within and we should handle it most carefully. Waiting for it to be collected. It'll be a good job when it does go,' she adds archly, 'as it's taking up precious space down here.'

Annie touches the package; it feels solid in places, softer and more fragile in others. 'To Lord Douglas . . . ' she says, thinking out loud.

'Yes, ma'am,' says Sarah, thinking what a strange house this is to work in. Unsettling noises from the basement at night as she tries to sleep in the small servants' hall, the body she saw Mr Meake bring in the other day. It is exciting, though, she thinks. Besides, her applications to other residences as a maid have thus far only met with rejection and so she must stay here until she secures another position. She has promised herself that she will hand her notice in with a show of great glee, an act she goes over in her head several times a day.

'Thank you, Sarah, carry on,' says Annie as she leaves, bumping into Mrs McGilliveray leaving the kitchen, carrying the ingredients for that evening's dinner.

Sarah catches the cook's eye as she comes in.

'Turns out *she* don't even know what it's in neither!' she says, eyes agleam.

Edward sits and fidgets in his dissecting room, excitement and adrenaline rushing through his veins. His letter accepting George Marshall's offer had been sent yesterday as soon as he'd managed to escape from Samuel's company. It should arrive, he hopes, by Tuesday morning and, if all goes to plan, his angel could be in London the following day.

He inhales, breathes in the scent of chemicals that lingers in the basement. He has been active all day since coming back from St George's, clearing out the spare cell for his new acquisition, preparing a sleeping area, organising a slop bucket and receptacles for food and drink. Earlier, he arranged for the disembodied wings from his broken angel to be readied for dispatched to the Douglases and now, in a moment of peace, he returns to his prayers. It is God's work that he does today. *God's work.* He exhales deeply.

Tomorrow, Edward will return to mounting his angel skeleton, a skilled job that takes time and patience and which he must complete to the level of perfection itself. He must go through his notes too, ready everything in preparation for the arrival of his new angel. So much to do! All things must be in their right place. He must check his files, copy his anatomical drawings, improve and edit his notes. He must preserve everything for posterity. He closes his eyes, tired.

He had prayed hard, so very hard, at St George's earlier. Please, I beg of you, oh Lord, let this third angel be the most magnificent of your gifts. He bows his head, puts his hands together once more, lips moving silently.

O most merciful Father, hear my prayer. I give humble thanks for the bounty that you have bestowed upon me and for the gifts that are yet to come. Glory be to the Father and to the Son and to the Holy Ghost. As it was in the beginning, is now, and ever shall be, world without end.

Amen.

'Anything?' Mary is with Charlie at their rendezvous on the corner of Leadenhall Street.

'Not much at first, miss, just the usual. Traders and post, but then there was a big package that went off at the crack of dawn. Huge it was, almost as big as me.'

'Where was it sent to?' she asks, intrigued.

'Not sure,' says Charlie. 'Sorry, miss, I followed it but I lost it round Bank way.'

'Oh well, no matter,' says Mary although in truth she is a little disappointed. In exchange for bed and board, Charlie is both helping Mary with her buttons and keeping an eye on the Meakes' residence. She isn't quite sure what she had been hoping for but Uncle Jos's words to her from this morning ring in her ears.

'You cannot keep on pursuing a dead end, Mary, we cannot afford for you to keep indulging yourself in this. It is not a story unless you can find *evidence*. Suspicion is nothing without confirmation of your misgivings.'

'Which is *exactly* what I am trying to do,' she had said, determinedly. 'Find out more, gain more knowledge. Like Miss Wiltshire always used to say—'

'Yes, yes – "Knowledge the wing wherewith we fly to heaven." Very apt, I'm sure.'

'Please, Uncle! I am doing all my other work, am I not? Unless you wish for me to take up a position at a factory – is that what you want?'

Jos had huffed. 'Of course not, and I understand, nay, I know all too well that it is my own fault we are in a somewhat more precarious position of late.'

'But you have not touched a drop since the fair,' Mary argued. 'Your work is returning to normal, we are surviving, aren't we? Please, Uncle, indulge me just this once. There is something peculiar afoot and I *must* find out what it is.'

Jos had looked at her with a mixture of reprimand and respect.

'One more week,' he had said. 'One more week, Mary – and if there is no progression in your findings, no actual *proof* of any of it, then you must let it drop. Otherwise, my dear, it is nothing but a wild goose chase.'

Annie's painting is coming along nicely. The blocks of colour, the outline of the shapes sitting on the canvas, the layers of oils building one by one. Edward's wings will be white as snow, his eyes green as a peacock's tail, the vibrancy of the colour echoed in the tranquil countryside glimpsed behind him. Edward himself, her painted angel, will be looking directly out, bold and proud, palms held open, hands reaching towards the viewer, a curve of a faint smile emphasising his high cheekbones.

He will be beautiful, she muses to herself. *He will be my masterpiece.*

The light for her is always the trickiest part, capturing the golden glow that speaks of warm evenings, of hope and fruitfulness. She will take her time to make sure it is just right. Marcus always used to tell her she had a tendency to rush things, a fault she has tried hard to correct over the years. But she had also learnt another important lesson from him.

'How on earth do you know when it is finished?' she had asked him many years ago after a frustrating day of trying to capture the long horizons of the Kentish sky in watercolour.

'Oh, my dear Miss Harding,' he'd said, warmly. 'No piece of art is *ever* finished, that is the simple answer. One only ever learns when to step away from it.'

Annie smiles as she returns to her work. She will breathe life into this canvas, make Edward seem as if he is really reaching out of it, as if he could take your very hand. She hums whilst she works, concentrating all her efforts on what stands before her, hoping beyond hope, although she knows it is ridiculous, that her labours will return her old Edward to her. This new version of him on canvas, it is a rebirth, an offering in order that the man she fell in love with can be promised back to her as if in a fairy tale.

Natalya has fallen into a whirlpool of her own thoughts. She nibbles at the dry bread her captor brings, wishing again she had never come to this cursed city.

She recalls the vision she had outside the church. All things are connected, she thinks. The trade card that led her here, the thief who stole her money. She thinks of her journey south, retracing her steps along the shoreline at Mersea, the uneven gravel slipping underfoot. Thinks too of Cata Sands and the white dunes of Tresness, of chambered cairns at Tofts Ness to the east of her beloved Sanday where old warriors still lay, hoping one day to wake from their long slumber. Sand and dust, water and waves . . . She pictures the same water whirling around the coastline of every island, connecting them all, every country that looks out towards the seas.

She holds her breath. All of it is contained within her. The waves of salt sea, rough grains of sand and smooth pebbles, ocean drift and the rage of storms, the stars reflecting back at her on a smooth sea, constellations twinkling under a crescent moon.

My islands. My beloved islands.

She breathes out. Her old life extinguished like the light of a candle, lost in a tangle of red-raw memories from which she will always carry the scars.

Such love. And *such loss*. The ditch by the side of the road; the pain and the anger; the blood and the anguish; the loss of it all. The fierce passion she would always feel for him – and the loss of *her*, her tiny fingernails, tiny eyelashes, the unbearable, overwhelming love . . .

It is only when she feels the tears drip into her lap that she realises she is crying.

Rose Cottage, Beauly, Inverness
Saturday 17th October

My dear Miss Bewdley,

Please forgive the delay in responding to you, my wife Marianne and I are holding vigil at my mother's bedside as we see her through what few remaining days she has left.

Your letter was most interesting and I thank you for confiding in me. However, I do feel that perhaps we have been taking advantage of your goodwill at St George's and that a period of rest from your voluntary work may do you the world of good.

I was most sorry to hear about the death of anyone seeking refuge in our beloved church, let alone a young woman, but Mr Meake is a man of medicine. I believe he would have treated the woman to the best of his abilities as he would any of his patients, including my own self. I should remind you too that Mr and Mrs Meake are much-valued members of the congregation and are always so generous in their donations to the church.

I wish you the best of health and both Marianne and I look forward to seeing you upon our return although, at this time, I cannot be certain of when that may be.

Sincerely yours.

Reverend JD Pennyforth

Miss Bewdley drops the letter as soon as she has read it, all hope falling to the floor with it. *He does not believe me.* Reverend Pennyforth thinks she has made it all up, that what she saw was simply an act of her imagination, conjured out of thin air. She sinks down into her armchair, lost and exhausted.

A pigeon taps loudly on her window, once, twice, before flying off. Is that a sign? she wonders. A bird, a *winged creature*, reminding her of that miraculous transformation she witnessed in front of the very altar itself?

She will write a letter to Mr Meake. Perhaps if she can speak to him again, in person, he might finally acknowledge what they saw, what she *knows* they saw. She dips an old quill pen in the ink, scribbling him a short note before absentmindedly stroking the underside of her chin with it. An idea comes to her and she wipes the nib dry before tugging it out to leave just the feather, which she tucks neatly inside the note to Mr Meake. Perhaps *this* will make him pay attention, she thinks. Perhaps this will remind him of the truth.

When she leaves her rooms and steps out into the street she is more than a little distracted, for she has just remembered the boy with the cut on his face and the young lady who visited her the other day. That boy, he had seen the feathers too! There *is* someone who might listen after all. Aaaah . . . She breathes out hope in the chill autumnal air, a cloud of hot breath sighed in front of her. She will find the two of them, track them down, tell them what really happened, tell them *everything*.

Alas, Miss Bewdley's attention is not on the road and,

although Queen Square is not often as busy as the surrounding area of Bloomsbury, she is not looking in the direction she heads in. A man on the other side of the road shouts at her, motions with his arm, but she only has a flash of puzzlement, for at the exact same moment that she finally registers his wave, the horse pulling hackney cab number 1,756 hurtles towards her, galloping with considerable speed as it mows her down.

A handful of minutes later, a pigeon flies overhead, oblivious to the commotion and carnage below and, as it does so, it sheds a sprinkling of tiny downy feathers that circle and dip, slowly floating down to earth.

As Miss Bewdley gasps her last, chest crushed by the horse's hooves, she will see these feathers drift down towards her and, in her last moments of consciousness, see it is a sign that God is welcoming her to the next life.

Her letter to Edward Meake is still clutched tightly in her right hand, even after her heart pumps its last, final beat.

'Ah, Jos, excellent. I am glad to find you on your own,' says Richard as he enters his friend's lodgings to find Jos scribbling away in a chaos of paper and ink.

'Oh?' says Jos, half-distracted and continuing to write as Richard takes a seat.

'It's about, um . . . Well, it's rather, I would say . . . it's about Mary.' His shyness overcomes him for a moment.

'What of her?' asks Jos, still not looking up, his pen scratching out an article.

'Jos, I know you are both in mourning still, but it cannot have escaped your notice' – Richard coughs, embarrassed – 'that . . . that she has become considerably more grown-up. It is surely only a matter of time before . . .'

'Ah,' says Jos. 'You think she should not be on this goose chase of the angel story? Forgive me, I'm always confused by feminine delicacies and where society's current thinking is as regards this or that. It's undignified for a young lady, is it?'

'That was not *quite* what I was thinking, no,' says Richard.

'Glad to hear it, I'm afraid she knows her own mind rather better than we do! I fear telling her *not* to do something will only encourage her further. She's as strong-willed as either of us, probably more so, eh?'

'Jos,' murmurs Richard, 'perhaps I should make myself clearer . . . '

'Good Lord!' says Jos, finally looking up. 'You mean to say . . . ? You think she will be attracting . . . *attention from men*?'

Thank goodness, thinks Richard. Jos has understood. His heart flutters, soars, sings. 'Well, yes. Yes, that was more along the—'

'Ah then, it's a good job you're here to keep an eye on her! I fear eighteen is still too young for me to lose her, particularly so soon after losing George. What on earth would I do without her, eh?'

Jos goes back to his writing for a moment before looking back up, concerned. 'You weren't thinking of any young man in particular, were you, Richard?'

'No, no. I should not have mentioned it, Jos. Please, forget I said anything.'

'No! I'm glad you did and I am so glad to have you back in London! You know we both think of you as family, as Mary's older brother? It's very kind of you to be this thoughtful towards her, towards both of us. Now, was there anything else? I must get on with this piece . . .'

Richard smiles, shakes his head, his heart now somewhere deep in the outer reaches of his toes. *Older brother.* It is not what he meant at all but now he has confused everything, muddled it up. He stands to leave, tongue-tied, ashamed to have brought Mary up so clumsily when they are still a family in mourning.

She has captured my heart, he thinks, blood rushing to his head, and I am not sure what to do about it except, perhaps – his heart plummets further for he still has all the impatience of youth – *wait*. An older brother, he thinks. Is that how Mary sees me? Is that how she has *always* seen me in fact?

This was not the scene he had written and played out in his head. It's a great shame, he thinks as he stands in the doorway, watching Jos work, that no one else appears to have learnt the lines he had written for them.

'I am afraid, Mr Covell, that Edward is *still* where he always is these days – in the basement,' says Annie, as they sit in the parlour where she pours him some tea.

'Annie my dear, you must stop him working himself into such a fervour!' exclaims Samuel. 'What *exactly* is he up to down there . . . ?'

Annie raises her eyebrow. 'Samuel, please. I have known you far too long for your mock concern to come across as anything other than inquisitiveness, which is, of course, why you bothered to visit in the first place.'

'*Mrs Meake!*' Samuel pretends to be offended.

'Come, let us at least have tea and pretend to be friends,' she says.

'Annie, we *are* friends are we not?' says Samuel, reaching for her hands.

He is shameless, she thinks. 'Mr Covell, you are an incorrigible flirt. Yes, we are *friends*, but you are here to see *Edward*, not myself.' She pulls her hands away.

'Of course, dear Annie.' He aims his most charming smile at her. 'But, it was *you* who requested my presence. It was *your* invitation that drew me here.'

He looks at her intently and Annie sees clearly now what a mistake it was to have consulted him upon the matter of children. If Edward ever found out, he would surely see it as a betrayal. She had invited Samuel to the house only because she was worried about her husband, worried about his increasingly erratic behaviour. She had thought, if he would not reveal his troubles to her, perhaps he might at least confide in his oldest friend.

'Besides, it is such a rare delight to see you,' Samuel continues. 'I see you so infrequently these days. I do so wish you would host another dinner; it feels like an age since you have done so. I suppose you are so busy with your painting and playing house and whatever else women do to pass the time and Edward is so busy with, well, whatever intriguing toys he has in the basement. Perhaps I should go down now and see him, find out what this is all about?'

Minutes later, impatience having got the better of him, Samuel is striding down to the basement, closely followed by a rather concerned Annie.

'Good Lord! Meake, what's this *door* doing here?' Samuel bellows through the oilcloth, putting his eye to the keyhole and trying to see through. He picks up Edward's bell that now sits beside the door and rings it loudly. 'Dammit, man, what on earth are you up to?'

Edward hears the commotion and comes to the other side of the gate. 'Samuel, I refuse to have a conversation with you here!' he snaps. 'I shall see you in the parlour within the hour, but you are disturbing my work without an appointment!'

'Since when did I need an *appointment* to visit my oldest

and dearest friend?' Samuel objects. 'Meake! Meake?' But there is no reply, simply the sound of Edward's feet heading away down the corridor.

'Annie, I believe he is still rattled about those damned lectures, would you believe?' says Samuel, shaking his head as they retreat back upstairs.

When Edward eventually emerges, Annie leaves the two men alone, returning to her small studio and hoping, *praying*, that Samuel can find out what is wrong.

Later, when she comes back down, she finds that her husband remains quietly furious with her. He paces around the room, still livid at having been interrupted in the delicate act of hanging the skeleton of his river angel.

'What on *earth* were you thinking, Annie? My work is not for anyone else's eyes, least of all Samuel's. I am not to be interrupted under *any circumstances*.'

'Edward, can you not see? You are not yourself! I had thought that if you will not tell me what troubles you, at least you might confide in your best friend.'

'I am *perfectly well*,' he snaps. 'Never better, in fact. And the next few days will provide me with a most crucial breakthrough, a further miracle, God willing!'

'Edward . . .' She goes to touch him but he flinches away. '*Please!* I cannot help you if you do not wish to be helped! Ever since we moved here, you have become increasingly distant and I do not know how to stop it!' she says, on the verge of tears now.

'Annie, I will tell you all in due course I *promise* you, but you will have to be patient with me – as I am with you and your artistic hobbies.'

He goes to leave, turning briefly before he does so. 'I shall not sup with you this eve, I will need to work late now – having been interrupted at such a critical moment.'

He leaves Annie in the empty parlour, her heart pounding. It is the first time he has ever used the word 'hobbies' for her artwork and it cuts deeply. *He is not himself.* The old Edward would *never* have said such a thing. I can but try, she thinks to herself. I can but keep on trying. The Edward she loves, the Edward of picnics and charm, of kindness and restraint, continues to fade before her. She feels him slip through her fingers like sand.

SOCIETY BALL.- Lord and Lady Douglas's annual autumn masquerade was held last night at their London residence near Regent's Park. Excellent bands and Music was enjoyed as part of the evening's sports and a handsome supper was provided to all who attended including Marquises, Turks and Princes. Lady Douglas was dressed in most splendid finery as the Angel of the Thames and sported a magnificent silk dress with impressive white angel wings the size of a small child, the likes of which have surely never before been seen in high society. A great deal of money was raised for charitable causes.

It is morning, a bright day full of sunshine, and Mary finishes darning a tear in her shawl before making a start on the next interminable batch of buttons when Richard comes bursting in, waving a copy of the *Morning Express*.

'If this is about the Angel of the Thames, Mr Gibbs, Uncle Jos is becoming increasingly keen that I leave the story well alone,' says Mary as the needle slips past her thimble, pricking her hand and causing her to yelp. 'Although given that he's at one of his endless board meetings at the Guinea Club, you can at least tell me anything of interest you may have gleaned before he comes back to spoil my fun.'

Richard smiles at her, before a worry surfaces as he remembers his previous conversation with Jos. 'Your uncle didn't mention anything about me coming over yesterday, did he?'

'No, why? Should he have done?'

'Oh, it's of no matter!' says Richard, relieved. 'It was nothing to do with the Angel of the Thames anyway, speaking of which . . .' He reads out the piece about the Douglases' party before throwing the paper down and pulling out a seat.

'You see?' he says with delight. 'It seems as if the Angel has captured the imaginations of even the highest echelons of society as well as your good self.'

'Hmm,' says Mary thoughtfully.

'I can hear the cogs whirling in your head,' Richard says, intrigued.

'No,' says Mary, shaking her head. 'It's nothing.' She returns to her sewing for a moment. 'Except . . . no.'

'Go on . . .'

'It's only that . . . There was a large parcel sent from Mr Meake's house the other day. I don't know where it went or what was in it but, *the size of a small child*. That's almost exactly how Charlie described it.'

'Ah, a coincidence!' says Richard. 'The same turn of phrase that's all.'

'Yes, of course. Yes.' Mary ponders the buttons in her hand, forehead screwed up in thought. 'Except – except, Richard, Lord Douglas is one of Mr Meake's better-known patients *and* they share a church. The Douglases are keen patrons of St George's, are they not?

'You think the parcel is a link?'

Mary bites her lip, eyes flitting around the room.

'Penny for your thoughts,' Richard says softly.

'You'll only laugh at me!' she says, ideas and images dashing around her head like a carousel.

'Miss Ward,' says Richard, 'you appear to have fallen entirely silent, something that I always find most troubling, rare as it is. Come, what are you thinking?'

'What if, Richard, what if those wings for Lady Douglas's fancy dress were not from a swan? What if they were from *some other creature* entirely? After all, it was you who told me what a hunch felt like, the idea of a story having legs. Imagine a story having *wings* . . .'

'I would say it sounds like a tall tale. A *very* tall tale.'

'Perhaps you're right,' says Mary, with a glint in her eye. 'But perhaps a visit to the maidservants of Lord and Lady Douglas may prove to be illuminating – tall tale or not.'

'You really won't let this lie, will you?'

'No, Mr Gibbs,' she says, biting off the end of the thread with her teeth. 'I bloody well will not.'

He gasps at her language and she delights in his reaction. 'Besides, Richard, what do I have to lose? If my suspicions about Mr Meake are unfounded, if this story is nothing but a fable, then all will be well and I'll be happy to be endlessly ridiculed about it for years to come.'

Richard laughs. 'You know, Miss Ward, I don't believe there is anyone else in the world quite like you.'

'Why thank you, Mr Gibbs. I shall take that as a compliment, even if you didn't mean it as one.' Mary stands up, wrapping her newly mended shawl around her. 'Well, then. Are you coming or not?' she says, reaching for her bonnet.

'Miss Ward, I fear this may be an entirely wasted journey and yet . . . Well, it's always an adventure with you, is it not?' he says, smiling at her.

'Excellent! Then *you* may pay for the cab, Mr Gibbs,' she says, giving him a warm grin as they depart her lodgings, leaving the paper behind, which, if either of them had looked at it more thoroughly, also contained news of a certain Miss Bewdley.

'Would you like the paper brought in, ma'am?' says Sarah archly as Annie surfaces for breakfast. If Edward made it to bed last night, he did so in such a manner as to not wake her – he was not there when she finally fell asleep and the bed was empty again when she awoke some little time ago.

'Yes, thank you, Sarah,' says Annie primly. 'I would ask, too, that you pay more attention to the dust in the hallway. I'm well aware that my husband's visitors bring the dirt of the streets in with them but I'm afraid to say your attention to detail there has been lacking in recent weeks.'

'Yes, ma'am,' says Sarah.

Annie doesn't have to even look at her to know she is rolling her eyes. She is not the most diligent of servants and Annie would be happy to be rid of her but for the fact that they have gone through a succession of servants in past years, the high turnover, she suspects, due to Edward's profession and the various experiments he undertakes. It had been hard enough to recruit the two full-time members of staff they had now and she could not bear to go through the hiring process again unless it was absolutely necessary.

She turns the paper and scans it as she sips her tea. But, as her eye alights upon a familiar name, the cup slips from her grasp, spilling its contents as it bounces once on the table before falling to the floor.

THE MORNING EXPRESS, Tuesday 20 October 1840

Fatal Cab Accident.- Yesterday morning, between nine and ten o'clock, the following dreadful accident occurred at Bloomsbury Way, which proved of fatal consequence to a respectable lady named Miss Amelia Bewdley, 62 years of age, residing at 40 Queen Square, Bloomsbury. It appears that the unfortunate woman stepped into the carriageway and fell underneath the horse of one of Hanson's patent cabs. The driver of the cab pulled up directly after the accident and maintained that he prevented the wheels passing over her, but the horse trod upon her before she could be extricated. Two lads who were on the spot at the time stated that they saw the approach of the cab proceeding at a canter. Immediately afterwards they heard the screams of a woman, and saw the deceased on the ground, but before they could stir to her rescue, the horse had passed over her breast and caused her instantaneous death. There seemed no blame attached to the driver.

Thomas Marshall reads slowly, carefully. 'We are to meet him at the Peacock Inn at Angel where we shall exchange the, er . . .'

'Peacock and Angel? Is this some sort of joke?' demands the rotund Mrs Marshall impatiently as she looks at her son, the youth who shot Etta with his crossbow. He reads Edward's letter, freshly arrived care of the Unicorn Inn.

'No, Ma, 'tis just a place name surely. Like the Angel in Ludlow. Or the Unicorn. 'Tis not uncommon for an area or tavern to be called such a thing.'

'Carry on, boy! Carry on!' says Mr Marshall. A whiskery-faced bully, he has a snotty nose and a persistent cough.

'Yes, Pa. Sorry, Pa,' says Thomas before continuing, 'Where we shall exchange the creature – he calls her an angel – for the same sum of money that was asked of Mr Covell.'

'The full money, all one hundred pounds?' asks Mrs Marshall greedily.

'Yes, Ma,' says Thomas. 'Upon receipt of the angel.'

'Ha! And does he say if he wants her alive or not?' asks Mr Marshall.

'Yes, Pa, yes, he does, he says so most strongly,' replies Thomas, although in truth he would have said anything to save Etta's life. She sleeps on the bed behind them and Thomas wishes he were brave enough to do something, exactly what he isn't quite sure, but *something*, *anything*.

'Thomas!' says his father, sharply. 'Idiot boy. What else is in the letter?'

'That's all, Pa,' says Thomas, folding it back up. ''Tis all.'

'And the name of this gentleman we are to meet again?'

''Tis a Mr Price, Pa.'

Edward is at least wise enough to use a pseudonym in his dealings with these people.

'Never heard of him,' his father sniffs.

'You hadn't heard of the other 'til that old rag came handed down to us,' snorts his wife.

''Tis no matter, my darling,' says Mr Marshall. 'For what matters who we sell her to as long as we get her off our hands and become rich in the process?'

He grabs her hands, whirling her around in a tight dance as Thomas looks away.

'And you can join in too, Thomas!' says his ma sharply. 'If it were not for you, we'd never have come into this good fortune. You're as deep in this as we are.'

'The idiot boy done some good after all,' adds Mr Marshall. 'Come now, we must make haste! If we are to be in London tomorrow, we must catch the coach this afternoon. Get your bags packed! For we are off to the capital!'

Thomas's heart sinks. There is something so fundamentally wrong about what they are doing, the selling and exchange of a life. Whatever she is, angel or woman, she can think and speak and feel and, Thomas thinks with overwhelming guilt, *she is so very frightened of us*. As his parents excite themselves with preparations for the journey, Thomas goes to the barn where he hid a cask of beer some while back. We tread on dangerous ground, he thinks as he drinks to numb his pain, dealing with men and matters we do not understand; it will not end well for us. And in that, at least, he will be proved correct.

'Oh, Annie, it is wondrous,' says Ellie, clapping her hands together with glee as she looks at the incomplete painting on the easel in Annie's study.

'You are too kind, Ellie, it is nowhere near finished,' says Annie, shyly.

'Marcus, come, tell her!' says Ellie.

'It is a most interesting composition,' Marcus says, loitering in the corner. 'I very much look forward to seeing it when it is finished.'

'Oh, Marcus, she was so reluctant to let us view it and that is such faint praise!'

'It's not *faint*,' Marcus defends himself. 'But the painting is half done, all the detail is missing and we all know that is Annie's true forte. The light is promising, the composition is, as I have already said, most interesting. But it is like looking at a half-constructed building, you cannot know the true sense of it until it is complete. Is that not so, my dear Annie?'

She smiles at him. The news about Miss Bewdley at breakfast had shocked and distressed her. It was an accident, she knew, but she had felt shaken by it, feeling it haunt her as she paced around the house, before she had thought to call for Ellie. Feeling calmer, knowing her dear friend was coming, Annie had returned to her painting, losing herself in her brushstrokes until Ellie arrived bringing with her the welcome accompaniment of their beloved Marcus.

'Now come,' says Marcus, cheerily. 'This house of yours, Annie, it has a suffocating air. Let us venture somewhere outdoors for our amusement, make the most of the autumn sunshine before the rains return.'

'Goodness me, yes!' says Ellie. 'It's such a treat for me to be with both of my dearest friends *and* away from the children!'

Annie and Marcus follow her out but he stops for a moment, pausing on the stairs, taking Annie's arm gently as Ellie disappears down into the hallway.

'Are you all right?' he asks, carefully.

'Yes, of course,' she says.

'And Edward?'

'He is very busy with his work.'

'Not too busy that he is neglecting you, I hope?'

'It is a large project he has embarked on and one he is taking most seriously.' Annie smiles, but Marcus sees the sadness in her eyes.

'Well, I shall be staying with Ellie and Stephen until next month and I hope you know that *whatever* troubles you, Annie, you may always talk to me. In strictest confidence.'

She nods. 'Thank you, Marcus, you are kind.'

'Come on then, let us get some fresh air,' he says, squeezing her arm affectionately as they walk slowly down the stairs together.

Unhappiness is a curse, Marcus thinks to himself, a damned curse.

GRAHAM JONES
The Angel Inn, Broad Street, Ludlow

This ticket for various reasons, should be preserved.

VERY REDUCED FARES to London, Tenbury, Worcester, Oxford, Newtown, Barmouth &c; also to Shrewsbury, Hereford, Aberystwyth &c.

The **Aurora** new and elegant light four-inside Coach (with lateral Springs on the improved principle for Safety), every Afternoon at Half Four except Sunday to Tenbury, Worcester, Oxford and London &c.

The **Bewdley Post Coach** every Morning at Seven (meeting the Birmingham coach at Bewdley and returning the same day).

The **Prince Regent** to Shrewsbury every day except Sunday, at Midday.

The **Holiday Coach** to Newtown, Mondays only at Four in the Morning (only during the Season).

The **Barmouth Coach** to Aberystwyth &c. Tuesdays and Thursdays at Ten in the Evening (only during the Season).

Please to observe that none of the above, or ANY of the Coaches from THE ANGEL INN call at, or have any connexion with The Charlton Arms on the right-hand side of the road going from Town.

COACH.
Carriage ... .
Porterage ... .
1840   £_____

TAKE NOTICE, That the PROPRIETORS of the Public Carriages, who transact their Business at this Office will not be answerable for any Package containing Cash, Bank Notes, Bills, Jewels, Plate, Watches, Lace, Silk or Muslins HOWEVER SMALL THE VALUE – nor for any other Package which, with its Contents shall exceed FIVE POUNDS IN VALUE – if lost or damaged, unless the Value be specified, and in Insurance paid *over and above* the common Carriage, when delivered here, or to any of their Offices or Agents in the different Parts of the Kingdom.

G. JONES AND CO., Proprietors

Etta is bundled into the coach known as the Aurora directly outside of Ludlow's Angel Inn, the start of her journey to the capital. The Angel sits right in the medieval heart of the market town, all black-and-white beams with round bay windows that look down onto one of England's most picturesque streets.

The Aurora is one of the country's fastest and finest coaches and Mr and Mrs Marshall have paid for all four seats inside direct to London, safe in the knowledge that the mysterious Mr Price will reimburse them upon their arrival.

'This lady is most poorly,' says Mrs Marshall as she elbows a casual passer-by out of the way. 'Please, let me get her inside as swiftly as possible.'

Mrs Marshall isn't sure if her prisoner is known here but it is best to be cautious, hence the tatty cloak she has wrapped her in and a veil she has draped from Etta's bonnet that hangs down, covering her face. Mr Marshall takes the seat opposite, his wife already next to Etta who is drugged to the point of lethargy. As for Thomas, he has been left behind after a terrible row in which Mr Marshall lost all control of his fiery temper.

'It's not right, all this, it's not right!' Thomas had said, voice quivering, emboldened by the quantity of beer he had downed. 'You cannot treat a person as a golden goose, not when she's one of God's own creatures!' It was the most he had dared challenge his parents in all his years and his reward was to be cuffed around the head, his father beating his ears until they swelled, ringing like church bells.

'She is one hundred pounds, that's what she is!' his mother had barked. 'One hundred pounds and the carriage paid for. We will be rich after this! *Rich*, Thomas! *That* is what matters!'

Thomas, sulking, kicks the door when he returns to the small, damp cottage where his family reside, scraping a precarious living from their tenant farmland. He had dropped his parents off outside the Angel earlier, minutes before the Aurora departed, not daring to meet his father's eye for fear of another beating.

Whilst his parents are on their way to London, Thomas will sit at home, brooding and mulling as his headache worsens and the bruises emerge. He will remember the time his father had, some years ago, in a fit of rage, beaten their kind-natured but elderly pony to death. Thomas had cried over the bloodied body until his father found him, beating him for his 'softness' too.

Thomas will feed and water their two current ponies with their stiff ears and earthy smell, their soft whiskers nuzzling at him. He will recall, as he brushes their velvety flanks, that his father refused to name the pair of them, saying 'they never last long enough to bother'. Thomas will remember too Etta's tears, her mouth gagged, eyes pleading at him. His guilt at having been part of something both miraculous and gruesome will eat away at him, nibbling at his soul, filling him with a belated sense of right and wrong. By the time his greedy parents return, hands filled with money and unaccompanied by any winged creature, he will be ready for them. Alas, though, his pricked conscience comes too late for Etta herself as she lies propped up in the corner of the Aurora, wedged between the carriage door and the ample girth of Mrs Marshall.

'Tenbury, Worcester, Oxford and London!' the coachman shouts whilst the roof above her creaks and shudders as the last customers begrudgingly take a seat outside, exposed to the inclement weather that looms.

'Ah,' Etta thinks drowsily, 'and so I am to be taken to London.' It is a place she has only ever been to once, aged just fourteen, when she was admired and gasped at as a curiosity. She remembers grasping fingers reaching for her arms and more than one lady asking to touch her curls as if she were a doll, being offended when she refused. She had found the city to be a place of noise and nonsense, a place in which she was expected to behave in a certain way as a young gentlewoman and to keep her quick intelligence firmly to herself. She had hated every single moment and vowed never to return, her pleas to her father so persistent that he eventually relented, promising her that he would never make her go back. After he had died, though, and Walter inherited almost all, Etta's invitations to the capital had dried up faster than a stream in a drought. The contents of her purse and expected inheritance had clearly meant more to some than the contents of her mind. It had been one of the few positive consequences of her father's death, she had thought. That those whose company she had not sought, no longer sought hers.

The coach judders forward, lurching and rattling down the hill and out of town, away from Etta's beloved hills and, as it does so, she feels part of her is left behind too.

Richard waits on the other side of the wide, well-kempt road, watching as Mary approaches the Douglases' grand residence near Regent's Park. He had been all set to go in himself until Mary pointed out that the young maid sweeping the steps was far more likely to talk openly and honestly to a fellow female.

'You mean I would intimidate her with my charm and good looks, Miss Ward?' Richard had asked, tongue firmly in cheek.

'Not *quite* how I would have phrased it,' Mary had said, with a grin, 'but let me try first, Richard, please. Give me an hour and then let us rendezvous at the lake by the Inner Circle of the park.'

'Miss Ward, I feel that you have abused my goodwill in order that I bankroll your cab journey here,' Richard had said, wryly.

'Mr Gibbs! How *ridiculous* you are! I very much appreciate your moral support and indeed, at times, your actual company. However, I do feel that perhaps what you might best offer the present situation is to retire to a nearby coffee house and leave the investigating to me.'

Richard watches her arrive at the curving avenue of houses on the other side of the street and laughs to himself as she swiftly talks her way in, disappearing down the servants' stairs and into the house without a backward glance. Oh, Miss Ward, you are *remarkable*, he thinks, warmth rising within him. He wishes again that he had been able to pluck up the courage to say something clearer to Jos about his intentions, but the moment has passed. Besides, he is now rather unsure of Mary's own feelings towards him. Sometimes there is such affection in the way that she looks at him but does she *really* view him as family, as an older brother? *We have become such good friends*, he thinks to himself. Yet, if he confesses his feelings and they are not reciprocated, it would drive a wedge between them. He fears it might ruin their friendship, that he could lose her easy, glorious company forever. No, he thinks. The stakes are too high.

There is one other thing too. Richard believes that honesty and openness must surely be the foundation of any relationship and there is something he has not yet told her, indeed has not told anyone in London. He remembers the letter from Edinburgh that unexpectedly turned up at his lodgings, the scribbled response he sent in return. We all make mistakes, he thinks. It worked out for the best in the end.

He watches the house for a moment, allows himself a smile and heads northwards, into the green environs and leafy paths of Regent's Park.

'They were a special delivery, miss,' whispers Emily Parton, one of the Douglases' many members of staff as she sneaks

Mary up the servants' stairs at the back of the vast, terraced house.

'And you don't know where they were sent from?'

'Afraid not, miss, no,' says Emily. 'Beautiful, they are though, over four foot high. She looked like an angel herself, she did.'

Emily opens a door, motions for Mary to go through. They are in a lavishly wallpapered corridor with rooms leading off in all directions. It is without doubt the biggest house Mary has ever stepped foot in and she is surprised at how oppressive the grandeur feels.

'Here, miss,' says Emily and raps on a door, listening carefully for a moment. 'All clear,' she whispers and Mary follows her into Lady Douglas's bedroom. It is a large room, almost as big as her entire lodgings with Uncle Jos. A four-poster bed draped in rich furnishings and a chaise longue dominate. There's a dressing table, two armchairs and a large grandfather clock, and the room smells of both wealth and polish. On the left, a further door leads to a dressing room and it is in there that Emily beckons her.

The dress hangs up on a hook and the sight of it takes Mary's breath away. It is *stunning* – pure white silk of the finest quality, but it's the wings she cannot help but be drawn to. They are *huge*. Larger and even more elegant than a swan's, they are a creamy white rather than the snow white of the bird. Mary reaches out, strokes the soft feathers in wonder.

'You can't help but touch them, can you, miss? I felt the same when I first saw them,' breathes Emily as Mary is struck dumb for a moment.

'They were short there,' says Emily, pointing. 'At the

top, I mean, as though some of the bone was missing. Apparently, it was a fair job to stitch them on so they sat right. They had to support some of it with whalebone, in the end, to stop it from tearing the silk. See, this bit here? And some of the feathers were bent too; I had to tidy them up a fair bit when it came back from the dressmaker.'

Mary examines the wings closely, feels the weight of them, measures the circumference of the large bone at the top with her finger.

'You've all done a marvellous job,' Mary says quietly, thinking of the wings she somewhat hastily made for Lou. 'May I take a feather as a souvenir?' She has wheedled her way into the house under the guise of being a seamstress for the opera and Emily clearly feels honoured that someone from such an exciting background has shown any interest in either her or her mistress's winged dress.

'I should say no, really, but I don't see why not – she won't ever wear it again.' Emily sighs as Mary reaches over and plucks out one of the longest feathers. 'I think the wings are due to be sent back so I'll have to unpick it all anyway.'

It's only as they go to leave that Mary notices the neat pile of brown paper sitting on the arm of one of the chairs. 'Is this what they were sent in?' she asks, eagerly.

'Might well have been, miss,' says Emily.

Mary carefully unfolds the paper, reads Lord Douglas's address – but there is another inked on there too, the sender's address, and it is the exact one that she was hoping to find. It is not quite proof of her suspicions, but still the excitement in her stomach makes her feel a little queasy.

'Thank you,' she says and offers Emily a coin, but the

girl refuses. 'No, miss, it's been a pleasure. If you ever do put on an opera with a costume inspired by it, then please think of me. It's rare I get time off properly but I'd very much like to know about it at least.'

Mary kisses her on the cheek. 'Thank you, Miss Parton,' she says as she goes to leave. 'You are a dear.'

When Mary finally catches up with Richard on the Broad Walk in Regent's Park, she is disappointed to find him less sanguine about her findings than she was hoping.

'I'm afraid, even if the wings *were* sent in that paper you found, all it proves is that they came from Meake's house and are to be returned there,' he says as they stroll along the avenue. 'It doesn't prove anything about which creature they may or may not have come from.'

'I know, I know – but there was the woman taken ill in the church, the same woman Charlie saw in the cab with feathers under her blanket. Miss Bewdley said the woman later passed away, but what if those wings were *hers*, Richard? What if he *murdered* her for them?'

'Mary . . .' Richard stops for a moment and takes her hands. 'Come now. Think clearly! Do not let your imagination run away with you. You have a connection between Meake and the wings, that is true. He may well have been the man who bought whatever body was dragged out of the Thames, although you have no *real* proof of that. All else is hearsay and conjecture. The wings could be from a swan he had been dissecting, the woman might have had feathers in her bonnet that fell into her shawl and were sticking up out of it. Yes, Meake reacted when you mentioned the word "angel" but that doesn't mean anything in itself.'

'You think there is no story here, then?' she asks, deflated.

'No, that isn't what I said — I would not have travelled with you here if I thought that was the case. All I said was to *think clearly*. You have but a handful of pieces from a jigsaw puzzle and from them you are prematurely guessing the shape of the final picture. Perhaps, although I think it is extremely unlikely, you are entirely correct in your guesswork, but in order to prove anything, you will need to gather more pieces of the puzzle first.'

'Then I must simply find more proof,' Mary says. 'And so I shall.'

'If there *is* any more proof to find, then of course you will,' says Richard, smiling at her. 'Of that I have no doubt whatsoever.'

Without thinking, without being able to stop himself, he lifts his hand to her face, gently strokes her soft, rosy cheek before, startled, realising what he's doing. They stare at each other for a moment, Mary wordless with surprise, Richard's heartbeat throbbing loudly in his head, the world suspended around them for a moment. *That wasn't meant to happen*, Richard thinks.

'M-Miss Ward,' he stutters as speech returns to him and he turns scarlet. 'Apologies. I, er, a fly on your cheek. Terribly sorry.' An awkward silence descends before Richard mercifully spots a sherbet stall and marches off to gather them some refreshment whilst Mary gently slides down onto a conveniently placed bench to regather her composure.

One more day, thinks Edward, for, all being well, it is tomorrow that his Salopian angel arrives in London. He recalls the letter, oh so full of promise, that Samuel threw into the fire. The wings upon her back, the young witness to the transformation . . . his heart lifts each time he thinks of it. He is concerned that his new angel has been injured, as the letter stated, but surely there is no better place for her than in his care? He imagines them on their way now, the Marshalls, his precious angel they accompany, coach wheels turning as the carriage rattles along country roads, bringing them ever closer to London, ever closer to him. He thanks God for giving him this latest, most fortuitous opportunity, prays for his angel's safe delivery.

Annie is still in her study, locked away on her mysterious painting – 'a surprise', she calls it. He knows she's upset with him for his secrecy around his own work, hiding her artwork as if he would care a jot about such a thing. His eye falls upon the day's papers and he sees the story Annie had earlier circled for him. Miss Bewdley, he thinks with relief, need no longer be a concern. The problem of Miss Bewdley has already been solved – praise be!

Restless and impatient for what tomorrow will bring, Edward unlocks the second basement cell, checking again that everything is in order. He ties the barking dog in the hallway for a moment but then a whim makes him open the door to the wingless creature and thrust the skinny black and tan mongrel inside.

'I shall give you the company you so clearly crave,' he says with a snarl. 'Careful, though, it might bite!'

The dog will keep her occupied, he thinks. Without her wings, she is of less value to him, but still, he finds himself fascinated by her. By her fierceness, her temper, her stubbornness.

He returns to his study, writes a note to Lord Douglas reminding him to return the wings. He would, of course, rather not have loaned them. Ideally he would not have let them out of his sight but he trusts Douglas and, exactly as he had hoped, it has brought him both favour and a decent sum of money – albeit not as much as he might have hoped. Why are the wealthy so loath to actually *spend* their money? he wonders.

Edward scratches his arm before stopping himself. He noted this morning, with clinical attention, that a mild red rash is beginning to spread away from the scab and along the rest of his arm. It is simply healing, he tells himself and, not for the first time, takes a sip of his own tincture mix to dull the itch.

Annie had feared it would be so and she was right. The dull ache in her lower belly, the inclination towards the heightened ends of her emotions and here it is. The brownish-red smear on the squares of paper in the privy, the slight sense of some inner workings sliding out. There will be no baby for them this time.

Another month, another cycle of the moon's circle overhead. Please, she prays quietly, *please*. I am a dutiful wife. Three years and more, all those consultations, all for nothing. Perhaps it is simply not God's will, she thinks. She remembers Samuel's suggestion that it is Edward who is at fault, but she dismisses it. *We must keep trying*, that is all, we must show God that we are not willing to give up so easily. If only Edward would come to bed at a sensible hour, if only he would stop losing himself in his work . . .

Annie cries for a while in the privy before wiping both her face and her below, tidying herself up as best she can before heading back to her bedroom to prepare for her monthlies. The pads of material hooked up beneath her undercarriage worn until semi-sodden then given to Sarah to be soaked like soiled babies' napkins before being boiled clean on washday.

The smell of her own self repulses her and she feels like a failure anew.

She does not mention it to Edward. She cannot bear to disappoint him too.

Edward is at the Peacock Inn long before the Aurora is due, impatient to meet his third angel. He finally finished hanging the skeleton of his river angel late last night, the joints perfectly positioned and fully movable. He has created a wheeled base for her to be mounted on, her small wings opened out and supported by metal struts. The wheels will be a great boon for his planned lectures so he can rotate and manipulate her by his side. She is magnificent, more impressive in some ways, Edward thinks, as a skeleton than she was as a body.

He fidgets whilst he waits inside the inn. The room he booked is already prepared and there is nothing else for him to do but wait. He had secured a much-needed short-term loan through a private financier, collected the bank notes this morning from the fine offices of Mr Thomas Middleton, a most obliging gentleman with an impressively wide ginger moustache and prodigiously long sideburns. One hundred and ten pounds is a huge sum to be made available at such short notice and Edward had been loath to borrow but it is not the first loan he has been forced to take out in recent months. Besides, he is certain of being able to repay it most handsomely in the near future – along with the extortionate interest rate. As soon as he is able to display his angels to his satisfaction, a veritable tidal wave of money will roll in.

There is a commotion outside and Edward rushes out, but only disappointment awaits – it is not his much-anticipated Aurora but the Peveril of the Peak, from way up north. The Aurora is now nearly an hour late and Edward's patience is fit to burst as he hovers outside the Peacock, watching and waiting.

'Make way, make way, this lady is *very* ill!' The Aurora jerks to a stop in front of the inn and a round woman – with a most unedifying visage, notes Edward – bursts out from the interior of the carriage. The outside passengers disembark from the roof and there is noise and chaos all around as both luggage and people tumble down. Edward weaves his way forward, pushing against the tide of confusion, to offer the woman his hand.

'Does your lady need medical attention?' he says loudly above the noise of the crowd. 'I am *Mr Price*, one of London's best surgeons!' He emphasises his false name, noting her eyes widening with recognition.

'George, George! It is the very man we were hoping to find,' she bellows back towards the coach before whispering to Edward. 'He will need a hand getting her out and into the inn. I presume a room is ready for us?'

Edward nods and the woman moves out of his way as he pushes himself into the carriage for a first look at his new angel. She is taller than he had expected but appears groggy and limp, a veil covering her face.

'Mr Marshall? I am Mr Price,' says Edward, briefly shaking hands but unable to take his eyes from the veiled creature. Well wrapped in an old cloak, her wings are not visible, but he notes with excitement that her shoulders appear promisingly bulky underneath the material.

It takes longer than Edward would like for them to get his new angel out of the coach and safely into the environs of the private room. He eyes the couple and finds them wanting. They are ill-educated, poor and coarse and he wishes to be rid of them as swiftly as possible.

'There!' says Mrs Marshall, all of aflutter as she sits, smoothing down her dress as Edward's angel, his precious winged woman, is placed gently on the chaise longue by the window near her husband.

'One hundred pounds and the return coach tickets, that's what we agreed, yes?' says George Marshall, keeping his narrowed eyes firmly on the fellow he knows only as Mr Price.

Edward ignores him.

'How and where is she injured?' he asks, watching his angel's chest rise and fall where she lies. He is hugely relieved to see her alive, but is concerned by her shallow breathing. He lifts her veil to see if her forehead is feverish and is startled both by the woman's beauty and the unexpected colour of her skin.

'She is . . .' He does not know what to say.

'Not what you had expected perhaps,' says George, Mrs Marshall motioning at him to continue, to seal the deal. 'But 'tis the wings that make her truly special, sir. My own son, with his own—'

'Yes, yes, that was in the letter, I remember.'

Edward cannot take his eyes off her. She is striking, *stunning*, even, with an elegant face and high cheekbones.

'It was a bolt, sir, a crossbow bolt. My son tried to stop her fleeing, see. 'Tis here.' Mr Marshall indicates with his hand and Edward draws back the cloak. Ah, the wings, his breath is sucked out of him. They are not the creamy white of his other two angels but a russet brown with streaks of darker colours.

'I will examine her before I settle the bill,' says Edward. 'Please avert your eyes.'

'No tricks,' growls Mrs Marshall.

'Let the gentleman have a look, Izzy,' her husband re-assures her. 'We have nothing to hide.'

Edward gently lifts his angel up, unhooks the cloak and rolls her onto her side. The wings are easily as large as the fallen creature in his basement but oh so different, full of colour and subtlety, they are more like those of an eagle than a swan. The angel murmurs as he turns her over and he allows his hand to brush against her feathers for a moment before lightly manipulating her wings, noting that they are attached by bone and sinew just as his other angels were.

'Where did you find her?' Edward asks as he removes her gloves, feeling the heat of her hands underneath. She has fine long fingers although her nails are short and, he notes, not particularly clean.

'My son found her in the woods far out to the west of Ludlow. 'Tis clear she was lost,' replies Mr Marshall.

'She has no name? Is not reported missing?' asks Edward

as he moves her onto her front, noting her wince as he does so.

'Would *you* have reported her?' asks Mrs Marshall, a touch of glee in her voice.

Edward remains silent as he softly rolls his angel back towards him, noting the loose linen wound around her abdomen. Her dress is of a considerably higher class than the Marshalls' own clothes and he wonders where exactly his angel might have originated. There is mud on the bottom of her skirt and it is clear from the marks on her dress that she has knelt in it at some recent point. He recalls the altar at St George's, for had his other angel not fallen to her knees during her transformation too?

'The injury is here, yes?' he asks and the Marshalls nod. Edward unwraps the linen, unpeels the cuts that have been made in the material of her dress and chemise to access the wound. There is a bandage over her skin and he is unable to see what damage has been done without removing it. He has brought his medical bag with him but he wonders if it isn't better to simply take her home.

'You are welcome to look, sir,' says Mrs Marshall. 'I am not unversed in herbal remedies and she is in little discomfort. She is healing well, but had a touch of fever, is all.'

'I am satisfied,' says Edward. 'You may have your money.'

'What will you do with her, sir?' asks Mr Marshall. 'If there is more money to be made, we feel strongly we would warrant a share in it.'

'I am a *scientist*, not a showman,' says Edward sharply. 'I am guided by God, not by money, I assure you. You have my name and address and I have yours – may we not trust

each other in the future as we have in the past days?'
Besides, he thinks to himself, these people are not endowed
with much intelligence; it is clear that they are out of their
depth and he wishes to be rid of them as swiftly and
permanently as possible.

This Mr Price is most businesslike, thinks Mrs Marshall,
impressed as her husband shakes hands with him.

As Edward's cab hurls him and Etta eastward and towards
St Mary Axe, so too do the Marshalls step back into the
Aurora later that afternoon to embark on their own return
journey home. By tomorrow evening they will finally be
home, exhausted and elated, and it is as they open their
front door that their son, racked with guilt about his part
in the whole sorry charade, will be ready and waiting for
them.

For now, though, safe in their ignorance and brimming
with cash, the Marshalls enjoy much ale and pie on their
long, bumpy and deeply uncomfortable coach journey
home, celebrating their good fortune and raising more than
one glass on the way to the good taste and deep pockets
of their benevolent saviour, Mr Price.

The dog and Natalya have reached an uneasy truce. She knows now, having seen it squat to urinate, that the dog is female. It carries with it a strong whiff of excrement and urine and is thin and angry, rib bones showing through its sides.

'Poor thing,' Natalya whispers softly and the dog whimpers. 'Ah, you know my voice from when I've spoken to you through the wall, don't you, friend?'

The dog yawns and Natalya half-smiles, the first time in an age.

'Ah,' she whispers, 'everyone's a critic . . .'

They had circled each other at first, the dog growling and baring its teeth. Natalya had grabbed her blanket, rolling it into a cylinder. It would not make for much of a weapon but it would, at least, protect her from any bites. She had emptied some of the watery beer into the pewter basin and put it down warily, the dog immediately lapping it up, growling at her between gulps, never taking its eyes off the unfamiliar person with whom it now found itself.

There was no longer any bread left but Natalya would

share that too when it next arrived. They sit as far away from each other as possible and Natalya's nose wrinkles at the animal stink that now pervades the room, adding to that of the slop bucket in the corner that she was forced to use earlier.

'But your own smell is not as bad as that of someone else's,' she whispers and the dog's ears prick up. 'Do you have a name?' she asks and the dog growls in response as it lies down, slowly and warily.

'You may tell me in your own good time, dog,' she whispers. 'I will not hurt you.'

Besides, thinks Natalya, if I can befriend you, you might obey me, not him. And that, she muses, may prove very useful indeed.

The very tips of someone's fingers are always so hard to get just right, ponders Annie as she looks over her painting with a critical eye. The underlying red is either not quite enough or it is too red and it's so *very* difficult to capture the faint blue of the blood vessels just underneath the skin. It is her least favourite part of any portrait. She would rather paint a thousand eyeballs moist with glistenings of white than a single foreshortened hand.

She is tired today, her monthlies draining her energy and enthusiasm. As she goes to add a small brushstroke to Edward's left hand, there is a knock on her study door and Sarah brings her a note.

'But this is addressed to my husband . . .' says Annie, puzzled.

'Yes, ma'am, but the boy who delivered it, he said it was from the lady who died and I thought it might be urgent,' says Sarah, bobbing with a curtsey. She wonders what her mistress is painting that so absorbs her and is desperate to take a look but the canvas faces away from her and Annie locks the door of an evening. *This house*, thinks Sarah with a fizzle of exhilaration, *is so full of secrets.*

'Which lady who died?' says Annie, turning over the note, puzzled.

'The one that got run over,' says Sarah.

'Miss Bewdley?' Annie asks, and Sarah nods. 'But why would it be urgent, Sarah? It can surely wait for Mr Meake.'

'Ah, but ma'am, thing is, the boy says she was *clutching it when she died*,' says Sarah gleefully. She had particularly liked this gruesome detail.

'Then I shall make sure my husband receives it as soon as he is home,' says Annie, putting the note to one side and dismissing Sarah. She resumes her painting, feeling the presence of the letter on her writing desk throughout.

Mary had been too full of excitement to sleep last night. The wings, there *is* something in it, there *must* be. And Richard, *Richard*, the way he had looked at her in the park. Her heart skips a beat. Had there *really* been something on her cheek? Or dare she believe he might have a fondness for her that is something more than the affection of a friend?

She'd fidgeted in bed until Charlie, top to toe, gave her an irritated nudge with his foot. She rolled onto her back, looking up at the hole in the plaster on the ceiling, the wooden struts behind it, a spider weaving its web across the gap. She lay like that until the sun stretched itself awake and the noise of the streets ratcheted up, all the time, thinking and hoping. But then the day had descended, the usual circuitous routines of cleaning and sewing and other mundane tasks.

Mary is just returned home, newly stocked up on tea leaves, soap and other household items, when Charlie bursts in as if his trousers were aflame. Mary drops her recent purchases on the table with surprise as the young boy beams at her, out of breath and over-excited.

'Lord, Charlie! You gave me a fright crashing in like that!' she says, relieved to see that the precious paper bag of tea hasn't split. 'Why such haste?'

'A carriage, miss, at Meake's house. I been keeping watch like you said but my legs was getting stiff so I took myself for a turn around the block. That passageway down the back of the row, s'where I saw him.'

'Mr Meake?'

'Yes, miss, and he had someone with him. A lady! She seemed asleep. He was carrying her down the back alleyway in his arms so I hid behind a bit of wall that jutted out and spied on him. She had a bonnet on and a veil so I didn't see her face. She was wrapped up in some kind of bulky cloak – but miss, she didn't have any gloves on.'

'She was alive, though?'

'Think so, miss, she was floppy though, but her hands, miss, her hands – they was brown!'

'A lady of colour?' Mary asks and Charlie nods, continuing at a rate of knots.

'He took her in the back way to the house, had a bit o' trouble with the door. As soon as he was in, I ran as fast as I could up to the other end of the passageway and . . .' He pauses for breath for a moment. '*The cab was still there!*'

'The one they travelled in?'

'Yes, miss! I got to him just in time, cabbie said he picked up the fare by the Angel, Peacock Inn he said.'

'Oh, Charlie! Charlie!' Mary claps her hands. 'That is most excellent news.'

'Oh, that ain't all, miss!' Charlie says with a grin.

'No . . . ?'

'No, miss, turns out he had to *clean the seat* inside after the fare.' Charlie triumphantly holds up a long brown feather. ''Cause there was feathers all over it.'

Mary's mouth falls open and she takes the feather, turning it over in her hand.

'Oh, excellent work, Charlie! Let me think. Most of the coaches will have already left for the day by now and I *really* should finish that next lot of buttons but—'

'But?' says Charlie hopefully.

'Well, it's a fair walk to the Angel . . . but I think you and I should perhaps pay a visit to the Peacock Inn.'

'Any chance of a cab?' asks Charlie, hopefully.

'No,' says Mary, conscious of reduced finances as she puts her shawl back on. 'But we have legs, don't we? And what did God give us legs for if we're not to use them? Come now, let us make haste!'

It is Wednesday and Edward should, by rights, be walking the wards of St Luke's but instead he has given permission for his deputy to take over for the day. Edward's attention, his entire being, is consumed only by what lies in front of him on his dissection table – his new angel. He has given her a fresh dose of laudanum and she is barely semi-conscious. He is still concerned about how hot she feels to the touch, agreeing with Mrs Marshall's diagnosis of a mild fever. Cutting open the bandage to inspect her wound properly, he is pleased to see that it is healing well. He suspects her thick woollen clothing prevented the bolt from going further in. If it had been a deeper injury, she would likely have died some while ago, he thinks, and he thanks God for saving her for him.

Edward has not encountered many people of colour this close up – although, of course, he has seen those with darker skin many times on the streets of London. The turbaned men selling rhubarb and spices, a handful of footmen, other servants, maids, dock workers and more. There was that well-known actor, some of the key aboli-tionists, and now here *she* is – *a beautiful, winged angel* given to him by the Almighty. Yet, Edward thinks, scratching his head, surely God made all superior people white? That was one of the bases for Empire, was it not? And yet, here in front of him, lies *the most perfect, most striking* out of all his three specimens . . . He cannot fathom it.

Edward cleans the scab gently before wrapping it in a fresh bandage. He will let his angel rest, wait for her fever to abate before he examines her further. Then, and only then, will he find out whether she too is a test from God, like the fallen creature or whether she, the third and most complete specimen, is in fact, his very own saviour.

Three angels in his basement. A trinity of gifts. A flicker of panic: *what if there are more?* Surely there can be no others? Surely God has chosen only him to receive such favours? He steels himself. God has guided him to this. To the three – one dead, one now broken and now this, the last of his gifts, the *most perfect of all*. He must show more gratitude. Three is, after all, a sacred number. The holy trinity. It is a message from the Almighty himself. The Father, the Son, the Holy Ghost. He must have more faith.

'The Lord giveth,' he murmurs to himself. 'Praise be to Him. The Lord giveth.'

Much to Mary's disappointment, she finds those who work at the Peacock Inn to be rather immune to the charms of both her and young Charlie. It's an extraordinarily busy place with a steady stream of guests coming and going, coaches arriving or being dispatched. It's a cacophony of chaos too – from the clatter of horses' hooves and the coachman's shouts, to the stallholders trying to sell passengers all manner of items for their journey. There are porters hoisting luggage to and fro and travellers from all manner of backgrounds, the well-to-do with their fine bonnets, ordinary folk wrapped up against the autumn chill with well-darned coats and scarves.

Eventually, after much patience, Mary pins down a porter with a moment to spare and so it is that she discovers six coaches arrived earlier in the day. Coaches from Yorkshire, Manchester, Ludlow, Rugby, Hereford and Cardiff. The Highflyer, the Peveril of the Peak, the Aurora, the Tally-Ho, the Bang-Up and the Prince of Wales. The woman whom Mr Meake took back to his house could have been on any one of the coaches and, potentially, from any stop along the way. By Mary's reckoning, that is at least thirty stops in towns or cities, not including any smaller villages where someone might hitch a ride if they knew the driver. She knows well that she would never be able to afford either the time or the money to venture to even a quarter of the stops and she and Charlie have all but given up when a shout stops them in their tracks. Mary turns to see a man running swiftly towards her, weaving through the traffic, wearing the coachman's distinctive red coat and tall black hat.

'Jonny said you were asking questions, miss,' says the man, out of breath. 'I'm Sayers, from the Peveril. What was it you're after, something about a passenger?'

'Yes!' says Mary. 'We're looking for a woman who arrived in London earlier today on one of the coaches. We think she was wearing a veil and may have been with a gentleman, tall with dark hair. She is, we believe, a lady of colour . . .' This is hopeless, she thinks, seeing Mr Sayers look at her blankly.

'She was wearing a blue dress,' Charlie pipes up. 'Bit dirty but well made and good quality. She had a dark cloak on over that, bit tatty. The bonnet was cream, same colour as some of the piping on her dress, what I could see of it anyway. The veil was dark, couldn't see through it. Tallish, I think, hard to say.'

'Oh, well remembered, Charlie!' says Mary, as Mr Sayers shakes his head.

'Not on my coach, I'm afraid, but if you can spare a few minutes, most of us are having some refreshments so you might ask the others. Mabbitt and Preston aren't there, that's the Aurora and Bang-Up, but the rest are.'

And so Mary finds herself welcomed into a small, wood-panelled room at the Peacock where the four coach drivers are doing their best to drink a barrel dry between them. There is no luck in identifying Charlie's mysterious woman, though, and Mary mentally crosses off four out of six on the list.

'That leaves just two tomorrow,' she says. 'We'll have to come back then, Charlie, and hope fortune may smile on us.'

Still, Mary thinks as they begin their long walk home, it is another little piece of the jigsaw and she keeps her fingers firmly crossed for the next day.

Etta comes to on a worn mattress in a small, windowless brick room. The walls are damp and she knows at once that she is underground. There is a whiff of something unpleasant, ammonia and worse, and she sneezes as it seeps up her nostrils. A small candle flickers in one corner of the tiny room with a chamber pot in another and a chair upon which sits some bread on a plate, a pewter tankard and some matches. She feels too tired to move but she can hear someone – or something – close by.

'Hullo?' she whispers, nervously. It is the first time she has spoken out loud for some days and her voice sounds hollow and empty.

A dog barks and howls back at her. *Oh*, she thinks, *a dog*, and she longs for Scout's velvety ears, the weight of his head upon her knee.

'Hallo?' says a voice suddenly and, for a moment, Etta thinks she dreamt it, that it was some kind of echo.

'Hullo? Can you hear me?' says Etta, struggling to stand. 'Can anyone hear me?'

'I hear you,' says a woman's voice close by. Her accent is one Etta has never heard before. Soft and lilting somehow.

'Where am I?'

'Ah, that I don't know. The man who brought me here, he is not a good man.'

'Are we in London?'

'I believe so, but I cannot be certain.'

Etta wobbles to her feet and the candlelight flickers with her movement. Looking at it, she estimates she has another half-hour or so before the light goes.

'There's a grill,' says Natalya. 'Higher up. For air. That's where I am, in the room next to you.' The dog barks. 'I have canine company and it stinks.'

Etta sees the grill and reaches up to it. She feels a slight puff of air as if someone is blowing at her. 'I cannot see you,' she says.

Natalya strikes a match and the light flickers around her. Etta sees the woman's pale face looking back at her, dark circles under her eyes.

'Oh,' Etta says, 'there you are.'

Natalya holds the match up, sees Etta's face in return. She catches a glimpse of Etta's wings, brown and copper like autumn leaves, sitting proud behind her.

'*So it is true . . .*' Natalya breathes. 'You have wings! Just as I once did.'

'*Once?*' whispers Etta, horror beginning to rise in her.

'Once,' says Natalya and holds the match up to her shoulders, turning to the side to let Etta see her bloodied, bandaged stumps for just a moment before the match burns to a cinder, plunging Natalya back into darkness.

Horror rises in Etta, the breath pushed out of her. She cannot speak. Her wings, whatever and why ever they were given to her, they are part of her. To mutilate someone in this way beggars belief. Fear overcomes her and she stumbles, breathlessly, down the wall to the uneven brick floor, collapsing onto the mattress, her wings scraping against the bricks as she does so.

'I said he was not a good man,' says Natalya's voice through the grate.

Etta, overwhelmed, closes her eyes as if it were all a nightmare she could simply shut out, but she knows, alas, she cannot.

40 Queen Square,
Bloomsbury,
London

Mr Meake,

I have pondered long and hard over this but I fear I must call on you once again. I believe both of us witnessed something spectacular, something extraordinary at St George's and I must discuss it with you at your earliest convenience.

I pray this letter reaches you safely and swiftly.

Yours, in deepest confidence,
Miss Amelia Bewdley

Edward screws up Miss Bewdley's letter and throws it into the hearth in his consulting room. She is dead, he thinks to himself, gone. It should not matter but he finds her inclusion of the feather disturbing. He holds it in his hand, brushing the barbs against his palm, before tossing it into the fire, screwing his nose up as the burning stench briefly fills the air before he heads back to the basement.

In his study downstairs, a small narrow room next to his dissecting room, Edward listens to the patter of the rain outside as he thinks. His study is full of taxidermied creatures, books and notes, bursting at the seams with proof of his many years of learning, of his version of the world around him, all annotated, edited and recorded, all filed and orderly, everything in its right place.

He scratches his arm and is irritated anew. The rains are heavy now, thudding at the small windowpane that only just clears the surface of the back yard. It is the sole window in this part of the basement and he is grateful for the tiny sliver of daylight. He wishes for a moment that he had installed gas lighting both here and in the holding cells. No matter, he thinks. He was right not to. Gas would eat up the air in such small spaces, it would have been an unnecessary extravagance.

He hears again in his head his fallen angel's roars as she transformed in front of him at St George's. What a gift to be given! A miracle! And yet she rejected it so thoroughly. He curses her every day for it, but the money that Lord Douglas had given him for the loan of the wings at least went some small way to softening the blow. He had not yet had a chance to follow up on his note requesting them to be returned. But it is all far less pressing now that he has been awarded his third, most complete, angel.

She was still resting when he checked on her and so he must be patient, must wait until tomorrow to find out what his angel truly is. But the rains outside, heavier than usual and building on the already overflowing medieval sewers that run like hidden rat tunnels underneath London's streets, will have an unexpected effect on Edward's still-forming plans.

★

'Was the letter from Miss Bewdley anything important?' Annie asks him later when he finally comes to bed.

'No,' he replies, calmly. 'I'm afraid she was suffering from delusions before she died and it would not be fair to share them with you.'

Annie watches him as he undresses before getting into bed, pulling the covers up, and turning his back on her. She reaches out to him for the warmth of his arms, to pull him towards her, but he flinches away.

'No, Annie. I'm tired,' he murmurs. 'Let me sleep.'

She listens to his breathing, slow and steady, watches his shoulders twitch as he falls asleep. She knows he is lying about the letter, but it is *why* he feels the need to that troubles her so.

After Etta had seen what little remained of her fellow prisoner's wings, there had been no more conversation between them. She is so fearful of what might be to come, of the thought of her own wings being forcibly removed, that she sits silent, on her tired mattress, legs hunched up, arms wrapped tightly around them. She imagines herself far away, back up Brown Clee with the wind rushing in her ears, clambering to the top of High Vinnalls with the skylarks crowding the skies, wandering across high ridges in the drovers' footsteps on the Kerry Ridgeway. She thinks of bracken and ferns, of apples ripening in the orchards, of damp October rain on the fertile earth. She thinks of ripe blackberries turning sticky-sweet on prickly brambles, of sloes and damsons and rosehips, fieldfares and redwings. She thinks of stoats and weasels, peregrines and sparrow-hawks, of buzzards and goshawks, kestrels and kites. She thinks of the unfurling fern and her little fossil of the same. She thinks of her wild hills of home, so brimful of life, of autumn stretching itself out along the fields as the greens turn to copper, rust and gold and the first frosts edge the leaves crisp with white.

Etta does not touch the bread or the drink. She misses the warmth and solace of her beloved Scout, her most loyal of friends, her dearest companion, so much so that she cries herself to sleep.

Next door, Natalya wonders if she has startled the other woman to death until she hears a faint gasp of sobbing and is, at least, relieved to know she is still alive. Natalya tries whispering through the grate but her attempts to start a conversation are futile. All becomes dark and still and so Natalya is alone again, bar the thin dog which sleeps curled up in the corner. The walls feel wetter today and the smell of mould is stronger but at least, muses Natalya with a grimace, it helps dampen the stench of dog.

Some time later, their gaoler comes to take Natalya's new neighbour away, but the dog barks and throws itself at the door with such ferocity that she is unable to hear anything else. Instead, Natalya sits and waits, waits until the dog has quietened, her own ears pricked, waiting in the darkness.

The other woman's wings are so very beautiful, Natalya thinks and wishes, with a pang that wounds her afresh, that she were still in possession of her own.

When Etta's captor unlocks the door to her cell, she stands, calmly waiting for him. Edward holds out his hand but she refuses to take it. Instead, he motions for her to follow him and she walks slowly behind, noting every detail of her surroundings on the way. The whitewashed walls of the short cellar hallway, the flickering gas lamps. A turn to the right that leads to a long hallway, cut off at the far end with a covered gate. A narrow oak console table sits, pushed up against the wall, on the right-hand side. Despite the gas lighting, it is still dark down here from the lack of windows and she can make out a servant shouting in what she assumes is a kitchen not far away. This is no hospital, then, Etta thinks. *This is someone's house.*

Edward gestures for her to move in front of him and she steps straight into his dissecting room. A skeleton with small wings faces her and Etta gasps, clutching her stomach.

Edward catches her eye and shakes his head. 'She was already dead,' he says. 'Pulled from the river. Drowned.'

Etta tries to remain calm on the outside but inside she is all atremble. *He is not a good man*, she thinks, recalling her fellow prisoner's words. She looks around, takes in everything she might learn about her captor from her new surroundings – the smell of chemicals, the eyes and bodies of various creatures in glass jars, the skulls looking down at her from the shelves – before she returns her gaze to him.

'I am not your plaything,' she says, clearly and crisply, as he looks at her with surprise. It is taking all her energy to concentrate and she now wishes very much that she had eaten at least some of the bread. 'You have no right to keep me here,' she adds, firmly.

'I bought you,' Edward says. 'Therefore you are mine.'

'I am afraid,' says Etta firmly, gaining in confidence, 'you appear to be rather late in your outdated attitudes. I am not a chattel to be bought and swapped at will.'

'No,' says Edward. 'Of course not. But you are, however, a scientific curiosity. And besides, you are safe here. Safer here than you would be outside, as I see you have already discovered.' He nods towards her wound.

'*Safe?*' Etta says sharply. 'Like my neighbour whose wings you mutilated?'

'She is not like you,' he says, defensively. 'She is fury and noise. She is a demon.'

They look at each other for a moment, sizing the other up. Etta decides to remain silent, to let him speak first, see what he will reveal when he does so.

'You are the third gift I have been given,' says Edward and Etta notices the fervour in his voice. He motions to the skeleton. 'The first was drowned, found in the Thames and God gave her to me. The second is in the cell next to you and—'

'And you pulled her wings off as if she were an insect,' says Etta coldly.

'Is that what she would have you believe?' Edward watches her, fascinated, from the other side of the dissection table. 'No. I am not guilty of that. She did it herself. Threw her own body against the wall until the bones at the top of her wings split and splintered of their own accord. I removed them only to prevent infection or further injury. I had very little choice in the matter, I can assure you.'

Etta frowns. Even if that is true, she thinks, does it make him any less in the wrong to keep them both down here?

'And then there is you,' says Edward. 'You are the third angel, my third gift.'

'I am no *gift*,' says Etta. 'I am myself.'

'No,' says Edward, unsettled by the frankness of his new angel. 'No, I—'

'Are you devout?' she asks, interrupting him, head tilted to one side. She is interested in his use of the word 'angel' to describe them.

'I am a man of *science*,' he says, proudly.

'You talk about God's gift as if this was all preordained, as if He had chosen you?

'The Almighty has chosen me, yes,' Edward replies, proudly, with a smile.

Ah, Etta thinks, so he is a religious zealot.

'I wish to examine you,' he says. 'See if your fever has abated further, although it seems you are recovering well enough. I wish to see if your wings are the same as the other angels'. They are different in colour but not, I believe, in structure.'

'You wish to dissect me?' she says, eyes narrowing.

'No. My word, *no*! I would much rather a live specimen than—'

Etta holds her hand up to silence him. *Specimen!* The word chills her even as a plan starts to form itself. 'You may examine my wings,' she says, frostily. 'That is all. You have ascertained, as God meant you to, that the other two were women in all senses bar the wings?'

He nods and she is relieved; it was guesswork on her part but she believes she is already beginning to get the measure of this strange fanatic.

'Then you have no need to examine me in the same way,' she says. She moves towards the dissecting table, sits elegantly on the edge, not daring to take her eyes away from him. 'There,' she says, tilting her face away as if from a bad smell.

'You will co-operate with me?' says Edward, barely believing his luck.

'I will co-operate with you, yes,' Etta says. 'For if the Almighty chose you, who I am to question His word?' She looks at him, waits for a flicker of doubt across his face but there is none to be seen.

'You must undress otherwise I cannot examine you properly,' Edward says, dry-mouthed.

She slides herself off the table and stands up facing him. She has never fully undressed in front of any man before and does not plan for this to be her first. She stares at him, holding his glance until he looks away.

'I will undress to my chemise and corset and no further,' she says, coldly.

He nods silently. Etta struggles to remove her layers and so he has to help her, carefully cutting open her coat and dress at the back in order for her wings to be freed. As Edward slowly examines them, a bell rings at the far end of the hallway. He ignores it but it is most persistent.

'Will you not answer it?' asks Etta, and Edward shakes his head. She watches him as he works in silence, notes his quick, draughtsman-like sketches. This man is troubled, she thinks. He is less interested in the reason *why* a handful of women should have grown wings, only in the fact that they have. He seems impatient for rewards in this life rather than the next, but perhaps she can use that to her advantage.

'Your accommodation is not conducive to my health,' she says, putting her torn coat back on.

'I apologise. I can only offer more blankets for now but—'

'Yes, that would be a start.'

'I must ask more of you,' he says, peering at her. 'The wings, you have not always had them?'

'No,' she says, warily.

'How did they appear?'

She tells him of the forest, of the crossbow, but she keeps the details scant. He has no right to be in possession of either me or my experiences, she thinks.

'What started your transformation?' he says, thinking of what he witnessed in St George's. 'Do you know?'

She hesitates for a moment for she does not know the answer to this. Yet the lie rises to her lips, unfurls in her mouth.

'I asked God,' she says and waits to see his reaction.

'Asked God? Asked Him for what?' he says, puzzled.

'To be His messenger on this Earth, to carry out His tasks.' Etta looks towards the heavens, warming to this new role of hers. 'To be an intermediary between mankind and the Almighty. To be *His* intermediary.'

Edward looks at her, eyes full of wonder. *He believes me*, she thinks, a sense of marvel rising within her.

'I did not know that He had chosen me to assist you,' she continues. 'That *you* had been chosen too. But now I see everything falling into place. His plan for all of us.'

'Yes,' says Edward, breathing deeply. '*Yes!*' He studies her for a moment. 'And before the wings? Where did you come from?'

'I was reborn when my wings came,' she says, thinking fast yet speaking slowly. 'Who or what I was before is of no bearing. I no longer recall any of it.'

When Edward is finished and Etta is returned to her cell, she waits until her captor's footsteps have faded into the distance and the dog next door has quietened again before whispering to her neighbour.

'I have spoken with him and watched him,' she says through the grate. 'And I believe our captor may not be entirely sane.'

'He only understands violence,' says Natalya and Etta shakes her head, although her fellow prisoner cannot see her.

'No, I don't think so. He is misguided, though – he thinks you are some sort of demon.'

Natalya laughs, a short chuckle that sets the dog off howling again. 'And what do you think?' she says.

'That you are a woman, like me, who has been given something you do not yet understand.'

Natalya remains silent for a moment. 'And you,' she says, after a while. 'What does he think of you?'

'That I am some sort of "gift" from God,' says Etta, thoughtfully. 'An "angel", but I feel we might play this to our advantage. I certainly do not wish to be a prisoner and I would hazard a guess that you feel the same. Given that you broke off your own wings.'

Natalya clenches her hands into fists as her anger silences her for a moment. The memory of dashing herself hard against the bricks, weeping as she did so, the sound of the bones cracking and splintering, the intense arrows of pain that shot through her, darkness falling as it overwhelmed her and she blacked out.

She inhales slowly. 'I did not want him to have them,' she says quietly. 'To have *me*.'

'Well then, let us try and thwart him further by getting out of here. I have no desire to be part of his collection either – dead or alive. Perhaps we may work together – if you are prepared to, that is?'

Natalya thinks for a moment. She does not know this other woman, but there is strength in her calmness and it garners Natalya's respect.

'Yes,' she replies. 'Of course. I will do anything that will get us out of here. *Anything.*'

And in the darkness, a flicker of hope glimmers within them. For the first time in days, and at precisely the same moment, their faces widen into genuine smiles.

Annie is beginning to feel short-tempered. She had agreed to see Samuel at St Peter's at his request, on a matter of utmost secrecy, and has been kept waiting outside his consultancy room for an intolerable amount of time. She has no desire to linger and is contemplating returning home in a fit of pique when the door opens and Samuel appears, all charm and smiles, to escort her in.

'This had better be good, Mr Covell,' she mutters. 'I feel *most* uncomfortable that you asked me here without my husband.'

'Mrs Meake – Annie – please. Sit down,' he says, all generosity and warmth as he guides her towards a large chair, which she perches on the edge of.

'Have you found out any more about Edward's state of mind?' asks Annie. 'Does he seem to you to not be his usual self?'

Samuel looks serious for a moment, thoughtful even. He sits down opposite her, ponders a while. 'You are quite right,' he says. 'He is *not* himself, I agree, but I'm afraid he will still not tell me anything. His lips are sealed.'

'I do hope you have not insisted I come all the way here just for *that* revelation, Mr Covell,' says Annie sharply.

'No,' says Samuel, drumming his fingers on the desk. 'But something has come to my attention and I thought it would be better to inform you of it first, discreetly.'

Annie brushes the front of her dress impatiently. 'Go on,' she says.

'In short, a senior role is set to come up – at the London Hospital.'

Annie looks at him, suspiciously. '*Which* role?'

'Head surgeon. Accompanied by the salary that one would expect for such a prestigious position.'

Neither of them say it out loud but both know full well that it is the job of a lifetime, the sort of role that comes up every few decades at most. It is, after all, one of the most esteemed positions in the entire country.

'Mr Covell, I don't understand. You are telling me instead of Edward because . . . because of what exactly?'

'Because, Annie, to put it plainly, I don't think he is well enough to go for it.'

'Ah. You mean *you* wish to apply for the position? To lobby the relevant persons for your own gain?'

'Annie! How little you think of me. I would gladly *share* the role with Edward, *that* is what I would propose *if* he was in his usual healthy mind. Believe me when I say I don't want a full-time role taking up all my efforts when I wish to pursue my own experiments. There are only so many hours in a day that a man can work, even one blessed with as much vigour as myself.'

'So, what *are* you suggesting?' asks Annie.

'I will speak to Edward about the role myself,' says Samuel. 'But I would be very grateful if you could tell me, discreetly, of his reaction after I have done so.'

Annie laughs. 'You wish for me to spy on my own husband?'

'Annie, come now. That is a little strong. A rather hysterical reaction, even by a woman's standards,' he says sharply as she purses her lips.

Annie stands to leave. 'I will see what his reaction is, but whether or not I report it back to you is something for my own conscience, Mr Covell.'

'Oh, Annie! Dearest Annie, come, do not be cross with me!' says Samuel, making no effort to get up. 'If Edward were a little less ruthless in his ambition, he could be genuinely great. But his hunger sometimes makes him appear pitiful. You know that as well as I! I am simply trying to help him, Annie, that is all.'

'Well then, perhaps he is no longer in need of your help,' she says, irritated. 'I shall show myself out, Mr Covell. Good day.'

She makes sure to slam the door behind her and Samuel laughs to himself as she does so. By God, he wishes he could have had her! That spark in her that is so often dimmed these days, it's good to know it is still there, hidden underneath.

Mary has emptied her pot of savings and is standing by her bed, readying herself for making a brave, some might say foolhardy, decision.

Earlier on, she and Charlie had gone to the Peacock Inn to track down the two remaining coach drivers. They'd had no joy with Mr Preston from the Bang-Up but had managed to catch the friendly Mr Mabbitt from the Aurora as he breakfasted. He had nodded as Charlie described their mystery woman.

'Yes, she came down to London yesterday,' he'd said. 'Friend o' yours is she? She didn't look the least bit well, I'm afraid. Travelling with two others. Hold on a bit . . .' He'd fished into a waistcoat pocket and pulled out a small pad which he methodically flicked through.

'Yes, that's it. A Mr and Mrs Marshall and your friend is down as a Miss Marshall. That her, is it? Funny thing though, there was another seat they took for a further Marshall, but a no-show on that one and they weren't keen on any others sharing with them, I can tell you that much. Caused a bit of a ruckus with a free seat inside and out of the cold. I hear, too' – he leant in, confidentially – 'they made a bit of a racket as they left yesterday as well. Less than two hours in London and straight back to Ludlow minus your friend. Can't be understanding some folks.'

'And you're sure they all got on together at Ludlow?' Mary had asked.

'Oh yes, miss, very sure. A Mabbitt sees everything,' he said with a wink. 'And they bundled your poor friend in very fast, I can tell you.'

'And are you driving back today, Mr Mabbitt?'

'No, miss, not 'til tomorrow. My daughter lives near and I've just become a grandfather for the third time. I'm on my way there now after finishing this lot.'

'Oh, congratulations! And would you mind me asking, when does the Aurora leave today?'

'Just under an hour and a half, miss. Regular as clockwork.'

Under two hours! Mary had thought. But that gives me no time at all. Dispatching Charlie with an urgent note for Richard, she had dashed home to pack an overnight bag.

She has just enough money to pay for a return journey and a bed for the night. It is all her savings. It is *everything*. Mary is grateful, for once, that Uncle Jos is away at one of his meetings at the Guinea Club, leaving her far from any influence he might try to exert over her.

'It is always an adventure with you,' Richard had said to her. Come then, she thinks. Let this be a new adventure. Do not dwell on what Uncle Jos would say if he were here. Think of what Uncle George would say – *he* would tell me to be bold, to be *courageous*!

As Charlie wings his way as fast as he can towards the offices of the *New Weekly*, Mary weighs up the situation. She is stepping into the unknown. She has never done anything as daring as this, never travelled as far away from home and, if nothing else, would like Richard's company at the least. She knows, though, that it cannot be guaranteed for she is unsure of his whereabouts and is doubtful her note will reach him in time. The thought of a long coach journey on her own is intimidating enough, let alone finding accommodation upon her arrival or making enquiries in an unfamiliar town. But she now has less than an hour until the coach leaves and she must make a decision straightaway.

It is a chance, she thinks, taking a deep breath, talking herself into it, a genuine chance to find out the identity of this woman that Mr Meake collected from the Peacock Inn. A chance to find out if she may indeed be what Mary thinks, *hopes*, she might be – impossible, glorious, a miracle. It is the only way to put her mind at rest. Time is slipping through her hands and she has but a handful of days left in which to show Jos that there is some basis to this story or to drop it completely. She must find out who this woman is, she *must*, and the only way she can do that is to retrace her footsteps, find out what happened, and build a case against Meake with facts. Find the evidence that Richard and Uncle Jos instructed her to. Build the jigsaw puzzle. She thinks of Miss Wiltshire's words: 'Knowledge the wing wherewith we fly to heaven.'

It is all my money, she thinks ruefully, looking at the small pile of coins in front of her. She puts her hand on them, feels the cool metal underneath. Yet, if it helps her get to the bottom of what is truly happening, what Mr Meake is doing, if it stops him from hurting anyone else, then surely it is worth every penny?

A scrap of brown paper sticks out from underneath the bed and she pushes it back with her boot before a thought strikes her. She picks up the paper, pulls it out and, with it, the clothes wrapped inside. They are the ones Lou gave her – the man's jacket and trousers complete with the accoutrements that Lou had been wearing when Mary had interrupted her at the penny gaff: the moustache, sideburns and a most excellent hat.

It is not proper for a single young lady to be gallivanting around the country in search of a story, thinks Mary, a sense of excitement rising within her. But for a *single young man*, well, surely that would be a most dandy adventure for a budding journalist?

She scribbles a note to her uncle. Decision made, she hastily starts to undress before she can change her mind.

Etta is deeply unhappy. The far corner of her small brick cell is beginning to seep with a most unpleasant-smelling liquid. It must be the rain, she thinks. She has heard of this in the big cities, of basements being full of effluent until the night-soil men carry it away and, worse still, of cellars lived in by people where the leaching of sewerage oozes directly through the walls.

She stands on her thin mattress as far away from the reeking corner as she can. 'Hallo?' she whispers and the dog barks, waking up her neighbour.

'Hallo?' Etta tries again and this time there is a groggy murmur of assent.

'Something is beginning to come through the walls in here,' says Etta. 'Some sort of noxious liquid. Is there any in yours?' She hears the strike of a match, sees a glimmer of light through the grill.

'No, the walls are damp but no worse than was already here.'

'I shall request that our captor put me in with you,' Etta says.

'You can ask him to put us in an inn, with soft pillows

and clean sheets, food that isn't bread, and wine instead of beer,' says Natalya sharply.

Etta smiles to herself.

Natalya softens. 'It'll be a tight fit if we are both to be in here, there is barely enough room to swing a cat. Or a dog, come to that.'

'We will be safer if we share the space,' says Etta.

'Safer?'

'He is a fanatic and I think we cannot be too wary of him. It would be safer to be together. However, I've been thinking. Why not encourage our gaoler a little further along in his beliefs? He already thinks that I am a gift from above.'

'And me?'

'He has already used the word "demon" to describe you,' says Etta, wryly.

Perhaps, Natalya thinks, this is worth a try. She laughs. 'Then I shall play my part,' she says. 'And I shall play it devilishly well.'

'Then I believe,' says Etta, 'we can push him right to the edge, tip him over and make good our escape.'

'To where?' asks Natalya.

'Anywhere,' says Etta, feelingly. 'For the love of all that is good in the world, anywhere but here.'

Richard makes it to the Peacock breathless and with a mere ten minutes to spare before the Aurora leaves. He has taken the liberty of sending a note to Jos saying he will accompany Mary but there is no sign of her anywhere and he has no idea what to do next. He strides up and down by the coach, looking both ways along the busy road with an air of panic until someone taps him on the shoulder from above with a walking stick.

'Young gent wants a word, sir!' says a bewhiskered old gentleman from the roof of the Aurora. Next to him, a young man with a terrible moustache is nodding his head in acknowledgement. He looks strangely familiar but Richard cannot place him.

'Mr Gibbs!' says the youth. 'Mr Gibbs, the journalist, it *is* you isn't it?'

But that is Mary's voice, he thinks. A voice he would know anywhere. He is struck dumb, his brain rendered temporarily useless as he gawps at the young man.

'If you are to catch the Aurora, then I'm afraid you must make haste,' the young man says, a twinkle in his eye.

Realisation dawns slowly on Richard. But this *is* Mary,

Mary dressed as a man, with facial hair. It is *impossible* that this youth is Mary and yet . . .

He bursts out laughing. 'Ah, *Mr Ward*!' he says, pointedly. 'Forgive me, I did not recognise you with your moustache.'

'It's a new look that I am trying,' says Mary, stroking the moustache as she does so, and Richard snorts.

'It makes you look older than your years,' he says drily.

'I shall take that as a compliment,' says Mary. 'For I am surely fortunate to be able to grow such a luxuriant moustache at my tender age, am I not?'

'You getting on?' asks the coachman and Richard nods.

'Are you going all the way to Ludlow too, Mr Gibbs?' asks Mary.

'I believe I am.'

'How fortuitous!' says Mary. 'For so am I. What a pleasant surprise!'

'Yes,' says Richard. 'Today has been rather full of them.'

'Here,' says the old gent, moving seats as Richard clambers up to take his place on the roof, 'it's clear the two of you are acquainted and I'm only going so far as Oxford, so I'll shift over in order that you can converse more easily.'

'Better hold on tight, Mr Gibbs,' exclaims Mary, eyes glittering, as Richard takes the space next to her just in time for the coach to lurch off, 'these coaches can be rather an adventure!'

It is only after Oxford that indoor seats finally become available. Richard and Mary relocate inside as the coach's lamps are lit, taking refuge from the increasingly chill wind. Alas, there are two other travellers going as far as Worcester who are already sitting within and it is not until they alight that Richard and Mary are able to talk freely. By that late point, however, Mary has already fallen asleep, head on Richard's shoulder as the coach rattles forward.

How she is able to sleep in this I don't know, thinks Richard with envy, feeling queasy at the carriage's constant lurching. The window next to him is fully open, giving a much welcome breath of cold air as he looks out at the darkness surrounding them. There is a distinct whiff of autumn, mouldering leaves beginning to rot down, joining the smell of damp hay scattered on the floor of the coach. The whole of the land is dozing off to sleep, Richard thinks. Winter is beginning to show its hand.

They clatter through the countryside and he knows it would be sensible for him to at least try and get some sleep but he cannot. Not with the rattling coach making so much noise. Not with her next to him. He looks down at her, eyes tightly shut, smile on her lips as she dreams of who knows what. He studies her for a moment, her cheeks, her eyelashes, her ridiculous false moustache. It has been a most unexpected day, but then is it not often so in her company? He resists the temptation to put an arm around her.

It is the first night that they will ever spend together.

Edward sits alone in his study, writing up his notes from earlier in the day. His new angel is endlessly surprising to him, as commanding as she is beautiful. He cannot take his eyes off her when he is in her presence, cannot stop thinking about her, and yet he still remains a little unsure of her.

When he helped her remove her clothes, he became suddenly self-conscious, aware of her warm breath, pulse beating silently in the smooth skin of her neck, the tight black curls of her hair . . . He had not felt that burn of desire since he fell in love with Annie. A wave of shame and guilt chills him as he recoils from his own thoughts. This is surely another test from God. He prays for forgiveness – from Annie, too – as he focuses his mind.

His new angel shines brightly, so very different to the other creature, brimful of anger, but there is a coolness to her too, a quiet resilience that the other did not display. He felt at one point a faint sense that perhaps she was mocking him but no, that cannot be. She is on His side, he reassures himself. He runs his hands through his hair as he goes back over his notes, editing and rewriting as he goes, exhausting himself further.

I can do this, I am worthy of this task, he says, trying to calm his nerves. He rubs his tired eyes, rolls his head to try and ease the stiffness in his neck. The enormity of it all! Part of him feels overwhelmed, wants to run upstairs, throw himself into Annie's arms, tell her everything; bury himself under the bedclothes and forget any of this has happened. But he cannot; he must face up to his duties. He must hold fast, put all things in order. These are his gifts from God and he must be grateful for them.

A huge bouquet of flowers has arrived and Annie is bemused. As an artist, she is well versed in the language of flowers and this bouquet is most confusing to her. There is delphinium for flights of fancy, maidenhair fern for discretion, ranunculus for radiance and charm, tea rose for remembrance and, most surprisingly, a single white rose for a new beginning, for everlasting love. It is a pretty thing to be sure, she thinks as she examines it, but it doesn't make sense. It would have cost a small fortune, too, given how much of the contents must have been grown in a hothouse at this time of year and she knows full well that Edward thinks flowers are a folly, a temporary indulgence and no more.

If not from Edward, then from whom? Not Marcus, she knows that much, he would never dare send something as overt as this, not now she is a married woman. *Ah, of course!* The answer forms itself in her head as she looks over the beautiful blooms – *this is Samuel Covell's work.* There is no note with the bouquet and indeed no need for one.

Annie is furious with him. A white rose. This is a step

too far. She will have stern words with him when their paths next cross.

She takes the flowers – with some difficulty as they are bulky in number – down to the kitchen, intending to ask Sarah to dispose of them as she sees fit, but Mrs McGilliveray distracts her with talk of menus and suppers and so the flowers are left to one side in the servants' hall. It is only much later, when Annie is readying herself for dinner, that Sarah mistakenly takes them back upstairs, displaying them in the entrance hallway on the sideboard next to the glass dome in which the clay Edward and Annie sit, smiling out upon the world without a care.

Edward is extremely concerned by the sodden and stinking corner of his new angel's small cell. London's damned medieval sewers, he thinks angrily. All things are bursting at the seams in this cursed city.

Etta watches him as he assesses the situation. 'How long do you plan to keep us down here?' she asks.

'It is a temporary measure,' he says. 'I am finalising my plans to reveal all to the world and so . . .'

'Your plans must surely be hastened with your own house crumbling around you,' she says, motioning to the walls.

'It is not crumbling!' he snaps. 'It is unfortunate timing, that is all.'

'I will share with the creature you call the demon,' she says. 'It is, after all, a temporary measure, as you say, and perhaps my presence will calm her.'

Edward looks at her, that faint sense of her mocking him rising again, but her face is expressionless and, besides, he has little choice. The other rooms in the basement – his study and dissecting room – only have locks on the inside and he has no desire to put her in either of them. They contain the sum of his life's work and, if she turned on him, as the demon had, she could destroy it all. He does not believe she would do such a thing, but still, an element of doubt remains.

'Let us go to your experiment room,' she says, 'so you may tell me of your plans.'

Edward eyes her curiously. 'Why would I do that?' he says.

'Because God wills you to. He has put His trust in you, has He not? And so you must put your trust in Him. He wishes me to hear of all your plans, for am I not sent by the Almighty Himself?'

She waits, head on one side, watching him. 'I will think upon it,' Edward says. He unlocks the door to his wingless angel, motioning Etta inside.

'You may go in,' he says. 'The dog will return to your cell.'

'The dog will stay,' says Etta.

'No,' says Edward and he gently pushes her in, grabbing the dog's collar as it angrily races towards him. He slams the door shut behind her, a gust of air extinguishing the candle within.

Etta stands in the darkness as the barking dog is locked up next door. She has well and truly sown the seed now. Let us see what mettle is in the man, she thinks, as Edward's footsteps pad away and the dog stops barking.

She knows the other woman is in here, can feel her breath, her presence. The dog truly does reek, she thinks to herself, but the other woman has cleaned as best she can with the wet rags that their captor brought down earlier and at least there will be no more of the dog's passings to sully the atmosphere.

'Hallo,' says Etta in the quiet dark. 'My name is Etta.'

'Hullo,' says the other woman in her soft voice. She moves closer, her breath warming Etta's face before she tightly embraces her, tears already beginning to run down her cheeks.

'I am Natalya.'

'I am glad *one* of us slept at least,' says Richard drily as Mary yawns herself awake on the last leg of the journey from Tenbury to Ludlow. They have been travelling in the cramped coach for the best part of an entire day and still have further to go before they reach their destination. There have been stops to light the lamps, stops for fresh horses, stops for sheep and cattle across the road, stops for mail delivery, stops for fords, stops for steep hills, stops for food and drink. It feels as if, Richard thinks wryly, there have been more stops than starts.

'Are we *still* not there?' asks Mary as she stretches, looking out of the Aurora's small windows to the rising peak of Titterstone Clee on the eastern horizon.

'Alas no,' says Richard. 'And you must look to your dreadful moustache. I fear the gum is weakening on the right-hand side.'

Mary licks a finger and lifts a corner of the moustache, wetting it underneath before firming it back down. 'And now?' she says, turning to him, and he responds with a snort.

'I wonder if you really are quite sane sometimes, Miss Ward,' he says warmly.

'And I you, Mr Gibbs,' she says, smiling back at him. 'After all *you* agreed to come with me. But if, perhaps, you could call me *Mr* Ward for now, that would be most agreeable.'

'Of course.' He nods. 'I had forgot, forgive me, *Mr Ward*. And so, dare I ask, what exactly your plan is when we arrive? I presume you had one before setting off on such a monstrously long journey or that at least your enviably deep bouts of sleep have given you inspiration.'

'Well, first, we must find out more about the Marshalls,' she says, thinking out loud as she stretches out the stiffness in her arms and legs in the narrow carriage. 'Who they are, where they live; and through that we will surely be able to trace our woman too, find out who she is and where she is from. I must build my case as you and Uncle Jos have instructed me to.'

'And how much money do you have for all this, O apprentice journalist?' he asks and she blushes at his frankness. Outside, the coach driver blows his horn loudly on the approach to Ludlow, alerting the town to the Aurora's imminent arrival.

'I have enough,' Mary says, quietly. 'The coach ticket was not quite as dear as I had expected.'

'We must also secure ourselves accommodation,' Richard says. 'We will not find out everything in a few hours.'

Despite the fact that they have already just spent a night together in the coach, the thought of them spending a night in an inn makes Mary's cheeks redden again. She had half forgot the journey would be almost a full day in length.

'I have a little money for that too,' she says, looking out of the window. 'That is not why I asked you to accompany me, Richard.'

'Oh, Mary – *Mr* Ward – that is not what I meant, only . . .'

'Besides,' she says, after a considerable awkward pause. 'I am over halfway through that review of yours and I shall get paid after that.' She turns and smiles at him and he smiles back, all tension between them gone in a moment. 'So there, Mr Gibbs.'

Both of them peer out of the Aurora's small windows, drinking in the scenery of the picturesque little town as they approach, clattering past the Charlton Arms and over the rushing river Teme at Ludford Bridge before proceeding up the hill into Ludlow proper, through the narrow medieval arch of Broad Gate and into Broad Street with its grand and imposing mansions.

As the Aurora slows to its final stop outside the Angel Inn, just before the Buttercross at the crest of the hill, Richard grins to himself and holds a hand out to Mary.

'Ah, *Mr* Ward, I do believe we have arrived.'

Etta and Natalya sit facing each other on the old mattress, light from the last remaining stub of a candle flickering upon them, their shadows playing against the wall. It is not much to illuminate the small space but it is enough.

'You did not react when you saw me,' says Etta. 'Through the grate, I mean.'

Natalya smiles at her. 'You weren't the first with wings I'd seen.'

'No,' says Etta. 'I mean *me*, I am—' She breaks off.

'Ah!' says Natalya, understanding. 'I'm from an island, people and boats from all over the world pass through our seas and ports.'

'Where are you from?' asks Etta. 'Which island?'

'Far north from here. Orkney. An island called Sanday.' She stops for a moment, the name sticking in her throat. 'It's as sandy as the name suggests. On a low tide, it grows in size and the beaches stretch right out to the horizon. It's a place of sea and sky, of wild weather too. It can rain and hail and burn your skin with sun and wind all in but a few hours. We say you can have all four seasons in a single day. There are other islands too, a whole archipelago of seafarers and explorers, fishermen and farmers, but Sanday is where I was born.'

'It sounds beautiful,' says Etta.

'Oh, it is! My favourite beach, at the Bay of Stove, is full of tiny shells of all different colours, pinks and purples, greys and blues. And it's noisy too – the eiders and terns, dunters and pickieternos we call them, oystercatchers and kittiwakes, selkies calling to each other in the shallows . . .' She swallows, her heart suddenly longing for those northern skies, for the freedom she no longer has.

'I'm sorry,' says Etta, reaching out a hand.

'And you?' says Natalya when she recovers herself. 'Where do you hail from?'

'By birth, from Jamaica, in the West Indies, but I have lived in the south of Shropshire, or Salop as some call it, since I was tiny, after my mother died. I fear no one will miss me from there though. My old friend Dorothy is already half-lost to another world. My maid Betsy, perhaps.'

'A maid? You are wealthy then? Your dress suggested as much.'

Etta grimaces, looks at the floor. 'In some ways, yes, and in others . . . My father was wealthy but, when he died, my half-brother inherited all. I have some freedom and a little money but I am left on the shelf and Walter – my half-brother, that is – he resents my very existence, he always has done.'

'Families are not easy,' says Natalya. 'Being linked by blood does not mean you are linked in other ways. Will none come looking for you, none wish to find you?'

'Walter will be glad I'm gone, that's the truth of it,' Etta says. 'And as for any others, well, I live a rather solitary life I'm afraid. It is something that chose me as much as I chose it. I'm a botanist, you see. I've devoted many years to the study of plants and my old friend, Mr Lawley, always used to say that companions were a distraction from the work in hand. I'm not sure that's entirely true, but there's certainly more than a grain of truth in it.' She thinks for a moment. 'Is Natalya a name from the islands? It seems to me something from further east.'

'Ah, I was named after my Russian grandmother. She used to tell us stories of her homeland, a land of ice and snow and white nights in the summer when the sun never set, full of wolves and palaces. It always seemed to me so far away. But she is where I get my stories from. I inherited both that and her name.'

'You tell stories then?'

'When there are people to listen to them. The islands are full of storytellers. The winter nights are dark and long – stories are a way of passing the time. And, if we are lucky, we catch a glimpse of the Merry Dancers.'

'The aurora borealis!' says Etta, with glee.

'You've heard of it?'

'Of course! What does it really look like? Does it move as much as they say?'

'Oh, it's like nothing else. Greens and violets shimmering across the sky. Wisps of smoke and dust, as though the Milky Way is alive and has ventured closer to look at us looking back up at it.'

'You speak of it with such love,' says Etta softly. 'Then how came you to London? Did our captor bring you here?'

'No. My cousin was here and I came looking for him, but he was long gone when I arrived, already dead and buried. Then the wings came . . .' Natalya stops. She is not ready to share the rest of her story, not yet.

'It's all right,' says Etta softly. 'You do not have to tell me.'

'But why us?' says Natalya suddenly. 'We are from different worlds, are we not? I'm a fisherman's daughter from the far north, you're an educated lady, a gentlewoman from inland. We are not the same age, the same colour in hair or eyes or skin, not the same height nor size. All that joins us together is our being women, is it not? So why us?'

'I don't know,' says Etta, thoughtfully. 'Truly. But I'm glad I'm not alone. That *we* are not alone – that we have each other even in these circumstances. And I am sorry for the other woman. The third with wings, the one found drowned in the Thames. I should very much like to have had this conversation with her too. I fear though, that this' – she motions to her own wings – 'was perhaps too much for her. And now we shall never know.'

They sit quietly for a moment before Natalya finds her voice again. 'What's it like where you are from?' she asks. 'In Salop.'

Etta smiles. 'Oh, it's a landlocked county, I think as far from the sea as is possible in all of England. The south is full of rolling hills and hedgerows, fields and forts. It's not wild, it's farmland and forest, mines and quarries, a scattering of towns and hamlets but it *feels* wild, somehow. There's a gorge not far away, steep in places where the river cuts through it, and high peaks with views towards mountains in the west and flat plains to the east.' She thinks for a moment. 'It's a place I can *breathe* in. I hadn't realised that 'til I was brought to London once as a child and felt suffocated, hemmed in by noise and people.'

'It sounds as if you feel it is part of you, somehow,' says Natalya, wondering.

'It is. It's all my world. My hills, my forests, my holloways – I think of them as mine, clambering up the peaks to see the world like a kite or kestrel might.'

'But that's how I feel! About Sanday! As if it flows through my veins – the sea, the fierce winds, all of it. Perhaps *that* is why we grew the wings? Because we are already wild inside?'

The candle burns itself out, suddenly plunging the cell back into darkness and the women into silence for a moment.

'I had, I suppose, some sort of vision before I changed,' Natalya says. 'Where time turned backwards before my eyes. Did you witness anything similar?'

Etta shakes her head. 'No. Nothing like that. I lost my companion, my dog, Scout. I loved him with all my heart but I cannot see that grief would have made me change in such a way – can you?'

An idea suddenly strikes Natalya, a question she would not have been bold enough to ask in the light. 'Are you, forgive my frankness, Etta, are you a mother by any chance?'

'Oh no,' says Etta. 'I am very much unmarried.'

'Ah,' says Natalya, sadly. 'As am I.' There is such deep sorrow in her voice that it marks the end of their conversation, for now at least.

In Ludlow, Mary and Richard have found out two things – firstly, that there are at least three Marshall families in and around town and, secondly, that there is barely any accommodation available. The first of the season's horse races starts the next day and the town's accommodation appears to be almost entirely taken up by rambunctious gamblers.

'We have but one room left,' says the cheerful woman who runs the Angel. ''Tis a big room, though, easy big enough for two and you are both but thin gentlemen.'

Richard looks at Mary. *We cannot share a room!* he thinks with both horror and excitement, it is most inappropriate. Yet they must find accommodation somewhere, for there are no coaches back until tomorrow and they have not yet spoken to any of the Marshall families.

'Take it or leave it, 'tis likely the last room in the whole of town, so . . .' the woman says with a shrug, drumming the tips of her fingers on the bar.

'Why then we shall take it, madam!' says Mary, much to Richard's surprise and they are soon led up a wide staircase to the second floor where the woman shows them a spacious room with a large window overlooking the street below.

'Make yourself comfortable, gents,' she says, shutting the door on them.

'This is *most* irregular, Mary,' says Richard, running his fingers through his hair, making it look even more unruly.

'Ah well!' says Mary. 'It's all they had. What were we supposed to do, sleep on the streets? It's a fine room anyway, finer than anything one could get in London for twice the price,' she says. She moves to the window and looks out, heart thumping at the thought of sharing a room with Richard.

'You must take the bed, of course,' says Richard, awkwardly, feeling flustered. 'I shall sleep in the armchair.'

'I sleep top to toe with Charlie,' says Mary. She continues to look out of the window as if she is distracted, allowing herself a grin as she bites her lower lip.

Richard looks at her back and is not sure whether she is, dare he hope, flirting with him or simply being naive.

'I fear we are both far too old for that,' he says, sternly. 'Come, let us leave our bags here and we can get our bearings now that we have secured a room.'

She turns to him, her face falling, yet she looks so funny with her dreadful moustache and sideburns and whatever she has done to her hair to make it look short that Richard cannot stop himself from laughing.

'Oh, Miss Ward,' he says, softening. 'Sorry, *Mr* Ward. What on earth will I do with you? Come, let us go and track down these Marshalls. After all, that is what we came for.' I will deal with the room situation later, he thinks, torn between exhilaration and fear. This could ruin both of them if anyone finds out.

★   ★   ★

As they head through town, making the most of the last hour of daylight, they pass by the magnificent St Laurence's, a cathedral in all but name, before walking past the building site of the new Assembly Rooms by the castle ruins. Mary tries to perfect her youthful swagger but it is very much a work in progress, thinks Richard with a grin. She didn't bring any of her three dresses in Jos's borrowed overnight bag and so she must keep up the pretence of being a gentleman the entire time they are away. Besides, he can hardly, hand on heart, tell her off for being impetuous, for taking risks – for surely this is one of the reasons he has fallen so in love with her.

Near the castle, on the narrow road called Dinham, Richard and Mary find the first Marshall family, ascertaining within minutes that they are not the same Marshalls who had so recently gone to London. There is one other family in town of the same name and Richard and Mary take a shortcut along the river before the last of the year's gnats become too bothersome. Ludlow is a surprisingly hilly town and autumnal landscapes – fields and hills and forests, roll away in all directions like folds in a dress. Greens and browns, velvets and silks, hedgerows like seams holding the whole countryside together.

'It's very beautiful here,' sighs Mary, and Richard nods.

'Quiet, though,' he says. 'Not like London.'

'Is this what Edinburgh is like?' she asks, eyes shining, and he laughs.

'Lord, no. Edinburgh is more like London. It is far bigger than this and some parts are – would you credit it, *Mr Ward*? – even hillier,' he says with a smile.

They walk in companionable silence for a moment as they pass Old Street Mill, before turning into Temeside where the second Marshall family are to be found. There they discover these Marshalls too have not travelled to London and, in fact, have no desire to ever visit the capital when, as they see it, they have all that they would ever need on their doorstep.

'That leaves us only the Marshalls near Onibury then,' says Richard, as he and Mary head back towards the Angel, the sun dipping down behind the roofs of the buildings, casting them into shadow. 'It's six or so miles from here and we will not make it by foot before the light goes. We must beg a ride, but I fear we will have to save that for the morrow.'

'Some of the other coaches are running early tomorrow too,' says Mary.

Richard nods. 'And we may also pick up gossip at the bar tonight — it's often a fine place to find stories when men's tongues are loosened by liquor.'

'Do you know,' whispers Mary, 'men's clothes are an awful lot more comfortable than women's? It is most freeing not to have to wear a corset *and* they are a damn sight less heavy than mine too. Lou said I might find it rather thrilling and she was right.'

'Ah, well,' Richard whispers back. 'I do hope you will not dress like that *all* the time from now on.'

'Not *all* the time,' says Mary with a grin, 'just, perhaps, *some* of the time . . . Anyway, come, I am ravenous, let us go and find something good to eat, Mr Gibbs, something good but something cheap to accommodate my most exacting budget.'

Annie is most disconcerted to find that Edward has invited Samuel for dinner. She had hoped the issue of the bouquet could be quietly resolved between the two of them at a later date but it is not to be. It also means putting out Mrs McGilliveray, who will be expected to produce a dinner suitable for a guest with almost no notice.

'I shall simply pour him some wine and all will be well!' says Edward. 'Don't fuss, Annie! He has what he calls an interesting proposition and I am eager to hear it.'

They will eat late tonight, late even by London standards, although it will end up being later still as Mrs McGilliveray fumes her way around the kitchen, clattering the pans and making as much noise as she can to show her displeasure.

Annie helps in the kitchen as much as she dare without further risking Mrs McGilliveray's ire, giving Samuel and Edward time to talk privately. Besides, she is still irked with Samuel – both by his request of her and the flowers he sent, blooms that carried with them all sorts of inappropriate and mixed messages along with their perfume. Annie is so busy bustling in the kitchen and then dressing for dinner that she doesn't see that Samuel's flowers have, in error, not only not been destroyed but are now displayed in the hallway near the front door.

Samuel and Edward are deep in conversation about the London Hospital vacancy when Annie finally appears in the dining room to join them.

'The most extraordinary role has come up!' says Edward, already buoyed up by wine as Annie takes her seat at the table. 'At the London Hospital of all places!'

Annie smiles and nods at him to continue, hoping her face does not give away the fact that she is already well aware of this.

'Samuel has proposed sharing the duties so we might both pursue other matters, but I've already said no to his kind offer.'

'Oh?' ventures Annie.

'I'm far too busy with my own project to take up even a part-time role elsewhere.'

This is not right, thinks Annie with concern. *He is not himself.*

'Edward, is this not the very role you have dreamt of, husband dear? Would this not be the ideal opportunity, the culmination of all your hard work over so many years?'

'The timing is off and I have other, more pressing, matters to attend to.'

'Ah, that is what I thought you might say, didn't I, Annie?' Samuel grins.

Edward looks at Annie as she glares at Samuel.

'You have spoken of this already?' he says, trying to hide his bemusement with a half-smile.

'Oh, she has not mentioned it then?' says Samuel, all

innocence. 'We saw each other yesterday and I told her then I was going to tell you of it.'

'No,' says Edward thoughtfully, staring at Annie. 'No. She didn't mention it.'

'No matter!' says Samuel. 'All is well! We shall wait, O Great Meake, for your reveal of this grand project that is consuming all your energies and, in the meantime, well, I hope you will permit *me* to apply for the London Hospital role.'

'With my blessing!' says Edward. 'Of course.'

'But, Edward—' Annie starts but she is silenced by a frown from her husband.

'A toast!' says Samuel. 'To the great Mr Meake!'

Annie finds it hard to stomach eating much and makes her excuses as early as possible leaving just the two old friends together, along with a large quantity of wine that they do their best to consume in its entirety.

It is only much later in the evening, when Edward is about to dispatch his equally inebriated guest home, when Samuel's tongue, loosened by wine, reveals that which it should not.

'I am so glad to see you in such good spirits,' slurs Samuel. 'It is excellent to see you cheered by whatever good fortune you've got tucked away downstairs. And I'm sorry, too,' he says and pats Edward on the arm with drunken affection.

'Sorry for what?' asks Edward, trying not to hiccup.

'You know,' Samuel motions towards Edward, the house behind him, 'no children . . .'

'Oh?' says Edward, confused, for he has never discussed this with Samuel before.

'You know she came to see me about it?'

'Who?'

'*Annie!*' Samuel whispers it at him, but his voice is too loud and her name echoes around the hallway. Edward cannot speak. He feels both suddenly sober and on the verge of vomiting, an unpleasant churn filling his stomach.

'But shh . . .' Samuel puts his fingers to his lips and winks. 'Patient confidentiality and all that.'

Edward feels breathless, his head filled with images of Samuel examining his wife, of her skirts pushed up. An ache throbs loudly inside his temples.

'She is *very* lovely,' says Samuel. 'I do hope you know that.'

It is the worst thing he could possibly say, fuelling the pictures that tumble over in Edward's head.

'You know you are my dearest friend,' Samuel slurs, as he attempts a drunken embrace with Edward before opening the front door and half-sliding, half-falling down the stairs. He heads off, waving behind him without a backward glance, weaving off down the street to find a cab to take him home.

It is only then that Edward notices, for the first time, the display of flowers in the hallway. His knowledge of flowers and what they represent is not as sharp as his wife's but he only needs know one flower for his envy and para- noia to start rising. For someone has sent Annie *a white rose* – the flower of everlasting love. Someone has *dared* send his wife a white rose.

He is so furious, so confused, so muddled in his thinking that in his drunken haze he cannot even bear to think of his wife's face, let alone confront her. He throws the flowers to the floor, stamping his anger out on them before kicking them to one side for Sarah to deal with in the morning.

Annie, with no knowledge of this latest outburst from Samuel, this unforgivable breach of confidence, waits for Edward in bed, hoping for a chance to explain what happened, why she visited his friend without his knowledge. She waits to explain her love, her loyalty, but alas, there is no opportunity for her to do so for Edward, sense of betrayal still rising, stumbles alone to the guest room to fitfully sleep away what remains of the night.

The curtains have been pulled, the door locked shut and Richard and Mary are alone in their large bedroom on the second floor of the Angel Inn where they must now negotiate the tricky situation of getting ready for bed.

'I shall wait outside,' says Richard awkwardly. 'Perhaps that is best.'

'Or you could simply turn your back?' says Mary, emboldened by the generous glass of port wine she had consumed at the bar earlier. 'That would be easier. Besides, there is no warmth in the corridor and the fire in here is still going, for now at least. There is no point in either of us catching a chill.'

Richard averts his glance. He does not, in truth, know where to look, and it takes all his willpower not to turn around. Mary hums as she undresses and he hears her clothes sliding off, buttons being undone, fabric moving across bare skin. He watches her reflection, guiltily, in the brass candlestick on the hearth before forcing his eyes shut.

'I am done,' says Mary as she slips into bed and he opens his eyes and turns around. Her moustache and sideburns are gone, her hair is loose on the pillow where she has unpinned it, and his heart is lost completely.

'I shall look the other way now,' Mary says, breaking the silence. He turns his back on her, suddenly self-conscious as he slowly undresses himself. Mary silently peeks, secretly watching him too, each item of clothing he removes peeling her own heart back, layer by layer.

So *this* is what he looks like underneath, she thinks. This delicious young man so familiar to her and yet so unknown. *He is so very beautiful*, she thinks, startled by the rush of heat that flows over her before she swiftly looks away.

'I am done,' Richard says, after a while, and Mary glances back at him, wild-haired in his thick white nightshirt. They stare wordlessly at each other for a moment, unblinking, before he looks away first.

'Ah, well,' he says with a sigh. 'It's a good job I came here after all. I dread to think what escapades you might have got into without someone to keep an eye on you.'

'Mmm,' says Mary, dry-mouthed all of a sudden, unable to speak for a moment.

'Jos said I was to be, er, an older brother to you, Mary and so I shall,' he says, with difficulty. 'So I am.'

'An older brother . . . ?' Mary murmurs, her heart deflating.

'May I take another blanket from the bed?' asks Richard. 'It is rather cold tonight.'

Mary nods and he slowly slides the blanket off the bottom of the bed, not taking his eyes from her.

'Goodnight, Mary,' he says, heart slowly breaking as he watches her pull the covers up high.

'Well, goodnight then, Mr Gibbs,' she says with an air of formality, rolling over onto her side – and with that, she blows out the candle.

Edward is still furious with Annie in the morning when he goes into the bedroom to change only to find her there, waiting for him. His head is sore, his heart too, and resentment teamed with the lingering alcohol in his system makes him short-tempered and rash.

'Edward, *please* give me a chance to explain what happened last night.'

'I should very much like to hear you try,' he says sarcastically as he stands by the window and looks out, his back to her where she sits on the edge of the bed.

'Samuel invited me to St Peter's the day before yesterday, on a matter of what he called urgency and secrecy. He told me about the vacancy at the London Hospital and asked me to relay to him, privately, whatever your reaction might be. To spy on you. I should have told you, and I'm sorry that I didn't, but I felt angry with him at having put me in a difficult position, angry that your own best friend would ask such a thing. That is all.'

'That is all, is it?'

'Yes! Of course it is!'

'Annie, you beggar belief sometimes. "That is all." Ha!

That is all, is it? And when were you planning to tell me about *the other matter*, eh?'

'What other matter?'

'*Your consultation with him!* With Samuel! About us, about our most private . . . ' Edward cannot bring himself to say it.

Annie fumes silently. 'He told you of that?'

'Of course he told me! The question is, why didn't you tell me yourself?'

'Oh, Edward, please! It was meant to be – I thought perhaps he could help. The one person we had not yet consulted. I thought—'

'No, Annie, you didn't think. You didn't *think* at all.'

'That is unfair, Edward!'

'Unfair! It is unfair for a man's wife to engage in secret meetings with another man, *that* is unfair! Why did you not tell me, Annie? Why keep it from me?'

Annie shakes her head. 'Why do you keep whatever it is that you're working on from me? Why do you not tell me of that?'

'Oh, so we are back to this again! I have already said a thousand times, I will tell you *everything*, Annie, but not yet. *Not. Yet.*'

They glower at each other, both furious, both feeling a sense of betrayal.

'I will say no more on the matter,' says Edward. 'Only that I am most displeased, with Samuel too, but *especially* with you. I would have expected more from my own wife.'

Annie is too upset and angry to respond but as Edward

goes to leave, he turns in the doorway a moment, a flicker of worry across his face.

'He did not . . . examine you, did he? Intimately, I mean.'

'Edward! No! Of course not!'

But her husband is already out of the room.

It is bright and early on Saturday morning and Mary and Richard stand outside a low, crumbling stone cottage six miles north of Ludlow, on the edge of the small hamlet called Onibury. They arrived moments earlier on a cart pulled by two ancient horses that seemed almost as old as the hill forts that scatter the landscape.

The Marshall family that Mary is hopeful will be found within do not seem to be particularly well liked in the local community. Richard had picked up at the bar last night both that the family kept away from Ludlow in the main, and that Mr Marshall was seen as somewhat of a bully.

'Come,' says Mary, nervous all of a sudden. 'Let us within.'

Richard holds her back, a look of concern upon his face. 'I'll go first,' he says, stepping forward to rap on the dilapidated wooden door.

'Hallo,' he says, loudly. 'Hallo! Is anyone in?'

He pushes at the door gently and it slowly creaks open as he steps into the shadows. He shivers for a moment, for there is no fire, no candle and no warmth inside and his eyes take a while to adjust to the dark, to notice the two large mounds on the floor, like sleeping dogs.

Richard moves towards them, waving his hand to bat away the flies that buzz around him before he realises what they are.

Bodies.

Two of them. Eyes staring but seeing nothing. A bolt in the chest of each.

Murder.

Richard swallows, bile rising, and turns to usher Mary out of the room but she is not behind him. Panicking, he stumbles back out of the cottage into the October sunshine only to find that she is not there either.

'Mary!' he shouts, fear making his voice tremble and his legs weak. '*Mary!*'

He looks around quickly, peers through the trees to see the outline of another building a little further away and he runs to it, runs as fast as he can.

An old barn and in much need of repair, the door is already open as he hurtles inside only to find Mary there, unharmed, standing stock-still, staring up at the ceiling. She turns to him, her face wet with tears, and it is only then that he realises what she was looking at. The shape in the darkness. A young man with a rope around his neck, gently swinging from a beam.

At breakfast, Edward announces, somewhat brusquely, that early next week he will host a dinner at home for the Society for the Promotion and Advancement of Knowledge followed, the same evening, by a presentation at the Royal Society. He tells Annie that he is to visit the Royal Society at Somerset House that very morning to confirm the date.

'And will I be allowed to see or know any more beforehand?' Annie asks, hopefully, trying to support him with her enthusiasm, but he shakes his head.

'Of course not!' he says sharply. 'Besides, you might only tell Samuel of it.'

Annie is so incensed that she leaves the breakfast table early. Another excitement for Sarah to report back to Mrs McGilliveray, she thinks, as she pulls the dining room door closed behind her with a bang.

Both Edward's reputation and his recent election to the Society for the Promotion and Advancement of Knowledge stand him in good stead when he arrives at Somerset House to discuss his plans. A senior figure at the Royal Society, one Professor James Bartley-Stewart, white-whiskered and with a particularly fine wart on his chin, listens to Edward's heartfelt pleas with interest, but his response is not what Edward had been expecting.

'Alas, Mr Meake, it is not *possible* to give you a slot in our lecture theatre,' says the professor, pulling at his whiskers as he speaks. 'After all, you are not currently a *member* of the Royal Society and our autumn lecture season is already an extremely busy one. It is a most irregular request and even more so at such short notice. I must say I am intrigued by what little you have told me, but wherever you do decide to hold your lecture, I would *very* strongly recommend that you allow a longer gap between the lecture itself and notification of the same. I fear holding a lecture within the same week of an invitation being sent out feels rather hasty, if you do not mind me saying so.'

'But, professor, it is *impossible* that I delay it any longer!' Edward says through gritted teeth. 'I have already explained! Due to circumstances beyond my control, the need to reveal my discoveries is most pressing. I *must* present my findings before the end of next week. I have made it clear, have I not, that it will be an event to change our understanding of everything? I cannot overstate what I have discovered, Professor. I believe – no, I know *for a fact* that I have within my grasp proof of God Himself.'

Bartley-Stewart eyes Edward carefully. 'Then I sincerely wish you the best of luck, Mr Meake,' he replies. 'I should like to be in attendance wherever you do decide to hold your lecture and I look forward to seeing whatever this exciting discovery is that you plan to reveal. But a word of caution, Mr Meake, I know you will not be holding your lecture here, for now at least, but I would remind you of the wisdom contained in the Royal Society's motto – "Nullius in verba".'

'Yes,' says Edward, sharply. "'*Take nobody's word for it*." Of course. But I am a man of *science*, Professor, and what I will reveal is something most extraordinary, something so miraculous that no one will have cause to doubt. It will, in itself, be proof enough. I look forward to welcoming you to what will be, I have no doubt, a lecture that will *change history*.'

Edward shakes Bartley-Stewart's hand, feeling the rejection many times over. How can this professor not see that he holds the understanding to all things? How *dare* he refuse him?

As Edward leaves Somerset House, passion and resentment rising, he takes comfort in the satisfaction he knows he will feel when Bartley-Stewart and the rest come swarming to him after all is revealed, begging him to join their various societies, clustering around him like wasps to the ripest and richest of the autumn apples. Still, he thinks, he must now find another venue – and with haste.

His feet carry him eastward down the Strand, not considering where he is going or why, but the sun peeps out from behind a cloud and he looks up for a moment. He is opposite Exeter Hall, the huge Corinthian pillars either side of the impressive steps welcoming him in. *Exeter Hall. Of course!* It is Providence that has brought him here. God Himself has guided my steps, Edward thinks, as he crosses the busy road and steps inside.

The grand doorway leads into a large open space with

two impressive curved flights of stairs, one on each side, leading up to the great hall, and a side entrance leading to the smaller hall. Mr Lambert, a helpful clerk, shows Edward around the cavernous building, both halls empty at this time of morning. The larger hall is not available for the coming Tuesday but, Mr Lambert assures Edward, the smaller hall seats up to 1,000 comfortably and, if his event is a success, he would be more than welcome to return to the larger hall at a later date.

'Oh, but it *will* be a success!' says Edward, greedy eyes taking in the innumerable wooden seats, the raised platform at the far end of the hall, the light streaming in from the high windows.

Mr Lambert nods, leaving Edward alone to wander around the vast space. He steps up onto the platform, turning to take in the entirety of the empty hall. In his mind's eye he imagines the unfilled chairs below him crammed with a sea of awestruck faces, mouths agape as he reveals his angels for the very first time.

A lectern stands centre stage from some previous event and Edward looks out from behind it. He imagines his angel skeleton on the far side of the stage, pictures the moment he introduces his live, most beauteous angel. He hears the gasps of wonder, of disbelief, imagines gently unfolding those spectacular russet wings, inviting one of his fellow members of the Society for the Promotion and Advancement of Knowledge onstage. He will ask this independent witness to touch his precious angel, to examine her in front of the crowd. He hears, in his mind, the collective breath of a thousand people held until she is declared entirely, wondrously, real. Edward beams as he imagines the applause, the thunderous roar of approval, the standing ovation, the glory! He stands on the stage, arms held out, bowing in each direction, smiling to himself as his imaginary crowd rise to their feet, cheering and applauding in a deafening rush of noise . . .

In a little over an hour, all is done. The hall is booked, the details confirmed. *And so it begins*, thinks Edward, with a sense of glee. He walks the two miles home to clear his head, pacing the streets to quell his feverish excitement. He passes close by St Paul's and, feeling that he has not perhaps given sufficient thanks today, steps inside the cathedral to pray. He thanks God for all that He has given him, the tests He has put him through, for choosing him above all others.

This is my time, thinks Edward, smiling as he leaves the cathedral, walking slowly down the wide steps. The Chosen One.

This is my time.

Mary is within a coffee house in Ludlow, her hands still shaking a little. Both she and Richard had already given a statement to Mr Tittensor, the town's one and only constable, and handed over the note that Mary had found on the floor of the barn, hidden amongst the hay where it had fallen from Thomas's fingers.

Every time Mary closes her eyes, she hears the faint squeak of the rope, sees the silhouette suspended in mid-air. It was not the first body she has ever encountered but it is the first suicide, and she very much hopes the last. She is only grateful that she did not bear witness to the bodies of the senior Marshalls in the house too, is glad that Richard protected her from that at least.

'Subject to fits of mental excitement induced by the injudicious use of stimulants,' Mr Tittensor had said, rolling each word around in his mouth like a toffee as he wrote it down in his neat copperplate writing. He'd looked up at them, pulled a face. 'Too much beer for a young man to handle. Temporary insanity is what the coroner will say, no doubt about it. Racked with guilt over "a miraculous brown angel", indeed. What nonsense the poor boy wrote in that note. Have you ever heard the like? The only thing I can't fathom, Mr Ward, Mr Gibbs, is the amount of money that was found . . . over a hundred pounds! A very strange affair all this, that's for certain. A very strange affair . . . '

Mary takes a deep breath, warms her hands on her coffee cup. She looks up to see Richard watching her, concern etched across his face.

'I'm all right,' Mary says quietly. 'Really I am. It was the shock.' She fingers her moustache, smoothing it down at the corner, as she looks around the coffee house, taking in the other small tables and the handful of men sitting at them. She listens to them rigorously debating everything from the current price of livestock and new political pamphlets to the best place to get a pair of boots mended. She idly wonders if Thomas Marshall ever ventured in here and sadness washes over her. She knows now that he never got to go to London, never got to see the world. The empty seat for Mr Marshall in the coach. The guilt that nibbled at him, waiting for his parents to return home, crossbow loaded, two straight shots . . . she swallows, seeing it in her imagination so very clearly.

'Come,' says Richard, standing up and tapping his hat firmly back on his mop of curls. 'The best medicine for despair is to do something about it. We know now that there was no Miss Marshall, but we are still looking for the same woman, a lady of colour, wearing a distinctive blue dress and a cream bonnet. We are not done yet, Mr Ward.' Richard takes a last gulp of his coffee, shuddering at the bitterness. 'Let that young man not have died in vain. Come, we have enquiries to make.'

When Edward returns home, he finds a package waiting for him from the Douglases' household. He has no need to open it for he knows already what it contains – the wings of his demon returned at last. He takes the parcel down to his study before inspecting the leaking cell. The mongrel stands on the floor, whimpering and shivering, an inch of foul liquid having now seeped its way through the brick walls, pooling on the flagstones in thick oily puddles. The dog growls at Edward as he steps inside although it can no longer snap at him now that it wears a muzzle. The stench of the dog fills Edward with revulsion. He could kill it, of course, but it would only mean more mess to clear up. He gives the animal a kick before locking the door behind him.

Edward scratches at his injured arm as he turns to the other cell. He had earlier examined the wound and was disappointed to see that the rash had spread further up towards his shoulder. No matter, though, the wound is healing and there is much else that needs to be done. He needs to measure his angel, for he wishes to commission a white flowing gown with slits for her wings to be slipped through. He will make her look spectacular. Oh, how he wishes for a moment that her wings were pure white, how much more perfect she would look! *No*, he thinks, catching himself. He must not be ungrateful! He prays again, thanks God profusely for His gifts. He unlocks the door, anticipating his angel's dark eyes boring through him, imagining how glorious she will look upon the stage at Exeter Hall. He smiles as she rises to her feet, follows him silently into his dissecting room.

'This coming week will be the one in which you are revealed to the world,' he says, excitedly. 'Tuesday. Tuesday evening and you will be presented to all! Is that not exciting?'

Etta's heart stops for a second. Presented, she thinks. As ladies of a certain standing are when they come of age, something she mercifully avoided for herself. She tries to remain calm. All those eyes staring at her. No, she will not allow it. She steadies her breathing. Calm, Etta, calm. Breathe . . .

'And the demon?' she asks, when she can find the words again.

'The demon will remain here.'

'And how do you propose to present me?'

'I will commission a gown in white to best show off your wings and your complexion. Silk, I think. Some simple and exquisite embroidery around the edges. Nothing to distract from the glory of your wings. '

Good, Etta thinks. A gown like that should take at least two days. Although, in truth, she has little sense of what day it now is, the presentation cannot possibly take place before the dress is ready. That gives her a little time in which to make good her escape. *Their* escape.

'All else is arranged, I presume?' she asks, haughtily. 'The invitations sent?'

'There is no need for you to concern yourself with such things but it will be done today. And best of all, I am to reveal you at one of the biggest venues in all of London!' His eyes gleam. 'At Exeter Hall on the Strand itself!'

She says nothing. This man's ambition rules his common sense, she thinks, taking precedence over his empathy, over his very humanity.

When he has finished measuring her, he takes her back to the cell, returning afterwards to bring a luncheon of cheese and bread. Natalya and Etta eat greedily when he has left and, when they are sated, Etta relays all that she has learnt. She has been watching and noting everything, paying particular attention to the door she believes may lead to the outside.

'We have two days in which to escape,' she whispers to Natalya. 'Perhaps more, but we cannot count on it. He does not see us as women, but as *creatures*, specimens to be examined, explored, used to make his own reputation.'

Natalya frowns and thinks for a moment. 'Imagine a God that can allow man to have such brutality, to see his fellow people in such a way. What kind of divinity would allow that, truthfully?'

Etta waits a moment. 'What made you lose your faith?' she asks quietly. 'You asked me before whether I was a mother. Did . . . did something happen to you?'

Waves of emotion rise up within Natalya like the storm before a flood. She cannot speak, cannot move, cannot express in words how hollow, how *empty* it makes her feel.

Silent tears fall from her eyes and drip onto her knees where she sits cross-legged.

Etta instinctively pulls Natalya towards her, holds her, hugs her, lets her sob out her sorrow, lets her wail and tremor and bawl until the sobs eventually slow and her tears fall less frequently.

Etta's arms are still tight around her when Natalya recovers her ability to speak.

'I had a baby girl,' she whispers, wiping her eyes and speaking slowly. 'She was *perfect*. So tiny, her little hands, each with perfect fingers and thumbs, tiny feet and tiny toes and tiny perfect nails on each and every one. She had eyelashes just like mine.'

She pauses, relives it all.

'She was perfect in every way except that she was born . . . She was born with no breath in her. Her eyes were closed, sealed shut to this world, as if she had already seen too much.'

She inhales, slowly letting the air fill her own lungs.

'I still don't know what colour her eyes were.'

'I am so sorry,' whispers Etta.

'I carried her for nearly nine months, felt her inside me, every kick, every wriggle, my belly swollen and for what? For *what*?'

She sobs again, allows herself to remember, allows it to come flooding back, the first time she has done so in such a long while.

'I gave birth to her in a field by the side of the road, steps away from a ditch, like an animal. I cut the cord myself, sat with her for two days, holding her close to me, tight against my breast, waiting, hoping to hear that first intake of breath. I sat there, *willing* her to open her eyes, to breathe, to cry.'

She runs her hands over her face, wipes her tears away.

'Two days I was lost to the world. Two days that felt like a lifetime. But her mouth, like her eyes, never opened, her cries never came. So I buried her myself, dug her grave with my own bare hands while my breasts leaked milk for a hungry mouth that never came to suckle. There is no marker where she lies, no stone with which anyone will remember her. Just an old blackthorn tree in the corner of a field to look over her.'

She turns to Etta, eyes wet with tears. 'You asked me when I lost my faith. Can you blame me?'

'No,' says Etta. 'I cannot.' She pulls her close, holds her tight. There are so many questions she wants to ask but she bites her tongue. Now is not the right time.

'Oh, I'm sorry,' she says. 'I am so, so sorry . . .' And Natalya begins to slowly, quietly, weep again.

With luck, Annie believes she can complete her painting today. It has come together faster and better than anything she has done previously and there is lightness in her heart as she concentrates, preparing to add the last few details, the final finishing touches. It is beautiful, she thinks, and yet she feels so very sad too. For her plan has not worked – the anger within Edward, his peculiar behaviour, it continues apace – her painting has not drawn it out of him at all.

It is whilst Edward is still at Somerset House that Sarah knocks on the door of Annie's study, bringing with her a note that Annie opens immediately. Sarah hovers in the doorway to see if a reply needs to be sent.

My dearest Annie,

Forgive me for inadvertently getting you into trouble with dear Meake. No offence was intended. I do hope the flowers I sent have arrived and are making your house as radiant as you, dear lady, are yourself.

Please, can we meet at the earliest opportunity? I beg to see you to explain my error in person.

With nothing but the highest of regards,

Samuel

Annie is furious. Confirmation that the flowers were indeed from him only makes her more irritated. And this propositioning of her . . . he knows *precisely* what he is doing, trying to drive a wedge between her and Edward at the exact time that she feels everything between them is already crumbling. He has worded his note carefully, the weasel, for she cannot show it to Edward without raising his suspicions further. So she does the only thing she can think of that will rid her of it. She rips it up and throws it onto the small fireplace in her room. The fire is low but the embers are still warm enough to swiftly transform it to ashes.

'Sarah,' says Annie, turning towards the door. 'I have instructions for you that I would like you to keep most discreetly, do you understand?'

Sarah nods, bobbing up and down as she does so. 'Yes, ma'am.'

'Mr Covell, the man who was here for dinner last night, you remember?'

'Yes, ma'am, never forget a face, ma'am.' Particularly not such a handsome one as that, thinks Sarah.

'Good. In that case, please remember this too. You are not to allow that man to set foot inside this house without my husband present. Do you understand?'

'Yes, ma'am.'

'Not under any circumstance may that man be allowed in without Mr Meake being in attendance.'

'Yes, ma'am. Not under any circumstance.'

'Good. Thank you, Sarah.'

Annie returns to her painting before realising that Sarah is still in the room. 'Was there something else?'

'Just that . . . C-could I please look at your painting, ma'am? It's just that I am so curious. I have never been any good at drawing and the like and . . . '

'I am afraid it isn't quite finished yet,' says Annie, blushing a little.

'Oh,' says Sarah, disappointed.

'But as long as you promise not to breathe a word of it to anyone – especially Mrs McGilliveray – then you may see.'

'Oh, ma'am, I promise, I do, I promise!'

'Come then,' says Annie, with a warm smile. 'Come.'

Sarah steps around to the side of the canvas and is taken aback to see the master of the house perfectly, nay *exquisitely*, rendered as an angel. He has a smile on his lips, arms beckoning outwards as if he were to pull you into the painting alongside him. He is more handsome on canvas than in reality, for Annie has painted him as he used to be, with kindness and joyfulness. His wings are magnificent. Snowy-white with gold edgings. Behind him lies a snippet of the most bucolic of countryside, all rolling green hills and oak trees. It is the most beautiful thing Sarah has ever seen, but she cannot say so for she is rendered entirely speechless by it.

'It is not *quite* finished,' says Annie, mistaking Sarah's silence for criticism.

'Oh, but it is, ma'am, it *is* finished!' Sarah gapes at it. 'It's perfect, ma'am, it's *perfect*.'

Annie is delighted with this response. 'Do not breathe a word to anyone,' she says, holding her finger to her lips and the maid nods, returning the gesture.

'I swear, ma'am, I swear,' she says. As Sarah goes to leave, she pauses by the door before shutting it.

'Thank you, ma'am,' she breathes. '*Thank you!*'

Their assets are few – a small table, a pewter jug and bowl, two tankards and a plate. They have a mattress, the slop bucket, four blankets, a single candle and perhaps half a dozen matches. It is not much with which to defend themselves or mount an attack.

Etta already knows their captor keeps the keys to the door in his waistcoat pocket. If they are to escape, they need those keys and both she and Natalya know he will not willingly give them up. Natalya is all for throwing the slop bucket over him, tossing a blanket over his head and overpowering him, but Etta is resistant to this. Edward is tall and strong and if it doesn't go to plan, there will be no second opportunity. Instead, Etta has persuaded Natalya of her part in something else, a little game to play with Edward's fevered mind.

The chance to put their new plan into action comes when Edward returns, later, to take Etta out of the cell. In his dissecting room she watches as he eagerly paces up and down, instructing her, preparing her for his presentation.

'You will obey my every command when we are at the

hall,' he says, words tumbling from his mouth. 'There are but a handful of days left and all must go to plan. The gown is ordered, the most expensive item of clothing I have ever purchased, but it will be worth every penny and more!'

Etta nods, brain whirling away as Edward tells her of where she is to be positioned, how she is to be revealed, where she will stand whilst strangers prod and poke at her. She is not to speak a word the entire time, a silent angel on stage, a puppet for her captor's ambitions. She fixes a smile on her face, all the while seething underneath.

'I will do whatsoever He requires of me,' she says piously, when he is done. 'I am guided by you as you are guided by Him. I will obey your every command.'

Edward nods, pleased.

'The demon I share the room with is increasingly calm,' she says, after a moment. 'I believe my presence has helped soothe her.'

'Excellent,' says Edward. 'And you are healing faster than I could have hoped for. All is proceeding as I would wish, as He desires in His great plan.'

'After I am presented,' Etta says, thoughtfully, 'where are we to go then? We cannot return to this basement, surely?'

Edward smiles. 'You will not have to, for you will no longer be a secret. Besides, I will have money, *lots of it*, from the audiences at the hall and with more to come. Much more! I will have the newspapers *begging* me to tell the full story. I could buy us the biggest suite in the finest of all the capital's hotels! It will be glorious.'

'Glorious,' says Etta, quietly. 'Yes, I imagine it will be.'

As he accompanies her back to her cell, they hear a strange wailing emanating from within. It is Natalya, screeching, crying and hysterical.

'The demon needs my presence,' says Etta as Edward unlocks the door. 'I will calm her.'

Natalya is all wildness, her hair loose, eyes rolling back in her head as she squeals and shrieks, throwing her fists against the wall.

Etta slowly but confidently steps towards her as Edward watches. She holds out a hand, palm outstretched.

'Calm yourself, demon,' she says, commandingly. '*Calm.*'

Etta touches Natalya's forehead and she immediately becomes silent, standing motionless as if in a trance, Etta's palm remaining on her.

'Calm,' Etta says again. '*Calm!*' before gently removing her hand as Natalya collapses into a crumpled heap. Etta turns to Edward, who is watching, open-mouthed.

'She will sleep for some while now,' says Etta, and nods for him to leave.

When Edward is gone, his footsteps echoing away into silence, Natalya waits for a while before bursting out laughing.

'Did I play my part well?' she says, clambering up from the floor and hugging Etta tightly.

'Most well!' Etta grins. 'For a moment, even *I* thought you were possessed, and judging by our gaoler's face, he was certainly convinced.'

Natalya releases her, holding her hands. 'Will it work, do you think?'

'I believe so. Let us hope so anyway!'

Etta feels that she is truly beginning to understand the fanaticism behind Edward's behaviour. She is not yet convinced that any attempt at escape will necessarily be successful – it is still too dependent on circumstances beyond her control for her to be certain – but she dare not say such a thing out loud for fear of shattering Natalya's confidence. She has become strangely fond of this broken, wild soul she shares the space with.

'Where will you go, afterwards I mean, when we get out? Will you return to Salop?' asks Natalya.

'I don't know,' Etta replies, truthfully. 'I do not know where I *can* go.' She turns, looks at her wings, touches the feathers. 'If I am seen with these, I fear history will repeat itself – others will want to possess me, experiment on me. And yet, for all that they have brought me, I would not now wish myself without them. I would dearly love to stretch them out, to see how they work, *if* they work, but I wish for no audience when I do so.'

'I should like to go home,' Natalya says, quietly, 'but they would not have me.'

'Your family?'

Natalya nods. 'They're not on Sanday anymore. Not for years now. A handful are still on mainland and the rest are gone.' She pauses a moment. 'One day, my father never came back from the sea. No sign of his boat, nothing. A storm far out must have taken him. My brothers already gone from the isles in search of other work. All that remained were my younger sister Catherine, my mother and myself. With no boat to sustain us, life became harder by the day until my aunt took us in on her farm on mainland, north of Stromness by the Bay o' Skaill.' She thinks for a moment. 'Have you ever worked on a farm?'

Etta shakes her head. 'No, I grow things, experiment with plants and so on, record and observe them, but nothing akin to farming.'

'Well, I can tell you farming is hard work. Very hard. Different to what I was used to on the smallholding, so many more animals, so much more to do. I worked in the dairy but it was always a given that, as the eldest, with no prospect of being married, I would stay at home, look after my mother in her dotage.'

'So what happened?' asks Etta.

'*He* happened,' she whispers. 'Robert Holroyd. The new farmhand.' She stops for a moment, closes her eyes, lets the memories flood back in – his hazel eyes, his broad shoulders, the smell of his hair, the curve of his neck, the warmth of his embrace. She remembers it all. The snatched moments in the hay barn as dusk fell and the lapwings cried their approval from the fields.

'He was the father of my little girl. And I *loved* him,' Natalya says, softly. 'We planned to marry and he went over the sea to Thurso for the rings. There was a jeweller he knew there, he said. But he never returned. I never saw him again, never found out what happened, where he had gone.'

'He disappeared?'

Natalya nods. 'Vanished. Perhaps misfortune befell him. Perhaps he ran away. And whilst I waited for news, my belly started to swell until it could be concealed no longer. And then all came tumbling out. I had brought shame on the family, a baby outside of wedlock. They disowned me. So one day I left, walked out of my life, out of my family, far away from the islands. And then I had my little girl . . .'

She swallows her words.

'I wound my way south through towns and ports and harbours, came to London in search of my cousin, in search of someone else who hadn't fitted in. I came for a new life and instead I found myself changed, captured, held prisoner.'

'I'm sorry,' says Etta, holding Natalya's hands tightly.

Natalya nods. 'And you? You said you were not married? Never been in love?'

Etta's thoughts turn to Henry Underwood. Those glorious days of laughter and hope, long walks in the sunshine, the exchanging of ideas and theories, the sheer delight in knowing his eyes were upon her.

'Oh, it's all so long ago now,' she says with a sigh. 'But yes. I believe I was in love once. And that he held some affection for me at one time too. But it was not to be. He chose someone else, someone less "challenging" and with considerably more money.'

'And there has been no other since?'

'I live a rather sheltered life,' says Etta. 'My circle is rather small. And a husband would have taken all that I had, my stipend, my cottage . . . Almost everything would have belonged to him, including the way in which I was free to live my life.'

'And there was no pressure from your family to marry? You said your mother died when you were little?'

Etta nods. 'I have no memory of her, in truth. When I

became old enough to understand the absence, I'd ask questions of my papa but he was always so reluctant to answer, preferring to talk about plants and botany instead. I wish I had pushed him further on it now. But perhaps, in all honesty, it is better that I do not know. I want so much to remember my father as an honourable man, but he was a widower when he went to the West Indies, my mother a freed slave. And I am no longer as naive as I once was. I like to think he fathered no others in his brief time out there, but I wonder now whether his reluctance to answer me may have lay in guilt or worse, in concealing the real truth of it all. And now it is too late – for I will never know.'

Natalya squeezes Etta's hands. 'But you are still you, Etta,' she says, softly, 'whatever the truth of it. You are your own person. Botanist. Wanderer. Dreamer.'

Etta smiles. 'Perhaps,' she says. 'My half-brother always said I was a difficult woman too.'

'A difficult woman?' Natalya laughs, half-sobbing, as she embraces Etta again, holding her tightly. 'I think maybe that is what I am too.'

It is the Bishops Castle mail-coach driver who recognises the young man's description of the woman. 'Ah, that'll be Miss Lockhart!' he says to the youth with the dreadful moustache. 'The one with the big black-and-white pointer, eh? Aye, she does sometimes go over Bishops Castle way but often walks back with the dog. I saw her . . . ' He thinks for a moment. 'Ooh, not for some while now.'

'And could you tell me, where does she usually reside?'

'Over towards Pipe Aston, Elton Hall. This something about her botanical studies, that it?'

'Why yes.' The young man smiles. 'Thank you, yes. That is *exactly* it.'

Mary dashes around the corner, interrupting Richard's conversation with a grocer to tell him of the latest development. He looks at his watch, consults the grocer as to the best route, and estimates that they have enough time to comfortably walk to Elton Hall and back before the Aurora leaves at half past four for its return trip to London.

'It *must* be her,' says Mary, as they walk swiftly over

Dinham Bridge and up over Whitcliffe Common, heading towards Pipe Aston. 'It *is* her, I can feel it.'

'Feelings,' he says, 'are less important than facts in this line of work, *Mr* Ward, and I would remind you of that. Still, the fresh air and an invigorating walk will no doubt do us both good.' He looks at her for a moment. 'Are you really all right, Mary? It was quite a shock this morning – for both of us.'

She nods. 'Better than I was.'

'And you understand now,' he says, 'what I meant about it not always being fun.'

'I know,' she says softly. 'And I'm so glad you were here. But I've been thinking, Richard, I never once thought this was as trivial as you did, and surely it's in the discovery, the reporting of the most serious of stories that one can make the most difference? That is true, is it not?'

Richard smiles at her. 'That is certainly true, yes. And spoken like a true journalist, may I add.'

It is a good hour's walk from the top of the common with views as far as the Long Mynd and the Clee hills as they walk along the quiet lane towards their destination.

'Ah,' Richard says, looking at the grand residence off to the left, perched on the slope of a hill. 'I believe *this* must be Elton Hall.'

A cart rattles past as they walk up the lengthy driveway towards the imposing building and Richard hails it to stop. 'We are looking for Miss Lockhart,' he says and the driver nods.

'Aye, well you won't find her in the big house, she's in the old gatekeeper's cottage.'

Richard and Mary exchange glances.

'If you head back the way you came and take the narrow path on the right afore the gates, that's the clearest way. And good luck too,' says the driver.

'Good luck?' says Mary.

'Aye, she can be rather testy at times, so I hear!'

The cart drives off as Mary and Richard turn tail and head back down the driveway.

'Rather testy,' says Mary, intrigued. 'I think I like her already.'

Betsy bobs a curtsey as she answers the door to the small cottage. 'If you are looking for Miss Lockhart, gentlemen, I'm afraid you're out of luck,' she says.

'Oh?' says Richard.

'She's not here and I dunt know when she's coming back.' Betsy peers at them closely. 'Are you some of her letter-writing friends?'

'Yes,' says Mary, stepping forward. 'I am Mr Ward and this is Mr Gibbs. We are very interested in botany, like Miss Lockhart. And you are?'

'Betsy Morgan, sir, her maid, sir.' Betsy curtseys and blushes. This young man with his distinctive moustache is a very pretty youth, she thinks.

'Miss Morgan, could I ask when you last saw Miss Lockhart?'

'Yes, of course, sir,' says Betsy. 'Thing is, I am rather worried about her, if truth be told.'

'Worried in what way?' asks Mary.

'She's gone missing, sir, since the day Scout died. Her dog, that is. I've not seen hide nor hair of her since.'

After Betsy has told them all about her mistress, shown them Etta's rickety cabin, and explained her strained relationship with her half-brother, Richard and Mary decide it's time to pay a visit to Walter in the main house.

'Surely he must be concerned about her, even given their differences?' says Mary as they approach Elton Hall's fine main door. 'Surely he will help us?'

'Hmm,' says Richard but he does not manage any more before the door opens. It takes some little persuasion for them to see Mr Lockhart in person, though, and they are kept waiting for so long that Richard begins to worry that the Aurora will depart without them, leaving them marooned in Ludlow for another day.

When Walter eventually admits them to the drawing room, he reacts with scorn. 'You are aware that what you say sounds utterly ridiculous?' he scoffs. 'My half-sister is a woman for whom a little knowledge has proved to be a dangerous thing. I don't believe for a moment that she is in London or that anyone has ever shown as much interest in her as to even contemplate kidnapping her.'

Mary congratulates herself that she manages to restrain her very strong desire to stick a pin in this pompous ass.

'She's a difficult woman, was upset about her rabid mongrel dying and she has gone off in a huff as she is wont to. That is all,' Walter adds, sharply.

'May I ask — has she stayed away for this long before, sir?' asks Richard.

'No, but she has become increasingly eccentric in the

years since my father died and I would not put it past her to continue to stay away to make a point – although what that point would be, and why, I am quite sure we are all past caring.'

'But surely, sir, her whereabouts are of *some* concern at least? As your half-sister, as a close relative?' says Mary through slightly gritted teeth.

'No,' says Walter. 'Absolutely not. We may have shared a father but we do not share a mother or indeed anything else bar a surname. She has proved herself to be nothing other than cantankerous and, in all honesty, a burden to myself and my real family. Why else do you think she moved to the old cottage?'

Perhaps because of your intolerable self, thinks Mary. 'We believe,' she says, 'and I say this most sincerely, sir, we believe her life to be in immediate danger, perhaps lost already.' She feels Richard glance at her.

'Well, I do *not* believe her life to be in danger,' says Walter. 'Even if what you tell me is true, then I have a great deal of pity for this man who you laughably believe has "taken" her. God only knows what he has let himself in for. Unless she returns shortly, I will have to move her to one of the outlying cottages anyway. I am constantly dismayed by her inappropriate behaviour; it brings all of us at Elton into disrepute. Now, unless you have some actual proof of these ridiculous tales – and no –' he holds his hand up to silence them – 'what you have told me so far is not proof of any kind, merely coincidence, rumour, and a note left by a young man who was clearly mentally deficient as well as a drunkard. And now, I'm afraid, I must end this conversation for I have business to attend to. I wish you good day.'

'It *is* her,' says Mary as they leave the house and head back to Ludlow on foot. 'It is her, I knew it!'

'Mmm,' says Richard. 'The timings work out, certainly, her mysterious disappearance, the fact no one has seen her since, the note from that poor young man . . .'

'We *must* get into Meake's basement,' says Mary. 'It is the only way we will find out for certain. We know he bought the body from Mr King—'

'No. We *believe* he did,' says Richard. 'Not quite the same thing.'

'Well, we know he took the woman from the church and now we have evidence that Miss Lockhart's disappearance is connected with him too.'

'That is all certainly true.'

'I don't want that young man to have died for nothing, Richard,' Mary says, quietly. 'He wasn't much younger than me.'

Richard glances at his pocket watch.

'Now then, we must make a decision . . .'

'We must return to London,' Mary says, firmly. 'We have found out all we can here. If there's any chance Miss Lockhart might still be alive, then it is now upon us to do everything we can to mount a rescue – particularly given that her brother is not prepared to assist in any way. Besides, I fear the glue on my moustache is wearing thin and I have no idea where to get new supplies from here.'

'Then we must hurry,' says Richard, 'for the Aurora departs rather soon.'

'We shall have to run for it,' says Mary. 'Something that is considerably easier in these clothes, I don't doubt. And if need be, I shall just have to hold my moustache on whilst we do so.'

She runs off a few paces, turning back briefly.

'*Come on, Mr Gibbs!* What are you waiting for?'

The invitations are drawn up and sent out, a notice placed in the papers for tomorrow. All is coming together, thinks Edward. The order for the white gown, made of the highest quality silk and edged with exquisitely subtle embroidery, will be delivered to him at the house by tomorrow afternoon – nearly a day earlier than expected. It never fails to surprise him what advantages money will buy. His beautiful, magnificent angel will look glorious on stage. How blessed is he that God has given him this extraordinary creature. *How blessed!* The power she holds within her, the way she calmed the demon, it is extraordinary, he thinks. Earlier, when she looked at him, he felt as if she could see into his very soul, and he, in return, was looking into the eyes of God Himself.

He has ignored the note from Thomas Middleton, his latest moneylender, asking politely for details of the first repayment. There are other notes too, from other lenders, despite him instructing them not to write to him at the house, but all is in hand. He will repay them a hundred times over, he thinks. He will be generous with his spending when all comes to fruition. He burns the note over a candle, watches it disintegrate as if it had never existed in the first place.

Annie is behaving strangely of late, going behind his back not just once but twice. Consulting Samuel about such a personal and sensitive matter, something he had no wish to discuss with his friend. *And* she had known about the London Hospital role without telling him. Twice betrayed. He remembers the bouquet he destroyed when he was drunk. That must have been from Samuel too, he thinks, paranoia rising. Edward knows Samuel has always been fond of Annie; he had told Edward more than once that he had won the best prize in all of London. No, no, Samuel would never do such a thing, he tells himself, but a niggle remains. Annie's old drawing master, Marcus, comes into his mind. He knows she has seen him several times of late. Might the flowers be from *him* in fact . . . ? Is she, Edward wonders, *having an affair*?

I must speak with her, Edward thinks. My standing will be affected if she is being disloyal. He stops himself, ashamed for a moment. And yet . . . do I trust her? he asks himself. Do I still *love* her, even? Come, I must talk with her. She must surely be calmer now, more rational. She will see why I was angry with her, why she was in the wrong. And, if the worst is realised, it is better to know now. Nothing must stand in the way of my presentation.

Annie is in her study, hiding from him, he thinks, as he knocks at the door.

'Come in,' she says, expecting Sarah and being most surprised when her increasingly estranged husband walks in instead.

'Edward?' she says, puzzled.

'I wished to talk to you in confidence,' he says, but Annie is distracted. Buoyed up by Sarah's earlier reaction to the painting, she is finally ready to reveal her work to a wider audience. Her last brushstroke done, she has spent the past hour tidying up her brushes and paints and now, as if he had tuned into her very thoughts, here is the man she most wants to show it to.

'But this is perfect timing!' she says, clapping her hands with glee.

Edward is confused.

'Yes!' she says. 'For *this* is what I have been working on, this is what has been absorbing all my energies. *Here.*' The light is still good enough at this time in the afternoon for her to turn the canvas around to face him and she does so.

Edward's heart stops. Time pauses as his chest tightens. A lump sits hard and solid in his stomach and he feels suddenly nauseous.

It is his own self, reflected as if in a mirror but – horror of horror – *with wings!* – just like the creatures that God has given him, *his gifts,* in their basement two floors down. It is as if his wife has looked into his soul and found him wanting. Is this a mockery? *Does she know?*

Fear and shock and anger well up in him. *Has she, in fact, known all along?*

Annie watches him, his face frozen – she cannot read him, cannot tell what he is thinking.

'Edward?' she ventures, picking at her fingernails nervously. 'Well?'

'Is this . . . ?' He can barely spit the words out. '*Some kind of a joke?*'

Annie is baffled. 'A . . . a joke? No, husband, this is – oh!'

She cannot speak further for he has slapped her hard and her hand goes up to her reddening cheek, feeling it smart underneath her palm.

'You think to mock me?' he snarls at her. 'You dare to laugh at my plans? How long have you known, eh? *How long have you known?*'

He goes to grab her and she shrinks away, hands skittering at her worktable, paints and brushes falling to the floor.

'Edward!' He has gone mad, she thinks, *he has gone mad!* Fear rises in her and for the first time in her life she is frightened, truly terrified, that he might kill her, that he might even be *capable* of killing her.

'What have you told Samuel? *What do you know?*' he shouts at her, spitting fury, his mouth bare inches from hers.

She shakes her head. She doesn't understand. It is *simply a painting*.

He grabs a pallet knife from behind her and slashes at the painting, gouging a tear in it as her breath is sucked out of her. All those hours of work, all those days, all that love and emotion, all those sketches and—

'No . . .' she murmurs. '*No!*'

She goes to hold his arm, to prevent him from damaging it further, but he pushes her away, slashing wildly at the canvas. Rips appear in his own painted face, down his arms, through his wings and hands.

He has destroyed it! she thinks as he continues his frenzy, gashing angry, deep cuts in her work.

Annie waits, watches him for a moment before quietly heading straight to her bedroom. She packs her overnight bag as fast as she can, noting with dismay that some of her mother's beloved trinkets are no longer in her jewellery box.

Edward does not even see her leave. He takes what remains of the canvas, glimpses of Annie's beautiful angel dangling from the wooden frame like shreds of flesh, out into the yard where, heart thumping and eyes still fierce with fury, he sets fire to it.

Just before Mary clambers up to the roof of the Aurora, she recognises Mr Mabbitt, the coachman, as he helps load up the carriage for the trip to London. He eyes her strangely in return.

'Have we met before, young sir?' he asks, staring at her curiously.

'I don't believe so. No,' says Mary. 'Perhaps you met a cousin of mine?'

'Hmm,' says Mr Mabbitt. 'A Mabbitt never forgets a face . . . I'll work it out. Meanwhile, I'll leave you in the capable hands of Mr Burden for your onward journey. I'm off for ale, pie and a lie down afore I take her back on the morrow.'

'Jolly good for you,' says Mary, giving him what she hopes is a manly pat on the shoulder before settling down on the roof. Richard climbs up to join her, taking the space next to her.

'Ah, the return journey begins, Mr Ward,' he says, leaning towards her. 'And yet I feel I have not quite fully recovered from our interminable outward-bound leg.'

'Then you must better learn to sleep in uncomfortable

situations, Mr Gibbs,' says Mary. 'I am somewhat fortunate in that it's always been a special talent of mine.'

'Well then, perhaps next time, Mr Ward, *you* may take the uncomfortable armchair,' he replies, amiably.

'Gladly, Mr Gibbs,' she says. 'But you offered first and it would have been awfully rude of me to refuse, would it not?'

He snorts and they smile at each other as the coach lurches off back down the hill and through Broad Gate.

'Heads!' yells the coachman and those on the roof collectively duck down, the stone arch missing their head by a handful of inches.

'Let's hope we are not too late,' Richard says and Mary nods, leaning against him for a moment, feeling his warmth alongside her in the chill October wind.

'There is an island far, far away that only a very few know about,' whispers Natalya as she and Etta lie close together on the ragged mattress, arms wrapped around each other for warmth.

'Mmm,' says Etta, sleepily.

'It lies off the coast of Sanday, to the south-east, not far away but far enough that none live there anymore. There are a few stone shacks that could, with a little effort, be mended, fixed up well enough to live in. There is a small shale beach to the south where the seals birth, selkies we call them, and a rocky harbour to the east that one can land a boat in if you know the waters. My father used to take us there sometimes. It's large enough to keep a few sheep, a cow or two, perhaps some goats and hens and, best of all, there's a spring tucked away in a rocky cleft on the west side.'

Natalya stops for a moment, thinks.

'*That* is where I should like to go,' she says, softly. 'It is a wild place, far from prying eyes. It would not be an easy life, but it would be a haven.'

She gently strokes Etta's wings, missing her own, wishing

with all her heart that she had not broken them off to spite him when, in fact, it only spited herself.

'Perhaps,' Natalya says, feeling the feathers between her fingers, thinking of starlit skies and the Merry Dancers, the rivers rushing and widening to join the seas. 'Perhaps it *is* the wildness within us that made us grow our wings. Perhaps it is because we see the world around us so clearly. Because we see it for what it is. A miracle of its own making. Wondrous.'

'Perhaps,' whispers Etta. She thinks of her fossils and her ferns, of opening her eyes in the depths of the forest, the autumn leaves spiralling down. How she felt everything around her, birdsong and breeze, the tree roots reaching out underneath her feet. How alive it all felt. How alive it made *her* feel, all things connected, from the insects in the soil to the clouds in the sky, from the red kite soaring far above to her own breath and heartbeat. All things held within her and she within them.

'Perhaps,' she repeats, softly. 'And perhaps the world is not ready for women such as us. Not yet.'

EXETER HALL, MR MEAKE'S LECTURE.- Mr Meake, eminent surgeon at St Luke's and recently appointed a member of the prestigious Society for the Promotion and Advancement of Knowledge, has announced a special lecture to take place at Exeter Hall, The Strand, on Tuesday 27 October. Mr Meake promises that those who attend will see scientific wonders, the likes of which have never been seen before, on these shores or elsewhere. He will present recent findings including a live specimen of 'an exceptional and miraculous' creature. He apologises for the short notice of the lecture but is most eager to share his findings with both the wider scientific community and the public at large. Tickets can be acquired through Exeter Hall or on the door. The event is highly anticipated and there is likely to be a full crowd in attendance. Mr Meake is also looking to repeat the same lecture in Birmingham, Manchester, Liverpool and Sheffield.

The introductory address at the Opening of the Session will be delivered by Mr Meake on 27 October at 8 o'clock sharp.

It is a marvel, Sarah thinks to herself, as she watches Edward calmly drink the tea that she has poured for him, that the master of the house is acting as if all is normal when they both know his wife is no longer within and, quite possibly, has no intention of returning. Sarah had collided with Annie, tears streaming down her mistress's face, at the bottom of the stairs yesterday as the young maid had finally got around to dusting the sideboard in the hallway.

'He has destroyed my work!' Annie had sobbed and Sarah's heart cracked for the loss of the beautiful painting.

'Oh, ma'am!' she had said sadly, noting the bag Annie carried. 'Where will you go?'

'To my true friends,' Annie had said. She nodded towards the stairs. 'Please, be careful of him, Sarah. He is no longer himself.'

He is a monster, thinks Sarah as Edward beckons her to the table for more tea. To have destroyed such a thing of beauty. *For shame.*

Edward may look calm on the outside but inside he is still seething. For Annie, for his *own wife*, to have painted him in such a manner. It cannot be a coincidence. Can it . . . ?

He is relieved to read his notice in the paper. Not long now until all will be revealed. He takes a deep breath. Annie will likely be at Mrs Bigsby's house, but he has much to do, notes to prepare for his lecture, and the gown for his angel will arrive today too. Annie must return, that is all. It is inconceivable that she disobey him like this. She must oversee the dinner for the Society on Tuesday for that is woman's work and he has no idea how to organise such a thing himself. So much to do, Edward thinks, and yet such little time in which to achieve it – even without going to today's service at St George's. He cannot bear to attend without Annie, cannot face the inevitable wave of questions about his wife's whereabouts. He knows, though, that their absence will be noted for the Meakes have never before missed even a single service.

Alas, there is more trouble in store for Edward for, as he finishes his breakfast, Mrs McGilliveray enters, bags packed and ready to leave. She hands him her resignation, a decision she knows was entirely the right one as he reacts first with fury and then with pleading desperation. His appeals for her to stay, at least another week, are met with stony-faced resistance, for his cook has, after some time of trying, found another position and Edward is left with only Sarah to assist him in the house.

All of this is Annie's fault! thinks Edward, as he angrily paces the hallway. She has ruined *everything*. Now I am to be left without a wife in attendance and – worse still – without a cook for the Society dinner. I will have to visit Annie, beg for her to come back! But no. No. He will not abase himself. *She* is the one who should, who *must*, God willing, come back.

'Sarah!' he yells and the beleaguered maid comes running up the stairs from the kitchen where she is trying to wash up, prepare luncheon and organise the laundry. She is so overwhelmed by all the tasks she is now expected to complete that she feels as if she might faint.

'Yes, sir,' she says, red-faced, bobbing a curtsey.

'What is Mrs Bigsby's address? Do you know it?'

'No, sir, 'fraid not, sir,' says Sarah, although, truth be told, she can remember it from the notes that Annie has sent, but she feels no inclination to assist this man even one tiny bit.

'We must find ourselves another cook!' he barks at her. 'As a matter of *urgency!*'

Edward steps into his consulting room for a moment and throws everything off his desk, paper flying towards the ceiling like doves, pens and inkwell crashing to the floor and smashing before he falls to his knees and prays.

How is this your will, God? Is this a further test? Help me! Help your servant. I act only for you, I act in your name!

He waits for an answer, for a sign, for *something*, but all is silent.

When Annie finally wakes after a deep and fitful sleep, Ellie is there beside her. It is no bad dream then, Annie thinks, overwhelmed by sorrow as her friend takes her hand. The loss of trust, the loss of the man she had loved so much, *still* loves so much.

'You must rest some more, Annie dear,' says Ellie, quietly.

'He is not himself,' Annie says. 'I don't believe he meant to hurt me, truly, Ellie.'

'Annie, my dear, your cheek is still pink from where he hit you and you have suggested that, of late, he has not been behaving as he should. But you must not think upon it now. Close your eyes and rest. Come,' she says, and she tucks Annie back into bed and kisses her on the cheek. 'We'll talk further when you are recovered more.'

'He is not himself, Ellie! Why destroy the painting? All that work I'd put in, all those hours. It was as if he was possessed! As if a devil had taken hold of him! He has never before raised a hand to me, never!'

'Get some rest,' Ellie says, firmly. 'You must stay as long as you need to. Rest first and we shall talk about it all later. Marcus will be back soon and—'

'Please don't let him go around there,' Annie pleads, squeezing Ellie's hand. 'I know Marcus will be angry, but *please* don't let him confront Edward. That is for me to do and me alone. Please.'

It isn't until Ellie promises that she will do whatever she can to prevent this that Annie finally lets go of her friend's hand.

'Oh, Annie,' Ellie says sadly. 'I know it is not helpful to say such a thing but I do so wish you had married Marcus all those years ago!' She leaves the room, gently shutting the door behind her.

No, thinks Annie. It is not helpful to think of such things – the mistakes we make, the paths we do not take – and yet, she thinks to herself, yes, I wish I had done so, too.

'I've often wondered what it might be like to live in a land full of forests,' murmurs Natalya, as she curls up next to Etta, pulling a blanket up to keep her warm.

'But there are forests on your isles, surely?' asks Etta, and Natalya chuckles quietly.

'Barely anything akin to what *you* might call a forest,' she says. 'The trees are mostly short, stunted even, and sparse too.'

'Why is that?' asks Etta, puzzled.

'The winds blow so fierce at times that . . .' Natalya pauses. 'I could tell you a story, if you like?' she says, shyly.

Etta smiles in the darkness. 'I would like that very much,' she says, and feels her companion shift, nestling into the crook of her arm and settling into position.

'Then I shall begin,' Natalya says, and Etta hears a new tone in her voice. 'Once upon a time, when wishes still came true, if you travelled far enough north, and went further still, you might find, with a fair wind behind you and the tide on your side, an island rising out of the foam-flecked sea. A large island with low cliffs and beaches, an island with moors and forests, lakes and streams, inlets and soft hills.

'In the midst of this island, in a low-lying dip, there lay a forest with all the trees of the world, but just one of each. Birch and cedar, oak and spruce, poplar and pine, elm and willow. There were trees too strange to imagine, trees from every corner of the earth. And just one of each.

'The forest had been on the island for as long as anyone could remember and each of the trees had just enough water, just enough soil and just enough sun to thrive. The trees would talk, too, talk to any who might listen. To each other, to the birds that sat on their branches, to the insects that alighted on their flowers, to the creatures that burrowed deep amongst their roots. On a quiet day, if all were still, even you might have been able to hear their whispers, hidden softly in the rustle of their leaves.

'One day, as the trees chatted amongst themselves, the birch noticed something different, something it had never seen before. A circle around the base of its own self, a ring of scarlet toadstools flecked with snow-white dots. A pretty thing, thought the birch, smugly, for none other had such decoration, such beautiful adornments.

'"Look at me!" said the birch. "Look how glorious I have become!" And each time the birch said it, each time the birch *thought* it, it grew, swelling with pride, reaching up a little further to the sky. As the days went by, the birch grew taller and taller and taller still, until all the other trees in the forest swayed in the breeze not just beside it, but below it too.

'"Look at me!" said the birch, as it towered above them. "Look how glorious I have become!" The birch rose further still, stretching out so high that it brushed the Sun as it passed by overhead at noon. But the Sun does not like to be touched and it burnt fierce and full, singeing the birch's branches, charring the ends.

'The birch was furious. The Sun had looked so pretty in its branches. A bauble with which to decorate itself. A shiny trinket to hold within its grasp. The birch stood silent for a while, waiting. When darkness fell, the Moon rose slowly above the horizon, a full, fat round Moon with a beaming face that smiled out over the forest, over the stars, over the deep blue sea. All was still. All were asleep. All except the birch.

'Only when the Moon passed by overhead, passed within reach of its branches, did the birch stir. It reached up, stretched out and grasped the Moon, holding it tight, the coolness of the light soothing its burns from the Sun. "Look at me!" said the birch, as the white light shone through its twiggy fingers. "Look how glorious I have become!"

'"Let me go!" said the Moon. "Please, let me go!" But the birch had no intention of letting go, for was this not the very *best* of ornaments it now held within its grasp? Alas, though, with the Moon held fast, time began to slow, for without the Moon's passage, the Sun could not, in turn, appear. Daybreak, sunrise, the seasons, all paused as time itself ground to a halt.

'"Let me go!" said the Moon. "Please, let me go!" Her pleading became louder but all was still, all were asleep. All except the birch. The Moon begged again, imploring the birch to release her from its branches, her voice becoming louder each and every time until, at last, the ears of one heard her plea. A Cattie-face, a short-eared owl, with eyes the colour of the Sun and wings of mottled brown. The call of the Moon rang in its little feathered head, waking it from its doze and it stretched its wings, flying high into the night sky to see if it could help.

"'Let me go!" said the Moon, one final time. "*Please, let me go!*" The Cattie-face saw the Moon helpless, imprisoned in the birch's branches and, talons out and beak sharp, pecked at the twiggy fingers tangled around the Moon. The Cattie-face pecked and pecked, scratched and clawed and scratched again, focusing on the charred ends where the Sun had burnt them earlier. The birch clung on, tried to swat the owl away, but the Cattie-face was persistent and as the birch stretched to knock it out of the sky, the Moon slipped out of its twiggy grasp, released back into the night sky where it belonged.

"'No!" said the birch, reaching upwards. "No!" but it was too late, for time no longer stood still. The Moon was free but she was furious too. She called to her friend, the North Wind, that cold, fierce wind that strikes fear into even the bravest of seafarers; she called for help and she called for vengeance. And the North Wind came and the North Wind blew. And it blew and blew and it blew so fast and so hard that all of the trees from all of the world were blown right back to the four corners of the earth from whence they came. Only a handful of trees clung onto the remote island, the birch, the oak, the rowan and the willow, and each and every one of them was ground down by the North Wind, reduced to a height where they would never, not a single one of them, ever again be able to reach as high as the Moon.

'And as for the Cattie-face, she was not lost. That little brave owl had her own reward as the Moon held her tightly, held her safe from the wind, asked what she might like as a gift in return for her help. "It is hard for owls to hunt at night," the Cattie-face said. "There is the Fox, the Badger, so many others who seek the same fare as I." And the Moon smiled, and she called to her friend, the Sun, and so it was that the Cattie-face was no longer obliged to hunt by night, but instead was allowed to hunt by the light of the day, the only owl to do so.

'And so that is why the trees are short and so very sparse on Orkney. And that is why, if one day you go to the island, with a fair breeze and the Sun high in the sky, you too might catch a glimpse of that same Cattie-face with eyes the colour of the Sun and her wings of mottled brown.'

Etta smiles in the darkness, hugs her friend tight to her.

'Thank you,' she whispers, her eyes full of tears. 'Thank you.'

It is late afternoon when an exhausted Mary and Richard finally arrive back in a very chilly London, having been delayed several times on their return journey. They stiffly disembark from the Aurora before heading straight to see Jos at his lodgings, to update him with all that they have learnt.

'Richard, thank goodness!' says Jos, standing up from his chair, his blankets falling to the floor as the young man sheepishly enters. 'But where on earth is Mary?'

A small young man with a terrible moustache sidles in behind Richard and Jos sees through the disguise at once.

'Good God, Mary! What on earth—?'

'It's all right, Jos,' says Richard, holding out a placating hand.

'No, damn it! It is not all right! It is far from bloody all right! What on earth do you mean by wearing such a thing? Where on earth did you get it from in the first place? Is this *your* doing, Richard?'

'Uncle, please!' says Mary. 'It is not Richard's fault, it was my own idea.'

'Then you have become more irresponsible than I

thought,' Jos fumes. 'D'you mean to say you've been wearing that ridiculous get-up the entire time you were away? And *you*, Richard, I thought you would have known better!'

Mary hangs her head in shame.

'Take off those ridiculous clothes!' barks Jos. 'What have you done to your hair too? My God, have you cut it all off?'

'No!' says Mary, on the verge of tears. 'It's just pinned up, look.' She takes off her hat and unpins her hair, letting it fall loosely down around her shoulders.

'You were supposed to look after her!' says Jos sternly to Richard. 'Yet you let her dress like a man!'

No, thinks Mary. *That is unfair.* She stands, chin up, back straight, defiant.

'No, Uncle Jos! Richard did not "let" me dress like a man, he had no choice in the matter. It was my doing and mine alone. I thought I would be safer dressed like this given that I was unsure if I was to be travelling on my own, if Mr Gibbs might not be able to accompany me. And – no, Uncle, let *me* speak for once – it has been a *revelation* to see what you, what all of you, can do with the freedom of your clothes. It is not my fault that I am born a woman. It is not my fault that I am not allowed to do this, that or the other, merely because of an accident of birth. I wore this for my own safety and I am *glad* I did so. Punish me if you will, but it is not Richard's fault. He has been nothing other than a kind and considerate companion, he has looked after me as a true friend and equal would!'

She pauses, takes a breath, as both men stand in silence,

dumbstruck by this outburst. 'Now, Uncle, I shall get changed into my old clothes and Richard can update you with all that has happened. You may be angry with me all you like, but you will have to wait, for we have important business to attend to.' She bows her head before heading to her bedroom, pushing the door closed behind her.

'Damn the girl,' growls Jos when he recovers the ability to speak. He eyes Richard, silently reprimanding himself for only now seeing the clear affection the young man and his niece hold for each other. How could he have been so blind?

'Whatever am I to do with the pair of you?' he sighs, shaking his head. 'You know, George always used to say the two of you were evenly matched. Even young Charlie said only yesterday he thought you meant to marry her.'

Richard's heart skips a beat, his mouth dry.

'And for God's sake, I hope you would!' says Jos. 'For I know this much if nothing else, no other damned man in the country – nay, the whole darned *world* – would take such a bloody-minded creature!'

And Richard cannot help but laugh, breaking the tension in the room. He is so tired from his journey, so full of emotion that he has to hold onto the back of one of the rickety chairs to prevent himself from crumpling to the ground. He wipes his eyes and pulls himself together as he drags out the chair and sits down on it with some relief.

'There is much to tell you, Jos,' he says, running his hands over his face, regaining some semblance of self-control. 'But we must be quick about it, for today is the day that we break into Meake's basement, come what may.'

As Jos frowns, Richard leans forward and whispers, 'I have not acted as anything other than her older brother as I promised you. That is all, Jos, I *swear*. I care far too much about the both of you to put anything at risk.'

'Come on then,' Jos says gruffly. 'Tell me all.'

Etta is thinking about her latest plan of escape. It is not particularly well thought through, but she has noted in which drawer Edward keeps the sharp knife he used to gently slice through her own woollen coat and dress. She saw, too, that there is no lock on that drawer, no keyhole with which to keep it fastened. The gown must arrive soon, she thinks, and that is when she will take her chance. Although the mind games she has been playing with Edward appear to be working, she is aware that time running out.

She has not yet told Natalya of this new element of her plan. It is a risk, that much is certain, but the risk is hers, not her friend's. She stands and stretches out, feels her wings unfold behind her, listens to Natalya's slow breathing as she sleeps, smiles as she remembers the story of the birch and the Moon.

Etta closes her eyes, imagines the wind in her face, the sound of birdsong, the feeling of life all around her. She slows her breathing. I cannot go back to Salop, she thinks. Scout is gone and what else is there to tempt me back? Certainly not Walter and his family. Dorothy is already half-lost, her mind, her memories washing away like marks on a beach as the tide comes in. And Etta's small handful of friends? Well, they were correspondents in truth, acquaintances more than anything, with their own busy lives to lead. She had been left behind, forgotten, destined to roam the lonely countryside without even the comfort of her dearest Scout. Her beloved hills had become her life and she loved them with all her heart, yet she had not ventured out of their safety for many a year now. Perhaps, she thinks, those same hills had become, in some small way, her prison too. She takes a deep breath, opens her eyes.

Besides, she thinks with a smile, looking towards her new-found friend in the darkness, I have always wished to go north. To explore the outer edges of nowhere, to see those remote and wild islands so full of new landscapes. New plants to study, new *everything*. From the forests and fields of Salop to fresh seas and skies. To machair sands and thrift, to orchids and the rare Scottish primrose, *Primula scotica*. To skuas and terns, to long beaches with tiny shells all the colours of the rainbow. To the Cattie-face that hunts in the day and the low-growing birches. Yes, she thinks. I would very much like to taste that salt wind on my tongue, to see those wide, northern skies, witness the 'Merry Dancers', as Natalya calls the aurora borealis, shimmering and stretching above the winter horizon. She feels a spark of excitement rising. For I have always wished to go north, have I not?

'Is Mrs Meake in?' asks Mary when Sarah, flustered and red in the face, opens the door.

'No, miss!' says Sarah, looking behind her to check that her master is nowhere near. '*She has left him!*' she whispers.

'*Left him?*'

Sarah nods, stepping outside and gently pulling the door to. 'It's most scandalous, I warrant you, but indeed she has. I saw her go with my own eyes!'

'Where might I find her? It's most urgent that I speak with her,' says Mary and Sarah notices the tall young man on the other side of the road, watching.

'Is that handsome fella, your beau?' she asks and Mary turns to see Richard waiting for her. Ah, she thinks with a smile, he has caught up with me then.

'No. Not quite. He's a family friend and it's – well, it's complicated.' Mary tries not to blush.

'Oh, ain't it always?' says Sarah, with a sigh.

'Why did Mrs Meake leave? Has Mr Meake's behaviour been strange of late?'

'Most strange!' says Sarah. 'But here, I shouldn't be seen talking to you. The cook is gone and there is much to do.'

'The cook has left too?'

Sarah nods. 'Handed her notice and left without the perquisites she was entitled to and everything. She said I should get out too, that there was something *rotten* in this house and she wanted no more part of it.'

'And Mrs Meake, is she quite all right?'

'Don't know, miss, only that she has gone to her friend's house.'

'Do you know the address? Please, we wish to help. We believe Mr Meake is not in his right mind. We think he may be responsible for some terrible things and we want to make sure that he is stopped.'

Sarah thinks for a moment before leaning forward, whispering the address in Mary's ear.

'Thank you,' says Mary, taking Sarah's hand and squeezing it. 'Thank you most kindly.'

'I would never breach a confidence under normal circumstances,' says Sarah. 'But he destroyed her painting, ripped it up and burnt it in the yard. I saw it beforehand and beautiful, it was. I think it broke her heart he could do such a thing.'

'I'm sorry to hear that,' says Mary. 'What was the painting of?'

'It was of him, her husband, but as an angel.' Mary's heart skips as Sarah continues. 'Last thing I'd have thought you could paint a man such as that as, but there we are.'

Mary thanks Sarah one final time before dashing across the road to where Richard waits.

'Jos is finding Charlie and will meet us here in an hour,' he says, eyes alight with excitement. 'And that is not all.

Happenstance would have me bump into a colleague from the *Express* as I came here. Meake is to announce his "findings" at Exeter Hall on the Strand on Tuesday evening.'

'But that is the day after tomorrow!' Mary says, and Richard nods.

'*And* the *Sunday Examiner* reports today that he plans to show a *live* specimen of "a rare and miraculous creature".'

'Richard! That must surely mean Miss Lockhart is still alive!'

He smiles, scratches his chin. 'We still don't quite know if any of this is true.'

'But the jigsaw puzzle is slotting into place, is it not? And whatever plans Mr Meake has to present his "findings", we must make sure they are thwarted.'

'How did you get on?' he says, looking back at the house. 'Did Mrs Meake refuse to see you?'

'No,' says Mary thoughtfully. 'She has left him! Come, I will tell you all on the way for I have found out where she is staying and we must make haste.'

Edward is in his dissecting room, ordering his notes and sketches. He is preparing for publication after his forth-coming lecture and is in a frenzied mood, collating, noting and stacking information and evidence.

He works at a speed that is both furious and intense and it takes almost all of his concentration to do so. He remains angry with Annie but he is disappointed too, his trust in her damaged. He still wishes for her to return, though, still wants his wife by his side throughout, but no matter, *she will return*, he thinks. And she will do so with her tail between her legs as soon as his lecture is done, as soon as his success and reputation is secured for all eternity.

He has already sent a note to one of the finer restaurants in the City, arranging for dinner to be delivered and served on the Tuesday, regardless of his wife's presence. It will be a tight fit with all thirteen of the Society around the dining table, he thinks to himself, so perhaps it is best she is not there to take up a space.

She will understand everything when she sees. God will make her understand. All that matters is the presentation. It is all he will allow himself to focus on. He knows the glories that will come afterwards will be unparalleled. *All will be well, God willing, for I am Your servant forever and ever. Amen.*

He hums to himself as he works, methodically moving his work from the dissecting room to his study, everything from the cloak that his angel of the Thames was found in to the ripped clothes of his demon. He lines up the notes and sketches of all three of his gifts, the jars of organs and body parts from his river angel.

As he returns to the dissecting room, he allows himself a smile of pride at the simple beauty of his winged skeleton, the exquisite mounting that he built for her. Now that he has cleared a little more space for himself, he is free to practise his lecture. He makes notes as he structures it, pacing around the room, finessing and annotating as he goes. It will be the brightest spotlight that has ever been shone on him and oh, he will be ready for it, *by Jove*, he will be ready for it!

He smiles to himself as his lips run over the words. It will be outstanding, he thinks, and is greatly pleased – nay, even overwhelmed – by his own magnificence.

It is most inconvenient that there should be any visitors today of all days, thinks Ellie as she is called downstairs, forced to leave Annie's bedside where they had quietly been talking of what had happened and what perhaps might be done.

A tall young man with curly hair waits in the drawing room, nervously twirling his hat in his hands whilst a young lady, dressed in black, stands, looking out of the window.

'I am Mrs Bigsby,' says Ellie. 'How can I help you?'

It is only when the young lady turns to face her that Ellie's face shifts from irritability to delight.

'Good Lord!' says Mary. 'Miss Wiltshire!'

'Mrs Bigsby for some long time, Mary!' says Ellie with a laugh as she runs over to her, holding her hands and whirling her around the room. 'And is this your own husband?' she asks, noting that both young persons blush crimson.

'Oh!' says Mary. 'No! This is Mr Gibbs, er, Richard – he is a friend of the family.'

Ellie smiles and shakes her head. 'I had not thought you to be in London still! It has been an age. And how is Jos? And dearest George?'

Mary's face falls.

'I am afraid George is no longer with us,' Richard says.

'Oh, Mary! Oh *no*, I am truly sorry to hear that, he was the best of men.' Ellie reprimands herself for not having noted Mary's mourning dress.

'Forgive me, but I had no idea the two of you were acquainted,' says Richard, puzzled.

'Oh, I did not recognise the name "Bigsby"!' says Mary. 'This is Miss Eleanor Wiltshire as was. She is the lady who was, for a brief time, my governess. You remember – "Ignorance is the curse of God, Knowledge the wing wherewith we fly to heaven"? It is many years ago now, though. I am surprised you recognised me, Miss Wiltshire.'

'Ah, you have a most distinctive presence. I am sure Mr Gibbs has noticed too,' says Ellie and Richard smiles, raising an eyebrow.

'I am afraid, though,' says Mary, 'we are not here to see you per se, dear Ellie, although there is much to tell you. We are here to see your friend. I believe Mrs Meake is here, is she not?'

Ellie nods, confused. 'Why, what is this about? I'm afraid, Annie, Mrs Meake, is rather fragile at the moment. I don't believe she should be receiving visitors of any kind.'

'We understand,' says Mary. 'And indeed it concerns her husband who we believe to be the cause of the upset – but it is also of the utmost importance. *Please* may we speak with her?'

'It is a grave matter,' adds Richard. 'I'm a journalist for the *New Weekly* and the *Morning Express* and Miss Ward and I have been investigating some most strange goings-on.'

'*Miss Ward has been investigating . . . ?*' says Ellie, amazed. 'Oh, but of course she has!' She smiles at Mary. 'I cannot truly be surprised by anything she might do.'

Richard nods. 'Miss Ward has, in fact, been the person who has driven the investigation. I cannot take any credit.'

Mary's heart glows as he says it, a feeling of pride rising within her. 'Please, Ellie, we *must* speak to her,' she says. 'I know it sounds ridiculous, fantastical even, but we believe a life may be in danger.'

'Very well,' says Ellie. 'I can but ask.'

Richard and Mary follow Ellie up to the first floor, waiting outside as she knocks on the bedroom door and enters, closing the door softly behind her.

'The infamous governess who said you were too difficult to teach, eh?' whispers Richard.

'I don't believe that is *quite* what she said Mr Gibbs,' says Mary. 'Oh, I do so hope she will see us!'

The door opens and Ellie holds it wide for them to enter. 'Come in,' she says.

Annie lies on the bed before them. Pale and worn-looking, she props herself up on an elbow. 'What is this about?' she asks, recognising Mary. 'I have seen you before, have I not?'

'I am Mary Ward and this is Richard Gibbs,' says Mary. 'We mean you no harm, Mrs Meake, I assure you. We come here in friendship and to ask for your help.'

'My *help*?'

'Your husband,' says Mary. She pauses for a moment. 'We believe he is holding someone – a woman – prisoner in your basement.'

Annie laughs, but this is ridiculous is it not? A prisoner! And in their basement! Then she thinks of the gate Edward had installed, the dog barking at all hours, his obsession with work. As she goes over memories, scenes in her head all jumbled up together, she has a sudden unsettling feeling and her face turns serious.

'I think you had better tell me everything, Miss Ward,' she says.

Edward unwraps the parcel on the dissecting room table carefully. He slices the string open with precision before gently peeling back the brown paper to reveal the white silk gown within.

It is *perfect*! He holds it up at arm's length, admiring the sheen of the cloth, the glimmers of light shimmering back at him from the gas lamps. His angel will look most spectacular in this!

He clears the table, moving the discarded wrappings to the sideboard, smiling to himself as he does so.

The gown is perfection itself. Now, he thinks, I must fetch my angel and see if it looks as magnificent on her as it does in my own hands.

It has long gone dark by the time Jos and Charlie arrive at St Mary Axe. They wait for Richard and Mary as instructed, but it is a cold night and Charlie is fidgety.

'You understand, if we must force our way in, that we will be breaking the law?' asks Jos and Charlie nods, grinning.

'Won't be the first time,' he replies with a wink.

'Hmm, well. I'll pretend I didn't hear that,' says Jos.

They are chilled as they wait, so much so that they are forced to circle the street to keep warm, stomping their feet and rubbing their hands as they do so.

'Feels like winter already,' says Charlie as they return to their vantage point opposite the Meakes' house. At the same moment, a cab rattles around the corner, pulling to a halt beside them. Richard jumps down from next to the driver as Mary opens the door and helps another woman out.

'Mrs Meake, I shouldn't wonder,' mutters Jos as they cross the road towards the small party.

Mary has already taken control of the situation.

'Uncle Jos, this is Mrs Meake. Mrs Meake, this is Jos

Ward, my uncle and a fellow journalist, and this is young Charlie Meckin who is helping us out. I am assured that he is most adept at picking locks should we need him to.'

The party nod acknowledgements at each other.

'Uncle Jos, you wait here,' Mary says. 'I will accompany Mrs Meake into the house through the front door and we will let Charlie in through the servants' entrance once we are inside. Richard will wait in the yard behind to help us out.'

Jos goes to protest but Mary stops him.

'No, Uncle. We need someone positioned outside the front too in case we need to raise the alarm or call for support,' she says firmly, and he does not dare argue with her.

'Ready?' she says and they all nod.

'Come then, Mrs Meake,' she says, taking Annie's hand as they cross the road and head up the steps to her front door, 'let us within,' and with that, she raps on the door as hard as she can.

Etta hears the door knock faintly in the distance as she stands in the dissecting room. The house feels peculiarly quiet today, she thinks to herself.

'Is it not *beautiful*?' Edward says as he holds up the white gown. 'Is it not perfect?'

'Yes,' she says and smiles sweetly, smiles for she has just now seen the knife that he used to undo the package left casually on the sideboard along with the discarded paper and string.

He is too close for her to get near it yet, though, and so she must change first. How ironic, she thinks, hope and excitement rising, nerves making her fingers tremor and her heart thud. How ironic that she will be dressed in pure white when she picks up that knife.

I am my own self, she says to herself. *I am Etta Lockhart and I am nobody's prisoner.*

'Avert your eyes,' she says after he hands her the gown. He turns away and she slowly takes off her torn coat, then her woollen dress, until she stands just in her chemise and corset. She feels dirty, as if she has not had a decent wash in days, which, indeed she has not, but the coolness of the fabric feels clean and fresh against her skin. It is cold down here, though, and she shivers as she slips the dress on.

'I am ready,' she says.

Edward turns to look at her, his mouth falling open at this vision before him. This beautiful angel with her perfect wings, her flawless face and the pristine white gown.

'Ahh,' he breathes, overcome by wonder.

God has guided him well.

Sarah has let them in and Annie and Mary head downstairs to the servants' hall where they open the door to Charlie. He gives a quick thumbs up to Jos before disappearing inside, where the trio of women wait for him.

The servants' hall is small and dark, open flame gas lights flickering, flaring up and fizzling down. There are shadows all around. It is cold and unsettling, thinks Mary with a shudder, even with the fire lit.

'The gate is through here,' says Annie. 'But it will be locked.'

'Please, ma'am,' whispers Sarah. 'Mr Meake is down here already. He came past me in the kitchen earlier and hasn't yet gone back up. I gave him a parcel that was delivered. Soft it was, felt like clothing of some kind.'

Annie and Mary exchange a glance.

'Sarah,' says Annie firmly, 'I wish you to go outside through the servants' entrance and stay with the man who is watching the house from the other side of the street. His name is Mr Jos Ward. Please tell him I sent you.'

'Yes, ma'am,' says Sarah, bobbing down.

'Wait a moment,' says Annie and Sarah turns. 'I have

not always been a good mistress to you, Sarah, but I thank you for everything you have ever done and for your kindness.' She kisses her on the cheek. 'Now run — go — for I cannot be assured of your safety in this house anymore.'

Sarah dashes out, taking one last look behind her, memorising everything in order to recount it to, well, someone, anyone, some day.

'Come,' says Annie and they follow her out of the servants' hall, past the stairs up to the ground floor, the kitchen on the right and the small wine cellar on the left. The hallway turns a sharp left and straight in front of them stands a metal gate covered on the other side with oilcloth.

'This is my husband's part of the basement. The gate he had installed so as not to be disturbed at his work,' says Annie, trying and failing to conceal her nerves.

'Charlie?' says Mary and the boy steps forward to look at the lock in more detail.

'I should, perhaps, try to talk to him . . .' says Annie.

'I'm not sure that is wise,' says Mary, but it is too late.

'Edward!' Annie shouts. 'Edward, husband are you there? I beg of you, open this gate. Husband! *Husband!*'

He is distracted, thinks Etta. They can hear his wife's voice from the hallway, the door to the dissecting room left open. Edward ignores the shouting but still, he is distracted.

'Will you not look to your wife?' says Etta, slowly.

'It is of no consequence,' says Edward but he is confused. Annie has returned. He supposes he must see her, but his angel is here and the two must not meet, not before his presentation is over and all is done.

'I shall put you back in your room,' he says reluctantly, for the cell is unclean and he does not wish to sully the gown.

'Then *you* must lead the way,' she says, motioning with her head.

As he steps out of the room, Etta dashes forward and grabs the knife from the sideboard.

He turns to see and is stunned to find her pointing the knife at him, eyes flaming.

'Edward!' yells Annie from the other side of the gate, picking up the bell and ringing it. 'Please! Open this gate.'

'*Open the gate!*' commands Etta fiercely.

'No,' he says, frowning. '*No!*'

'Edward, if you do not open this gate, then *we* will open it for you!' says Annie loudly. 'There is a locksmith here and he will open it on my say-so.'

'Open it,' says Etta firmly as she moves towards him. 'Or I will slice you open instead.'

'But it is not . . . this is not God's will.' He stumbles as he takes a step backwards down the hallway. 'You are my angel! *God gave you to me!*'

'Open the gate or so help me God, I will slit your throat open as neatly as you sliced off her wings,' she says. Her voice as full of ice as her eyes are of fire.

'Please, I cannot!' he says. 'I cannot. I will lose everything.'

'Yes!' she says, jabbing the knife in his direction. 'You can and you *will*.'

But Etta has no need to put her threat into practice for Charlie's attempt at lock-picking has succeeded.

Mary reaches for Charlie's hand instinctively, holds it tight as the gate slowly swings open to reveal Mr Meake standing in the hallway in front of them and behind him, behind him . . . No, she will never know quite how to describe it. This elegant woman with her brown skin and black curls, huge russet wings fanning out behind her, white gown like something from a painting draped around her. She will never know how to tell of the blaze in the woman's eyes, the power that emanates from her. She is a goddess. She is a miracle. It is the most impossible, most magnificent, most wondrous sight.

Annie gasps. She cannot take it in. She cannot process it. This extraordinary creature here, in her own basement! How long has she been here? *How long has he kept her here?*

Etta takes the initiative as all fall silent around her.

'Give me the keys to the cells!' she says, but Edward has his back to her. The gate opened, he is undone, unable to take his eyes away from his wife who looks at him with such horror, stares at him as if he were a monster.

Mary is the first from the servants' side of the gate to recover her senses. Charlie is all eyes, he cannot speak, cannot think. She bends to his ear. 'Charlie, go out and tell Uncle Jos what has happened. We shall meet you out there shortly. Flag down a cab so we can make good our escape at the end of the street.'

Annie steps forward, walks slowly up to her husband.

'Give me the keys,' she commands, steel in her voice now.

'Annie . . . please . . .' But his secret is out, the genie cannot be put back into the bottle – all is lost, and he has nothing else to say.

'They are in his waistcoat pocket,' says Etta from behind him and Annie reaches into Edward's pocket and takes them. He offers no resistance, feeling as if all the bones in his body are disintegrating, as if he is nothing but jelly.

'What have you done?' she whispers angrily to him. '*Oh, Edward! What have you done?*'

Mary runs forward, dashing down the hallway, past Annie and Edward as Charlie heads outside.

'Miss Lockhart?' Mary says as Etta looks down at her, eyes piercing through her. 'I am Mary Ward and I am here to rescue you.'

'Then you must make haste,' says Etta, puzzled as to how this young woman can possibly know her name. 'For I am not alone down here.'

'Mrs Meake, the keys,' says Mary, turning back for a moment as Annie throws them to her. She catches them, following Etta around the corner to Natalya's cell. Hands trembling, Mary unlocks the door and is appalled by what she sees. The tatty mattress, the thin, pale woman wrapped in a blanket, with huge dark blue eyes, black circles beneath them.

'Come, my dear friend,' Etta says, holding out her hand to Natalya. 'It is time we left, is it not?'

Natalya, not quite daring to believe that she, that both of them, might truly be free, stands stock-still for a moment.

'Come,' Etta says. 'Time is of the essence, friend.'

Natalya reaches out, takes the offered hand and pulls Etta towards her, hugging her tight.

'You must let the dog out too,' Natalya says to Mary over Etta's shoulder. 'For we are not monsters. Not like him.'

Mary, fumbling, unlocks the other door as Etta and Natalya step out into the hallway, hands tightly clasped.

'Come, little one,' says Etta and the dog quietly, nervously, steps out, thin tail tucked up tightly by her undercarriage.

'All are out!' cries Mary as she steps back into the hallway. 'All are freed!'

Annie and Edward still face each other in silence, so much to say and no way of saying it. She goes to step past him and he stops her, grabs her arm tightly, fingers digging hard into her.

'Please, Annie, *please*. Let me—'

She unpeels his fingers one by one, her anger giving

her strength as she pushes him away. He grabs at her again, arms flailing, but it is too late, she is by the door of his dissecting room. She looks in, sees the skeleton from the river, bony wings held in place by metal rods.

'My God, Edward!' she sobs, turning to him full of horror. '*What have you done?*'

'It's not what you think!' he says, rooted to the spot. 'Annie! Please! It's not – she was already . . . This was for both of us, this was all for you!'

Etta, Natalya and Mary watch from the far end of the hallway as Annie howls at Edward, tears falling down her cheeks.

'No, Edward! *No!*' she says, voice trembling. 'This was *you* and you alone! You have only *ever* thought of *yourself!*'

Annie turns her back on him, walks to join the small group of women at the end of the hallway. She looks Etta and Natalya in the eye, these two women who have been held down here. *Kept as prisoners by her own husband.*

'I am sorry,' Annie says, sobbing. 'I am so sorry. I had no idea!'

'Please,' says Natalya, her own eyes brimming with tears. 'I need fresh air, I cannot bear it down here a moment longer.'

Mary interrupts. 'Mrs Meake! The fastest way out?'

Annie motions up the handful of steps to the back door and Mary unlocks it with Edward's keys. They struggle to pull it open, though, for the door is stiff with the cold, swollen by the recent heavy rains. Mary batters her fists against it.

'Richard! Help us! *Help us!*'

Behind them, Edward stands in the hallway, dazed as if in a dream. He closes his eyes a moment. This is not real, he tells himself. *None of this is real.* He is powerless, impotent, unable to move as all his dreams crumble into nothing around him, dissolving into thin air.

Annie joins Mary, trying to pull the door open. Natalya stands behind them, exhausted, leaning against the wall holding onto the dog's collar, her other hand held tight by Etta, but Etta's attention is elsewhere. She is not quite done with their captor yet.

Etta thinks for a moment, anger welling within. She gives Natalya's hand one last squeeze before letting go. She turns, walks back towards Edward as he stands, broken, a puppet of a man in the hallway.

'You were chosen by no one,' Etta says to him, clearly and fiercely, keeping her distance. 'You are no "messenger of God"! You have not been guided by anyone or anything other than your own greed and ambition.'

He stands by the narrow table, defeated. There will be no glory for him now. No fame and fortune. All is lost.

She plucks a feather from her wing, holds it up to the nearest flickering gas light and watches as the flame takes hold.

'*You are merely a man,*' she says, holding up the fiery feather. She gathers her energy, feels the fury in her belly and she blows it towards him, a fearsome blast that comes from the hills, the skies, from the wild within her.

It is at that same moment that Richard manages to kick the door open and a draught of cold, sooty London air gusts in. As Richard helps Annie and Natalya out into the yard, Etta's lit feather flies down the corridor towards Edward, alights on his narrow oak console table and, in an instant, sets the beeswax polish aflame. The small blaze travels swiftly over the wooden cladding that runs below the dado rail, taking seconds to spread as it stretches itself down the hallway, licking and spitting as it goes.

Etta watches for a moment, the elemental nature of the flames lighting something within her own self. And then she too is gone, the last Edward will ever see of his beloved angel.

Outside, it is freezing cold as Mary helps Etta up the steps and into the yard. Etta gasps as she takes her first breath of outdoor air for some many days.

'Are you hurt?' Mary asks and Etta shakes her head, overwhelmed for a moment. This is freedom, she thinks, breathing deeply in: air and sky and earth.

Richard is too startled, too surprised to speak. This winged creature in front of him, this miraculous woman stepping from the basement. He had not really considered, not really thought it was possible and yet . . .

'This is Mr Gibbs,' says Mary. 'He helped me find you.'

'Thank you,' says Etta, finding her voice again and holding out her hand as Richard, dumbfounded, shakes it.

'I thank you too,' says Natalya. 'Both of you.'

'I didn't know there was more than one of you here,' says Mary, amazement whirling inside of her. 'Are you . . .?' She looks at Natalya. 'You are not by any chance the woman from St George's? The church in Bloomsbury where a lady fell ill, is that you?'

Natalya looks at this young woman, marvels at how on earth she could know such a thing and nods slowly.

Mary considers her and frowns. 'But I thought you were dead,' she says, almost to herself.

'No! *NO!*' a wail goes up. Annie's voice. The orange glow of the fire is visible through Edward's small study window that looks out into the yard, smoke already beginning to billow out of the back door.

'Fire!' says Richard and, before anyone can think to stop her, Annie dashes back inside. Richard turns to Mary and she already knows what he will do, perhaps even before he does. They look deep into each other's eyes – a moment that lasts a fraction of a second but feels like a lifetime – before he turns and runs into the house after Annie.

'Richard! *Richard!*' Mary screams after him, but it is too late.

She goes to follow him, but the dog stands in front of her, blocking her way and barking as Richard disappears into the smoke.

'Richard!' she yells again, panic rising, heart thumping. '*Richard!*'

Annie coughs, holds her arm over her mouth as she stumbles down the steps into the basement.

'Edward!' she shouts. '*Edward!*'

Smoke fills the hallway and she cannot see him. She checks the empty dissecting room before fumbling her way forward as the wood cladding burns to her right, perilously close to her dress.

'*Edward!*'

He is in his study, the door locked from the inside. He ignores her as she raps on the door and peers through the small glass panel.

He has his head in his hands. '*Are we not in our own way gods you and I?*' Then this *was* a test. This was *all* God's test and he has failed Him – for do not medicine and morality come hand in hand? His angel told him that his ambition blinded him and he cannot face the world without her, cannot face the hordes at Exeter Hall, cannot face his beloved Society ever again. He has nothing to offer. All the promises he has wrought and all for nothing. All is lost. All is turned to dust. He used God's creatures for his own gain, deluded himself with his own greatness when he was, all along, as his angel had said, *merely a man*. A man with foibles and faults, hopes and dreams. He has torn up his own life, ripped it into shreds just as he destroyed Annie's painting. He unpeels the bandage on his arm, looks at the scar, at the angry rash that spreads up and over his skin as he recalls the inscription at St Luke's, words that now cut him deeply. *Miseratione non mercede*. For compassion not for gain.

'Edward! Please! *Do not do this! Edward!*'

He hears Annie banging at the door, but he ignores her. She will never look at me in the same way, he thinks, calmness and acceptance coming over him. What is done cannot be undone. It is too late for redemption. His path is set, perhaps was set for him all along. He recalls a passage from Isaiah.

When thou passest through the waters, I will be with thee; and through the rivers, they shall not overflow thee: when thou walkest through the fire, thou shalt not be burned; neither shall the flame kindle upon thee.

Then he prays:

'Our Father, which art in heaven,
Hallowed be thy name;
Thy kingdom come;
Thy will be done;
In earth as it is in heaven.'

Richard stumbles forward in the smoke, feels his way along the hallway to where Annie is and grabs her by the shoulder. She resists at first, but she is tired and she can see through the glass that her husband, stubborn and determined as ever, has already made up his mind.

'Edward!' she tries one last time, her fists thumping at the door. '*Edward!*'

> 'Give us this day our daily bread.
> And forgive us our trespasses,
> as we forgive those who trespass against us.
> And lead us not into temptation, but deliver
>   us from evil,'

She sobs as Richard scoops her up, tries to carry her out, but the smoke is thick, she is heavy in her woollen clothes and the fire is unbearably hot. He staggers slowly with her in his arms, coughing and choking along the hallway, carefully trying to avoid the flames that flicker and taunt them from all directions. He gathers every ounce of energy he has, each footstep a battle with his own self. He roars as he tries to move forward, pushing himself on but it is so very, very hard . . .

> 'For thine is the kingdom, the power,
>   and the glory,
> for ever and ever.
> Amen.'

The fire sighs with relief as it explores Edward's dissecting room, fingers of flames licking their way towards his specimen jars full of flammable liquid. Aaah, the fire whispers, aaah . . .

The explosion feeds the fire, transforming it into a raging furnace.

Charlie has dutifully obeyed his instructions. A cab is waiting at the end of St Mary Axe and he runs back to tell Jos just as the explosion blows out the windows in the servants' hall at the front of the house.

Jos panics. His beloved Mary, *my God*! He cannot lose her too, cannot even contemplate the possibility of doing so. He runs to the house, bellowing, shouting Richard's name too, but the flames are already travelling up from the basement's polished wooden stairs to the ground floor, licking at the new wallpaper, feeding on the rich wool carpets that were so recently put in.

Charlie meanwhile is shouting, 'Fire!' as loudly as he can, running towards Leadenhall to raise the alarm, Sarah, who he dispatches to do the same, pelting off in the opposite direction.

By the time the first Merryweather fire engine arrives, horses' hooves clattering along the street, the fire, an ever-hungry beast, has already moved up to the first floor. Annie's sketches, her paints, her paper – all are consumed in the blaze along with everything that remained in the basement: the skeleton of the Angel of the Thames, all of

Edward's jars, bones, specimens and medical notes, the mattresses in the cells, the blankets his angels once wrapped themselves in – all are now turned to smouldering ash.

It is only twenty feet or so but to Mary it feels like miles. As Etta holds the dog back by its collar, Mary runs towards the basement door, bile rising in her throat as fear almost overwhelms her.

Richard.

Please.

Please let him be safe.

I cannot—

Please.

The heat pushes her back like a wall of resistance then he bursts out, coughing, stumbling. Face black with soot, eyes streaming from the smoke, Annie in his arms like a dead weight, eyes closed and overcome by it all.

Richard falls to his knees in the yard, the cold flagstones sending a welcome chill through him as Annie rolls out of his arms and onto the ground, senseless but safe.

'You bloody idiot!' sobs Mary. 'You *bloody idiot,* Richard!'

'Sorry,' he mutters, looking up at her as she throws herself at him, pummels him with her fists for a moment before holding him as tightly as she can, as she has wanted to for so long now. She digs her fingers deep into his hair, feels his warmth wrap around her as his arms clasp her tightly in return and she sobs into his chest.

Etta watches, sighs, breathes in London air. Ash and soot.

She turns to Natalya. 'I, for one, have had enough of

cities,' she says softly, as she looks again at the fire, tendrils of flame now reaching through the roof. 'Perhaps it is time we were going.'

'Where?' Natalya asks. 'And how?'

But Etta only smiles at her as she steps forward, brings her close.

'Put your feet on mine,' she says. 'Hold your arms around me. As tight as you can,' and Natalya does so, wrapping herself around Etta and her white silk dress.

Etta looks up at the sky, takes a deep breath, and stretches her wings. She opens them out, lets them softly beat for the first time.

She looks back at Natalya and their eyes lock. 'I have no idea if this will work,' Etta whispers and they both smile.

Charlie and Jos burst through the back gate just in time as Richard motions to his beloved Mary.

'Look,' he coughs. 'Look!' And she turns her head.

For Etta's wings, those magnificent russet wings, beat slowly at first, lifting her and Natalya up for a moment, just an inch or two. Then, as they beat faster, as strength turns to confidence, Etta rises, holding Natalya close, her friend's eyes scrunched tight with both fear and excitement. The sky opens and Etta's wings hum, slicing through the air like a knife as she ascends, as she *flies* for the very first time.

'*Open your eyes!*' Etta whispers in Natalya's ear, as she marvels at all she has become.

The ash from the burning house falls around them, swirling around the yard and fluttering down, looking for all the world like the first flakes of winter snow.

The eyes of all those present stay on Etta, Natalya clutched tightly to her, mesmerised as the impossible becomes possible. They watch her, this woman with wings, this strange wonder, as she rises up in the sky above the chimneys of Leadenhall, far above the highest buildings in all the capital, until she disappears into the clouds, swallowed up by the night sky.

DESTRUCTIVE FIRE.- Between nine and ten o'clock on Sunday night, a fire broke out in the residence of acclaimed surgeon Edward Meake of St Mary Axe, Leadenhall. In a few minutes after the discovery of the fire, the engine and men from the City station arrived followed by the West of England engine and a half-dozen others belonging to the brigade and, being plentifully supplied with water, played with such effect upon the burning mass as to confine it to the individual house in which the fire originated but not before the whole of the residence was destroyed. By midnight, all fears of further danger were at an end. A large body of the police under Mr Superintendent Randall Hawkins, newly installed in the role from the western board of the United States, were on the spot during the raging of the fire and rendered efficient service in keeping back the populace and in assisting the firemen in their operations. We are moved to report that the surgeon Mr Meake, of St Luke's Hospital, appears to have perished in the fire although no accident befell any other individual. Mr Meake was due today to have presented his recent scientific findings at Exeter Hall on the Strand. An inquest will take place at the Rising Sun on Thursday afternoon and a service to mark Mr Meake's contribution to medical science will be held at St George's, Bloomsbury this Friday. He is survived by his widow.

When Edward's father is told of his last remaining son's death, his face remains immobile, held in place by the muscles that – much like Edward for so many years – no longer obey his command. When he is left alone, after his wife leaves him, sobbing into her handkerchief as she closes the bedroom door behind her, a single tear rolls down his cheek, falls onto the pillowcase where it blots like ink on paper.

Annie does not go to the memorial service, does not step foot in the east of the city, and does not see Edward's family ever again. She gathers herself up as small as she can and hides from the world. She stays in Ellie's house, in the nursery on the top floor, sleeping in the oldest child's bed. She is full of sorrow and anger, confusion and guilt. Her own husband – he had done such terrible things. And yet there was wonder too, the beauty of that creature! I am a widow now, she thinks with an empty heart, and shrinks just a little more.

If only Annie could see a little way ahead, if only she could be comforted by what is still to come. For in just over a year's time, she will be atop a mountain in the

Canary Isles, looking out at a landscape that seems to her as if it is from some other world entirely. Wide plains and colours which look stranger than the surface of the moon itself, mountain breezes playing with her hair, her bonnet long since discarded on the ascent, her skirts whipping around her, a sense of triumph at having conquered the peak; she will turn to Marcus, standing beside her, looking out at the view, and she will smile, happiness returned to her, as she begins to unpack her travelling watercolour set, the china mixing tiles, the sponge, the brushes and the glass water pot which she will fill from her flask.

She will stand for a moment, close her eyes, breathe in the warm, clean air, feel the sun tickle her skin, knowing that the freckles will appear like paint spatters on her face and hands and she will not care what society – nay, the entire world, thinks of her. For, like a piece of art herself, she has learnt the correct time to step away from it.

London is so very noisy with the clatter of cabs and carriages, livestock, street vendors and more that, to Richard's consternation, it is very hard to find somewhere quiet enough outdoors to have an intimate conversation.

He walks silently beside Mary and her newly acquired dog, rescued from the Meakes' basement, now named Millicent, Millie for short – although the black and tan mongrel seems blissfully unaware of this as yet.

Richard had caught a chill after the fire and spent a few days recovering in bed from both that and the effects of smoke inhalation. Although Mary and Jos had visited his bedside, discussed the wonders of what they had all seen and the sorrow of being unable to share it with the wider world, this is the first time he has spent alone with Mary since. It is strange, too, for although he feels he has at least a novel's worth of words within him, he does not seem able to recount them.

'I hope you don't mind, Mr Gibbs, but I've already delivered that review of yours directly to Mr Ashman himself,' says Mary as they walk slowly along the park's small avenue of trees.

Richard nods, his mind elsewhere.

'And, I am pleased to say, he has already commissioned another two reviews from me,' Mary adds. 'So no more button sewing for Mr Gidley, thank goodness!'

Richard nods again. 'Mmm. Excellent good. Of course.'

It is not the reaction Mary was expecting. It is most un-Richard-like to be quite so serious and intense, so preoccupied, and it troubles her. He is behaving *very* oddly today, she thinks, turning up at their lodgings and insisting he speak privately with her on a matter of utmost importance. Jos was already out on a lead for a story and Charlie was soon to leave for the penny gaff where Lou had conjured up some more odd jobs for him. Mary had suggested a walk instead, to make the most of the last of the autumn sunshine.

'Besides, Millie needs to learn how to navigate the roads, poor thing. Who knows how long she'd been cooped up down there?' she had said, patting the dog's head, but Richard's face was all anxiety and it unsettled her, even more so since he hadn't managed more than a handful of words the entire way to the park.

'Shall we sit for a moment?' he says suddenly, motioning to a bench. She smooths her dress and sits, Millie at her feet, as Richard takes his place next to her.

They are silent for a while, Richard fidgeting and looking out into the distance. Lord, this is hard, he thinks to himself. All those glorious spars with her, all the time he has felt so at ease in her company – and yet now she is the hardest, most impossible person in the world for him to talk to.

'This is really rather difficult, Miss Ward,' he says suddenly.

'I fear I have not been entirely honest with you about several matters.'

'Oh?' she says.

'This is really . . . This is very . . .'

'Richard, are you sure you're quite all right?' she asks, worried.

'Mary . . . I . . .' He takes a deep breath. 'Oh, Lord! Mary, look, when I was in Edinburgh, I formed an attachment. There, it is out.'

Oh. But Mary cannot think more than that, the air squeezed out of her chest and all hope with it. All those times he had looked at her so intently, all those awkward moments where she had dared hope . . . *Oh*.

'Please. Let me explain . . . she was the daughter of one of the journalists on the paper I was editing. I saw her almost every day and I'm afraid I mistook familiarity for—'

'Mr Gibbs,' says Mary, forming the words with some difficulty as her heart splinters, shatters into a million tiny sharp pieces, 'you do not need to explain. Who you do or do not form an attachment to is surely none of my business.'

'Mary, *please!*' He holds up his hand. 'I had thought myself, oh Lord! Look, I had thought myself to be rather in love with her. But I was wrong. By God, I was *so very wrong*. It was a brief attachment, a mistake on both sides. In fact, she wrote recently to invite me to her wedding, to the person she always ought to have married, and I'm very happy for them. I am. But that's *not it,* Mary, that's not what I'm trying to say . . .'

He falls into silence for a moment as Mary feels utterly bewildered.

'The thing is, the truth of it is . . . I didn't know what it felt like. To be in love. *Truly* in love. And then, when I came back, for George's funeral, I . . .' He clears his throat. 'And you were there and – *by Jove*, this is difficult! And. Well . . .'

He looks at his feet for a moment.

'I thought I would die in that fire,' he says quietly. 'I thought I would perish and never be able to tell you the truth and I swore to myself that if I got out of there, if by *some miracle* I got out of there alive, then I would tell you *everything*. All of it, honestly and truthfully. No secrets, Mary, none.'

He shuffles his feet, swallows, summons up his courage and takes a deep breath.

'Mary – *you* were the reason I came back from Edinburgh,' he says softly, still not daring to look at her. 'You *are* the reason I came back.'

He leans forward and his hat falls off, tipping itself into his lap just as he catches it. Mary bites her lip, tries not to laugh or cry although she wishes *oh so much* to do both.

'It is your curls, Mr Gibbs,' she says, eyes twinkling. 'They resent being contained within the confines of your hat.'

Richard looks at her, the first time he has done so since they sat down and he feels as if his heart might burst. They look into each other's eyes, whirlpools of possibility.

He takes her hands, feels their fingers entwine.

'I know you are in mourning,' he says softly. 'I know you are still only eighteen, but I will wait, Mary. I will wait a thousand years if I have to. I know there is so much you want to see and do and I will help you, however I can. Just please, *please*, tell me that I am right to hope, right to hope beyond hope that my affections might be returned, if not today, then some day. *One day*. Please.'

Mary cannot speak. She swallows, tries to think of something to say. She squeezes his hands.

'Oh, Richard,' she says, smile spreading across her whole face. 'You know, I never did think of you as an older brother.'

He reaches out a hand, strokes her cheek. She closes her eyes for a moment, inhales happily, before opening them again.

'If you tell me there's a fly on my cheek *this* time,' she says with a wicked grin. 'I might get rather cross.'

But instead he pulls her towards him, warm lips meeting for the first time as their hearts sing in unison.

John Brown, broad of chin, kind of heart and getting on in years, waves to the two figures in the boat as they push off from the beach below his crofter's cottage. They have achieved a great deal in a relatively short period of time, he thinks with respect. They have breathed new life into the old croft on the small island, created a home where there had not been one for many years. They keep themselves to themselves, yet they are not unfriendly. The taller one, the one with the hunchback and the pretty dark skin, it's a shame she must cover her shoulders so with that big shawl wrapped around so tight. She is friendly enough, but her pale stepsister with the wary eyes, she has taken longer to get to know. And yet he is rather fond of them both, he thinks, as he prepares his pipe, their vessel receding on the horizon as it heads off towards the little island, a blizzard of hopeful gulls following like a cloud, mistaking it for a fishing boat.

We all have our secrets, he thinks as he squints at them, laughing and chatting as they cut through the waves. For it is only since the pair of them arrived that he has spotted a strange thing in the skies. His eyes are not good enough these days to be able to say without doubt what exactly it is, but it is the biggest bird he has ever seen, that much is certain. Bigger than the sea eagles, bigger even than the albatrosses he saw when he was out at sea. It is almost, he has thought for a while now, as big as a person . . .

He has his suspicions, ah, that he does, but, he thinks with a smile, he will not tell a soul of them. He taps his pipe out on the low stone wall, looks up and gives them one last, final wave.

Acknowledgements

The Gifts is, obviously, a work of fiction. I've bent and distorted facts, dates, and locations to make this world feel real. Any mistakes and errors in it are mine and mine alone.

Many of the characters are inspired by real life people from both the Georgian and Victorian era. Edward by Astley Cooper (Queen Victoria's surgeon) with a dash of John Hunter; Etta by Mary McGhie; Mary by George Eliot and Harriet Martineau; Annie by, amongst others, Annie Swynnerton; Natalya by a mix of glorious storytellers from both now and the past including the extraordinary Orcadian writer, George Mackay Brown.

A note on the use of gas – in 1840, many of the streets of London were lit by gas lamps as were many theatres and shops. Whilst gas in the home came, *en masse*, somewhat later, some houses in the capital did feature gas lighting at this time. As Edward is already seriously over-spending, I thought it was exactly the sort of thing a show-off like him might have invested in.

I've been unbelievably lucky to work with the amazing team at Manilla Press. Whilst it's my name that's on the cover, I owe a true debt of gratitude to the brilliant wonders that have helped make this an actual physical book and one that is so beautiful to look at.

To Sophie 'The Great' Orme for seeing the potential in a rough-cut stone, and for cutting and polishing it with me.

To all of Team Manilla – in particular: Katie Lumsden and Katie Meegan for eagle eyes and wise words; Felice McKeown and Grace Brown for marketing magic; Nick Stearn for his stunning cover design; Karen 'Stretchy' Stretch and Clare Kelly for publicity brilliance; Jenny Richards for understanding what's in my head visually; and to Sally Taylor for her exquisite illustrations.

To my amazing agent and dear friend Anwen for giving me the confidence to keep on writing.

To Hannah Khalil for being my ever-inspiring writer twin.

To Naomi 'Nay' Luland for keeping faith in me over two decades.

To Rachel Buchanan for early feedback and all the chats.

To Jules Woodman for first telling me about Shropshire botanist Mary McGhie.

To Jane Packer for saving me from embarrassment on all things medical.

To Alex Snow for veterinarian advice, wild cake, and secret wanders.

To Mireille Harper for thoughtful feedback and generosity of spirit!

To Laura Wildgoose from the beautiful Wildegoose Nursery for botanical checks.

To Kathie Touin Brown for guidance on all things Orkney.

To the Griffiths family – particularly Sian for 'crackling' support.

To Dulcie at Mostly Flat – May the Great Goblin rise again one day!

To Julia Walling for helping me embrace my inner hermit and for Etta's cabin.

To Stephenjohn Holgate for wise words of advice and general brilliance.

To Iran for roses, barefoot walking, and cups of tea.

To Jon Saxon and Adam Tutt for letting me borrow The Blood Bay and The Blue Boar and relocate them from Ludlow to London.

To Robin Dance for twinkly-eyed mischievousness.

To Dorothy Blackwell at the Back to Backs in Birmingham and all those at the Judge's Lodging in Presteigne.

To the parentals and all the extended family for all their support.

To Sara-Jane Arbury, Jonathan Davidson, Jon Bruford, Simon Bolton, Tariq Jordan, Abby Harrison, Polly Shepherd, Ali G (not that one), Katy Moran, Jane Hobson, Natasha Farrant, MG Leonard, Lesley Parr, Zara McCartney-Hubbard, Ruth Cairns, KB, Jackie Morris, Nicola Davies, Rebecca F John, Stacey Halls, Thi Dinh, Maura Wilding, Lucy Hirschman, Magic Deb, Simon Thomas, Stanton Stephens, Claire Preston, Chlöe Alexander, Ruth at Booka, and Sarah Odedina for kind words and support – I cannot tell you how much it's meant to me. Thank you from the bottom of my heart!

To the entire brilliant Writing West Midlands team for tea, cake and kindness – particularly to Liv Chapman for helping me through 'suspended terror'.

A special thank you to Rachel, Ange, Sarah, Laura, Rich, and the team at Moniack Mhor. I was lucky enough to be awarded The Bridge Award/Moniack Mhor Emerging Writer Award in 2018. It gave me thinking, wandering, and writing time at a truly magical place and I began writing *The Gifts* when I was there.

In memory of the lovely Nick 'Ferg' Ferguson whose wise advice about knowing when the right time to step away is has stuck with me for all these years.

To all the friends and family whose names I've borrowed for cameo roles – you know who you are!

Thank you too to my canine pals – Scout, Dennis, Roscoe, Brian, Spud and in memory of lovely Millie.

And lastly and most importantly, my heartfelt thanks to Rob – for putting up with me.

Bibliography

Annie Swynnerton – Painter and Pioneer, Christine Allen and Penny Morris

Crucial Interventions, Richard Barnett

Victorian News and Newspapers, Lucy Brown

Digging up the Dead, Druin Burch

Untold Histories – Black people in England and Wales during the period of the British slave trade 1660-1807, Kathleen Chater

The Victorian Flower Garden, Jennifer Davies

The Victorian Kitchen Garden, Jennifer Davies

Night Walks, Charles Dickens

Around the World in 80 Trees, Jonathan Drori

Sex and Sexuality in Victorian Britain, Violet Fenn

The Butchering Art, Lindsay Fitzharris

The Victorian City, Judith Flanders

The Victorian House, Judith Flanders

Cranford, Elizabeth Gaskell

How to be a Victorian, Ruth Goodman

Britain's Black Past, edited by Gretchen Holbrook Gerzina

Black Victorians – Black Victoriana, edited by Gretchen Holbrook Gerzina

George Eliot – The Last Victorian, Kathryn Hughes

Victorians Undone, Kathryn Hughes

Dirty Old London, Lee Jackson

Titterstone Clee, Everyday Life, Industrial History and Dialect, Alf Jenkins

Wildlife in the Marches, Mark Lawley

The Concise Gray's Anatomy, C.H. Leonard

Bringewood Chase and Surrounding Countryside, David Lovelace

The Old Ways, Robert MacFarlane

Beside the Ocean of Time, George Mackay Brown

Greenvoe, George Mackay Brown

Hawkfall, George Mackay Brown

Pictures in the Cave, George Mackay Brown

The Victorian Domestic Servant, Trevor May

The Victorian Schoolroom, Trevor May

London Labour and the London Poor, Henry Mayhew

London's Underworld, Henry Mayhew

Mayhew's London, Henry Mayhew

Victorian Lady Travellers, Dorothy Middleton

The Victorian Hospital, Lavinia Mitton

The Mitchell Beazley Pocket Guide to Wild Flowers, Peter D Moore

The Knife Man, Wendy Moore

Black and British: A Forgotten History, David Olusoga

The Routledge History of Sex and the Body: 1500 to the Present, edited by Sarah Toulalan and Kate Fisher

Victorian London, Liza Picard

Walking on the Orkney and Shetland Isles, Graham Uney

The Life and Times of Mortimer Forest in a Nutshell, Julia Walling (Butterfly Conservation)

If Walls Could Talk, Lucy Worsley

St George's Bloomsbury, London, World Monuments Fund publication

Back to Backs, National Trust publication

The British Newspaper Archive

Hammond Turner Button Museum

If you wish to follow in any of the characters footsteps, here are some places you might like to visit.

London
The Old Operating Theatre
Charles Dickens's House/Museum
The Post Office Museum
St George's, Bloomsbury
Dennis Severs's House

Ludlow and the Midlands
The Blood Bay, Ludlow
The Blue Boar, Ludlow
The Angel Inn, Ludlow
Ludlow Museum Resource Centre
The Judge's Lodging, Presteigne
Elton Hall, Elton (not open to the public)
St Leonard's Church, Ludlow
The Back to Backs, Birmingham

Orkney
The Kirbuster Farm Museum
Stromness Museum
The Orkney Museum, Kirkwall
Westray Heritage Centre
Sanday Heritage Centre

Reading Group Questions

1. *The Gifts* follows multiple characters. Who was your favourite? Who did you feel was the central character?
2. How does this novel explore gender? Do you think Edward would have reacted differently if he had found winged men, not women?
3. What role does religion play in the novel, and how do religion and science both clash and complement each other?
4. Both Etta and Annie sketch and draw. What role do you think art plays in the novel?
5. How does the historical and geographical setting affect the story? How do you think a phenomena like this would be treated in a different time and place?
6. What do you think of Edward, and how did you opinion of him change throughout the novel?
7. What do you think the significance of the title is?
8. What do you think Edward and Annie's life would have been like if Edward hadn't discovered the 'angels'? Does Edward's obsession change him, or was he always going to be the person he becomes?
9. Natalya tells stories, Mary, Richard and Jos all write, and myths circulate about the 'angels'. What role does story-telling play in the book?
10. Etta, Annie and Mary are all orphans, and Mary has recently lost one of her parent figures. Edward has a strained relationship with his father, as does Natalya with her mother. How does the novel explore the complicated relationships between children and their parents?
11. Why do you think Etta and Natalya grow wings?

Hello dear reader!

Thank you for picking up *The Gifts*, I do so hope you enjoyed it.

I've always believed that all stories begin with a 'what if?'. What if a whale swallowed a ship whole? What if Gods were real and lived alongside us? What if our souls were known as daemons and visible to others?

What if a woman grew wings . . . ?

Just over eleven years ago, I left my life in London behind and moved to a small medieval town in south Shropshire, where forested hills fringe the horizon, capped with remnants of Iron and Bronze Age forts. I felt stories, like wisps of autumn mist, gather around me as I walked the forests and fields, the hills and valleys, engraving myself into the ground as the seasons changed – much like Etta does.

Everywhere I looked, I saw traces of the past, the signs of humans long gone – from medieval burgage layouts and disused quarries to abandoned villages and Neolithic burial cairns. The Industrial Revolution had scarred the landscape here but everywhere I looked, there was nature too, clawing its way back. Nuthatches and peregrines, skylarks and sparrowhawks.

I wanted to know more and so, through books and museums, word of mouth and stories, I fell backwards in time, discovering great Victorian scientists, geologists and botanists, a flourishing of ideas and knowledge. And yet, the women were largely absent, a handful of pioneers, the rest reduced to wives, mothers or siblings of these same men. What if I were to write about them then, these forgotten women, the ones who did not, *could not*, open the door of opportunity, but who had, against the odds, nudged it open regardless, allowing others to follow in their footsteps? The sort of women for whom there would never be any glory or fame, those whose names and achievements have long since disappeared in the mists of time. And so, I started to assemble my female cast – an aspiring botanist, an artist, a gifted young journalist and a storyteller. Glorious women with curious minds, women who sought enlightenment for its own sake. Glorious women with impossible wings . . .

Of course, I then needed an adversary for them, not just in terms of the wider society, but in an individual too, someone clever and ambitious, someone who could be spurred on by ideas of fame and fortune. Surgery in early 19th century London was dangerous and exciting, wildly competitive and yet rudimentary. It felt inevitable that Edward would be a surgeon, viewing the winged women as his route to success with disastrous consequences.

The Gifts is, I think, a book about many things, a slice of imagined history woven with inspiration from real-life 19th century figures; it explores the dangers of ambition, the power of friendship and the nature of enlightenment. Both Etta and Natalya 'open their eyes' to nature too, something that is dear to my heart – I truly believe that our relationship with the natural world, as the climate crisis unfolds, has never, in human history, been more important. Above all though, it is a book about women; strong, determined, glorious women who fought to be seen for themselves.

Thank you so much for reading *The Gifts* and, if you would like to hear more about my books, you can visit www.lizhyder.co.uk and sign up to become part of my free Readers' Club. It only takes a moment to join, there are no catches, Bonnier Books UK will keep your data private and confidential and never pass it on to a third party. I promise not to spam you with loads of emails too! I'll just get in touch every now and then with news about my writing. And of course, you're welcome to unsubscribe whenever you want.

If you would like to get involved in a wider conversation about *The Gifts*, you can find me on both Twitter and Instagram as @LondonBessie or tag me in at #TheGifts. I love it when readers get in touch! And, if you wanted to, please feel free to review it on Amazon, Goodreads, any other e-store, or on your own social media.

Very best wishes,

If you enjoyed *The Gifts*, be sure to look out for . . .

THE ILLUSIONS

At a time of extraordinary change, two women must harness their talents to take control of their own destiny . . .

Bristol, 1896.
Used to scraping a living as the young assistant to an ageing con artist, Cecily Marsden's life is turned upside down when her master suddenly dies. Believing herself to blame, could young Cec somehow have powers she little understands?

Meanwhile Eadie Carleton, a pioneering early filmmaker, struggles for her talent to be taken seriously in a male-dominated world, and a brilliant young magician, George Perris, begins to see the potential in moving pictures. George believes that if he can harness this new technology, it will revolutionise the world of magic forever – but in order to achieve his dreams, he must first win over Miss Carleton . . .

As a group of illusionists prepare for a grand spectacle – to mark both the retirement of legendary master The Professor and the announcement of his successor – Cec, Eadie and George's worlds collide. But as Cec falls in love with the bustling realm of theatre and magic, she faces the fight of her life to save the performance from sabotage and harness the element of real magic held deep within her.

***The Illusions* is the captivating new novel from the much-lauded author of *The Gifts*. Inspired by real-life illusionists and early film pioneers, this astonishing story of women and talent, magic and power, sweeps you into a world where anything is possible and nothing is quite as it seems . . .**

Coming soon. Read on for a sneak peek . . .

Bristol, March 1896

A storm is coming. It lingers in the air, dances in the trees, and blows at the roof tiles, trying to prise them from their holds. The rusting weathervane at the top of St Andrew's rattles as it swings in circles, uncertain of which direction to blame for the sudden gusts and gales that make the church's resident barn owls hide in the bell tower, huddled together for warmth.

Beneath them, a small crowd of men and women gather in the midst of the graveyard, holding tightly onto their bonnets and hats as the wind tries to snatch them away and cast them off into the black of the night. Arter Evans, an ageing con artist with a knack for the theatrical, tries his best to hold both their attention and his lantern, a battle he is in danger of losing. The deep and often empty pockets of Arter's frayed woollen coat carry a smattering of coins from his audience and they clink faintly as he picks up a small bronze bell from the top of an old headstone, ringing it loudly to mark the start of proceedings.

His accomplice, Cecily Marsden, barely hears the bell from where she is hiding, crouched behind a large moss-covered gravestone in the far corner of the dank churchyard. The wind is doing its best to steal the sound away, but it is not that. Cec, as she prefers to be called, is focused entirely on something else. Over the past eight months or so, ever since a chance encounter in a room above a tavern in a grubby corner of London, Cec has developed a serious interest in card tricks – an obsession almost. Since then, she has practised secretly at every spare moment, sewing hidden pockets into her dresses so her two already dog-eared packs are accessible whenever she chooses. She has practised in bed, when Arter was out on drunken binges, lost to the bottom of the bottle in the darkest alleyways of whichever town they found themselves in. She has practised, as she does tonight, whilst waiting for a show to begin. She has begged and borrowed tricks from card sharps in the many taverns and inns they have passed through on their way to Bristol. She has even – although she would never admit it – practised in rare, quiet moments whilst sitting on the toilet, dress hitched up above her knees. She has become truly skilled now, having swiftly mastered the basics – switching cards, marking a deck, fanning and shuffling – confident in all manner of tricks. But she has never dared share it, not with Arter, nor anyone else. It's the only thing she has that is hers, *all hers.* Her very own secret. But never before has young Cecily Marsden achieved this . . .

The wind blows around her as her mouth falls open, her left palm facing outward, empty. Leaves and tiny twigs, white petals from early blossoms circle her like a small faint tornado in the dark. In front of her, out of reach and about a foot away, a playing card is held up without her even touching it. Just as she witnessed that night in London eight months or so ago, a secret rehearsal no-one else was meant to see. But that night there were gossamer threads, thin as a spider's web, strung across the stage. Concealed paper hooks on the back of the cards. A clever trick, nothing more. Tonight though, there is no thread, no trick of the light, no hidden hooks, nothing except Cec and an impossible card. The four of diamonds, freshly plucked from her pack, hangs suspended in mid-air, stubbornly resisting the wind's power. Held up with – well, she is not entirely sure. It is unbelievable. It is *impossible.*

Cec gasps and the card suddenly falls to the ground like a dead weight. She pounces on it, scooping it up and tucking it first back into the pack, then into her hidden pocket. All of this in but a moment. Her mind whirls, trying and failing to understand as she attempts to steady herself for her performance, wrestling her mind back to Arter.

'Ladies and gentlemen!' He bellows throatily as the audience shiver, nudging each other. 'Tonight, you will witness a genuine spectre. The famed ghost of St Andrew's, the Lady in White. Tonight, ladies and gentlemen, at the stroke of midnight . . .' He pauses for effect. '*She will walk again!*'

There is an intake of breath from the audience and Arter nods, pleased, before continuing on.

'Hers is a story of tragedy. An echo from the past of an exquisite young beauty who fell in love with a handsome, dangerous–'

It takes all of Cec's effort to listen to him, her mind still reeling, as the wind steals Arter's words away. She puts a hand to the pocket of her stiffly starched dress, feels the solidity of the cards underneath her costume. It must have been her imagination. A vision caused by an empty stomach. But it wasn't. She *knows* it wasn't . . .

'The Lady in White, now abandoned by her lover, lost and alone,' Uncle Arter continues as the wind alters its course again and Cec strains to focus. 'She came to this very church to pray for her soul, to pray for redemption. She knelt down on the cold flagstones, her hands clasped together. And when she was done, she rose, entering the door of the tall tower you see before you, and she started to climb, up those steep stone steps to the very top, where she looked out upon her last night on earth–'

The first chime for midnight rings out – Cec's cue to begin her part in tonight's charade – and the barn owls take flight from the bell tower, scattering across the graveyard, skimming the heads of the crowd, before disappearing into the night.

'Hark!' cries Uncle Arter theatrically, eyes wide, a hand cupped to his ear. 'The Lady in White will soon appear!'

Cec concentrates, trying to wipe the four of diamonds from her mind. Candles are no good in weather such as this, so she must make do with a small oil lamp but the wind snatches the flame away as she tries to light it. She curses quietly, adjusting her bonnet and pulling her stiff veil down before trying her matches again. The fifth chime already echoes around the graveyard by the time the Lady in White finally emerges from the dark, her ghostly lamp lighting her way, reflecting the luminous paint of her stiffly starched costume as Cec glides smoothly, silently, around the front of the church to gasps of astonishment.

'Three times she will encircle the church! Three times she will search for her lost lover!' Arter cries, motioning towards her, trying to make himself heard above the clanging bells of St Andrew's.

Cec walks slowly, each foot placed purposefully on the uneven path. A quick learner, she has made various improvements to Arter's acts since he took her on five years ago, when she was just eleven. She has continued to tweak and perfect things even when he discourages her. To her mind, there is always *something* that can be made better. The veil draped over her bonnet hides her intricate make-up, a semi-skeletal face, carefully drawn on with the aid of a stick of charcoal. Tonight, she has darkened the ring around her left eye socket and drawn on a more defined nose cavity. After the third and final circuit of the church, she is to remove her veil and reveal her face. She had been hoping tonight that someone might faint when they see it, by far her favourite reaction, but as she disappears into darkness around the far side of the church, her mind again slips back to her impossible four of diamonds.

'Here she comes again!' cries Uncle Arter, moments later as the Lady in White re-emerges, somewhat out of breath, for Cec has pelted around the back of the church as fast as she can. 'See how she *glides*!'

Cec walks steadily, focusing on her feet, as she again reaches the far end of St Andrew's. She turns the corner, lifts her skirts, starts to run around the back of the church, relieved this is the final circuit, but it is so very dark now and a large branch from a nearby oak, loosened by the wind, has fallen ahead of her. She trips, groaning as her ankle twists, folding beneath her. Crumpled on the ground she reaches out, feeling her foot to check no bones are broken. A clipped ear will await if she doesn't finish the show – she knows Arter's ways well enough – so she forces herself to stand, testing her weight, but her smooth glide, practised to perfection, is impossible without just a little rest. She leans on the cold stone walls of the church, knowing both Arter and the audience will be impatient for the Lady in White's final appearance.

Cec grimaces as she comes back into view, grinding her teeth and trying not to hobble, but as thunder rumbles above, the wind picks up speed and, in full sight of the audience, grabs her ghostly bonnet and loosens it, snatching it from her and carrying it away, the veil trailing in its wake.

'Her head! The Lady in White's head!' screams one woman before she flees, certain for the rest of her days that she saw the decapitated head of a spirit flying over the church. The hysteria quickly spreads and the audience scatter. One lingerer spies Cec as she glares at him in pain, and all *he* sees is a rotted skeletal face, scowling at him. He gives a piercing shriek as he pelts off, his wife running to catch up with him.

Arter holds his hands out, begs for money from those who hadn't already paid but it is too late, for the entire audience, like the owls of St Andrew's, have vanished into the night. Cec, when she is confident they are all alone, hobbles over to him and Arter holds his hand out to show that half the coins he collected were simply buttons and badges. The perils of collecting money in the dark.

'What happened?' he snaps. 'What the hell happened?!' He cuffs Cec around the ear, too fast for her to dodge.

'Ow!' she cries, glaring at him. 'It wasn't my fault! I *told* you the storm was coming, but oh no, *you* were the one who insisted we still do it tonight.'

'Ah well . . .' he grumbles at the reprimand. 'Sorry Cec. Shouldn'a hit you.'

She purses her lips in anger and he shrugs, picking out the few coins in his palm and slipping them into his coat.

'Not enough for a decent meal,' he says, sorrowfully. 'Not for both of us anyway.'

Cec feels her belly rumble, drowned out by the thunder echoing around the churchyard.

'What now then?'

'Home,' he relies. 'Sleep it off. See if tomorrow brings better luck.' He shuffles his feet for a moment before looking back at her.

'Come on then,' he says, ''fore the rain comes.' And with that he's off, moving with great loping strides, his coat flapping out behind him. For a fleeting moment she hates him. Loathes him with every inch of her being. Five years since this old trickster with his grey-streaked hair and sallow cheeks plucked her from the streets, the small girl with a big mouth and a knack for fast learning. Five years of Arter's broken promises. Of scraping by, scratching a living from their wits, of half-empty bellies, of famines rather than feasts. She forgets for a moment how much fun he can be, how generous and silly, how he can transform himself in the blink of an eye. She forgets how he has used more and more of her ideas in their little scams, how much she's learned from him, how she'd be lost without him. All she can think of in that moment is her hunger, her resentment and fury. She *knows* he'll drink it. The money. That once again she'll fall asleep, blanket wrapped tightly around, only to wake and find Arter gone or already half-cut in his bed, with a stench of beer and gin hovering around him like a cloud. Cec hates him for it. Despises him even as she reluctantly follows him onto Regent Street and uphill, beside the grand terraced houses, filled with folk who never know what it is to go hungry. She hates them too. All of them.

Arter disappears underneath a tower of scaffolding, Cec lagging behind, ankle still bothering her. Another house being done up, painted and preened. More money wasted on frivolities when others starve. She clenches her fists as she thinks of it, growling to herself, wishing for revenge on the lot of them.

'Come on!' Arter bellows over his shoulder, not bothering to look back, and Cec glares at him, her nails digging hard into her palms as she struggles to contain her temper.

She sees it happen almost before it does. A sense of inevitability like a cup balanced on the edge of a table you know will fall. Time seems to stretch, expand, as the wind roars furiously across the whole of the city. The house's wooden scaffolding turns towards her. A twist in its legs. A lean to one side as if all three storeys of it are curious to see her. She sees Arter, underneath, the scaffolding forming a tunnel around him, the full moon bright just for a moment. His distinctive silhouette, the top hat that had seen better days, his long coat fanning out behind. Just a glimpse of him, black and white, before the scaffolding groans and splinters, collapsing in on itself like a tower of cards, swallowing him up within it.

A cloud of sawdust lingers for a moment, before the storm whips that away too, revealing the damage that has been done. Huge planks of wood snapped like matchsticks, piled up like a small mountain. Chaos. And there is Arter. Trapped in the midst like a broken bird. One corner of his coat flapping, black and useless, like a snapped wing.

Cec runs to him, forgetting the pain in her ankle, forgetting everything. Her breath comes fast and hard as she clambers over the broken timbers to reach him, splinters of wood digging into her hands and knees, sharp as needles. But it is too late. Arter stares into nothingness, a puzzled look on his face, a frown of bewilderment.

Arter.

The wind whistles triumphantly as rain starts to patter down, light at first and then heavier, harder. Cec's hair comes loose from its pins, whipping across her face like wet rope as she stares at Arter's body. At his crushed hat. At his torn and flapping coat. In the outstretched palm of his right hand lay the buttons from earlier and, after a moment, Cec reaches down and takes them, rolling them in her left hand like rosary beads before putting them in her pocket, next to her beloved cards.

She can barely remember what life was like before Arter. She feels as if he has always been there. But now he is gone and, for the first time in years, she is once again all alone.

She is all alone now.

Cec isn't sure how long she stands there for, but it must be for some while as she suddenly realises that she is soaking wet and shivering, drenched through by the storm which still rages around her. She barely remembers what happens next only that she has some vague notion that, despite all her mixed feelings about him, Arter must not be left here like this, must not be forgotten. Her feet develop a mind of their own, taking her to the one person in all of Bristol that might be able to help, to a house that if you'd asked her earlier, she would have denied she could even have found again. And yet here she is, face still streaked with make-up despite both the rain and her tears, standing outside the home of Mr Roderick Skarratt, knocking on the door with her fists until she is let inside, dripping pools of water in the dark hallway. And then there is light and warmth and soft carpet underfoot, a room with three unfamiliar faces and Skarratt himself sat around a table. A fire flickering in the hearth. Half-drunk glasses of port, plates with scatterings of crumbs.

Skarratt stands and he is both shorter and yet more imposing than she remembers.

'What is the meaning of this?' he asks, sharply. He comes

closer to her, his face appearing fuzzy at the edges somehow, black ink bleeding around her vision.

'You're Arter's girl? That's right, isn't it?'

He glances back at his companions as Cec nods, trying to remain steady on her feet as the shock of it finally hits her. Arter's staring eye, his outstretched palm . . .

She nods as a sob starts to rise up.

'It's Arter, sir. It's about Arter–'

She feels Skarratt's hand on her arm, fingers tight, holding her up as her legs start to feel less solid.

'It's . . . he's–' The words elude her for a moment before she howls them out, a wail of loss, of disbelief. 'He's dead sir. *Arter's dead!*'

The blackness around Skarratt's face spreads slowly inwards and all Cec can think about is the four of diamonds, the way she had controlled it, despite the storm. Her searing anger with Arter moments before his death. The way time had seemed to stretch. The scaffolding shifting towards her before falling down on itself, crushing both Arter and her whole world in a moment.

Her last thought as she feels herself falling down into the darkness, her vision vanishing to a pinhole, is that somehow *she* did it. The scaffolding. Her clenched fists . . .

I killed him, Cec thinks. *I killed him.*

And the words dance inside her head for a moment, pattering like the rain on the window outside.